"Finally, someone has done justice to Colette's masterpiece! Rachel Careau's new translation is incredibly smooth and elegant and amazingly accurate. Colette is the most difficult of French writers to translate and Careau has done an astonishingly fine job with the *Chéri* novels. Let's hope she continues with more of Colette's novels. Required reading."

—Elisabeth Ladenson, professor of French and comparative literature at Columbia University

"'Aren't I splendid?' Chéri asks, and to his arrogant query this grand translation offers a positive response. Even as the splendor of lyric effusion and inevitable tragic ending remind us of *Der Rosenkavalier*, this literary masterpiece of musical interpretation and understatement grabs us with its pity, wit, and layers of lamentation for the ruin of youthful beauty and for the simultaneous self-discovery enacted by character and reader."

—Mary Ann Caws, Distinguished Professor Emerita of comparative literature, English, and French at the Graduate Center of the City University of New York

"This is a refreshing and modern new translation of two of Colette's most fascinating works. The translation itself is natural and readable, and perfectly suited to contemporary audiences. Lydia Davis's foreword provides an engaging backdrop to the stories and to their author."

—Kathleen Antonioli, associate professor of modern languages, Kansas State University

CHÉRI

AND

THE END OF CHÉRI

COLETTE

CHÉRI

AND

THE END OF CHÉRI

TRANSLATED BY RACHEL CAREAU

W. W. NORTON & COMPANY

Independent Publishers Since 1923

Translation copyright © 2022 by Rachel Careau
Foreword copyright © 2022 by Lydia Davis

Originally published in French as *Chéri* and *La fin de Chéri*

For information about permission to reproduce selections from this book, write to
Permissions, W. W. Norton & Company, Inc., 500 Fifth Avenue, New York, NY 10110

For information about special discounts for bulk purchases, please contact
W. W. Norton Special Sales at specialsales@wwnorton.com or 800-233-4830

Manufacturing by Lakeside Book Company
Book design by Chris Welch Design
Production manager: Julia Druskin

Library of Congress Cataloging-in-Publication Data

Names: Colette, 1873–1954, author. | Careau, Rachel, translator. |
Colette, 1873–1954. Fin de Chéri. English.
Title: Chéri : and, The end of Chéri / Colette ; translated by Rachel Careau.
Other titles: Chéri. English
Description: New York, NY : W. W. Norton & Company, [2022]
Identifiers: LCCN 2021052468 | ISBN 9781324006374 (hardcover) |
ISBN 9781324006381 (epub)
Subjects: LCSH: Middle-aged women—Fiction. | Courtesans—Fiction. |
Young men—Fiction. | France—Fiction. | LCGFT: Novels.
Classification: LCC PQ2605.O28 C513 2022 | DDC 843/.912—dc23
LC record available at https://lccn.loc.gov/2021052468

W. W. Norton & Company, Inc., 500 Fifth Avenue, New York, N.Y. 10110
www.wwnorton.com

W. W. Norton & Company Ltd., 15 Carlisle Street, London W1D 3BS

1 2 3 4 5 6 7 8 9 0

CONTENTS

FOREWORD

The Case of Colette

As I have been reading Rachel Careau's brilliantly ingenious, close new translation of *Chéri* and *The End of Chéri*—together constituting, really, the strangest of love stories—I have also been exploring other work by Colette, such as her novel *Green Wheat* and extracts from her early fiction and memoirs, and browsing through what her contemporaries wrote about her. I have been musing over the literary figure she presents and over her reputation here in the United States as opposed to in France, attempting to reconcile the two and to form a more complete and accurate notion of this important writer.

Whereas it is not infrequently said, in France, that she is second only to Proust in importance, in twentieth-century French literature, here in the United States, she is a case apart. She is not always mentioned in the same lists or with the same solemnity as her compatriots Camus, Duras, Sarraute, Butor, Céline, Gide, and others, even though she has many admirers in this country and her works have enjoyed numerous film and television adaptations and have a well-established place, here, in college and graduate course reading lists.

Is she hurt, even in our day, by the fact that she is a woman writer and especially one reputed to write mainly about love, though in fact she wrote about so much more (war, nature, childhood, criminal life, theater, etc.)? Perhaps the fault is our "provincialism," as one Colette-loving friend of mine has said, or, I would add, our relatively narrow acquaintance with the large body of her work, which amounts to forty, fifty—or is it eighty?—books. (Counts vary.) To any French reader, after all, her work is available in its entirety, whereas monolingual Anglophone readers have access only to those books that a publisher has chosen to bring into English, via a translator who may or may not be faithful to Colette's very individual style.

I wonder if our appraisal of her has been too influenced by our association with the 1944 novella *Gigi*, perhaps her most famous story, and, even more, its adaptations? Could it be that some seventy years ago, the winsome Audrey Hepburn, though chosen by Colette herself to play Gigi in the Broadway play, did her a lasting disservice? On this side of the ocean, we have Broadway and Hepburn, while on the other, there is the Legion of Honor, the nomination for a Nobel Prize . . .

I'm also speculating about her name. Just a suspicion—but how many, even among those who read her most enthusiastically here in the United States, must assume that "Colette" is a first name, and a diminutive at that, perhaps similar to certain other rather charming-sounding French words familiar to us ending in *-ette*: *soubrette*, *mignonette*, *midinette*, *coquette*, and the now rejected, as demeaning, *suffragette*? The *New Yorker* writer Janet Flanner, reporting during many years from her base in Paris, respectfully refers to her as "Madame Colette," as do the writer's own fan correspondents. But to most others, she has always been, as they beautifully say, a mononymous author (accent on the second syllable).

"Colette," however, is not a diminutive, nor a first name, but the surname of her father, Jules-Joseph Colette, a military man who, in heroic action, lost a leg in the 1859 war in Italy. "Colette," or "Captain Colette," or simply "the Captain," as his affectionate wife called him, is tenderly described by his daughter, in her memoirs *Sido* and *Le képi*, as a would-be writer who in fact wrote very little, mainly verses that his daughter criticized for their excessively flowery lyricism. Instead, she says, he dissipated his desire to write in arranging on his worktable, and cherishing, the paraphernalia of writing: blotting paper, pens, nibs, an ebony ruler, sharpened pencils of different colors, sealing wax, and so forth, objects coveted, and sometimes stolen, by the adolescent Colette. Most extraordinarily, when he died, he left behind, high up on a shelf, a row of beautiful volumes he had bound himself, complete with titles of projected works on their spines and filled with fine cream-laid paper—but the pages were blank. The family used them, thereafter, for jam pot wrappings, cutlet frills, drawer liners (Colette's mother), for scribbling (her grandchildren), and for writing out medical prescriptions (Colette's doctor brother).

Both parents, it seemed, were readers: when ill, Colette's mother requested oranges and the newspaper; her father would recite to his daughter a high-flown kind of lyric verse that she firmly rejected. These were evidently the examples constantly before young Sidonie-Gabrielle Colette as she was growing up, the youngest child: an older half sister with her nose always in a book; the father the dreamer, who "often made us laugh . . . told a good tale, embroidering recklessly"; the mother the down-to-earth amateur naturalist, industrious, articulate, who wrote so fluently, honestly and gracefully, herself, about love and life, though mainly, or only, in personal letters.

I can imagine—speculating again—that if our associations with her surname had been more like those we have with certain other strong, prominent women writers, such as the stony Stein or the dark Woolf, we might have been biased to view Sidonie-Gabrielle Colette in a different light. (True, the formidable Woolf never appeared on the music hall stage.)

After all, consider the high honors that came her way throughout her life—inducted into the Belgian Royal Academy in 1935; elected to a seat on the prestigious Goncourt Academy in 1944 (preceding Jean Giono and serving with Raymond Queneau); later elected its president; nominated for the Nobel Prize in 1948; recipient of the Legion of Honor in September of 1920, alongside Proust and their mutual friend the poet Anna de Noailles; and, after her death, the first French woman of letters to be honored with a state funeral.

———

The better acquainted one becomes with Colette and her work, the more she acquires definition as the emphatic, no-nonsense, many-faceted person she evidently was, a woman sexually liberated who scorned prejudice—most varieties, in any case. She becomes more clearly visible as a person driven by a boundless, restless energy that finds its outlet in many forms and genres. One commentator characterized her as "eager" and "courageous." The word that occurs to me is "appetite"—she had such appetite not only for life, love, the natural world, experience, but also for variety, innovation, and, as we hear from several sides, for hard work right up to the end.

She was a sensualist, a lover of food who gathered mushrooms in the Bois de Boulogne and ate them there, raw; advised us to add sugar cubes to our *bœuf à la mode*, as our grandmothers used to do. She knew her plants and animals, like her mother, the names of sea-side plants and the preferred food of a swallow, and did not flinch from wringing the neck of a sick bird; so close to her own pets that her second husband used to say, "When I enter a room where you're alone with your animals . . . I feel I'm being indiscreet."

Besides working as a mime and as an actor both early and later in her life, she was also a journalist and editor, not to mention librettist, screenwriter, touring lecturer, writer of film subtitles, amateur photographer, correspondent from the front during World War I, and broadcaster during World War II. Flanner reports that in 1939, Colette, on special assignment as a courtroom reporter for the paper *Paris-Soir*, wrote a "brilliant" article on the charmingly honest, intelligent, and articulate serial killer Eugen Weidmann, a scoundrel so popular with the people of Paris that his execution by guillotine was the last to be carried out in public.

———————

The young Colette was described by Cocteau as "thin, thin . . . a sort of miniature fox in cycling dress . . ." In contrast, by 1929, when she was in her fifties, she is portrayed by Flanner as "a short, heartybodied woman with a crop of wood-colored hair, with long, gray luminous eyes and a deep alto voice . . . [who] still speaks French with a racy Burgundian accent."

It was in the landscape of Burgundy that Colette grew up, free to roam all day on her own. During these years she evidently absorbed her deep knowledge of and love for nature, the knowledge that informs all her work, either in literal descriptions or in metaphorical images. "I was at liberty to keep up as best I could," she writes in the autobiographical *La maison de Claudine* (*My Mother's House*, as translated by Una Vincenzo Troubridge and Enid McLeod), "with my long-legged brothers as they ranged the woods in pursuit of swallowtails, white admirals, purple emperors, or hunted for grass snakes, or gathered armfuls of the tall July foxgloves which grew in the clearings already aglow with patches of purple heather. But I followed them in silence, picking blackberries, bird cherries, a chance wild flower, or roving the hedgerows and waterlogged meadows like an independent dog out hunting." When the children eventually returned, "our anxious mother's keen sense of smell would discover on us traces of wild garlic from a distant ravine or of marsh mint from a treacherous bog. The dripping pocket of one of the boys would disgorge the bathing slip worn in malarial ponds, and the 'little one' "—that is, Sidonie-Gabrielle—"cut about the knees and skinned at the elbows, would be bleeding complacently under plasters of cobweb and wild pepper bound on with rushes." The four children, in her depiction of them, were contentedly occupied from morning to night with reading, nature exploration, scientific invention, and music; kind to one another and, strangely, by preference quite silent.

And the amateur psychologist will peer in vain into this apparently happy childhood in search of hints as to what might have determined her later preoccupation with unconventional love relationships, in her life and in her fiction. Her parents were, she says, in love with each other, both respectful and tender, and at the same time utterly discreet—a courtly kiss on the hand was cause for a blush.

Despite the freedom of her childhood, one of the themes in her work became the place of woman in society and her struggle to liberate herself from its constricting norms. To set her novels within the special world of the "kept" man or woman was to choose a setting beyond the reach of those confines.

The circles she moved in were, naturally, those of artists and writers, but also, at different times in her life, those of the demimonde and the haut monde. It was at one salon, that of Madame Arman de Caillavet's Wednesdays, in the mid-1890s, that she first met the young Proust, who evidently pursued her to the point of irritation.

I particularly delight in her account of the moment, since it shows the two so young—still in their twenties—one eager (Proust) and one intolerant (Colette), decades before they will both, as esteemed writers, be awarded the Cross of the Legion of Honor. She writes: "I was hounded, politely, by a pretty, young literary-minded boy . . . My little flatterer, thrilled by his own evocations, never left me. . . ." She was further put off by "his overweening politeness, the excessive attention he paid to those he was talking to." And yet, years later, when he had aged and was suffering from ill health, she was kinder, describing his pallor and his shadowed eyes, and how, as a group of friends were leaving him, late one evening, the silence of the night and the mist surrounded him "with a halo exactly suited to his decline and his prestige."

In these circles, gender identification was often fluid. Her friends and acquaintances were not only heterosexual but also bisexual, lesbian, and gay. And this fluidity was reflected in her fiction, where she often described a young man as feminine and, recurringly, a female character as "virile," whether it was a girl of fifteen growing into womanhood while at the same time as strong and athletic as a boy, or an older woman becoming more masculine as she aged, sometimes attractively so, sometimes hideously.

Here, too, with regard to age and aging, Colette upended conventional attitudes in her life and her fiction. She herself was married, first, to a man fourteen years older; second, to a man a few years younger; and last, till her death, to a man sixteen years younger. Her years-long affair with a man a full thirty years younger is notorious, though this relationship was apparently not the model for *Chéri*.

In *Chéri*, and especially *The End of Chéri*, the attractiveness of an aging woman, in this case Léa, is convincingly and repeatedly evoked from Chéri's point of view, even by contrast with the lovely young Edmée, who becomes Chéri's wife. In fact, that is the pathos of *The End of Chéri*, finally—how deeply bound Chéri has become to Léa, how perfectly attuned he has grown to be, to this relationship, this "intimate earthly paradise in which Léa and Chéri had lived together for years," as *The End of Chéri* has it. It is a relationship that has no future, no longer any possible life, and yet which—perhaps because he was so young when he first entered into it—Chéri has come to need, desire, and look to for sustenance.

Chéri and *The End of Chéri* were written some six years apart, yet, strikingly, the two novels, though each fully realized on its own, are enhanced by each other, seem almost necessary to each other, once one has experienced them both. *Chéri* ends at a logical point—the main action, the relationship, has come to a conclusion—and yet it has a deceptive innocence, by itself, without its sequel; it is confined to a smaller dimension; we view it, and see it, differently before we have gone on to read *The End of Chéri*. In a parallel fashion, the latter has a darkness absent from the former, a fatality lacking to the former, a deepening of themes begun in the former, that make it a more intensely disturbing, even tragic, novel. And yet for its full import, its full impact, it requires the earlier novel, the earlier part of the story, the sunnier aspect of Léa and Chéri together.

Chéri, in the second novel, is older, and has been through the war. He has also been fatally changed (warped?) by a love that is now and forever out of reach. The woman he loved is still there, she is even, in one sense, available to him, but she has changed, physically, the woman he knew has been subsumed in this different woman, the relationship is no longer possible, and at the same time, for Chéri, no other relationship is possible.

"No one," remarks a critic, in a 2011 article revisiting Colette's *The Vagabond*, "writes about relationships as perceptively as Colette," and it is true that in the two *Chéri* novels, especially,

Colette paints each shade of feeling and perception as exactly as elsewhere she paints the modulations in the surface of the sea or the color of the flower petals in the Paris garden of Chéri's mother. This same critic describes her as "mistress of metaphor and sparkling detail"; Colette conveys the smell of a bedroom in *The End of Chéri* by evoking "old bachelors and cologne," and startles us by comparing the gay men in Proust's *Sodom and Gomorrah*, the opening of which she found so "stunning," to cuttlefish who "propagate at every step their personal cloud."

———

"**O**h, how I like Colette's way of writing!" André Gide wrote exuberantly in his journal in 1941, going on to perfectly sum up some of her writing's most important qualities: "What unerring boldness in the choice of words! What a nice feeling for the nuance! And all without seeming to pay attention—the exquisite result of a painstaking elaboration." We can add to this: her meticulous care for accuracy, her spurning of the sentimental. Proust's biographer Jean-Yves Tadié mentions, also: "terseness . . . geometrical precision, [and a] surface decorated with a few golden touches." It is a style from which Colette, ever self-critical, carefully "weeded out," as she said, any possible "unintentional lines of verse." Her sentiment was balanced by her toughness and wit.

It is a style that some earlier translators perhaps found either too challenging or too unprofitable, so that earlier English versions of certain works may read more smoothly and conventionally than is really representative of the innovation and boldness of Colette's unusual style, which Gide so admired and which Rachel Careau has so painstakingly and inventively reproduced in the present translation.

—————

One commentator, Robert Phelps, wrote some ten years after her death, that "[Colette] also knew ... that to be born sentient and watchful is a daily miracle: that the *paradis terrestre*, the earthly paradise around us, is as wondrous an index of heaven as any we shall ever know; and that to abide here, even as an exile, for seven or eight decades, is a blessing—because it is a chance to watch, to 'look for a long time at what pleases you.' " And it was also up to the writer, Colette said, to find "*un mot meilleur, et meilleur que meilleur*"—"a better word, and better than better"—with which to convey it to others. Thus, the mistress of metaphor and sparkling detail. As to the daily miracle, she added, when still in her early sixties, in her acceptance speech to the members of the Belgian Royal Academy, "to be astonished is one of the surest ways of not growing old too quickly."

Did Sidonie-Gabrielle Colette, before her death at eighty-one, become one of those androgynous older women who people her novels? Perhaps, to some eyes, but she never lost the devotion of her last husband, and when Julien Green visited her late in her life, as she received her visitors from her bed—where she would continue writing almost to the end—he found her unchanged since before the war, "and no one could look at her without loving her. Her large eyes are the most beautiful ones I have ever seen in a woman ... brimming over with soul and sadness."

Lydia Davis

TRANSLATOR'S NOTE

It can seem, today, that Colette's life, or more accurately her myth, has come to overshadow her art in the public imagination. This myth, in the sense not of a fiction but of an amplified and idealized conception, is apparent in the countless readily available photographs of Colette, photographs that attest to a potent mystique and that have become iconic to the cult of Colette: A self-assured Colette, looking worldly-wise beyond her fifteen years, half reclining in a hammock, wearing a sailor dress and broad-brimmed hat, her sinuous braids like twin bullwhips. A deceptively ingenuous Colette, as the little faun in *Le désir, la chimère et l'amour*, with diminutive goat horns and furred ears, looking straight into the camera, her slightly melancholic, triangular face cradled in her hands. The sensational Colette of her music hall years, scandalously exposing one breast in *La chair*, or lying Sphinx-like at the feet of her costar-lover "Yssim" (Missy) in drag, in *Rêve d'Égypte*, before the kiss that provoked an opening-night riot at the Moulin Rouge. Or perhaps most famously, an ambiguously seductive Colette *en travesti*, wearing a dark suit, striped vest, and tie, a lighted cigarette balanced between her second and third fingers, her head tilted coyly to one side.

Regarding her legacy as a writer, she herself, as Julia Kristeva has remarked, undeniably "muddied the waters: scandalous woman, sexual woman, she played with that a great deal." She had what Angela Carter memorably described as an "uncompromising zeal for self-exploitation," and was therefore never averse to creating a sensation in either her professional or her personal life. Professionally, she reinvented herself over the years in ways that surprised and sometimes shocked: from writer to music hall mime, to war correspondent, editor, crime reporter, stage actor, advice columnist, beauty product entrepreneur, and, ultimately, Grand Officier of the Légion d'honneur and luminary of the Académie Goncourt. Her very name became a medium for her reinventions: born Sidonie-Gabrielle Colette, called Gabri within the family, known to her mother as Minet-Chéri, she became Colette Willy after her first marriage and then, after her second, Colette de Jouvenel, before finally, in 1923, signing herself, with the economy typical of her prose, simply Colette.

Personally, her life was endlessly complicated. Its more lurid (and mythologized) facts are well known. Her first marriage, at the age of twenty, to the louche journalist and writer "Monsieur Willy" (Henry Gauthier-Villars), fourteen years her senior, with his "obscene German postcards" and his "trunk loads of pornographic books": he published her first novels under his own name, and appropriated, then sold, the rights. Her five-year affair (not her first with a woman) with the lesbian transvestite the Marquise de Belbeuf, born Sophie-Mathilde-Adèle-Denise de Morny, called Missy, niece of Napoleon III and great-granddaughter of the Empress Josephine: Colette, in her devotion, wore a bracelet engraved with the words *J'appartiens à Missy* (I belong to Missy). Her second marriage, to the aristocratic future statesman Henry de Jouvenel: with Sidi, as she called him, Colette enjoyed the title of baroness and a material comfort she had lacked with Willy, but like Willy, the handsome, seductive Jouvenel betrayed her openly and repeatedly. Her semi-incestuous five-year affair with her stepson Bertrand de Jouvenel: she initiated the liaison when he was seventeen and she forty-seven and still married to his father. Less known, because less sensational, are the details of her third—happy—marriage, to the steady, urbane Maurice Goudeket, who would remain devoted to her, as she was to him, for the last thirty years of her life, through her long decade of crippling arthritis, her immobilization and confinement to "the raft"—her divan-bed in the entresol apartment at the Palais-Royal—and her apotheosis in the Académie Goncourt. Still less known are some of the more unattractive aspects of her story: the indifference and neglect that characterized her relationship with her daughter, Colette de Jouvenel, known as Bel-Gazou, and the unsavory fact that she wrote for collaborationist journals during the Second World War.

Colette was born into modest circumstances, on January 28, 1873, in the village of Saint-Sauveur-en-Puisaye, in rural Burgundy, and although she moved to Paris at the age of twenty and, except for brief visits, never returned, she always retained her country girl's love of the woods and of flower gardens, her naturalist's fascination with the characteristics and behaviors of plants and animals, her folk wisdom and rural know-how. She made her home in Paris until her death in 1954, becoming the quintessential Parisian, as much a fixture of the Palais-Royal as its stone arches and columned arcade, yet she never ceased to draw on her provincial roots, famously retaining her rolled Burgundian *r*'s, consciously playing "to the tension in French culture between the nostalgic idealization of a rural past, and the sense of national identity as sophisticated, urban, and intellectual," as Diana Holmes has noted. This, too, became part of her myth, and the source, perhaps, of her particular attraction for the French.

So potent a myth has the power to obscure another Colette, Colette the artist—sedulous, stylistically disciplined, precise, a writer who, as Maurice Goudeket recalled, "loved certain words for themselves, quite apart from the idea which they represent . . . loved them for their music," but also for their specificity, for their "homely technicality." She was known to be prodigiously hardworking, taking on overlapping projects and putting in long hours at her desk: according to Goudeket, during periods of intense concentration she was "capable . . . of working eight or ten hours at a stretch" and "was not far at such times from a sort of trance-like state." She wrote some fifty books (seventy-three, claims Janet Flanner), including novels, memoirs, collections of journalism and short stories, and a book of literary portraits of flower bouquets; among her books are *The Vagabond*, *My Mother's House*, *Break of Day*, *The Pure and the Impure*, and *The Cat*. Her collected works fill four volumes and a staggering 7,488 pages in the Bibliothèque de la Pléiade edition.

Paradoxically, Colette's particular discipline perhaps manifests itself more in what is left out of her books than in what is put in. She subjected her texts to what Marie-Christine Bellosta has described as "a stubborn eradication of everything that wasn't absolutely indispensable," and indeed, what becomes most apparent to the reader of her work in the original French is its extreme and seemingly effortless economy: it contains no excess, no ornament, nothing beyond the essential. Her sentences can feel skeletal, the flesh carved away to convey their meaning with the fewest possible words. A master of concision, subtraction, condensation, renunciation, she is always trying to do more with less: "You become a great writer," she states, "as much through what you refuse your pen as through what you grant it."

Her refusals take several forms. Notably sparing is her use of the kinds of words that create smooth transitions within a sentence, such as coordinating conjunctions (*and, but, yet*, and so forth) and relative pronouns (*who* and *which*, for example)—the connective tissue of language. Compound predicates often take the form *a, b, c*, omitting the coordinating conjunction that commonly precedes the final element in a series, so that she tends to write sentences like *Elle abaissa son regard, rencontra celui de Chéri, sourit* (She lowered her eyes, met Chéri's, smiled). She makes frequent use of comma splices, as, for example, in *Il allait disparaître, il se retourna* (He was about to slip away, he turned around), both eschewing the *and* or *but* that might otherwise connect the two independent clauses and declining to subordinate one clause to the other so as to clarify the logical connection between them (*As* he was about to slip away, he turned around). She manages without *who* clauses when she can, so that, for example, she will write *Chéri, debout dans le cadre de la porte, Chéri venu sur ses pieds ailés et muets* (Chéri, standing in the doorframe, Chéri borne on his winged, silent feet) rather than clutter a sentence with a superfluous relative pronoun. All these choices tend to make her writing a bit jagged and syncopated, the transitions a bit abrupt.

She is sparing, too, with adjectives. Already at ten years old, Colette displayed this aversion to embellishment. Her father, Jules-Joseph Colette, a former captain in the Zouaves, had lost his leg at Melegnano fighting for Napoleon III. Ever after an aspiring writer, he valued Colette's critical opinions and once read to her "a lovely piece of oratorical prose, or an ode, smooth lines, lavish in their rhythm and rhyme, as sonorous as a mountain storm," to which, Colette recalled in *Sido*, she "listened, severely." When he had finished, she shook her head and pronounced her judgment: "Still too many adjectives!" Even at so early an age, she was an unsparing and astute critic.

Her antipathy to ornament also leads her to forgo long, flowing sentences, complex syntax, and lavish descriptions—elements that she must have attributed to what she disparagingly called "literature." As literary editor of *Le Matin*—a job she held from the end of the Great War until early 1924, and throughout the composition of *Chéri*—Colette read the stories of a young Georges Simenon. Summoning him to her office, she told him: "You know, I read your last story . . . It isn't right. It's almost right, but it isn't right. You're too literary. You must not make literature. No literature! Suppress all the literature and it will work." Forty years later, Simenon reflected: "It's the advice that's been the most useful to me in life."

This antipathy is evident in *Chéri*, where, for example, Colette eschews the picturesque, refraining from describing Italy's Lake District (where Chéri and Edmée spend their honeymoon) or the Côte d'Azur and the Pays Basque (where Léa travels to try to forget Chéri), to focus on the principal locales in which the story's action takes place—the pink cocoon of Léa's home on the avenue Bugeaud, Charlotte Peloux's villa on the boulevard d'Inkermann in Neuilly, Desmond's rooms at the Morris Hotel, and Chéri and Edmée's mansion on the avenue Henri-Martin. By restricting herself to a relatively small number of places and characters, and limiting their description to a few dominant features—focusing, for example, on Chéri's satanic eyebrows and quivering nostrils, on Léa's honest blue eyes and slackening neck—Colette is able to achieve a unity of expression that makes these novels feel taut but never thin.

This stripped-down quality, this lack of literary affectation, is what André Gide is responding to when he writes to her on December 11, 1920, to congratulate her on *Chéri*, which had been published in book form by Fayard the previous July: "What I particularly like in your book is its spareness, its divestment, its nakedness." And it's in part because of this economy, this directness, that her writing still feels fresh and vital and approachable today.

Economy of style doesn't, however, preclude a linguistic richness. Within its stylistic austerity, Colette's work is remarkable for the range of its vocabulary as well as for the variability of its diction, which shifts seamlessly from high to low, from classical and archaic to contemporary, from rare and literary usages to the regionalisms and contemporary argot that, along with her keen ear, lend verisimilitude to her dialogue—in Colette's own words, "loose, rapid, malleable dialogue" that is truly "the slack and living language that we speak in daily life."

All these hallmarks of Colette's writing, from its terse style to its wide-ranging vocabulary, present challenges to the translator. Extreme economy is difficult to translate, or at least to translate well, as if the words, without their synovial fluid—the conjunctions and relative pronouns of smoothly flowing sentences—are bone on bone. The translator who wishes to respect Colette's style must avoid the temptation to flesh out, to fill in, to adorn. Similarly, the translator must resist the urge to "correct" Colette's comma splices and sentence fragments, or her exuberantly mixed metaphors, which appear not to have troubled her, so that she could write, for example, *Desmond mordait à même la paix avec une fureur guerrière, dont les rapides fruits étonnaient Chéri* (Desmond bit straight into peacetime with a warlike fury, whose rapid fruits surprised Chéri), and *Chéri, bondissant de quatre marches en quatre marches, trouva son ami qui semblait boire, lèvres au calice, la ténébreuse haleine du récepteur* (Chéri, bounding four at a time up the steps, found his friend, who seemed to be drinking, lips to the chalice, the obscure breath of the receiver). And the translator must become a detective, sleuthing out the more obscure words—the rare senses of familiar verbs, the neologisms, the street vernacular—that surprise again and again in her work.

Skeletal, flesh, connective tissue, synovial fluid, nakedness: it is not surprising that metaphorical references to the body frequently arise when we try to describe Colette's work, because Colette devotes at least as much attention to her characters' physical being and transformation as to the evolution of their psychological states. Physical features, gesture, movement, stance, all take on primary importance in Colette's presentation of character. In this, Colette demonstrates what I. T. Olken has identified as her "preference for an idiom that externalizes and materializes thought and feeling," as though she were depicting a nonhuman species. Indeed, the character of Chéri—beautiful, taciturn, instinctual—is more intuitive animal than thinking being.

———

Chéri and *The End of Chéri*, though they were conceived independently and published six years apart, arguably form a single novel, considered by many to be Colette's masterwork. To the poet Anna de Noailles, somewhat disingenuously, Colette once described *Chéri* as "a little novel about sad people almost unworthy of suffering." Writing to the critic Jean de Pierrefeu, however, she softened her stance: "To be drawn towards the pitiful—Léa, and Chéri even more than she, are the pitiful living among the pitiful—is that so base? . . . It seems to me that I've never written anything so moral as *Chéri*." Indeed, the portion of nobility that Colette accords to Léa and Chéri—each after a different fashion—allows the suffering of these two "pitiful" beings to move us, in spite (or perhaps because) of their flaws.

Chéri appeared in 1920, eight years after the opening of the story it tells, which unfolds between June 1912 and spring 1913 (specifically May, since the chestnut trees are in bloom), in Paris and Neuilly. The plot, like Colette's style, is economical, and easily recounted. Léa, an aging courtesan of forty-nine at the end of a successful career, learns that her twenty-five-year-old lover, the flawlessly beautiful but emotionally opaque Chéri, is soon to enter into an arranged marriage, bringing an end to their six-year affair. Léa and Chéri part without bitterness, Chéri marries, grows dissatisfied—unable to forget Léa—and, for a time, leaves his docile young wife, Edmée. Léa, meanwhile, has departed Paris to travel so as to make a clean break. When Chéri discovers that Léa has returned, he goes home to his wife, but he is drawn back to Léa's for one last night, after which, unable to accept the signs of her aging, he leaves Léa definitively.

When *The End of Chéri* begins, we are on the other side of the First World War. The year is 1919 (so Chéri tells us), the month June, although Colette's timeline is a bit hazy: At the close of *Chéri*, it's May 1913, Léa has turned fifty, and Chéri is twenty-five. But partway through *The End of Chéri*, Chéri laments, "I'm thirty years old!" on the one hand, while on the other estimating that Léa would now be "fifty-eight, perhaps sixty." Chéri would have been thirty in spring 1918; Léa, fifty-eight in 1921, sixty in 1923. Other details point to a date later than June 1919, such as Chéri's bringing up "the Lenoir boy's accident" (probably a reference to an actual event that took place in September 1919) and Léa's mention of dining at Montagné's (presumably Prosper Montagné's Paris restaurant of that name, which didn't open until 1920). Since we know that Christmas 1918 has come and gone, we can state with certainty that the Armistice has passed and that we are at least some months into life in a postwar context. The plot, again, is stripped down, and the timeline even more compressed than that of *Chéri*, the events taking place between June and either September or October (here again, there is confusion) of the same year. Chéri, now a decorated soldier, has returned from the trenches to a changed world in which he can't find his place. Emotionally estranged from his dynamic, independent, and unfaithful wife, disenchanted with both money and pleasure, Chéri spends his nights as a solitary walker. Encouraged by his mother—Léa's treacherous friend and fellow courtesan Charlotte Peloux—Chéri visits Léa, in a scene that Judith Thurman calls "probably the greatest Colette ever wrote." But Léa is no longer the Léa of *Chéri*: comfortable in her retirement, she has taken on a "sexless dignity" and "immense" physical proportions that repel Chéri, and he flees. Visiting a bar unchanged since his boyhood, Chéri has a fateful reunion with the Girlfriend, an aging, destitute, and kindly former prostitute from Léa's circle. She invites him to her apartment, where he takes refuge alongside a wall of photographs of a Léa who no longer exists, as his foreseeable end inexorably plays out.

Loss reverberates through these two books. Léa's loss of beauty and femininity and a way of life, Chéri's loss of definition and purpose, his loss of connection to others—Edmée, Desmond, even his wounded fellow soldiers—the culture's loss of the carefree innocence and gaiety of the Belle Époque, Léa and Chéri's shared loss of each other: all these losses might have plotted similar courses for Léa and Chéri. But unlike Chéri, Léa has been compensated for her losses: in exchange for her beauty and femininity, she has gained "newfound strengths," among them "a tranquil virility" (virility in a woman being a virtue that Colette proudly ascribes to herself in *L'étoile Vesper*). Léa's resilience and adaptability cause her life's trajectory, like that of Edmée and of Charlotte Peloux, to arc upward, whereas the force of memory ineluctably draws Chéri into a downward trajectory from which he cannot break away. "In *Chéri* and *The End of Chéri*," Colette herself remarked in 1926, "I simply wanted to say that when an older woman has a relationship with a very young man, she is less likely than he to remain indelibly marked by it. Try as he may, in all his relationships to come, he will be unable to avoid recalling the memory of his old mistress." Chéri has been indelibly marked—condemned—by his relationship with Léa.

At the time that Colette made this observation, after the publication of *La fin de Chéri*, she herself had been the older woman whose memory would mark a very young man. Her relationship with her stepson Bertrand had ended in 1924 or 1925. Public knowledge of their liaison and their respective ages at the time of the publication of *Chéri*—forty-seven and seventeen—gave rise to much speculation about whether Bertrand had been the original of Chéri. Bertrand himself put an end to the speculation with the publication in 1986 of his disclaimer in volume 2 of Colette's *Œuvres* in the Pléiade edition: the composition of *Chéri* had preceded their relationship. It was a pure instance of life imitating art.

Among the actual models for Chéri, Colette told Bertrand in 1922, was Auguste Hériot, the heir to the fabulous Grands Magasins du Louvre fortune, with whom she had begun an affair in 1910, when she was thirty-seven and he twenty-four; Bertrand, however, discounts the likeness. Colette put forth the Belle Époque actress Suzanne Derval as an inspiration for the character of Léa; other demimondaines whom Colette personally knew—among them the celebrated courtesans Liane de Pougy (who had been Hériot's lover before Colette) and La Belle Otero—no doubt played a part as well. The "manly" character of the Baronne de La Berche, "burdened with a sexual aberrancy," certainly owes a debt to Missy, the Marquise de Belbeuf. But all were clearly only partial models.

The character of Chéri began life as Clouk. Rich, docile, sniffling, a bit pathetic, Clouk was the subject of five short stories published in *Le Matin*, the first on August 11, 1911, and the remaining four between June 27 and December 27, 1912. In the intervening months, from January 25 to April 4, 1912, he was superseded by Chéri—still rich but slightly malevolent and, quite unlike Clouk, possessed of head-turning good looks. After 1912, both characters would disappear entirely until Chéri's resurrection in 1919, when Colette began the composition of *Chéri*. It was beyond Colette's powers, it would seem, to sustain her interest in so pitiful a being as Clouk.

In *Chéri* and *The End of Chéri*, all of Colette's skills as a novelist are on view: the freshness and detail of her descriptions, her precise evocation of the physical world through sensory imagery, her convincing portrayal of her characters' complex and shifting inner lives, motivations, and desires, her brilliant construction of scenes, her clear-eyed depiction of the social life of the Parisian demimonde before and after the First World War, her keen awareness of nuances of social distinction, her biting humor. To have achieved all this in so few strokes, to have arrived at the depth and complexity of these two novels with such economy of expression, underscores Colette's mastery as a writer.

Among her contemporaries, it was not only André Gide who admired Colette. She first met Marcel Proust at the Wednesday salons of Madame Arman de Caillavet on the avenue Hoche in 1894 or 1895, and although they fell out of touch for twenty years beginning in 1897, they began corresponding again in December 1917, when Colette sent Proust a copy of *Les heures longues*, a collection of her wartime journalism. They exchanged books and letters from then on, until Proust's death in 1922. Responding to Colette after she had sent him a copy of *Chéri* in 1920, the year in which they had both been awarded the rank of Chevalier of the Légion d'honneur, Proust wrote, "It is I who am proud to be decorated alongside the author of the ingenious *Chéri*. [. . .] You are well aware that I am the admirer, and you the admired." In 1927, five years after Proust's death, Paul Claudel called Colette "the greatest living writer in France," an assessment reiterated by her fellow French writers in a 1935 poll, in which she was declared "the greatest living master of French prose." More recently, her admirers have ranged from Edmund White to Philip Roth, both of whom named *Chéri* as one of their favorite books; and Julia Kristeva devoted volume 3 of her trilogy *Female Genius: Life, Madness, Words* to Colette, calling her "the priestess of the mot juste" whose work is moreover a "hymn to jouissance . . . articulated for the first time in the voice and by the pen of a woman, a Frenchwoman."

————

Given that Colette is, in the words of her biographer Yvonne Mitchell, "appallingly difficult to translate," it's not surprising that there have been so few translations made of *Chéri* and *La fin de Chéri*. I am aware of three previous English translations of *Chéri*, by Janet Flanner (1929), Roger Senhouse (1951), and Stanley Appelbaum (2001). Of *La fin de Chéri*, there appear to be still fewer: Viola Gerard Garvin's (1933) and Roger Senhouse's (1951). Flanner's and Garvin's translations are all but unavailable; Senhouse's translations have been much reprinted and have long been the standard versions.

For the prospective translator of these books, Senhouse has set the bar high, since his translations have considerable charm. Roger Henry Pocklington Senhouse (1899–1970) was a British translator and publisher marginally associated with the Bloomsbury group. Educated at Eton and Oxford, in 1936 he became co-owner, with Frederic Warburg, of Secker & Warburg, the house that would later publish his translations of *Chéri* and *La fin de Chéri* in England. His knowledge of French was impressive, if not above the occasional mistake, and he had a good ear. Nevertheless, his translations are not without flaws, and while some of those flaws can be considered minor, others are more serious.

Readers of a seventy-year-old translation by a Briton will expect the occasional Briticism and dated word or turn of phrase. Dated language and unfamiliar dialect, however, can sometimes baffle or even

mislead modern American readers. From their very first words—
"Give it me, Léa"—Senhouse's translations of *Chéri* and *La fin de
Chéri* announce their Britishness, and although we are unsurprised
by such run-of-the-mill Anglicisms as "petrol" for gasoline, "lorry"
for truck, or "chap" for fellow, other locutions are more mystifying,
and we may well scratch our heads when presented with "ha'porth"
for *sou* (a five-centime piece), "done a bunk" for *fichu le camp* (cleared
off), "wheezes" for *trucs* (tricks), and "skivvy" for *rosse* (a good-for-
nothing). More problematic still, for example, is Senhouse's substitu-
tion of the British exclamation "Oh my sainted aunt!" for *Mes amis!*
(My friends!)—an error in judgment that he compounds a few lines
later by rendering *n'invoque pas ta vermine d'amis ici* (don't invoke
your low-life friends here) as "Don't invoke your wretched aunt in
my house." Léa's admonishment feels oddly ungrounded, since it is
the first and last reference anywhere to any aunt of Chéri's. Similarly, dated language such as "shan't," or "stuff!" for *poésie*, poses
little difficulty, but "Odol" for *dentifrice* is nowadays obscure.

Senhouse was, of course, a product of his time and place, and his
choices reflect his milieu. But other kinds of choices can rightly be
called flaws. The flaws in Senhouse's translations can roughly be
assigned to the following six categories: omissions; mistranslations;
inconsistent translations; embellishments; alterations; and disregard
for sentence structure, paragraphing, and space breaks.

Senhouse's most glaring omission occurs on the second page
of *Chéri*, where he leaves out one entire sentence, *Il penchait sur la
femme couchée un rire provocant qui montrait des dents toutes petites et
l'envers mouillé de ses lèvres* (He pitched over the reclining woman a
provocative laugh that displayed his tiny teeth and the moist inside
of his lips)—an inauspicious beginning. Other, smaller omissions—
excluding from Léa's internal discourse the repetition of "national
Harpy" in reference to Charlotte Peloux in the first chapter, for

example, or rendering the sneering moniker *Berthellemy-le-Desséché* (Berthellemy the Desiccated) simply as "Berthellemy"—occur throughout the two books, sometimes softening the text's bite (as in these two cases).

More prevalent are Senhouse's mistranslations. To give but a few examples: Chéri does not dine on "a roast bird" at a grillroom with Desmond, but rather—indulging a peculiarly French appetite—on roasted songbirds (*des oiseaux rôtis*). (Appelbaum follows Senhouse's lead, then compounds the error by rendering the phrase "roast chicken.") Chéri doesn't insinuate that the Baronne de La Berche leaves the president of the Ranch company's board of directors to "cover her face in flour" but rather to down a bottle of cheap white wine (*s'appuyer un kil de blanc*). When Léa tells Chéri that he looks as if he's been *battu de l'oiseau*, she's not saying, "You've been fluttering your wings too much," but rather that he looks "like the quarry struck by the hawk"—that is, as if he's been beaten down by misfortune and has lost his courage (according to *Le Littré*, the metaphor comes from falconry and refers to an avian predator beating its prey with its wing). In describing her landlady to Chéri as *un oiseau aux yeux de pervenche*, the Girlfriend isn't saying that she has "periwinkle blue eyes, and *a head like a bird*" but that she's "a creature with periwinkle blue eyes"—*oiseau* meaning a person, an individual. And when Chéri, returning home late one night, calls, *Petit greffier, viens*, to the gray cat that escapes through the opened front door, he's saying, "C'mere, little puss," not "Come here, little clerk of the courts."

Inconsistencies can result from mistranslations or inattention and can confuse the mental picture we make as we read, as well as chip away at the unity of the text. Is a *bergère*, to take one example, a "basket chair," a "wickerwork chair," or an "armchair"? Senhouse has all three.

Senhouse's embellishments (by which I mean *additions* to the text) are unfortunately numerous, and not only change the meaning but also add fat to Colette's lean style. *Chaises maigres et solides* (delicate but sturdy chairs) becomes "spindly yet strong *Sheraton* chairs"; *le faisait repeindre en vert* (would have it repainted in green) becomes "would have it repainted a *similar muddy* green"; *un cheval de douairière* (a dowager's horse) becomes "a *quiet* horse *appropriate* to a dowager"; *tout ce que je ne t'ai pas appris* (everything I didn't teach you) becomes "*the wisdom and kindness* you never learned from me"; *un brave type* (a decent guy) becomes "a *rare* good sort"; *pour souiller et pour nuire* (to sully and disparage) becomes "to spatter and wound *one whom he had loved*"; *pour un gigolo* (over a gigolo) becomes "over some *wretched* gigolo"—the list goes on and on. Senhouse sometimes supplies a missing word that Colette has deliberately left out, "dumbing down" the text as if the reader could not be relied on to catch the allusion, so that *le svelte lys verdissant* (the slender greenish lily) becomes "*her* slim lily-green *son*," in case we have missed the allusion to Chéri (Appelbaum renders this "his slender greenish-white face," losing the figurative lily entirely), and *après le jour de la surprise devant la glace* (after the day of the surprise in front of the mirror) becomes "even after surprising *Edmée* in front of the looking-glass." Finally, Senhouse has a tendency to turn all metaphors into similes, weakening Colette's metaphoric language, so that, for example, *le doux bruit d'étrave fendant une eau calme* (the gentle sound of a bow cleaving calm water) becomes "a sound *like* the ripple of a ship's prow cleaving calm waters," *renversa une tête blessée* (tipped back a wounded head) becomes "tilted his head back *as if he had been struck*," and *Le vent, créé par la vitesse, lui plaquait au visage le battement d'une sèche serviette chaude* (The wind generated by his speed hit him in the face with the slap of a hot dry towel) becomes "The breath of wind raised by the speed of his motor was *like* a hot dry towel being flapped in his face."

Alterations (by which I mean *substitutions* for the words in the text) also abound in Senhouse's translations: for example, *la porte de son ancienne chambre* (the door to his old bedroom) becomes "the door of his *nursery*"; *il ne faut pas toucher à la hache* (you mustn't touch the ax) becomes "Never play with cold steel" (missing the allusion to "*Ne touchez pas à la hache,*" Montriveau's words of warning to the Duchesse in Balzac's *La duchesse de Langeais,* said to be the words of Charles I to his executioner); *Je ne sais pas si trois déménagements valent un incendie* (I don't know whether three moves equal a fire) becomes "*The proverb may well be true that* three moves are as bad as a fire" (although it is indeed a proverb, Colette never says so); *les 'espoirs'* (the "hopefuls") becomes "*white* hopes," and *un chinois* (a Chinese), "a Chinee" (tainting the text with a racist ideology that is absent in the original French); *cette philosophie culinaire* (this culinary philosophy) becomes "this *obsession* with the kitchen"; *le ciel* (the sky) becomes "the *vault of the heavens*"; and *la blessée nue* (the naked victim) becomes "the wounded *Circassian.*"

The final category of flaws in Senhouse's translations—disregard for sentence structure, paragraphing, and space breaks—encompasses the greatest number of Senhouse's transgressions. Of course, a translation that doggedly follows the sentence structure of its source text will be a poor translation indeed; but whenever syntax represents an author's deliberate choice, as distinct from the conventions of the language, its idiosyncrasies should be respected as far as possible within the limits of the target language. Time and again, Senhouse's sentences bear little or no syntactic relationship to Colette's. The order of phrases is modified; long sentences are broken up into shorter ones; short sentences, expanded into longer ones. Too often, Senhouse is loose and flabby where Colette is tight and lean. Finally, Colette's paragraphing is repeatedly disregarded, and space breaks are sometimes overlooked.

The cumulative effect of all these flaws is to radically alter Colette's style. In doing so, Senhouse does a great disservice to English-language readers of these masterpieces of concision by obscuring the very essence of her greatness.

———

The First World War—the Great War, as it was then called, or, in French, *la guerre de quatorze*, *quatorze-dix-huit*, or simply *quatorze*—is at once clearly present and virtually absent in these books. In *Chéri*, it lies in the future, beyond the characters' ken; but as readers we bring to the novel our knowledge of the world-changing convulsions that are to come. In *The End of Chéri*, the war's consequences are everywhere evident, but the war's trauma is suppressed. There are no combat flashbacks, no heroic accounts of bravery under fire; we are shown only the redheaded boy Pierquin's death, briefly, and Chéri's ignominious response.

Colette herself had experienced the war firsthand, both at home and at the front. In October 1914 she had served as a nurse at a temporary hospital set up at the Lycée Janson-de-Sailly, working long shifts tending soldiers critically wounded in the war, while her then husband, Henry de Jouvenel, was serving at the front in Verdun. Remarkably, not long after, she left Paris to join him there, remaining for several months, living in hiding, witnessing barrages and air battles. Later, in mid-1915, she went to Rome on assignment as a reporter for *Le Matin*. Her war experience no doubt underpins her depiction, in *The End of Chéri*, of Edmée's "heap of wounded," and we can hear the echo of her own observations of shell-shocked young ex-soldiers in postwar Paris in Léa's counsel to Chéri.

Despite Colette's stated intention, these are novels about more than the indelible mark left by an older mistress on a much younger man. In *The End of Chéri*, Chéri's trauma is twofold: for Chéri, "there was Léa, the war . . ." His longing to return to Léa is also a longing to return to an unchanging prewar state. War inevitably brings change, and in the aftermath of the war, everyone around him has adapted, has changed: Desmond grips Chéri's hand "in a hand that had changed"; Léa says to him, "I've changed, eh, kid?"; of Charlotte Peloux and Edmée, he observes, "Their whole world changes, and exists to change." But seeing Léa's pearls, he thinks, "*They* haven't changed! They and I haven't changed": only he is incapable of adaptation, incapable of change. The war serves to throw this truth into sharp relief. Rather than expanding outward and forward into the future, like the lives of those around him, Chéri's life moves inward and backward, folding into itself like "his index finger against a small projection of threaded steel."

Rachel Careau

CHÉRI

"Léa! Let me have your pearl necklace! Do you hear me, Léa? Let me have your necklace!"

No response came from the big wrought-iron and embossed-copper bed, which shone in the darkness like a suit of armor.

"Why wouldn't you let me have your necklace? It suits me as well as it does you, or even better!"

At the click of the clasp, the bed's lacework shook, two magnificent bare arms with delicate wrists lifted two beautiful, idle hands.

"Leave it alone, Chéri, you've played with that necklace enough."

"I'm having fun . . . Are you afraid I'll steal it from you?"

In front of the sun-pierced pink curtains he was dancing, all black, like a graceful devil against a blazing furnace. But when he stepped back toward the bed, he became all white again, from his silk pajamas to his suede babouches.

"I'm not afraid," the sweet, low voice replied from the bed. "But you're wearing out the string of the necklace. The pearls are heavy."

"They are that," Chéri said with respect. "He didn't skimp on you, whoever gave you this piece."

He stood in front of a long mirror mounted on the wall between the two windows and contemplated his image, that of a very beautiful, very young man, neither tall nor short, his hair blue-tinged like a blackbird's feathers. He opened his nightshirt, revealing a firm olive chest, thrust out like a shield, and the same rosy sparkle played across his teeth, the whites of his dark eyes, and the pearls of the necklace.

"Take off that necklace," the female voice insisted. "Do you hear what I'm saying?"

Motionless before his reflection, the young man laughed softly:

"Yes, yes, I hear. I know perfectly well that you're afraid I'll take it from you!"

"No. But if I gave it to you, you'd be capable of accepting it."

He ran to the bed, threw himself onto it in a ball:

"Would I ever! I'm above conventions. I find it idiotic that a man can accept from a woman one pearl on a stickpin, or two for studs, but thinks himself dishonored if she gives him fifty . . ."

"Forty-nine."

"Forty-nine, I know the number. Tell me it doesn't suit me! Tell me I'm ugly!"

He pitched over the reclining woman a provocative laugh that displayed his tiny teeth and the moist inside of his lips. Léa sat up in bed:

"No, I won't say that. First of all because you wouldn't believe it. But can't you laugh without crinkling your nose like that? You'll be quite pleased when you have three wrinkles at the corners of your nose, won't you?"

He stopped laughing at once, flattened the skin of his forehead, tucked in the underside of his chin with the skill of an old coquette. They eyed each other with hostility, she propped on her elbows among her lingerie and lace, he sitting sidesaddle at the edge of the bed. He was thinking: "She's got a nerve, telling me about the wrinkles I'll have." And she: "Why is he ugly when he laughs, he who is beauty itself?" She reflected for a moment and finished her thought aloud:

"It's just that you look so nasty when you're cheerful . . . You laugh only out of spitefulness or sarcasm. It makes you ugly. You're often ugly."

"That's not true!" Chéri cried with irritation.

Anger knitted his eyebrows across the bridge of his nose, widened his eyes, full of an insolent light and fortified with lashes, half opened the chaste, disdainful arc of his mouth. Léa smiled to see him as she loved him, rebellious, then submissive, uncomfortably enslaved, unable to be free; she placed a hand on his young head, which impatiently shook off the yoke. She murmured, the way one calms an animal:

"There . . . there . . . What's this . . . what's this, now . . ."

He collapsed onto her beautiful, broad shoulder, pressing his forehead and nose into it, hollowing out his customary spot, already closing his eyes and seeking the protection of his long morning nap, but Léa pushed him away:

"None of that, Chéri! You're having lunch with our national Harpy and it's twenty to twelve."

"No! I'm having lunch with the boss? You, too?"

Léa slipped back lazily into the depths of the bed.

"Not me, I'm on vacation. I'll go have coffee at two thirty, or tea at six o'clock, or a cigarette at quarter to eight . . . Don't worry, she'll still see enough of me . . . And besides, she didn't invite me."

Chéri, who was on his feet sulking, lit up with mischief:

"I know, I know why! We're having the right sort of people! We're having the lovely Marie-Laure and her pest of a child!"

Lea's big blue eyes, which were wandering, fixed on him:

"Really? Charming, the girl. Less so than her mother, but charming . . . Take off that necklace, now, I mean it."

"Too bad," Chéri sighed as he unfastened it. "It would look nice in the wedding basket."

Léa lifted herself up on one elbow:

"What wedding basket?"

"Mine," Chéri said with a comical self-importance. "MY wedding basket for MY jewelry for MY marriage . . ."

He leapt into the air, landed on his feet again after a proper entrechat-six, pushed aside the portiere with a butt of his head, and disappeared, crying:

"My bath, Rose! As high as it'll go! I'm having lunch with the boss!"

"That's that," Léa mused. "A lake in the bathroom, eight towels swimming in it, and razor scrapings in the sink. If only I had two bathrooms . . ."

But she told herself, as on other occasions, that it would mean getting rid of one closet, and trimming off part of the dressing room, and concluded, as on other occasions:

"I'll just put up with it until Chéri's marriage."

She lay down on her back again and noticed that Chéri had, the previous evening, thrown his socks on the mantelpiece, his drawers on the bonheur du jour, his tie around the neck of a bust of Léa. She smiled in spite of herself at this ardent masculine disorder and half closed her large, tranquil eyes, which were a youthful blue and had kept all their chestnut-brown lashes. At forty-nine years old, Léonie Vallon, known as Léa de Lonval, was ending a successful career as a well-paid courtesan and obliging girl who had been spared life's flattering catastrophes and noble griefs. She kept her birth date a secret; but she freely admitted, letting fall on

Chéri a look of voluptuous condescension, that she was reaching the age where she was due some small pleasures. She loved order, beautiful linens, mature wines, well-thought-out meals. Her youth as a fawned-over blonde, then her maturity as a rich demimondaine, had countenanced neither angry outbursts nor equivocation, and her friends remembered one Drags Day, around 1895, when Léa replied to the assistant editor of *Gil Blas*, who had called her "dear artist":

"Artist? Really now, dear friend, my lovers are awfully indiscreet . . ."

Her contemporaries were jealous of her unshakable health, young women whose backsides and stomachs already bulged beneath the fashions of 1912 scoffed at Léa's shapely breasts, the latter and the former equally envied her Chéri.

"My goodness!" Léa would say. "There's no reason to. They can have him. I don't keep him on a leash, and he goes out by himself."

About this, she was half lying, proud as she was of a liaison—she sometimes said "adoption," owing to her penchant for sincerity— that had now lasted six years.

"The wedding basket . . . ," Léa repeated. "Marrying off Chéri . . . It's not possible, it's not . . . human . . . Giving a girl to Chéri—why not just throw a doe to the dogs? People don't know what Chéri is."

Between her fingers, like a rosary, she rolled the necklace flung onto the bed. She took it off at night now because Chéri, who was mad about beautiful pearls and stroked them lovingly each morning, would have noticed too often that Léa's thickening neck was losing its whiteness and showed slack muscles under the skin. She fastened the necklace at her nape without getting up and took a mirror from the bedside table.

"I look like a gardener," she judged bluntly. "A vegetable farmer.

A Norman vegetable farmer who goes out into the potato fields wearing a necklace. It looks about as good on me as an ostrich plume stuck up my nose, and I'm being polite."

She shrugged her shoulders, harshly judging everything that she no longer liked about herself: a bright, healthy complexion, a bit red, a complexion that came from fresh air, suited to setting off the strong blue of her eyes encircled with darker blue. Her proud nose still found favor with Léa; "Marie-Antoinette's nose!" maintained Chéri's mother, who never failed to add: ". . . and in two years, our good Léa will have Louis Seize's chin." Her mouth, with its tightly spaced teeth, which almost never erupted in laughter, smiled often, in harmony with her large, languidly blinking eyes, a smile praised, rhapsodized, photographed a hundred times over, a deep, trustful smile that others could never tire of.

As for her body, "Everyone knows," Léa would say, "that a good-quality body lasts a long time." She could still show off that big white body tinged with pink, endowed with the long legs and straight back found among the nymphs in Italy's fountains; her dimpled buttocks, her high-set breasts, could hold out, Léa would say, "until well past Chéri's marriage."

She stood up, wrapped herself in a dressing gown, and opened the curtains. The midday sun entered the cheerful, overly decorated pink room whose luxury was dated, double lace panels at the windows, rosebud-pink faille on the walls, gilded woodwork, electric lights veiled in pink and white, and antiques upholstered in modern silks. Léa would not relinquish either this cozy room or her bed, a considerable, indestructible masterpiece of copper and wrought iron, severe to the eye and cruel to the shins.

"No, no, really," Chéri's mother would protest, "it's not as ugly as that. I myself love that room. It's an era, it has its own style. It's like Païva."

Léa smiled at this memory of the "national Harpy" as she tied up her unruly hair. She hastily powdered her face when she heard two doors slam shut and the smack of a shod foot against a delicate piece of furniture. Chéri returned in pants and a shirt, his ears white with talc, his mood aggressive.

"Where's my stickpin? Unholy mess! Are people swiping jewelry now?"

"Marcel put it in his tie to go grocery shopping," Léa said gravely.

Chéri, devoid of humor, bumped up against the pleasantry like an ant coming upon a lump of coal. He stopped his menacing pacing and found nothing to answer but:

"That's charming! . . . And my boots?"

"Which?"

"The buck!"

Léa, sitting at her dressing table, looked up with too-gentle eyes:

"I don't put the words in your mouth," she slipped in caressingly.

"The day when a woman loves me for my intelligence, I'll be done for," Chéri retorted. "While I'm waiting, I'd like my stickpin and my boots."

"Why? You don't wear a stickpin with a suit jacket, and you've already got shoes on."

Chéri stamped his foot.

"I've had enough of this, no one takes care of me here! I've had enough!"

Léa put down her comb.

"Fine! Leave."

He shrugged his shoulders rudely:

"So you say!"

"Leave. I've always loathed guests who ransack the kitchen and plaster cream cheese on the mirrors. Go to your sainted mother's, my child, and stay there."

He couldn't withstand Léa's gaze, lowered his eyes, protested like a schoolboy:

"So, what, I can't say a thing? Will you at least lend me the car to go to Neuilly?"

"No."

"Because?"

"Because I'm going out at two and Philibert's having lunch."

"Where are you going at two?"

"To perform my religious duties. But if you want three francs for a taxi . . . Fool," she resumed gently, "I may go have coffee at Madame your mother's at two. Aren't you pleased?"

He shook his head like a baby ram.

"People snap at me, people refuse me everything, people hide my things from me, people . . ."

"Won't you ever be able to dress all by yourself?"

From Chéri's hands she took his tie and knotted it.

"There! . . . Oh, that purple tie! . . . By the way, it's perfectly appropriate for the lovely Marie-Laure and her family . . . And you wanted a pearl even, on top of that? Little nabob . . . Why not some earrings? . . ."

He gave in to it, blissful, limp, irresolute, captive once again to an indolence and a pleasure that closed his eyes . . .

"Nounoune darling . . . ," he murmured.

She brushed his ears, straightened the fine, bluish part that divided Chéri's black hair, touched his temples with a perfume-moistened finger, and kissed him quickly, because she couldn't resist his tempting mouth breathing so close to her. Chéri opened his eyes, his lips, stretched out his hands . . . She pulled away:

"No! Quarter to one! Run off, and don't let me see you again!"

"Never?"

"Never!" she told him flatly, laughing with an impassioned affection.

Alone, she smiled proudly, let out a ragged sigh of stifled desire, and listened to Chéri's footfalls in the building's courtyard. She saw him open and close the gate, move off on winged feet, only to be greeted by three ecstatic errand girls walking arm in arm:

"Oh, my, my! . . . It's impossible, he can't be real! . . . Do we dare ask to touch him?"

But Chéri, unmoved, didn't even turn around.

"My bath, Rose! The manicurist can go; it's too late. The blue tailored suit, the new one, the blue hat, the one lined in white, and the little shoes with straps . . . no, wait . . ."

Léa, her legs crossed, felt her bare ankle and shook her head:

"No, the laced blue kid ankle boots. My legs are a bit swollen today. It's the heat."

Her aging maid, coiffed in tulle, looked at Léa knowingly:

"It's . . . it's the heat," she repeated obediently, shrugging her shoulders, as if to say: "We know . . . Everything must wear out . . ."

Now that Chéri was gone, Léa again became animated, precise, alert. In less than an hour, she had been bathed, rubbed with sandalwood-scented alcohol, her hair coiffed, her shoes donned. While the curling iron heated, she found time to dissect the butler's account books, to summon the valet, Émile, to show him a blue haze on a mirror. She cast around her a confident eye, which was almost never deceived, and lunched in a joyful solitude, smiling at the dry Vouvray and the June strawberries served with their stems on a Rubelles plate as green as a wet tree frog. An enthusiastic eater in bygone days must have chosen, for this rectangular dining room, the large Louis XVI mirrors and English furniture of the same period, airy china cabinets, tall footed sideboard, delicate but sturdy chairs, everything in an almost black wood, embellished with fine garlands. The mirrors and solid silver serving pieces received the abundant daylight, the green reflections of the trees along the avenue Bugeaud, and Léa, as she ate, scrutinized the red polishing powder that lined the chasing of a fork, closed one eye to better judge the sheen of the dark wood. The butler, standing behind her, dreaded these games.

"Marcel," Léa said, "your wax has been gumming up for a week or so."

"Does Madame think so?"

"She thinks so. Add some spirits when you heat it in the double boiler, it's simple to redo it. You brought the Vouvray up a little early. Draw the blinds as soon as you've cleared the table, we're up against some real heat."

"Very well, madame. Will Monsieur Ch . . . Monsieur Peloux be dining?"

"I think so . . . No *crème-surprise* tonight, let's just have strawberry sorbet. Coffee in the boudoir."

As she rose, tall and straight, her legs visible beneath the skirt hugging her thighs, she had time to read the "Madame is beautiful" in the butler's restrained gaze, which didn't displease her.

"Beautiful . . . ," Léa thought as she went up to the boudoir. "No. Not anymore. Now I need white linens near my face, very pale pink for my underclothes and negligees. Beautiful . . . Bah . . . I hardly need to be anymore . . ."

Yet she didn't allow herself a nap in her painted-silk boudoir, after her coffee and newspapers. And it was with her battle face on that she commanded her chauffeur:

"To Madame Peloux's."

———

The lanes of the Bois, dry beneath their new June greenery, which the wind parched, the octroi gate, Neuilly, the boulevard d'Inkermann . . . "How many times have I taken this route?" Léa wondered. She counted, then wearied of counting, and listened, as she slowed her step on Madame Peloux's gravel path, for the sounds that came from the house.

"They're in the conservatory," she said.

She had put on more powder before arriving and drawn her blue veil, a fine mesh like fog, down under her chin. And she replied to the valet who invited her to come through the house:

"No, I'd rather go around through the garden."

A true garden, almost a park, encircled a vast villa, all white, typical of Paris's outer suburbs. Madame Peloux's villa had been called "a country estate" in the days when Neuilly was still on the outskirts of Paris. The stables, now become garages, the outbuildings with their kennels and washhouses, attested to it, as did the size of the billiards room, the vestibule, the dining room.

"Madame Peloux has a sound investment here," piously repeated the old parasites who came, in exchange for dinner and a glass of brandy, to play a hand of bezique or poker against her. And they would add: "But where does Madame Peloux not have her money invested?"

As she walked in the shade of the acacias, between clumps of blazing rhododendrons and rose-covered arches, Léa heard a murmur of voices, pierced by Madame Peloux's nasal trumpet and the burst of Chéri's dry laugh.

"That child laughs badly," she mused. She stopped for a moment, to better hear a new female voice, faint, pleasant, quickly drowned out by the formidable trumpet.

"That's the girl," Léa thought.

She took a few quick steps and found herself on the threshold of a glass-enclosed conservatory, from which Madame Peloux dashed forward, exclaiming:

"Here's our lovely friend!"

This little barrel, Madame Peloux, in reality Mademoiselle Peloux, had been a ballet dancer from the ages of ten to sixteen. Léa would sometimes search Madame Peloux for something that might recall the former blond, plump little Eros, or the dimpled nymph, but found only her large, implacable eyes, her delicate, harsh nose, and a coquettish manner she had, still, of placing her feet in fifth position like members of the corps de ballet.

Chéri, resurrected from the depths of a rocking chair, kissed Léa's hand with an instinctive grace, and ruined his gesture with:

"Drat! You've worn a veil again, I detest that."

"Would you leave her alone!" Madame Peloux interjected. "You don't ask a woman why she's worn a veil! We'll never make anything of him," she said tenderly to Léa.

Two women had risen in the pale shadow of the straw blind. One, in mauve, held out her hand rather coldly to Léa, who gazed at her from head to toe.

"My God, you're beautiful, Marie-Laure, there's nothing as perfect as you!"

Marie-Laure deigned to smile. She was a young redheaded woman, with brown eyes, who enchanted without gestures or words. She pointed, as if playing the coquette, to the other young woman:

"But do you recognize my daughter, Edmée?" she said.

Léa held out to the girl a hand that was taken only slowly:

"I should have recognized you, my child, but a schoolgirl changes quickly, and Marie-Laure changes only to disconcert us more each time. Are you finished with boarding school now?"

"I should hope so, I should hope so," Madame Peloux exclaimed. "You can't hide it under a bushel basket forever, this charm, this grace, this marvel of nineteen springs!"

"Eighteen," Marie-Laure said graciously.

"Eighteen, eighteen! . . . Yes, of course, eighteen! Léa, do you remember? This child took her first communion the year that Chéri left school, you must remember! Yes, nasty brat, you left and we were each as panic-stricken as the other!"

"I remember very well," Léa said, and she exchanged with Marie-Laure a little nod—something like the "touché" of honest fencers.

"You must marry her off, you must marry her off!" continued Madame Peloux, who never repeated a basic truth fewer than two times. "We'll all attend the wedding!"

She beat the air with her little arms, and the girl looked at her with an ingenuous fright.

"She's the perfect daughter for Marie-Laure," Léa thought, observing her closely. "She possesses discreetly everything that her mother possesses flamboyantly. Fluffy hair, ash-colored, as if powdered, restless eyes that stay hidden, a mouth that refrains from speaking, from smiling . . . Exactly what Marie-Laure needed, though she must hate her even so . . ."

Madame Peloux intruded a maternal smile between Léa and the girl:

"How well they've already been getting along in the garden, these two children!"

She indicated Chéri, standing in front of the wall of windows and smoking. He clenched his cigarette holder between his teeth and threw back his head to avoid the smoke. The three women looked at the young man, who, his head tilted back, his lashes half-closed, his feet together, immobile, nevertheless seemed a winged figure, hovering motionless in the air . . . Léa didn't mistake the bewildered, defeated expression in the girl's eyes. She allowed herself the pleasure of making her start by touching her arm. Edmée shuddered all over, pulled back her arm, and whispered timidly:

"What? . . ."

"Nothing," Léa answered. "I dropped my glove."

"Let's go, shall we, Edmée?" Marie-Laure ordered nonchalantly.

The girl, mute and obedient, walked toward Madame Peloux, who beat her little wings:

"Already? Oh no! We'll meet again! We'll meet again!"

"It's late," Marie-Laure said. "And you're expecting a lot of people, on a Sunday afternoon. This child isn't used to so many people . . ."

"Yes, yes," Madame Peloux cried tenderly, "she has lived so shut in, so alone!"

Marie-Laure smiled, and Léa looked at her as if to say: "Your turn!"

". . . But we'll come again soon."

"Thursday, Thursday! Léa, are you coming for lunch as well, on Thursday?"

"I'm coming," Léa answered.

Chéri had rejoined Edmée at the threshold of the conservatory, where he stood beside her, spurning any conversation. He heard Léa's promise and turned around:

"That's that. We'll go for a ride," he proposed.

"Yes, yes, that's just the thing at your age," Madame Peloux insisted fondly. "Edmée will go with Chéri in front, he'll drive, and the rest of us will go in the back. Youth takes precedence! Youth takes precedence! Chéri, my love, will you ask for Marie-Laure's car?"

Though her chubby little feet rolled from side to side on the gravel, she led her visitors as far as the bend in a path, then abandoned them to Chéri. When she returned, Léa had removed her hat and lit a cigarette.

"How handsome they are, the two of them!" Madame Peloux said breathlessly. "Right, Léa?"

"Ravishing," Léa exhaled with a plume of smoke. "But it's that Marie-Laure! . . ."

Chéri came back in:

"What has Marie-Laure done?" he asked.

"What beauty!"

"Oh! . . . Oh! . . ." Madame Peloux said approvingly. "It's true, it's true . . . that she was quite pretty!"

Chéri and Léa looked at each other and laughed.

" 'Was'!" Léa said emphatically. "But she's youth itself! She hasn't got a wrinkle! And she can wear soft mauve, that dreadful color that I hate and that hates me back!"

The large, pitiless eyes and slim nose turned away from a glass of brandy:

"Youth itself! Youth itself!" Madame Peloux shrieked. "Sorry! Sorry! Marie-Laure had Edmée in 1895, no, '94. At the time, she had cleared off with a singing instructor and ditched Khalil-Bey, who had given her the famous rose diamond that . . . No! No! Wait! . . . That was one year earlier! . . ."

Her trumpeting was loud and out of tune. Léa put a hand over her ear, and Chéri sententiously declared:

"An afternoon like this would be too lovely if it weren't for my mother's voice."

She looked at her son without anger, accustomed to his insolence, sat down in a dignified manner, her feet dangling at the bottom of a bergère armchair too high for her short legs. She warmed a glass of eau-de-vie in her hand. Léa, balanced in a rocking chair, from time to time cast a glance at Chéri, Chéri sprawled on the cool rattan, his suit jacket open, a half-extinguished cigarette on his lip, a lock of hair across his brow, and under her breath she flatteringly called him a beautiful scoundrel.

They remained side by side, without straining to please or speak, peaceful and happy in their way. Long experience with one another rendered them silent, restored to Chéri his listlessness and to Léa her serenity. Because of the increasing heat, Madame Peloux lifted her narrow skirt up to her knees, displaying her little sailor's calves, and Chéri furiously tore off his tie, a gesture that Léa rebuked with a "tt . . . tt . . ." of her tongue.

"Oh, leave him alone, the dear," Madame Peloux protested, as if from the depths of a dream. "It's so hot . . . Would you like a kimono, Léa?"

"No, thank you. I'm fine."

The abandon of these afternoons disgusted her. Never had her young lover caught her in disarray, nor with her bodice open, nor in slippers during the day. "Naked, if you wish," she would say, "but not half-dressed." She picked up her illustrated magazine again but didn't read it. "This old mother Peloux and her son," she thought, "put them in front of a generous table or take them out to the country—presto: the mother strips off her corset and the son his vest. Like barkeeps on vacation." She looked vindictively at the barkeep in question and saw that he was sleeping, his lashes lowered over his white cheeks, his mouth closed. The exquisite arc of his upper lip, lighted from below, held at its apexes two points of silvery light, and Léa admitted that he looked far more like a god than like a wine seller. Without getting up, she delicately plucked from between Chéri's fingers a smoking cigarette and threw it in the ashtray. The sleeper's hand slackened and let fall like limp flowers its slender fingers, armed with cruel fingernails, a hand not feminine but a little lovelier than one might have wished, a hand that Léa had kissed a hundred times without servility, kissed for pleasure, for its perfume . . .

Over the top of her magazine, she looked at Madame Peloux. "Is she sleeping, too?" Léa liked the fact that the siesta of mother and son gave her, since she remained wide awake, an hour of mental solitude in the heat, shadow, and sun.

But Madame Peloux wasn't sleeping. She sat Buddha-like on her bergère, looking straight ahead and sucking on her fine champagne with the application of an alcoholic infant.

"Why isn't she sleeping?" Léa wondered. "It's Sunday. She lunched well. She's expecting the old troublemakers of her day at five o'clock. Consequently she should be sleeping. If she's not sleeping, it's because she's up to some mischief."

They had known each other for twenty-five years. The hostile intimacy of loose-moraled women whom a man enriches and then deserts, whom another man ruins, the fractious friendship of rivals lying in wait for the first wrinkle or white hair. The companionship of pragmatic women, skilled at financial games, but the one a miser and the other a sybarite . . . Such bonds matter. Another, stronger connection came to unite them later in life: Chéri.

———

Léa remembered Chéri as a little boy, a marvel in long curls. When very small he was not yet called Chéri, but only Fred.

Chéri, by turns forgotten and adored, grew up among pale housemaids and lank, sardonic valets. Though by virtue of his birth he had mysteriously brought affluence to the household, you never saw any *miss*, any *Fräulein*, near Chéri, who was protected, with a clamor, from "those ghouls" . . .

"Charlotte Peloux, woman of another age!" the elderly, dried-up, expiring, and indestructible Baron de Berthellemy would say familiarly. "Charlotte Peloux, in you I salute the only woman of easy virtue who dared to raise her son as the son of a hooker! Woman of another age, you don't read, you never travel, you look after your lonely fellow man, and you leave your son to be raised by domestics. How pure that is! How like About! How like even Gustave Droz! And to think that you know nothing about either!"

Chéri consequently knew all the joys of a debauched youth. Before he'd outgrown his lisp, he took in the servants' gossip. He shared clandestine suppers in the kitchen. He bathed in iris milk in his mother's bathtub, or washed up hastily with the corner of a towel. He suffered indigestion from sweets, and hunger cramps when his dinner was forgotten. Half-naked and suffering from a cold, he got bored at the Flower Festivals, where Charlotte Peloux exhibited him sitting among damp roses; but he managed to entertain himself royally at twelve years old, in a clandestine gambling hall where an American lady gave him fistfuls of louis d'or to wager and called him "little masterpiece" in faulty French. Around the same time, Madame Peloux inflicted a private tutor on her son in the person of an abbot, whom she let go after ten months "because," she confessed, "seeing that black robe dragging all over the house made me feel as if I'd taken in a poor female relation, and God knows there's nothing more depressing than a poor relation in your home!"

At fourteen, Chéri had a taste of school. He didn't believe in it. He defied any jail and escaped. Not only did Madame Peloux find the energy to imprison him again, but what's more, faced with her son's tears and abuse, she fled, her hands over her ears, crying, "I don't want to see this! I don't want to see this!"—a cry so sincere that she in fact left Paris, accompanied by a young man with few scruples, only to return two years later, alone. It was her last amorous weakness.

She found Chéri grown too quickly, gaunt, dark shadows veiling his eyes, wearing horse trainers' suits and speaking more crudely than ever. She beat her breast and dragged Chéri out of boarding school. He stopped working entirely, wanted horses, cars, jewels, demanded round monthly allowances, and when his mother beat her breast, squawking like a peahen, he cut her off with these words:

"Ma'am Peloux, don't get worked up. My revered mother, if there's only me to bankrupt you, you'll really risk dying nice and cozy under your American quilt. Having a trustee doesn't appeal to me. Your dough is mine. Let me handle it. Friends come cheap, at the cost of some dinners and champagne. As for the ladies, you don't exactly expect me, Ma'am Peloux, since I'm the way you've made me, to give them more than the tribute of an artistic trinket—if that!"

He pirouetted as she cried softly and declared herself the happiest of mothers. When Chéri began to buy cars, she trembled afresh, but he advised her: "Eye on the gasoline, please, Ma'am Peloux!" and sold his horses. He was not averse to dissecting the two chauffeurs' books; his calculations were fast and accurate, and the figures that he jotted down on paper, slender, emphatic, quick, clashed with his rather slow and clumsy handwriting.

As he turned seventeen, he was becoming an old man, a nitpicking annuitant. Still beautiful, but thin, and short of breath. More than once, Madame Peloux met him on the cellar stair, on his way up from counting the bottles in the wine racks.

"Would you believe it!" Madame Peloux said to Léa. "It's too wonderful!"

"Much too," Léa replied. "It will end badly. Chéri, show me your tongue!"

He stuck it out with an irreverent grimace, and other ugly manners that didn't shock Léa, too close a family friend, a sort of indulgent god-mother whom he addressed with the familiar *tu*.

"Is it true," Léa interrogated him, "that someone saw you at a bar with old Lili last night, sitting on her knees?"

"Her knees!" Chéri joked. "She hasn't had knees for a long time! They've been buried."

"Is it true," Léa insisted more severely, "that she made you drink gin with pepper? Do you know that that makes your mouth smell bad?"

One day, Chéri, hurt, had answered Léa's inquiry:

"I don't know why you're asking me all this, surely you must have seen what I was doing, because you were there, in the little storage room in back, with Patron the boxer!"

"That's perfectly true," Léa answered, expressionless. "Patron has nothing of the little deadbeat about him, you know? He has other charms than a cheap little mug and eyes swimming in brown butter."

That week, Chéri caused quite a sensation each night in Mont-martre and Les Halles, with ladies who called him "lover boy" and "my vice," but nothing excited him, he suffered from migraines and a throaty cough. And Madame Peloux, who would confide to her masseuse, to Madame Ribot, her corset maker, to old Lili, to Ber-thellemy the Desiccated, her new anxieties—"Ah, for us mothers, what a calvary life is!"—passed with ease from the state of happiest-of-mothers to that of mother-martyr.

———

One June evening, which brought Madame Peloux, Léa, and Chéri together in the Neuilly conservatory, altered the destinies of the young man and the mature woman. For one evening, chance scat-tered Chéri's "friends"—a minor wholesaler of liqueurs, the Bax-ter boy, and the Vicomte Desmond, a parasite scarcely come of age, scornful and demanding—and returned Chéri to his mother's house, toward which habit led Léa as well.

Twenty years, a past made up of similarly dull evenings, the lack of acquaintances, as well as a certain distrust and a certain cowardice that, toward the end of their lives, isolate women who have loved only passionately, kept these two women in each other's presence for another evening, as they awaited still another evening, each suspecting the other. The two of them looked at the uncommunicative Chéri, and Madame Peloux, lacking the strength or authority to care for her son, confined herself to hating Léa a little each time a gesture inclined Léa's white nape and ruddy cheek close to Chéri's pale cheek and translucent ear. She would happily have bled that robust womanly neck, where Venus's rings were beginning to ravage the flesh, so as to tint the slender greenish lily with pink, but she would never even have thought of taking her beloved to the country.

"Chéri, why are you drinking brandy?" Léa scolded.

"So as not to offend Ma'am Peloux, who would be drinking alone," Chéri answered.

"What are you doing tomorrow?"

"Dunno—you?"

"I'm leaving for Normandy."

"With?"

"That's none of your business."

"With our good Spéleïeff?"

"You must be joking, that's been over for two months, you're out of touch. Spéleïeff is in Russia."

"Chéri dear, what are you thinking?" Madame Peloux sighed. "You forget the delightful breakup dinner that Léa treated us to last month. Léa, you haven't given me the recipe for the langoustines that I so enjoyed!"

Chéri straightened up, his eyes sparkling:

"Yes, yes, langoustines in cream sauce, oh, I'd like some!"

"You see," Madame Peloux reproached, "he has so little appetite, yet he'd have eaten langoustines . . ."

"Peace," Chéri commanded. "Léa, are you heading to the leafy shade with Patron?"

"Of course not, dear; Patron and I are just friends. I'm leaving by myself."

"Rich woman," Chéri blurted out.

"I'll take you along, if you want, we'll do nothing but eat, drink, sleep . . ."

"Where is your little backwater?"

He had gotten up and stood right in front of her.

"Can you picture Honfleur? The Côte de Grâce? . . . Sit down, you're looking green. You know that carriage gate, along the Côte de Grâce, where we always used to say as we went past, your mother and I . . ."

She turned toward Madame Peloux: Madame Peloux had disappeared. This kind of discreet escape, this vanishing, was so little in keeping with Charlotte Peloux's habits that Léa and Chéri looked at each other and laughed in surprise. Chéri sat down beside Léa.

"I'm tired," he said.

"You're running yourself down," Léa said.

He straightened up conceitedly:

"Oh, you know, I'm still in pretty good shape!"

"Pretty good . . . perhaps for others . . . but not . . . not for me, for example."

"Too green?"

"Just the word I was looking for. Will you come to the country, everything strictly aboveboard? Good strawberries, crème fraîche, tarts, little roasted chickens . . . Now, that's a good regimen, and no women!"

He let himself slip onto Léa's shoulder and closed his eyes.

"No women . . . Great . . . Léa, tell me, are you a buddy? Yes? Well then, let's go. Women . . . I'm over them . . . Women . . . I've seen them all."

He said these crude things in a sleepy voice, and Léa listened to its full, sweet sound and felt his warm breath on her ear. He had grasped Léa's long necklace and was rolling the large pearls between his fingers. She slipped her arm under Chéri's head and drew him close to her, without any ulterior motive, trusting in her familiarity with this child, and she rocked him.

"I'm comfortable," he sighed. "You're a buddy, I'm comfortable . . ."

She smiled as if she had received the most precious praise. Chéri appeared to be falling asleep. She looked closely at his lashes, lying sparkling, as if wet, on his cheek, and at that gaunt cheek that bore the marks of a cheerless fatigue. His upper lip, shaved that morning, was already blue-tinged, and the rosy lamplight gave a false color to his mouth . . .

"No women!" Chéri declared, as if dreaming. "So . . . kiss me!"

Surprised, Léa didn't stir.

"Kiss me, I say!"

He said it as an order, his eyebrows knitted, and the brilliance of his suddenly reopened eyes unsettled Léa like an abruptly switched-on light. She shrugged her shoulders and placed a kiss on his forehead, so near to her. He wrapped his arms around Léa's neck and bent her toward him.

She shook her head, but only up to the instant their mouths met; then she remained absolutely still and held her breath, like someone listening. When he let her go, she pushed him away from her, stood up, took a deep breath, and arranged her hair, which had not been disarranged. Then she turned around, a little pale, her eyes grown dark, and said in a joking tone:

"That was bright!"

He lay in the depths of a rocking chair and kept silent, his active eyes taking her in, so full of challenge and questioning that after a minute she said:

"What?"

"Nothing," Chéri said. "I know what I wanted to know."

She blushed, humiliated, and cleverly defended herself:

"What is it you know? That I like your lips? You poor kid, I've kissed uglier ones that way. What does it prove? You think I'm going to fall at your feet and cry: Take me! So have you only been with young girls? Thinking that I'm going to lose my head over a kiss! . . ."

She had become calmer as she spoke and wanted to demonstrate her composure.

"Tell me, kid," she pressed as she leaned over him, "do you think nice lips will mean anything in my memories?"

She smiled down at him, sure of herself, but she was unaware that something lingered on her face, a very faint sort of quivering, an enticing distress, and that her smile looked like the smile that follows a fit of tears.

"I'm quite calm," she continued. "Even if I kissed you again, even if we . . ."

She stopped herself and pouted scornfully.

"No, honestly, I don't see us in that position."

"You didn't see us in the position we were in just now, either," Chéri said, taking his time. "And yet you stayed there for a good long while. Do you think about the other possibility, then? *I* didn't say anything to you about it."

They sized each other up like enemies. She was afraid of showing a desire that she hadn't had time either to entertain or to conceal, she had something against this child, who had instantly become cold and perhaps mocking.

"You're right," she conceded lightly. "Let's forget about it. I'm offering you, as we were saying, a meadow in the country where you can tuck yourself away, and good food . . . Mine, which speaks for itself."

"We'll see," Chéri answered. "Would I take the open Renouhard?"

"Naturally, you wouldn't leave it for Charlotte."

"I'll pay for the gasoline, but you'll feed the chauffeur."

Léa burst out laughing.

"I'll feed the chauffeur! Oh! Oh, the son of Madame Peloux indeed! You forget nothing . . . I'm not the prying type, but I'd like to hear what pillow talk between a woman and you would be like."

She fell into a chair and fanned herself. A sphinx moth and big mosquitoes with long legs were circling the lamps, and the scent of the garden, because night had fallen, was becoming a country scent. A whiff of acacia blew in, so distinct, so potent, that they both turned around as if to see it walking.

"It's the pink-flowered acacia," Léa whispered.

"Yes," Chéri said. "But as if, this evening, it had drunk from the orange tree blossoms!"

She gazed at him, vaguely admiring his having come up with that. He inhaled the perfume like a willing victim, and she looked away, suddenly afraid that he might call her to him; but he called her nevertheless, and she went.

She went to him to kiss him, with a rush of spite and selfishness and punishing thoughts: "Hold on now . . . It's quite true that you have nice lips, this time I'll take my fill of them, because I want to, and then I'll leave you, too bad, I couldn't care less, I'll go . . ."

She kissed him so fully that they broke free from each other drunk, deaf, breathless, trembling, as if they had just been fighting . . . She stood up again in front of him—he hadn't stirred, still lay in the depths of the armchair—and she silently challenged him,

"Well? . . . Well? . . ." and expected to be insulted. But he held out his arms to her, opened his beautiful, fragile hands, tipped back a wounded head, and between his lashes revealed the twin glimmer of two tears, while he murmured words, moans, an entire tender, animal song in which she distinguished her name, some "darling's," some "come here's," some "never leave you's," a song that she listened to bent over him and full of anxiety, as if she had unintentionally done him a very great wrong.

Whenever Léa remembered that first summer in Normandy, she would observe equitably: "I've had wicked infants funnier than Chéri. Kinder, too, and smarter. But all the same, I've never had another quite like him."

"It's strange," she confided, at the end of that summer of 1906, to Berthellemy the Desiccated, "there are times when I think I'm sleeping with a Negro or a Chinese."

"Have you ever had a Chinese and a Negro?"

"Never."

"And so?"

"I don't know. I can't explain. It's an impression."

An impression that had come to her slowly, together with an astonishment that she had not always known how to hide. The first memories of their idyll abounded solely with images of mounds of fine food and choice fruits, and with an epicurean farmer's concerns for her table. She could still picture an exhausted Chéri, paler in the broad sunshine, dragging himself along the Normandy hedgerows, falling asleep on the warm copings of ornamental ponds. Léa would wake him to stuff him with strawberries, cream, frothy milk, and corn-fed chicken. With wide, empty eyes, as if stunned, he would follow the swarm of mayflies around the basket of roses at dinner, check his wristwatch for his bedtime, while Léa, disappointed but bearing no grudge, mused about the promises the kiss in Neuilly hadn't kept, and simply waited:

"Up to the end of August, if necessary, I'll keep him in the fattening cage. And then, back to Paris, whew! I'll return him to his beloved studies . . ."

———————

She went to bed mercifully early so that Chéri, sheltered against her, nuzzling her with his forehead and nose, selfishly hollowing out the right spot for his night's rest, might fall asleep. Sometimes, the lamp extinguished, she would follow a pool of moonlight shimmering on the parquet. She would listen, as they mingled with the gentle lapping of the aspen and with the crickets, which never died down night or day, to the great hound-dog sighs that heaved Chéri's chest.

———————

"So what is it that's keeping me awake?" she wondered vaguely. "It's not this boy's head on my shoulder, I've borne heavier . . . How beautiful the weather is . . . For tomorrow morning, I've ordered him a good porridge. You can already feel his ribs less. So what is it that's keeping me awake? Oh, of course, I remember, I'm going to have Patron the boxer come, to train the boy. We have time, between Patron and me, to really dazzle Madame Peloux . . ."

She would fall asleep, stretched out on the cool sheets, lying absolutely flat on her back, the wicked infant's black head lying on her left breast. She would fall asleep, to be awakened sometimes—but so seldom!—by an insistent demand from Chéri, toward daybreak.

The second month of their retreat had indeed brought Patron, his big suitcase, his little pound-and-a-half dumbbells and his black tights, his six-ounce gloves, his leather boots laced down to his toes; Patron with his girlish voice, his long lashes, covered in skin so beautifully tanned, like his suitcase, that he hardly looked naked when he took off his shirt. And Chéri, by turns surly, listless, and jealous of Patron's serene strength, began his unglamorous, productive physical education with slow, repeated movements.

"One . . . sss . . . two . . . sss . . . I don't hear you breathing . . . three . . . I see your knee cheating . . . sss . . ."

The leafy canopy of lindens filtered the August sun. A thick red mat, thrown over the gravel, painted the two naked bodies of instructor and pupil with purple reflections. Léa would watch the lesson intently. During the fifteen minutes of boxing, Chéri, intoxicated with his newfound strength, would get carried away, risk low blows, and flush with anger. Patron bore the swings like a wall and from the Olympic heights of his glory would let fall on Chéri oracles weightier than his celebrated fist.

"Hmmm! That's an inquisitive left eye you have. If I hadn't prevented it, it would have come over to see how my right glove is stitched together."

"I slipped," Chéri fumed.

"It's not about balance," Patron continued. "It's about character. You'll never make a boxer."

"My mother's against it, what a pity!"

"Even if your mother weren't against it, you wouldn't make a boxer, because you're malicious. Malice doesn't go with boxing. Isn't that so, Madame Léa?"

Léa smiled and savored the pleasure of being warm, staying still, and watching the games of these two naked young men, whom she silently compared: "Isn't he magnificent, this Patron! He's as magnificent as a building. The boy's ripening nicely. Knees like his don't roam the streets, and I should know. His back, too, is . . . no, will be marvelous. Where the devil did old mother Peloux cast her line . . . And the muscles at the base of his neck! A real statue. How nasty he is! He laughs, you'd swear a greyhound was about to bite . . ." She felt happy and maternal, and bathed in a tranquil virtue. "I would happily exchange him for another," she thought, seeing Chéri naked in the afternoons under the lindens, or Chéri naked in the morning atop the ermine throw, or Chéri naked in the evening beside the big tub of lukewarm water. "Yes, beautiful as he is, I would happily exchange him, if it weren't a matter of conscience." She confided her indifference to Patron.

"And yet," objected Patron, "he's got a good build. You already see muscles on him like on guys who aren't from around here, colored guys, even though he's as white as they come. Little muscles that don't show off. You'll never see biceps like cantaloupes on him."

"I should hope not, Patron! But *I* haven't taken him on for boxing!"

"Of course," Patron agreed, lowering his long lashes. "You have to reckon with feeling."

He bore with embarrassment Léa's overt voluptuous allusions and smile, those insistent smiling eyes that she rested on him whenever she spoke of love.

"Of course," Patron continued, "if he doesn't completely satisfy you . . ."

Léa laughed:

"Completely, no . . . but I draw my reward from the most noble springs of selflessness, like you, Patron."

"Oh! Me . . ."

He feared and hoped for the question that didn't fail to follow:

"The same as ever, Patron? Do you still dig your heels in?"

"I still dig my heels in, Madame Léa, I've gotten another letter from Liane, in the midday mail. She says that she's alone, that I have no reason to dig my heels in, that her two boyfriends have gone away."

"Well?"

"Well, I think it isn't true . . . I dig my heels in because she digs her heels in. She's ashamed, she says, of a man who has an occupation, especially an occupation that forces him to get up early in the morning, train every day, give lessons in boxing and calisthenics. No sooner do we see each other again than there's a scene. 'People will think,' she cries, 'that I'm not able to support the man I love!' It's a fine sentiment, I don't deny it, but it's not to my way of thinking. Everyone has his peculiarities. As you have said so well, Madame Léa: it's a matter of conscience."

They were talking in whispers under the trees, he modest but naked, she dressed in white, her cheeks tinged a robust pink. They relished their reciprocal friendship, born of a similar inclination toward simplicity, toward health, toward a sort of nobility of the lower classes. Yet Léa wouldn't have been shocked had Patron received, from the beautiful, upper-crust Liane, substantial gifts. "You scratch my back and I'll scratch yours." And she tried to subvert Patron's "peculiarity" with arguments based on an old-fashioned fair-mindedness. Their lingering talks, which each time roused the same two gods—love and money—would stray from money and love to return to Chéri, to his blameworthy education, to his beauty, "basically harmless," as Léa would say, to his character, "which was nonexistent," as Léa would say. Talks that satisfied their need to confide and their loathing for new words and new ideas, talks disrupted by the ridiculous appearance of Chéri, whom they had believed to be asleep or driving down some hot road, Chéri who would suddenly materialize, half-naked but armed with an account book, his fountain pen behind his ear.

"Behold Mr. Bracket!" Patron said admiringly. "He's the spitting image of a bank teller."

"What's this?" Chéri shouted from a distance. "Three hundred and twenty francs' worth of gasoline? Someone must be drinking it! We've gone out four times in two weeks! And seventy-seven francs' worth of oil!"

"The car goes to the market every day," Léa answered. "On that subject, your chauffeur came back for three extra helpings of leg of lamb at lunch, it seems. Don't you find that that exceeds our agreement a little? . . . When you can't stomach a bill, you look like your mother."

Lacking a riposte, he remained uncertain for a moment, rocking on his slender feet, suspended with that alate grace of a little Mercury that made Madame Peloux swoon and squeal: "Me at eighteen years old! Winged feet, winged feet!" He searched for some bit of insolence and his whole face quivered, his mouth half-open, his brow thrust forward, in a tense bearing that accentuated the peculiar satanic bend of his raised eyebrows across his temple.

"Come on, stop searching," Léa said simply. "Yes, you hate me. Come give me a kiss. Handsome devil. Fallen angel. Little ninny . . ."

He came, vanquished by the sound of her voice but offended by her words. Patron, in front of the couple, allowed the truth to bloom anew on his pure lips:

"As far as physique goes, you have an attractive physique. But me, when I look at you, Monsieur Chéri, it seems to me that if I were a woman, I would say to myself: 'I'll come back in ten years or so.' "

"Do you hear, Léa, he says in ten years or so," Chéri slipped in as he pushed aside his mistress's inclined head. "What do you think of that?"

But she didn't deign to listen, and patted the young body that owed her its renewed vigor, all over, on his cheeks, on his legs, on his bottom, with a nanny's irreverent pleasure.

"What satisfaction does being nasty give you?" Patron asked Chéri.

Chéri enveloped the Hercules slowly, completely, in a barbarous, inscrutable gaze, before answering:

"It soothes me. You wouldn't understand."

To tell the truth, after three months of intimacy Léa had understood nothing about Chéri. If she still spoke—to Patron, who now came only on Sundays, to Berthellemy the Desiccated, who would arrive without invitation but leave two hours later—of "returning Chéri to his beloved studies," it was out of a sort of tradition, and as if to excuse herself for having kept him so long. She would set deadlines, each time missed. She was waiting.

"The weather's so beautiful . . . and besides, his running off to Paris last week tired him . . . And besides, it's better for me to get good and sick of him . . ."

She was waiting in vain, for the first time in her life, for what she had never before lacked: trust, calm, confessions, sincerity, the indiscreet effusiveness of a young lover—those hours of blackest night when the almost filial gratitude of an adolescent unrestrainedly pours forth tears, confidences, resentments, on the warm breast of a mature and dependable friend.

"I've had them all," she would reflect stubbornly, "I've always known what they were worth, what they were thinking, and what they wanted. But this kid, this kid . . . That would be going a bit too far."

Strong now, proud of his nineteen years, cheerful at mealtime, impatient in bed, he gave away nothing of himself but his body, and remained as mysterious as a courtesan. Affectionate? Yes, if affection can show through the involuntary cry, the clutch of arms. But his "nastiness" would reappear with his speech and his vigilant determination to be evasive. How many times, toward dawn, Léa holding her tamed, satisfied lover in her arms, his eyes half-closed with a gaze and lips to which life was returning as if each morning and each embrace reimagined him more beautiful than he had been the previous day—how many times, vanquished at that hour by her longing to conquer him and the voluptuous satisfaction she would take in hearing him confess, had she pressed her forehead against Chéri's:

"Speak . . . talk . . . tell me . . ."

But no confession arose from his arched lips, and hardly any words other than sullen or intoxicated invectives, along with this name "Nounoune," which he had given her when he was small and which today he called out to her from the depths of his pleasure, like a cry for help.

"Yes, I'm telling you, a Chinese or a Negro," she confided to Anthime de Berthellemy; and she added, "I can't explain," unruffled but at a loss to describe the impression, vague but strong, that she and Chéri didn't speak the same language.

September was drawing to a close when they returned to Paris. Chéri went back to Neuilly to "dazzle" Madame Peloux from the very first evening. He would brandish chairs, crack nuts with a single blow, jump onto the billiard table, and play cowboy in the garden, chasing the terror-stricken guard dogs.

"Whew," Léa sighed when she returned home alone to the house on the avenue Bugeaud. "How nice, an empty bed!"

But the next evening, while she was savoring her ten o'clock coffee, not admitting to herself that she found the evening long and the dining room enormous, the sudden appearance of Chéri, standing in the doorframe, Chéri borne on his winged, silent feet, drew from her a nervous cry. Neither tender nor talkative, he ran to her.

"Are you mad?"

He shrugged his shoulders, he didn't deign to make himself understood: he ran to her. He didn't ask her: "Do you love me? Were you already forgetting me?" He ran to her.

A moment later, they were slipping into the hollow of Léa's double bed forged of steel and copper. Chéri feigned sleep, languidness, to be better able to clench his teeth and close his eyes, in the grip of a fit of silence. But she listened to him all the same, as she lay against him, she listened with delight to the slight vibration, the remote and seemingly captive tumult, that resonates in a body that denies its anguish, its gratitude, and its love.

"**W**hy didn't your mother tell me about it herself last night at dinner?"

"She thought it more appropriate that it be me."

"Really?"

"So she said."

"And you?"

"And me, what?"

"Do you think it more appropriate, too?"

Chéri looked at Léa uncertainly.

"Yes."

He appeared to consider, and repeated:

"Yes, it's better, come on."

So as not to embarrass him, Léa turned her eyes toward the window. A warm rain was darkening the August morning and falling straight onto the three plane trees, already turning brown, in the tree-lined courtyard. "You would think it's autumn," Léa silently observed, and she sighed.

"What's wrong?" Chéri asked.

She looked at him, surprised:

"But there's nothing wrong, I don't like this rain."

"Oh, I thought . . ."

"You thought?"

"I thought that you were upset."

She couldn't help laughing openly.

"That I was upset because you're getting married? No, listen . . . you're . . . funny . . ."

She rarely burst out laughing, and her gaiety offended Chéri. He shrugged his shoulders and lit a cigarette with his habitual grimace, his chin too taut, his lower lip stuck out.

"It's wrong of you to smoke before lunch," Léa said.

He replied with some impertinence that she didn't hear, occupied as she suddenly was with listening to the sound of her own voice and the echo of her mechanical daily admonishments, reverberating to the depths of the past five years. "It makes me feel as if I'm seeing an endless reflection in a pair of mirrors," she thought. Then, with a little effort, she floated back toward reality and good spirits.

"Luckily I'll soon hand over the instructions regarding tobacco on an empty stomach to someone else!" she said to Chéri.

"*She* has no say in the matter," Chéri declared. "I'm marrying her, aren't I? Let her kiss the tracks of my divine feet, and be eternally grateful for her destiny. And that'll do."

He exaggerated the protrusion of his chin, clenched his teeth on his cigarette holder, parted his lips, and thus succeeded only in resembling, in his immaculate silk pajamas, an Oriental prince gone pale in the impenetrable shadows of palaces.

Léa, unruffled, hugging against her body a pink dressing gown whose particular pink she called "obligatory," was brooding over thoughts that she found fatiguing and that she decided to fling, one by one, against Chéri's feigned calm:

"Well, why are you marrying this girl?"

He leaned both elbows on a table, unconsciously imitated Madame Peloux's studied expression.

"You understand, my dear . . ."

"Call me 'madame,' or Léa. I'm neither your maid nor a pal your own age."

She spoke curtly, sitting up straight in her armchair, without raising her voice. He wanted to counterattack, braved her beautiful face, a bit ravaged under the powder, and her eyes, which enveloped him in a light so blue and pure, but then he softened and yielded in a manner that wasn't customary for him:

"Nounoune, you ask me to explain to you . . . Certainly, I must settle down. And besides, there are substantial interests at stake."

"Whose?"

"Mine," he said without smiling. "The girl has a considerable personal fortune."

"From her father?"

He toppled over backward, his feet in the air.

"Oh, I don't know! You ask so many questions! I think so. The lovely Marie-Laure isn't withdrawing one and a half million from her own purse, is she? One and a half million, and some high-society jewels."

"And you?"

"*I* have more," he said proudly.

"Then you don't need money."

He shook his sleek head, where the light traced blue moiré waves.

"Need, need . . . you know very well that we don't understand money the same way. It's something we don't agree on."

"I'll grant that you spared me this topic of conversation for five years."

She leaned over, placed a hand on Chéri's knee:

"Tell me, kid, how much of your income have you saved, over the past five years?"

He played the buffoon, laughed, rolled around at Léa's feet, but she pushed him away with her foot.

"Honestly, tell me . . . Fifty thousand a year, or sixty? Let's hear it, sixty? Seventy?"

He sat down on the rug, tipped his head onto Léa's knees.

"I'm not worth that much, then?"

He stretched out in the broad morning light, turned his neck, opened his eyes wide, eyes that appeared black but whose dark russet color Léa knew well. With her index finger, as if to point to and choose what was rarest amid so much beauty, she touched his eyebrows, his eyelids, the corners of his mouth. At times, the form of this lover whom she slightly despised inspired in her a sort of respect. "To be that beautiful is a kind of nobility," she thought.

"Tell me, dear . . . And the young lady, in all this? How is she with you?"

"She loves me. She admires me. She doesn't speak."

"And you, how are you with her?"

"I'm not," he answered simply.

"Charming love duets," Léa said dreamily.

He raised himself up halfway, sat cross-legged:

"I think you're awfully concerned about her," he said severely. "Don't you think about yourself, then, in this disaster?"

She looked at Chéri with a surprise that made her appear younger, her eyebrows raised and her lips half-open.

"Yes, you, Léa. You, the victim. You, the sympathetic figure in the matter, since I'm jilting you."

He had gone a bit pale and seemed, in treating Léa harshly, to have hurt himself. Léa smiled:

"But, my dear, I have no intention of changing anything in my life. For a week, I'll come across a pair of socks, a tie, a handkerchief, in my drawers from time to time . . . And when I say a week . . . my drawers are very tidy, you know. Oh, and then I'll remodel the bathroom! I'm thinking about pâte de verre . . ."

She fell silent and took on a greedy expression, drawing a vague plan in the air with her finger. Chéri's vindictive stare was unrelenting.

"You're not pleased? What did you expect? That I would go back to Normandy to hide my grief? That I would lose weight? That I would stop dyeing my hair? That Madame Peloux would rush to my bedside?"

She imitated Madame Peloux's trumpet, fluttering her forearms:

" 'The shadow of herself! The shadow of herself! The poor woman has aged a hundred years! A hundred years!' Is that what you expected?"

He had listened to her with a stiff smile and a quivering of his nostrils that may have indicated emotion:

"Yes," he cried.

Léa placed her smooth, bare, heavy arms on Chéri's shoulders:

"You poor kid! But I would already have had to die four or five times, by that reckoning! Losing a little lover . . . Replacing a wicked infant . . ."

She added, in a quieter, milder tone:

"I'm used to it."

"As everyone knows," he said bitterly. "I don't give a damn! *That*, I really don't give a damn about—not having been your first lover! What I would have wanted, or rather what would have been . . . appropriate . . . decent . . . is that I be your last."

With a roll of his shoulders, he dislodged her superb arms.

"Basically, I'm saying this, you see, for your own sake."

"I understand perfectly. You're worried about me, I'm worried about your fiancée, that's all very well, very natural. It's obvious that everyone concerned has a noble heart."

She stood up, waiting for him to answer with some boorishness, but he fell silent, and it pained her to see on Chéri's face, for the first time, a sort of discouragement.

She leaned over, placed her hands under Chéri's armpits:

"Come on, let's go, put your clothes on. I just have to get into my dress, I'm all set underneath, what would you expect us to do at a time like this, if not go to Schwabe's to pick out a pearl for you? I have to give you a wedding present."

He leapt up, his face gleaming:

"Super! Smart, a pearl for my shirt! One that's a little pinkish, I know the very one!"

"Not on your life, a white one, something masculine, come on now! I know the one, too. It's ruin for me again! How much money I'll save, without you!"

Chéri reverted to his reticence:

"That—that depends on my successor."

Léa turned around at the threshold of the boudoir and displayed her gayest smile, her strong gourmand's teeth, the clear blue of her skillfully bistered eyes:

"Your successor? Forty sous and a packet of tobacco! And a glass of cassis on Sundays, that's all he's worth! And I'll provide dowries for your kids!"

They both became very cheerful in the weeks that followed. Chéri's official engagement kept them apart each day for a few hours, sometimes a night or two. "You must build trust," Chéri maintained. Léa, whom Madame Peloux kept away from Neuilly, gave in to curiosity and asked a hundred questions of the self-important Chéri, who was weighed down with secrets that he spilled no sooner than he'd reached the doorstep, and who played the prankster each time he was reunited with Léa:

"My friends!" he cried one day, as he capped Léa's bust with his hat. "My friends, the things we've seen at Peloux's Palace since yesterday!"

"Take your hat off there, for starters. And then don't invoke your low-life friends here. What is it this time?"

She was scolding, though she was laughing already.

"Tempers are flaring, Nounoune! Flaring between those ladies! Marie-Laure and Ma'am Peloux are battling it out over my contract!"

"Really?"

"Yes! It was a magnificent scene. (Stash the hors d'oeuvres so that I can do Ma'am Peloux's arms for you.) 'Her assets protected! Her assets protected! Why not a trustee? It's a personal insult! An insult! The statement of my son's inheritance! . . . Let me tell you, madame . . .' "

"She called her 'madame'?"

"As broad as an umbrella. 'Let me tell you, madame, that my son hasn't had a sou of debt since coming of age, and the list of investments bought since 1910 amounts to . . .' Amounts to this, amounts to that, amounts to my nose, amounts to my behind . . . In a word, Catherine de Médicis, and what's more a diplomat, I'm telling you!"

Léa's blue eyes glistened with tears of laughter.

"Oh, Chéri! You've never been so funny in all the time I've known you. And the other one, the lovely Marie-Laure?"

"Her! Oh, dreadful, Nounoune. That woman must have two dozen corpses behind her. All in jade green, her red hair, her skin . . . well, eighteen years old, and that smile. My revered mother's trumpet didn't make her bat an eyelash. She waited for the end of the charge before answering: 'It would perhaps be better, dear madame, not to mention too loudly how much your son saved in 1910 and the years after . . .' "

"Wham, in the eye! . . . In yours, that is. Where were you, during all this?"

"Me? In the big bergère."

"You were there?"

She stopped laughing and eating.

"You were there? And what did you say?"

"A witty remark . . . naturally. Ma'am Peloux was grabbing some priceless object to avenge my honor, I stopped her without getting up: 'Gently, my adored mother. Do as I do, do as my charming mother-in-law does, who is all light . . . and sweetness.' At which point I got the communal estate limited to property acquired after the marriage."

"I don't understand."

"The famous sugarcane plantations that poor little Prince Ceste left to Marie-Laure in his will . . ."

"Yes . . ."

"Forged will. Ceste family very worked up! Trial possible! Do you get the picture?"

He was jubilant.

"I get the picture, but how do you know this story?"

"Ah! So here it is. Old Lili has just swooped down with all her weight on the Ceste boy, who is seventeen years old and full of pious sentiments . . ."

"Old Lili? How awful!"

". . . and the Ceste boy murmured this idyll to her, between kisses . . ."

"Chéri! I feel sick to my stomach!"

". . . and old Lili passed the tip on to me at Mother's afternoon get-together last Sunday. Old Lili adores me! She's full of esteem for me because I never wanted to sleep with her!"

"I should hope not," Léa sighed. "Be that as it may . . ."

She was reflecting, and Chéri found her lacking in enthusiasm.

"Well, say it, aren't I splendid? Say it!"

He leaned over the table, and the sun playing on the white table-cloth and dishware illuminated him like footlights.

"Yes . . ."

"Be that as it may," Léa thought, "that nuisance Marie-Laure literally called him a pimp . . ."

"Is there any cream cheese, Nounoune?"

"Yes . . ."

". . . and he didn't hit the roof any more than if she'd thrown him a flower . . ."

"Nounoune, will you give me the address? The address where you get the coeurs à la crème, for the new cook I've hired for October?"

"You must be joking! They're made here. You don't find mussel sauce and vol-au-vent without a cook!"

". . . it's true that for five years I've practically supported this child . . . But he still has three hundred thousand francs' allowance. So there. Can you be a pimp when you have three hundred thousand francs' allowance? It's not a matter of numbers, it's a matter of mentality . . . There are some guys whom I could have given a half million to and who wouldn't have been pimps for that . . . But Chéri? And yet, I've never given him money . . . Still . . ."

"Still," she burst out, "she called you a pander!"

"Who?"

"Marie-Laure!"

He lit up with a childlike expression:

"Did she? Did she, Nounoune—was that really what she meant?"

"So it seems to me."

Chéri lifted his glass, filled with a Château-Chalon wine the color of eau-de-vie:

"Three cheers for Marie-Laure! Quite a compliment, isn't it? And if someone said as much of me when I'm your age, I would ask for nothing more!"

"As long as you're happy . . ."

She listened to him distractedly till the end of lunch. Accustomed to the half silences of his wise friend, he contented himself with the daily maternal chidings—"Take the crusty part of the bread . . . Don't eat so much of the fresh crumb . . . You've never known how to choose a fruit . . ."—while, secretly glum, she rebuked herself: "Yet I ought to know what I want! What would I have wanted? That he stand up: 'Madame, you insult me! Madame, I'm not what you think!' I'm really to blame. I raised him in a cocoon, I spoon-fed him everything . . . Who would have guessed that one day he would want to play the part of pater-familias? It didn't occur to *me*! And supposing it had occurred to me, as Patron says: 'It's in the blood!' Even if he had accepted Liane's proposals, Patron's blood would have boiled if talk had drifted in that direction within his earshot. But Chéri has Chéri's blood. He has . . ."

"What were you saying, kid?" she interrupted herself. "I wasn't listening."

"I was saying that never, do you hear me, never will anything else have made me laugh so much as my scene with Marie-Laure!"

"So," Léa concluded to herself, "this is what makes him laugh."

She stood up wearily. Chéri wrapped an arm behind her waist, but she moved it away.

"What day is your marriage, again?"

"A week from Monday."

He appeared so innocent and so detached that she became alarmed:

"It's extraordinary!"

"Why extraordinary, Nounoune?"

"You don't even seem to be thinking about it!"

"I'm not thinking about it," he said in a calm voice. "Everything is settled. Ceremony at two o'clock, that way we don't have to lose our heads over a big luncheon. Afternoon tea at Charlotte Peloux's. And then the sleeping cars, Italy, the lakes . . ."

"Are the lakes back in fashion again, then?"

"They're back in fashion. Villas, hotels, cars, restaurants . . . Monte Carlo, you know!"

"But her—there'll be her! . . ."

"Of course there'll be her. There won't be much of her, but there'll be her."

"And there will no longer be me."

Chéri wasn't expecting this little remark and showed it. A sickly roll of his eyes, a sudden discoloration of his lips, disfigured his face. He carefully caught his breath so that she wouldn't hear him breathing, and returned to his usual self:

"Nounoune, there will always be you."

"Monsieur gratifies me."

"There will always be you, Nounoune . . ."—he laughed awkwardly—"as soon as I need you to do me a favor."

She said nothing. She leaned over to pick up a fallen tortoiseshell comb and stuck it in her hair, singing softly. She continued her song complacently in front of the mirror, proud of having mastered herself so easily, of having dodged the only emotional moment of their parting, proud of having held back the words that must never be said: "Speak . . . beg, insist, cling to me . . . you have just made me happy . . ."

Madame Peloux must have been talking a lot and for a long while before Léa's entrance. The blaze of her cheekbones increased the sparkle of her large eyes, which conveyed nothing but watchfulness, an indiscreet and inscrutable attention. She wore, that Sunday, a black afternoon dress with a very narrow skirt, and no one could have failed to notice that her feet were very small or that her belly was drawn up tight at the waist. She stopped talking, drank a mouthful from a slender chalice that grew warm in her palm, and dipped her head toward Léa with a languorous contentment.

"Isn't it beautiful out? What weather! What weather! Would anyone think it's October?"

"Oh, no! . . . Certainly not!" two fawning voices answered.

A river of red salvia stirred gently along the length of the path, between banks of asters of an almost gray mauve. Clouded yellow butterflies were flying as in summer, but the scent of the sun-warmed chrysanthemums found its way into the open conservatory. A yellow birch quivered in the wind, above a Bengali rose garden that detained the last bees.

"And what," Madame Peloux proclaimed, with sudden lyricism, "—what is this weather, next to what *they* must be having in Italy?"

"There's no denying it ... Indeed! ..." the fawning voices answered.

Léa turned her head toward the voices, frowning:

"If only they didn't talk," she murmured.

Sitting at a gaming table, the Baronne de La Berche and Madame Aldonza were playing piquet. Madame Aldonza, a very old ballet dancer with swaddled legs, suffered from polyarthritis and wore her black-lacquered wig askew. Opposite her and towering above her by a head and a half, the Baronne de La Berche squared a country priest's inflexible shoulders, a large face that old age had rendered frighteningly masculine. She was all hair in her ears, bushes in her nose and over her lip, hairy fingers ...

"Baronne, you won't get around my ninety," Madame Aldonza said tremulously.

"Mark it down, mark it down, my good friend. What *I* want is for everyone to be happy."

She cursed unremittingly and concealed a brutish cruelty. Léa considered her as if for the first time, with disgust, and turned her face back to Madame Peloux.

"At least Charlotte has a human appearance ..."

"What's wrong with you, Léa? You're not feeling out of sorts?" Madame Peloux inquired tenderly.

Léa arched her beautiful back and answered:

"Of course not, Lolotte darling ... It's so pleasant at your house that I'm taking life as it comes ... ," even as she was musing, "Careful ... there's savagery in her, too ... ," and her face put on an appearance of self-satisfied comfort, of satiated reverie, which she underscored by sighing:

"I ate too much . . . I'd like to lose weight, now! Tomorrow I'm starting a diet."

Madame Peloux beat the air and simpered:

"Grief isn't enough for you, then?"

"Haw-haw-haw!" Madame Aldonza and the Baronne de La Berche guffawed. "Haw-haw-haw!"

Léa stood up, tall in her autumn dress of a muted green, beautiful beneath her otter-trimmed satin hat, young among these ruins whom she scanned with a kind eye:

"Oh, my dears! . . . Give me a dozen of these griefs, so that I might lose two pounds!"

"You're splendid, Léa," the Baronne barked at her in a puff of smoke.

"Madame Léa, may I have that hat when you get rid of it?" old Aldonza begged. "Madame Charlotte, do you remember your blue one? It lasted me two years. Baronne, when you've finished ogling Madame Léa, will you deal me some cards?"

"Here they are, sweetie, wishing you luck with them!"

Léa stood for a moment on the threshold of the conservatory, then went down into the garden. She picked a Bengali rose, which shed its petals, listened to the wind in the birch tree, the streetcars on the avenue, the whistle of a train on the Ceinture. The bench she sat down on was warmish, and she closed her eyes, letting the sun warm her shoulders. When she opened her eyes again, she quickly turned her head toward the house, certain that she would see Chéri standing on the threshold of the conservatory, his shoulder leaning against the door . . .

"What's wrong with me?" she wondered.

Bursts of high-pitched laughter, a little hubbub of welcome in the conservatory, saw her stand up, trembling a little.

"Am I becoming high strung?"

"Oh, there they are, there they are!" Madame Peloux trumpeted.

And the Baronne's strong bass voice chanted:

"The li'l couple! The li'l couple!"

Léa shuddered, ran to the threshold, and stopped: there before her were old Lili and her adolescent lover, Prince Ceste, who had just arrived.

Perhaps seventy years old, a corseted eunuch in her portliness— old Lili was often said to be "beyond bounds," though what bounds those were was never specified. An eternal childlike gaiety shone in her round, pink, made-up face, where her large eyes and very small mouth, thin and sunken, flirted shamelessly. Old Lili kept up with the fashions scandalously. A striped skirt, Revolution blue and white, held the lower part of her body in check, a small blue spencer gaped over a chest with the puckered skin of a tough turkey; a silver fox couldn't hide her bare neck, like a flowerpot, a neck as broad as a belly, which had sucked up her chin . . .

"It's repulsive," Léa thought. She couldn't take her eyes off some particularly grim-looking detail, the white felt Breton, for example, girlishly set at a backward tilt on a wig of short, pinkish-brown hair, or the pearl necklace, now visible and now buried in a deep ravine that in bygone days had been called "Venus's ring" . . .

"Léa, Léa, my good friend!" old Lili exclaimed, hurrying toward Léa. She walked with difficulty on round, swollen feet, bound up in buskins and straps with bejeweled buckles, and was the first to congratulate herself:

"I walk like a little duck! It's a style all my own! Guido, my obsession, do you recognize Madame de Lonval? Don't recognize her too much, or I'll take out your eyes . . ."

A thin child with Italian features, enormous empty eyes, a weak receding chin, quickly kissed Léa's hand and returned to the shadows without saying a word. Lili snatched him as he passed and pinned his head against her grainy chest, calling on all present to witness.

"Do you know what this is, madame, do you know what this is? This is my true love, mesdames!"

"Behave yourself," Madame de La Berche's masculine voice advised.

"Whatever for? Whatever for?" Charlotte Peloux said.

"For the sake of decency," the Baronne said.

"Baronne, you're unkind! Aren't they sweet, the two of them! Oh," she sighed, "they remind me of my children."

"I was thinking of them," Lili said with a delighted laugh. "It's our honeymoon, too, the two of us, Guido! We've come to learn the news of the other young couple! We've come to find out *everything*."

Madame Peloux became stern:

"Lili, you don't expect me to tell you risqué stories, do you?"

"Oh yes, indeed I do," Lili cried, clapping her hands. She attempted to skip but managed only to lift her shoulders and hips a little. "That's how I am, that's what you get with me. The sin of listening! No one will break me of it. This little rascal here knows something about it!"

The silent teen, thus incriminated, didn't open his mouth. His black pupils went back and forth across the whites of his eyes like alarmed insects. Léa, frozen, watched.

"Madame Charlotte told us about the ceremony," Madame Aldonza bleated. "Under the orange tree blossoms the young Madame Peloux was a dream."

"A Madonna! A Madonna!" Charlotte Peloux corrected at the top of her lungs, aroused by a saintly delirium. "Never, never have you seen such a sight! My son was walking on clouds! On clouds! . . . What a couple! What a couple!"

"Under the orange tree blossoms . . . do you hear, my obsession?"

Lili murmured . . . "Tell me, Charlotte—and our mother-in-law? Marie-Laure?"

Madame Peloux's pitiless eyes glittered.

"Oh, her! . . . Unseemly, absolutely unseemly . . . All in tight-fitting black, like an eel out of water; her breasts, her belly, you could see everything! Everything!"

"My word!" the Baronne de La Berche grumbled with a martial fury.

"And that look she has as if she's sneering at people, that look as if she always has cyanide in her pocket and a pint of chloroform in her reticule! Well, unseemly, that's the word! She gave the impression of having only five minutes to spare—her mouth barely wiped: 'Good-bye, Edmée, good-bye, Fred,' and she was gone!"

Old Lili was breathless, sitting on the edge of an armchair, her small grandmotherly mouth, wrinkled at the corners, hanging half-open:

"And the advice?" she blurted out.

"What advice?"

"The advice—oh my obsession, give me your hand!—the advice to the young bride? Who gave it to her?"

Charlotte Peloux looked her up and down with an offended expression.

"That was perhaps done in your day, but it's an outmoded custom."

Lustily, the old woman put her fists on her hips:

"Outmoded? Outmoded or not, what could you know about it, my poor Charlotte? People marry so seldom in your family!"

"Haw-haw-haw!" the two helots guffawed incautiously . . .

But a single look from Madame Peloux filled them with consternation.

"Peace, peace, my little angels! You each have your paradise on earth, what more could you want?"

And Madame de La Berche extended a peacemaking policeman's strong hand between the two ladies' flushed faces. But Charlotte Peloux could sense a contest like a purebred horse:

"If you're looking for a fight, Lili, you won't have trouble finding it here! I owe you respect and with good reason, otherwise . . ."

Lili shook with laughter from chin to thighs:

"Otherwise you would get married just to refute me? Come on, it's not difficult to get married! *I* would marry Guido, if he were of age!"

"Really?" said Charlotte, who with that forgot her anger.

"Really! . . . Princesse Ceste, my dear! The *piccola principessa*! *Piccola principessa*! That's what he calls me, my little prince!"

She gripped her skirt and spun around, disclosing a gold chain in the probable whereabouts of her ankle.

"Only," she continued mysteriously, "his father . . ."

She trailed off, and motioned to the silent boy, who spoke quietly and quickly, as if he were reciting:

"My father, the Duc de Parese, wants to cloister me in a convent if I marry Lili . . ."

"In a convent!" Charlotte Peloux shrieked. "In a convent, a man!"

"A man in a convent!" Madame de La Berche brayed in her deep bass. "Good Lord, how exciting!"

"They're savages," Aldonza lamented, joining her shapeless hands.

Léa stood up so abruptly that she knocked over a full glass.

"It's clear glass," Madame Peloux noted with satisfaction. "You'll bring good luck to my young couple. Where are you rushing off to? Is your house on fire?"

Léa had the strength to let out the faintest of secretive little laughs:

"A fire, perhaps . . . Shh! No questions! Mystery . . ."

"No! Again? Impossible!"

Charlotte Peloux whined enviously:

"Though I thought you had a funny look . . ."

"Yes, yes! Tell us everything!" the three old women yapped.

Lili's padded palms, old mother Aldonza's deformed stumps, Charlotte Peloux's hard fingers, had seized hold of her hands, her sleeves, her gold mesh bag. She tore herself away from all these paws and managed to laugh again mischievously:

"No, it's too early, it would spoil everything! It's my secret! . . ."

And she rushed into the vestibule. But the door opened in front of her and a desiccated old-timer, a sort of bantering mummy, took her in his arms:

"Léa, sweetheart, give your little Berthellemy a kiss, or I won't let you pass!"

She cried out in fear and impatience, slapped away the gloved bones that held her, and fled.

————

Neither on the avenues of Neuilly nor on the lanes of the Bois, blue beneath the rapidly falling dusk, did she allow herself to think. She shivered slightly and rolled up the car window. The sight of her tidy house, her pink bedroom, and her boudoir, overly furnished and overly flowered, comforted her:

"Quick, Rose, a fire in my bedroom!"

"But the heater is set at seventy as in the winter: Madame was wrong to take only a fur neckpiece. The evenings are deceptive."

"A hot-water bottle in my bed right away, and for dinner a big cup of well-thickened chocolate, with an egg yolk beaten into it, and some toast, some grapes . . . Quick, my dear, I'm freezing. I caught a chill in that heap in Neuilly . . ."

In bed she clenched her teeth and stopped them from chattering. The warmth of the bed relaxed her tensed muscles, but she didn't yet let down her guard, and the chauffeur Philibert's account book kept her busy until the arrival of the chocolate, which she drank piping hot and frothy. She chose the Chasselas grapes one by one, swinging the cluster by its stem, a long cluster, amber green in the light . . .

Then she switched off the bedside lamp, stretched out in her favorite way, flat on her back, and let herself relax.

"What's wrong with me?"

She was again gripped by anxiety and shivering. The image of an empty doorway haunted her: the door of the conservatory flanked by two clumps of red salvia.

"It's unhealthy," she thought. "You don't get into such a state over a door."

She could picture the three old women as well, Lili's neck, the beige blanket that Madame Aldonza had dragged with her everywhere for the past twenty years.

"Which of the three will I look like in ten years?"

But this prospect didn't fill her with terror. Yet her anxiety grew. She wandered from image to image, from memory to memory, seeking to distance herself from the empty doorway framed with red salvia. She was getting tired of being in her bed and trembled slightly. Suddenly an uneasiness, so vivid that she at first believed it to be physical, brought her to her feet, contorted her mouth, and wrung from her, with a ragged breath, a sob and a name:

"Chéri!"

There followed tears, which she couldn't immediately master. As soon as she regained her self-control, she sat down, dried her face, switched the lamp on again.

"Oh," she said. "I see."

She took a thermometer from the bedside table, put it under her armpit.

"Ninety-eight point six. So it's not physical. I see. It's because I'm suffering. I'm going to have to work it out."

She took a drink, got up, washed her inflamed eyes, powdered herself, poked at the logs, went back to bed. She felt wary, mistrustful of an enemy she was unacquainted with: grief. Thirty years of a straightforward, congenial, often passionate, sometimes grasping life had just turned their back on her and left her, at close to fifty, young and seemingly vulnerable. She laughed at herself, no longer felt her grief, and smiled:

"I think I lost my mind a little while ago. There's nothing wrong with me anymore."

But a movement of her left arm, involuntarily open and rounded so as to receive and shelter a sleeping head, brought back all her pain, and she sat up with a start.

"Well! This is going to be great," she said out loud, harshly.

She looked at the time and saw that it was barely eleven o'clock. Overhead, the elderly Rose's muffled footsteps went past, reached the stairs to the attic floor, faded away. Léa resisted the urge to summon her deferential old servant for help.

"Oh no! I don't want any trouble with the servants, now, do I?"

She got up again, dressed herself warmly in a quilted silk robe, took the chill off her feet. Then she half opened a window, strained her ears to hear she knew not what. A wet, gentler wind had brought clouds, and the Bois, very close by, still leafy, was murmuring in gusts. Léa closed the window again, picked up a newspaper, and read the date:

"October twenty-sixth. It's been just a month since Chéri was married."

She never said "since Edmée was married."

Unwittingly copying Chéri, she still hadn't counted this young shadow of a woman as a living being. Chestnut-brown eyes, very beautiful ash-colored hair, a bit crimped—the rest dissolved in her memory like the contours of a face seen in a dream.

"They're making love in Italy, at this hour, no doubt. And it doesn't matter to me in the least . . ."

She wasn't boasting. The picture she painted of the young couple, the familiar positions she conjured, Chéri's face itself, unconscious for a moment, the white line of light between his languid eyelids, all of it excited in her neither curiosity nor jealousy. But an animal spasm took hold of her again, bent her body, faced with a nick in the pearl-gray woodwork, the mark of one of Chéri's brutalities . . .

"The beautiful hand that left its trace here has turned away from me forever . . . How well I speak! Apparently grief's going to make me a poet!"

She walked around, sat down, went back to bed, waited for daylight. Rose, at eight o'clock, found her sitting at her desk and writing, a sight that worried the elderly maid.

"Is Madame unwell?"

"So-so, Rose. Age, you know . . . Vidal wants me to have a change of scenery. Will you come with me? It's shaping up to be a bad winter here, we'll go eat a little oily cooking in the sun."

"Where?"

"You're too inquisitive. Just have the trunks taken out. Beat my fur rugs well . . ."

"Madame is taking the car?"

"I think so. I'm even sure. I want all my conveniences, Rose. Just imagine, I'm leaving all by myself: it's a pleasure trip."

For five days, Léa made the rounds of Paris, wrote, telegraphed, received wires and letters from the South. And she departed Paris, leaving Madame Peloux a short letter that she had nevertheless started over three times:

My dear Charlotte,
You won't hold it against me if I leave without saying good-bye to

you, and keep my little secret. I'm just a big fool! . . . Oh well, life is short, it should at least be happy.

I send you a very affectionate kiss. Give my regards to the child when he comes home.

Your incorrigible,

LÉA.

P.S. Don't go to the trouble of coming to interview my butler or concierge, no one knows anything at my house.

"**D**o you know, my beloved angel, that I don't find that you look very well?"

"It's the night on the train," Chéri answered briefly.

Madame Peloux didn't dare to say all that she was thinking. She found her son changed.

"He's . . . yes, he's cursed," she decided; and she managed out loud with enthusiasm:

"It's Italy!"

"If you wish," Chéri conceded.

Mother and son had just eaten their breakfast together, and Chéri had deigned to praise with some flattering blasphemies his "concierge's café au lait," a thick, light, sweet coffee that was gently reheated over embers, after pieces of buttered toast had been broken into it, and continued to cook slowly, concealing the coffee under a succulent crust.

He was cold in his white wool pajamas and clasped his arms

around his knees. Charlotte Peloux, anxious about her appearance in front of her son, was christening a marigold-yellow dressing gown and a morning cap, close fitting at the temples, which lent the starkness of her face a sinister-looking importance.

Since her son was looking at her, she simpered:

"You see, I'm adopting the grandmotherly style! Powder before long. Do you like this cap? It's eighteenth century, isn't it? Dubarry or Pompadour? What do I look like?"

"You look like an old convict," Chéri flung at her. "You just don't do that kind of thing, or at least you give warning."

She groaned, then guffawed:

"Ha-ha! You really can be scathing!"

But he didn't laugh, and looked out into the garden at the thin coating of snow, fallen overnight on the lawn. The spasmodic, almost imperceptible bulging of his jaw muscles alone betrayed his agitation. A frightened Madame Peloux copied his silence. The muffled trill of a bell reverberated.

"It's Edmée ringing for her breakfast," Madame Peloux said.

Chéri didn't answer.

"So what's wrong with the heater? It's cold in here," he said after a moment.

"It's Italy," Madame Peloux repeated lyrically. "You've come back here with your eyes and your heart filled with sunshine. You've arrived at the North Pole! The North Pole! The dahlias haven't bloomed in eight days! But don't worry, my precious love. Your nest is coming along. If the architect hadn't had a paratyphoid fever, it would be done. I had warned him; if I told him once, I told him a hundred times: 'Monsieur Savaron . . .' "

Chéri, who had gone to the window, abruptly turned around:

"What's the date on that letter?"

Madame Peloux stared with a little child's wide eyes:

"What letter?"

"That letter from Léa that you showed me a little while ago."

"It wasn't dated, my love, but I received it the day before my last Sunday in October."

"OK. And you don't know who it is? . . ."

"Who *what* is, my treasure?"

"You know, the guy she left with?"

The stark face of Madame Peloux became mischievous:

"No, can you imagine! No one knows! Old Lili is in Sicily and not one of those ladies has caught wind of anything! A mystery, an agonizing mystery! But you know me, I *have* picked up little bits of information here and there . . ."

Chéri's black pupils moved across the whites of his eyes.

"What gossip?"

"About a young man . . . ," Madame Peloux whispered. "A young man who's rather . . . rather disreputable, if you know what I mean! . . . Very good looking, however!"

She was lying, choosing the basest conjecture. Chéri shrugged his shoulders:

"Oh, for God's sake! . . . Very good looking! That pathetic Léa, I can just see it, a strapping young man from Patron's school, with black hair on his knuckles and damp hands . . . Listen, I'm going back to bed, you make me sleepy."

Shuffling along in his babouches, he returned to his bedroom, lingering in the long corridors and on the broad landings of the house, which he seemed to be seeing for the first time. He bumped into a bulging wardrobe and was surprised:

"The devil take me if I remembered there was a wardrobe there . . . Oh yes, I remember vaguely . . . And this guy here, who can he be?"

He was examining an enlarged photograph, hung gloomily in

its black wood frame, near a piece of polychrome crockery that was equally unfamiliar to Chéri.

Madame Peloux hadn't moved in twenty-five years and preserved in their place all the successive errors in her ridiculous and acquisitive taste. "It's the house of an ant that's gone nuts," reproached old Lili, who herself had an appetite for paintings, but more particularly for avant-garde painters. To which Madame Peloux replied:

"Why tinker with what works?"

Was a corridor of sea green—hospital green, Léa would say— beginning to flake? Charlotte Peloux would have it repainted in green, and jealously sought, so as to replace a chaise longue's garnet-colored velvet, the same garnet-colored velvet . . .

Chéri stopped on the threshold of an open bathroom. The red marble of a sink top was fitted with monogrammed white basins, and two electric wall lamps supported lily-shaped shades made of pearls. Chéri raised his shoulders to his ears as if he had been hit by a draft:

"Good Lord, but this heap is ugly!"

He set off again hurriedly. The window at the end of the corridor he was pacing was adorned with a border of small red and yellow stained-glass panes.

"As if I need that to boot!" he grumbled.

He turned left and opened the door—the door to his old bedroom—roughly, without knocking. A little cry burst forth from the bed, where Edmée was finishing her breakfast.

Chéri closed the door behind him and gazed at his young wife without approaching the bed.

"Good morning," she said to him, smiling. "How surprised you look to see me!"

The reflection off the snow illuminated her with a blue, even light. Her frizzled ashen-chestnut hair was undone, and didn't quite cover her low, elegant shoulders. With her cheeks white and rosy to match her nightgown, her pink mouth paled from fatigue, she was a freshly painted picture, unfinished, and slightly remote.

"Won't you say good morning to me, Fred?" she insisted.

He sat down close to his wife and took her in his arms. She leaned backward slightly, pulling Chéri with her. He rested on his elbows so as to look more carefully at this creature beneath him, so young that weariness had not yet removed her bloom. Her lower eyelids, puffy and full, without the slightest wrinkle, seemed to fill him with wonder, as did the silvery smoothness of her cheek.

"How old are you?" he asked suddenly.

Edmée opened her eyes, which she had tenderly shut. Chéri saw their hazelnut color, the small, square teeth exposed by her laughter:

"Oh! Let's see . . . I'll be nineteen on January fifth, try to remember it! . . ."

He abruptly pulled back his arm and the young woman slid into the hollow of the bed like an untied scarf.

"Nineteen, that's incredible! Do you know that I'm over twenty-five years old?"

"Of course I know, Fred . . ."

He took a honey-colored tortoiseshell mirror from the bedside table and gazed at himself in it:

"Twenty-five years old!"

Twenty-five years old, a face of white marble that appeared invincible. Twenty-five years old, but at the outer corners of his eyes, and under his eyes as well, delicately doubling the classical shape of his eyelids, two lines, visible only in direct light, two lines, traced by a hand so dreadful and so unthinking . . . He put down the mirror:

"You're younger than I am," he said to Edmée. "I find that shocking."

"I don't!"

She had answered in a mordant tone that was full of insinuation. He paid no attention.

"Do you know why my eyes are beautiful?" he asked her with great earnestness.

"No," Edmée said. "Perhaps because I love them?"

"Mere poetry," Chéri said, shrugging his shoulders. "It's because I have eyes shaped like a sole."

"Like a . . ."

"Like a sole."

He sat down close to her to demonstrate.

"Look here, the corner closest to the nose, that's the head of the sole. And then the top goes up, that's the back of the sole, whereas underneath, it continues straighter: the belly of the sole. And then the corner of the eye that's elongated toward the temple, that's the tail of the sole."

"Oh?"

"Yes, if I had eyes shaped like a flounder, which is to say as rounded on the bottom as on top, I would look stupid. There you have it. You've got your diploma, but did you know that?"

"No, I must admit . . ."

She fell silent and remained dumbstruck, because he had spoken sententiously, with unnecessary severity, like certain eccentrics.

"There are moments," she thought, "when he's like a savage. A creature from the jungle? But he doesn't know anything about plants or animals, and at times he seems not even to know about humankind . . ."

Chéri, sitting up against her, had one arm around her shoulders and with his free hand fondled the small pearls, very beautiful, very round, perfectly matched, of Edmée's necklace. She inhaled the perfume that Chéri used immoderately, and went limp, intoxicated, like a rose in a hot room.

"Fred . . . Come to bed . . . we're tired . . ."

He seemed not to hear. He fixed on the pearls of her necklace a stubborn, anxious look.

"Fred . . ."

He flinched, stood up, furiously stripped off his pajamas, and threw himself stark naked into bed, seeking a spot for his head on a youthful shoulder whose delicate clavicle still protruded. Edmée yielded her body, hollowed out a space at her side, opened her arm. Chéri closed his eyes and became still. She remained cautiously awake, a little breathless under the weight, and thought he had fallen asleep. But after a moment he turned over with a jump, imitating the grunt of an unconscious sleeper, and rolled himself up in the sheet on the other side of the bed.

"As usual," Edmée noted.

————

She was to wake up all winter in that square, four-windowed bedroom. The bad weather hampered the completion of a new house, on the avenue Henri-Martin, as did the caprices of Chéri, who wanted a black bathroom, a Chinese sitting room, a basement equipped with a swimming pool and a gym. To the objections of the architect, he responded: "I don't give a damn. I'm paying, I want service. I don't care about the cost." But at times, he fiercely dissected an estimate, asserting that "you don't dupe young Peloux." Indeed, he would expatiate on standard pricing, asbestos cement, and colored stucco with an unexpected ease and an accurate memory for figures that compelled the contractors' respect.

He seldom consulted his young wife, though he made a show of his authority to impress her, and took care, on occasion, to conceal his uncertainty by issuing sharp commands. She discovered that while he instinctively knew how to work with color, he scorned the beautiful forms and characteristic features of styles.

"You burden yourself with a heap of trouble, you, what's-your-name . . . uh . . . Edmée. A decision concerning the smoking room? Well, here's one: Blue for the walls, a blue that's not scared of anything. A purple carpet, in a purple that knows its place before the blue of the walls. And then, in all that, don't be afraid of black, or gold for the furniture and knickknacks."

"Yes, you're right, Fred. But it will be a little relentless, those lovely colors. It will lack charm, a light note, a white vase or a statue . . ."

"Certainly not," he interrupted rather inflexibly. "The white vase, that will be me stark naked. And don't let's forget a cushion, a thingy, some whatever in pumpkin red, for when I lie around stark naked in the smoking room."

Secretly attracted and repelled, she cherished such visions, which transformed their future residence into a sort of dubious palace, a temple erected to the glory of Chéri. But she didn't fight, gently angled for "some small spot" for a tiny, precious set of furniture, upholstered with stitching on a white background, a gift from Marie-Laure.

This gentleness, which concealed a will so youthful yet already so well trained, earned her four months of camping out at her mother-in-law's, and of evading, throughout those four months, the constant monitoring, the traps daily set for her serenity, for her already timid gaiety, for her diplomacy; Charlotte Peloux, excited by the proximity of so tender a victim, would lose her head a little and squander her arrows, bite indiscriminately . . .

"Some self-control, Madame Peloux," Chéri called out from time to time. "Who will you murder next winter, if I don't stop you?"

Edmée would look up at her husband with eyes in which fear and gratitude trembled together, and tried not to think too much, not to look at Madame Peloux too much. One evening, Charlotte, as if oblivious, thrice called out Léa's name in place of Edmée's over the chrysanthemum centerpiece. Chéri lowered his satanic eyebrows:

"Madame Peloux, I believe you're having memory problems. Do you think a rest cure would be appropriate?"

Charlotte Peloux fell silent for a week, but Edmée never dared to ask her husband: "Was it on my account that you got angry? Was it really me you were defending? It wasn't the other woman, the one before me?"

Her childhood, her adolescence, had taught her patience, hope, silence, the agile handling of the captive's weapons and virtues. The lovely Marie-Laure had never reprimanded her daughter: she confined herself to punishing her. Never a harsh word, never a tender word. Isolation, then boarding school, then the further isolation of a few vacations, frequent banishment to a decorated room; finally the threat of marriage, any marriage, from the moment the too-beautiful mother's eye discerned in her daughter the dawn of another beauty, a timid beauty, seemingly oppressed, and all the more affecting . . . Compared to this mother of unfeeling ivory and gold, the straightforward malice of Charlotte Peloux was all roses . . .

"Are you afraid of my revered mother?" Chéri asked her one evening.

Edmée smiled, pouted unconcernedly.

"Afraid? No. You jump when a door slams, but you're not afraid. You're afraid of the snake that slithers under it . . ."

"Quite the snake, Marie-Laure, eh?"

"Quite."

He waited for a confidence that didn't come, and with one arm clasped his wife's slender shoulders companionably:

"We're orphans of a sort, aren't we?"

"Yes, we're orphans! We're so sweet!"

She pressed herself against him. They were alone in the conservatory, Madame Peloux was upstairs preparing her poisons, as Chéri put it, for the following day. The night, already cold behind the windowpanes, reflected the furniture and lamps like a pond. Edmée felt warm and protected, confident in the arms of this man she did not know. She raised her head and cried out in astonishment, because he had tipped a magnificent but despairing face toward the chandelier, closing his eyes on two tears, held suspended and glistening between his lashes . . .

"Chéri, Chéri! What's wrong?"

In spite of herself, she had called him by this too-affectionate pet name that she had wished never to utter. He responded to the cry distractedly, and brought his gaze back to her.

"Chéri! My God, I'm afraid . . . What's wrong?"

He pushed her away a little, held her by her arms in front of him.

"Oh! Oh, this little girl . . . this little girl . . . What are you afraid of, then?"

He offered her his velvet eyes, more beautiful for their tears, peaceful, wide open, unfathomable. Edmée was about to beseech him to stay silent, when he spoke:

"How stupid we are! . . . It's this idea that we're orphans . . . It's idiotic. It's so true . . ."

He recovered his air of comical importance and she took a breath, certain that he would say nothing more. As he began to put out the candelabras carefully, he turned toward Edmée with a vanity that was either very innocent or very sly:

"Well, why wouldn't I, too, have a heart?"

"**W**hat are you doing there?"

Though he had questioned her almost inaudibly, the sound of Chéri's voice struck Edmée to such a degree that she bent over as if he had pushed her. Standing beside a wide-open desk, she placed both hands on some scattered papers.

"I'm tidying up . . . ," she said in a weak voice. She lifted one hand, which stopped in midair as if it had gone numb. Then she seemed to awaken and quit lying:

"Here it is, Fred . . . You had told me that for our upcoming move, you couldn't stand personally taking charge of what you want to bring: this room, this furniture . . . I wanted, in good faith, to tidy up, to sort . . . and then, the poison came over me, the temptation, evil thoughts—*the* evil thought . . . Forgive me. I have touched things that don't belong to me."

She trembled bravely and waited. He kept his forehead inclined, his hands closed, in a menacing attitude, but he seemed not to see his wife. His gaze was so veiled that she retained, from that time forward, the memory of a colloquy with a pale-eyed man . . .

"Ah!" he said finally. "You were searching . . . You were searching for love letters."

She didn't deny it.

"You were searching for my love letters!"

He laughed his awkward, unnatural laugh. Edmée blushed, hurt:

"You think I'm stupid, obviously. You're not the type of man not to have put them away for safekeeping or burned them. And anyway, after all, it doesn't concern me. I'm getting only what I deserve. You won't hold a grudge against me for it, Fred?"

She was expending some little effort in entreating him, and was intentionally making herself pretty, her lips pouty, the upper part of her face hidden in the shadow of her fluffy hair. But Chéri's demeanor didn't change, and she noticed, for the first time, that his beautiful, unvarying complexion was taking on the transparency of a winter-white rose, and that the oval of his cheeks had grown thinner.

"Love letters . . . ," he repeated. "It's a scream."

He took a step and picked up a fistful of papers, which he plucked out one by one. Postcards, restaurant checks, letters from suppliers, telegrams from girlfriends met for a night, messages sent pneumatically from freeloading friends, three lines, five lines; a few cramped pages, slashed with the sharp-edged handwriting of Madame Peloux . . .

Chéri turned toward his wife:

"I have no love letters."

"Oh!" she protested. "Why do you want . . ."

"I don't have any," he interrupted. "You can't understand. I hadn't realized it. I can't have love letters, since . . ."

He stopped.

"Oh! Wait, wait. There was nevertheless one time, I remember, I hadn't wanted to go to La Bourboule, and so . . . Wait, wait . . ."

He opened drawers, feverishly threw papers on the carpet.

"This is too much! What did I do with it? I would have sworn it was in the upper left . . . No . . ."

He shut the empty drawers roughly and fixed a weighty gaze on Edmée:

"You didn't find anything? You didn't take a letter that began: *Of course not, I'm not annoyed. We should always separate for a week every month*, and then it continued with I can't remember what, about a honeysuckle that was climbing up the window . . ."

He fell silent because his memory failed him, and made an impatient gesture. Edmée, tensed and slender before him, didn't falter:

"No, no, I didn't *take* anything," she stressed with curt annoyance. "Since when am I capable of *taking*? So you've let a letter that's so precious to you lie around? I need not ask if such a letter was from Léa!"

He flinched faintly, but not as Edmée was expecting. A stray half smile passed across his beautiful, inscrutable face, and, his head inclined to one side, his eyes attentive, the exquisite arc of his mouth slack, he listened perhaps to the echo of a name . . . All of Edmée's youthful strength, tender and undisciplined, burst out in cries, in tears, her hands in contorted gestures or open so as to scratch:

"Go away! I hate you! You've never loved me! You care no more for me than if I didn't exist! You hurt me, you despise me, you're coarse, you're . . . you're . . . You think only about that old woman! You have the tastes of a madman, of a degenerate, of . . . of . . . You don't love me! Why, I wonder, why did you marry me? . . . You're . . . You're . . ."

She shook her head like an animal gripped by the neck, and when, choking, she tipped her head back to take a breath, he could see the small, milky-white, matched pearls of her necklace gleam. Chéri gazed with amazement at the disordered movements of this charming, supple neck, at the hands knotted together in entreaty,

and above all at those tears, those tears . . . He had never seen so
many tears . . . Who, then, had cried in front of him, for him? No
one . . . Madame Peloux? "But," he mused, "Madame Peloux's
tears don't count . . ." Léa? . . . No. He searched, in the most hidden recesses of his memory, for two eyes of an honest blue, which
had shone only with pleasure, mischievousness, and slightly
mocking affection . . . What a lot of tears there were in this young
woman who thrashed before him! What do you do with so many
tears? He didn't know. Nevertheless he stretched out his arm, and
since Edmée drew back, perhaps fearing some brutality, he placed
his beautiful, smooth, perfume-infused hand on her head, and he
stroked this disordered head, trying to imitate a voice and words
whose power he knew from experience:

"There . . . there . . . What's this . . . What's this, now . . . there . . ."

Edmée suddenly dissolved and fell onto a seat, where she curled
up tight and began to sob passionately, with a frenzy that resembled
turbulent laughter and fits of joy. Her graceful, bowed body was
bounding, heaved by grief, jealous love, anger, unconscious submis-
siveness, and yet, like the wrestler in the midst of the match, like the
swimmer in the trough of a wave, she felt herself bathed in a new
element, pure and bitter.

———

She cried for a long time and recovered only slowly, during lulls
pierced by great jolts and quivery gasps. Chéri had sat down close
to her and continued to stroke her hair. He had passed the peak of
his own emotion, and was getting bored. He scrutinized Edmée,
flung diagonally across the hard couch, and he disliked the way this
sprawled body, with its dress lifted up and its scarf undone, heightened the room's disorder.

However soft had been his sigh of boredom, she heard it and sat up.

"Yes," she said, "I exhaust you . . . Oh, it would be better . . ."

He interrupted her, dreading a torrent of words:

"It's not that, only I don't know what you want."

"What do you mean, what I want . . . What do you mean, what I . . ."

She showed her tear-inflamed face.

"Listen to me closely."

He took her by the hands. She wanted to break away.

"No, no, I know that voice! You're going to give me some far-fetched argument! When you take on that voice and that look, I know you're going to prove to me that you have an eye like a mullet and a mouth shaped like the number three lying on its back! No, no, I don't want to hear it."

She was recriminating childishly, and Chéri calmed down, realizing that they were both very young. He shook the warm hands he was holding:

"Will you just listen to me! For God's sake, I'd like to know what you reproach me with! Do I go out in the evening without you? No! Do I often leave you during the day? Do I carry on a secret correspondence?"

"I don't know . . . I don't think so . . ."

He turned her from side to side, like a doll.

"Do I have a separate bedroom? Do I make love to you badly?"

She hesitated, smiled with a suspicious shrewdness.

"You call that love, Fred . . ."

"There are other words, but you wouldn't like them."

"What you call love . . . couldn't that be, really, a . . . a sort . . . of pretext?"

She added hastily:

"I'm generalizing, Fred, you understand . . . I'm saying, it *could* be, in certain cases . . ."

He let go of Edmée's hands:

"That," he said coldly, "is a gross mistake."

"Why?" she asked in a feeble voice.

He whistled, his chin in the air, as he moved off a few steps. Then he came back to his wife, looked her up and down as if she were a stranger. A dreadful beast has no need to pounce to cause fear. Edmée saw that his nostrils were flared and the tip of his nose was white.

"Well! . . ." he exhaled, looking at his wife. He shrugged his shoulders and made an about-face. At the end of the room, he turned around and came back.

"Well! . . ." he repeated. "She speaks."

"What?"

"She speaks, and what does she say? She's taking liberties, upon my word . . ."

She stood up in a rage:

"Fred," she cried, "you won't speak to me in that tone again! Who do you take me for?"

"For a blunderer, didn't I just have the honor of telling you?"

He touched her shoulder with a hard index finger, she suffered from it as if from a grievous wound.

"You've passed your graduation exam, isn't there somewhere a . . . a sentence that says: 'Don't touch the knife, the dagger,' something?"

"The ax," she said mechanically.

"That's it. So, my dear, you mustn't touch the ax. Which means to wound a man . . . regarding his favors, if I may put it that way. You've wounded me regarding the gifts that I give you . . . You've wounded me regarding my favors."

"You . . . you speak like a cocotte!" she stammered.

She was turning red, losing her strength and her composure. She hated him for remaining pale, for retaining a superiority whose whole secret consisted in the carriage of his head, the steadiness of his stance, the ease of his shoulders and arms . . .

The hard index finger again pressed into Edmée's shoulder.

"Excuse me, excuse me. It would no doubt shock you if I claimed that on the contrary you're the one who thinks like a tart. When it comes to such assessments, you don't fool young Peloux. I know a bit about 'cocottes,' as you call them. I know quite a bit about them. A 'cocotte' is a lady who generally manages to get more than she gives. Do you understand?"

She understood above all that he was no longer addressing her with the familiar *tu*.

"Nineteen years old, white skin, vanilla-scented hair; and then, in bed, closed eyes and slack arms. That's all very nice, but is it really that uncommon? Do you think it's really that uncommon?"

She flinched at each word, and each sting awakened her to the battle of female against male.

"It might possibly be uncommon," she said firmly, "but how would you know?"

He didn't answer, and she hastened to register an advantage:

"*I*," she said, "I saw men in Italy more beautiful than you. It's nothing out of the ordinary. My nineteen years are as good as the next woman's, one handsome boy is as good as another handsome boy, come, come, everything will settle itself out . . . A marriage nowadays means nothing. Instead of embittering ourselves with ridiculous scenes . . ."

He stopped her with an almost forgiving shake of his head:

"Oh, poor kid! . . . It's not so simple . . ."

"Why? There are quick divorces, for a price."

She spoke with an escaped schoolgirl's curt demeanor, and it was pitiful to see. Her hair swept up above her forehead, and the gentle, shrouded outline of her cheek, made her anxious, intelligent eyes darker, the eyes of an unhappy woman, eyes that were perfect and definite in an uncertain face.

"That wouldn't settle anything," Chéri said.

"Because?"

"Because . . ."

He inclined his forehead, where his eyebrows tapered into pointed wings, shut his eyes and opened them again as if he had just swallowed a bitter mouthful:

"Because you love me . . ."

She noted only the return of the familiar *tu* and, above all, the sound of his voice, full, a bit subdued, the voice of better times. Deep down inside she agreed: "It's true, I love him; at the moment, there's nothing that can be done."

The dinner bell rang in the garden, a too-small bell that predated Madame Peloux, a bell from a provincial orphanage, sad and clear. Edmée shuddered:

"Oh, I don't like that bell! . . ."

"Oh?" Chéri said distractedly.

"In our home, they will announce meals rather than ring for them. In our home, we won't have these boardinghouse ways; you'll see, in our home . . ."

She spoke as she followed the hospital-green corridor, without turning around, and didn't see, behind her, the savage attention that Chéri gave to her last words, nor his silent half laugh.

He walked along lightly, stimulated by a muted spring that could be sensed only in the moist, erratic wind, in the intense earthy perfume of the squares and small gardens. A plate-glass window from time to time reminded him, as he passed, that he was wearing a becoming felt hat, pulled down over his right eye, a loose light-weight overcoat, large light-colored gloves, an earthenware-colored tie. The silent tribute of women followed him, the most inexperienced among them devoting to him that fleeting amazement that can be neither dissimulated nor feigned. But Chéri never looked at women in the street. He had just set off from the building on the avenue Henri-Martin, having left the interior decorators with a few orders, contradictory but barked out in a masterful tone of voice.

At the end of the avenue, he lingeringly inhaled the vegetal scent that came from the Bois on the heavy, moist wing of the westerly wind, and hurried on toward the Porte Dauphine. In a few minutes, he had reached the bottom of the avenue Bugeaud, and stopped dead.

For the first time in six months, his feet were treading the familiar path. He opened his overcoat.

"I walked too quickly," he thought. He set off again, then stopped once more, and this time, his gaze was directed at a precise spot: fifty yards away, head bare, a chamois leather in his hands, Ernest the concierge, Léa's concierge, was "doing" the brass on the gate in front of Léa's building. Chéri began to hum as he walked, but he realized from the sound of his voice that he never hummed, and he fell silent.

"How's it going, Ernest, still at work?"

The concierge's face lit up cautiously.

"Monsieur Peloux! I'm delighted to see Monsieur, Monsieur hasn't changed."

"Neither have you, Ernest. Is Madame well?"

He spoke in profile, keeping watch on the closed blinds on the second floor.

"I think so, monsieur, we've gotten only a few postcards."

"Where from? From Biarritz, I imagine?"

"I don't believe so, monsieur."

"Where is Madame?"

"I would be at a loss what to tell Monsieur: we transmit Madame's mail—what little there is of it—to Madame's lawyer."

Chéri pulled out his billfold, looking at Ernest cajolingly.

"Oh! Monsieur Peloux, money between us? You wouldn't want to do that. A thousand francs wouldn't make a man talk if he knows nothing. If Monsieur wants the address of Madame's lawyer . . . ?"

"No, thank you, honestly. And when is she coming back?"

Ernest spread his arms:

"That's another question that's outside my jurisdiction! Perhaps tomorrow, perhaps in a month . . . I'm keeping things up, as you see. With Madame, you have to be careful. If you said to me, 'Look who's coming around the corner of the avenue,' I wouldn't be surprised."

Chéri turned around and looked at the corner of the avenue.

"Is there nothing else Monsieur Peloux wants? Was Monsieur passing by on a stroll? It's a lovely day . . ."

"No, thank you, Ernest. Good-bye, Ernest."

"Always at your service, Monsieur Peloux."

Chéri went up as far as the Place Victor-Hugo, twirling his cane. He tripped twice and nearly fell, like people who think they're being keenly watched from behind. Having reached the railing of the Métro, he rested on his elbows, leaning over the black-and-pink shadow of the underground, and felt crushed by fatigue. When he straightened up, he saw that the gaslights on the square were being lit and that night was tinting everything blue.

"No, can it possibly be true? I'm ill!"

He had touched the depths of his gloomy reflections and was struggling to bring himself back. The requisite words finally came to him.

"Come on now, for God's sake . . . Young Peloux, are you going off the rails, my good friend? Don't you know that it's time to go home?"

This last word called to mind the vision that an hour had sufficed to banish: a square bedroom, Chéri's big childhood bedroom, an anxious young wife, standing against the window, and Charlotte Peloux loosened up by a martini cocktail . . .

"Oh no," he said out loud. "No . . . That's all over."

At a wave of his raised cane, a taxi stopped.

"To the restaurant . . . uh . . . to the Blue Dragon restaurant."

———

He crossed the grillroom to the strains of violins, bathed in an atrocious electric light that he found invigorating. A maître d' recognized him, and Chéri shook his hand. Before him, a tall, gaunt young man stood up, and Chéri sighed tenderly:

"Ah, Desmond! And here I was, so wanting to see you! You turn up at just the right moment!"

The table where they sat down was decorated with pink carnations. A small hand, a large aigrette, waved toward Chéri from a neighboring table:

"It's the Kid," the Vicomte Desmond warned him.

Chéri didn't remember the Kid, but he smiled to the large aigrette, touched the small hand with the end of an advertising fan without getting up. Then, in his gravest lady-conquering manner, he looked an unfamiliar couple up and down, because the woman had forgotten to eat ever since Chéri had sat down near her.

"He looks like a cuckold, that guy, doesn't he?"

To whisper these words, he had leaned in close to his friend's ear, and the joy in his expression sparkled like welling tears.

"What have you been drinking since you got married?" Desmond asked. "Chamomile tea?"

"Pommery," Chéri said.

"Before the Pommery?"

"Pommery, before and after!"

And opening his nostrils, he inhaled, in his memory, the rose-scented effervescence of an old champagne from 1889 that Léa used to keep for him alone . . .

He ordered the dinner that a milliner out on the town might choose, cold fish with port wine sauce, roasted songbirds, a piping hot soufflé whose center concealed an acidic red glaze . . .

"Hello there," the Kid cried, waving a pink carnation toward Chéri.

"Hello there," Chéri answered, lifting his glass.

The bell of an English wall clock chimed eight o'clock.

"Oh, drat!" Chéri grumbled. "Desmond, leave a message for me over the telephone."

Desmond's pale eyes were hoping for revelations:

"Go ask for Wagram 17-08, have them give you my mother, and tell her we're dining together."

"And if it's young Madame Peloux who comes to the telephone?"

"The same thing. I'm very free, you see. I've broken her in."

He drank and ate a great deal, very concerned with seeming solemn and blasé. But the least burst of laughter, a crashing of glass, a tawdry waltz, intensified his pleasure. The steely blue of the gleaming woodwork took him back to memories of the Riviera, at the hour when the too-blue sea darkened around a patch of molten sun. He forgot his ritual cold indifference, the kind affected by very beautiful men, and began to scan the dark-haired lady facing him with his accomplished gaze, setting her entire body aquiver.

"And Léa?" Desmond asked suddenly.

Chéri didn't flinch, he was thinking of Léa.

"Léa? She's in the Midi."

"Is it all over with her?"

Chéri placed a thumb in the armhole of his vest.

"Oh, naturally, you understand. We parted very decently, as very good friends. It couldn't last a lifetime. What a charming, intelligent woman, my friend . . . Anyhow, you knew her! A broadmindedness . . . Quite remarkable. My dear fellow, I confess, if there hadn't been the issue of age . . . But there was the issue of age, and isn't it . . ."

"Obviously," Desmond interrupted.

This young man with faded eyes, who thoroughly understood the arduous and delicate vocation of a parasite, had just given in to curiosity, and reproached himself for his recklessness. But Chéri, at once circumspect and stimulated, didn't stop speaking about Léa.

He said sensible things, filled with conjugal good sense. He praised marriage, all the while doing justice to Léa's virtues. He extolled his young wife's obedient sweetness so as to find the opportunity to criticize Léa's strong-minded character: "Oh, the brazen woman! I assure you, that woman had her own ideas!" He pushed his confidences further, so that, with regard to Léa, he verged on severity and even impertinence. And as he spoke, sheltered behind the imbecilic words whispered to him by a persecuted lover's distrust, he savored the subtle joy of speaking about her without risk. A little more, and he would have sullied—even as he celebrated in his heart the memory he had of her—her sweet and effortless name, which he had denied himself for six months, the entire merciful image of Léa, leaning over him, lined with two or three big, serious, irreparable wrinkles, beautiful, lost to him, but—alas!—so present . . .

Around eleven o'clock they got up to leave, their enthusiasm dampened by the nearly empty restaurant. At the neighboring table, however, the Kid was attending to her correspondence and asking for some *petits bleus*. She raised her inoffensive, pale sheep's face toward the two friends when they passed:

"Hey, aren't you going to say good evening?"

"Good evening," Chéri conceded.

The Kid, admiring Chéri, called on her girlfriend to bear witness:

"Can you believe it! And to think that he has so much money! Some guys have everything."

But Chéri offered her only his open cigarette case; and she became acerbic.

"They have everything except the know-how to use it . . . Go home to your mother, honey! . . ."

"Actually," Chéri said to Desmond when they reached the street. "Actually, I wanted to ask you, Desmond . . . Wait until we're away from this narrow alleyway where we're trampled underfoot . . ."

The mild, moist evening caused walkers to linger; but the boulevard, after the rue Caumartin, was still waiting for the theaters to let out. Chéri took his friend's arm:

"So, Desmond . . . I'd like you to go back to the telephone."

Desmond stopped.

"Again?"

"You'll call Wagram . . ."

"Seventeen-o8 . . ."

"I adore you. You'll say that I felt unwell at your house . . . Where do you live?"

"At the Morris Hotel."

"Perfect . . . Say that I'll return tomorrow morning, that you're making me mint tea . . . Go on, friend. Here, you'll give this to the little kid at the telephone, or else keep it yourself . . . Come back quickly. I'll wait for you at a table outside the Weber."

The tall, obliging, and haughty young man left, crumpling the bills in his pocket, without allowing himself a critical remark. He returned to find Chéri bent over an untouched orangeade, in which he appeared to be reading his destiny.

"Desmond! . . . Who answered?"

"A lady," the messenger said laconically.

"Which one?"

"I don't know."

"What did she say?"

"That it was fine."

"In what tone of voice?"

"In the one I repeated it to you in."

"Oh, good—thanks."

"It was Edmée," Chéri thought. They walked toward the Place de la Concorde, and Chéri had again taken Desmond's arm. He didn't dare admit that he was feeling very weary.

"Where do you want to go?" Desmond asked.

"Oh, my friend," Chéri said with a sigh of gratitude, "to the Morris, and right away. I'm dead tired."

Desmond forgot his composure:

"What, really? We're going to the Morris? What do you want to do? No joking, eh? Do you want . . ."

"To sleep," Chéri answered. And he closed his eyes as if he were ready to drop, then opened them again. "To sleep, to sleep, do you hear me!"

He clenched his friend's arm too tightly.

"Let's go," Desmond said.

In ten minutes they were at the Morris. The sky blue and ivory of a bedroom, the faux Empire of a small sitting room, smiled at Chéri like old friends. He took a bath, borrowed a too-tight silk shirt from Desmond, went to bed, and, wedged between two thick soft pillows, sank into a dreamless contentment, into a sleep, black and deep, that protected him on all sides . . .

Shameful days slipped by, which he counted. "Sixteen . . . seventeen . . . When three weeks have passed, I'm going home to Neuilly." He didn't go home. He was lucidly gauging a situation that he no longer had the strength to remedy. Sometimes, at night, or in the morning, he flattered himself that his cowardice would end in a few hours. "No longer the strength? Excuse me, excuse me . . . Not *yet* the strength. But it's returning. At noon on the dot, what would I bet I'll be in the dining room on the boulevard d'Inkermann? One, two, and . . ." Noon on the dot found him in the bathtub, or driving his car with Desmond at his side.

Mealtimes granted him a moment of conjugal optimism, as punctual as a feverish attack. Sitting down across from Desmond at their bachelor table, he would see Edmée appear and would silently muse over the inconceivable deference of his young wife: "She's too sweet, that girl! Have you ever seen a darling of a woman like that? Not a word, not a complaint! I'm going to give her one of those bracelets

when I go home. Ah, upbringing . . . talk about Marie-Laure for raising a girl!" But one day, in the grillroom of the Morris, the appearance of a green dress with a chinchilla collar, like one of Edmée's,
had colored Chéri's face with all the marks of an abject terror.

Desmond was enjoying life and putting on a little weight. He
reserved his arrogance for the moments when Chéri, urged to visit
"an extraordinary Englishwoman, foul with vice," or "an Indian
prince in his opium palace," flat-out refused, or agreed with an
undisguised contempt. Desmond no longer understood Chéri, but
Chéri was paying, and better than in the best times of their youth.
One night, they met up with the pale Kid, at the home of her friend,
whose dull name everyone always forgot: "What's-her-name . . .
you know very well . . . the Kid's girlfriend . . ."

The Girlfriend smoked opium and gave it to others to smoke.
Just beyond the entrance to her modest mezzanine apartment,
seeping gas and cooled drugs wafted, and she won her visitors
over with a maudlin cordiality, a constant inducement to sadness, which were not innocuous. Desmond had been called, at
her home, "a big desperate kid," and Chéri "a beauty who has
everything and is only the more wretched for it." But he didn't
smoke, looked at the box of cocaine with the repugnance of a
cat awaiting a purgative, and sat nearly all night on the matting,
his back against the low padding on the wall, between a sleeping
Desmond and the Girlfriend, who didn't stop smoking. Nearly all
night, sober and distrustful, he inhaled the aroma that satisfied
hunger and thirst, and he seemed perfectly happy except for the
fact that he often gazed, with a tiresome and searching fixity, at
the Girlfriend's withered neck, a reddened, grainy neck on which
gleamed a necklace of fake pearls.

Once, Chéri stretched out his hand, stroked with his fingertips
the henna-colored hair at the Girlfriend's nape; he weighed the

large, hollow, light pearls, then pulled back his hand with the nervous quiver of someone who has caught his fingernails on fraying silk. Shortly after, he got up and left.

––––––––

"**H**aven't you had enough," Desmond asked Chéri, "of those clubs where we eat, where we drink, where you consume no women, and of this hotel where people slam the doors? And of the nightclubs where we go in the evenings, and of veering in your sixty-horsepower from Paris to Rouen, from Paris to Compiègne, from Paris to Ville d'Avray . . . What about the Riviera! The fashionable season down there isn't December or January, it's March, it's April, it's . . ."

"No," Chéri said.

"Well then?"

"Well then nothing."

He softened disingenuously and assumed what Léa used to call his "enlightened enthusiast's face."

"My dear fellow, you don't understand the beauty of Paris at this time of year . . . This . . . this indecision, this spring that can't brighten, this soft light . . . whereas the banality of the Riviera . . . No, don't you see, I like it here."

Desmond nearly lost his valet's patience:

"Yes, and then perhaps young Peloux's divorce . . ."

Chéri's sensitive nostrils turned white.

"If you have a scheme with a lawyer, dissuade him at once. There will be no young Peloux's divorce."

"My dear fellow! . . ." protested Desmond, who tried to appear offended. "You have a strange way of acting toward a childhood friend, who at every opportunity . . ."

Chéri wasn't listening. He leveled at Desmond a thin chin, a mouth that he pursed like a miser's mouth. For the first time, he had just heard a stranger disposing of his property.

He reflected. Young Peloux's divorce? He had spent many an hour of the day and night musing, and at such moments those words signified liberty, a sort of childhood regained, perhaps even better . . . But the voice, intentionally nasal, of the Vicomte Desmond had just elicited the necessary image: Edmée leaving the house in Neuilly, determined beneath her little driving hat and long veil, and going to an unknown house, where there lived an unknown man. "Obviously, that would settle everything," Chéri the bohemian admitted. But at the same time, another oddly timorous Chéri objected: "You just don't do that kind of thing!" The image became clearer, gained color and movement. Chéri heard the low, harmonious sound of the gate, and saw, from the other side of the gate, on a bare hand, a gray pearl, a white diamond . . .

"Good-bye . . . ," the small hand said.

Chéri stood up, pushing back his seat.

"It belongs to me, all of that! The wife, the house, the rings, they belong to me!"

He hadn't spoken aloud, but his face betrayed such a barbarous violence that Desmond believed the final hour of his prosperity had come. Chéri took pity, without kindness:

"Poor kitty-cat, are you scared to death? Oh, this old military aristocracy! Come on, I'm going to buy you drawers just like my shirts, and shirts just like your drawers. Desmond, is it the seventeenth?"

"Yes, why?"

"The seventeenth of March. You might as well say spring. Desmond, fashionable people, and I'm talking about truly elegant people now, women or men, can they wait any longer before outfitting themselves for the coming season?"

"Hardly . . ."

"The seventeenth, Desmond! . . . Come on, everything's all right.

We're going to buy a big bracelet for my wife, an enormous cigarette holder for Ma'am Peloux, and a tiny little stickpin for you!"

———————

He likewise had, on two or three occasions, the staggering premonition that Léa was about to return, that she had just come home, that the blinds on the second floor had been opened, permitting a glimpse of the flowered pink of the half curtains, the pattern of the long appliquéd drapes, the gold of the mirrors . . . April 15 passed and Léa didn't come back. Irritating events scratched at the dull course of Chéri's existence. There was the visit of Madame Peloux, who thought she would die when she saw Chéri flat as a greyhound, his mouth shut and his eyes darting. There was the letter from Edmée, a perfectly coherent and surprising letter, in which she explained that she would remain in Neuilly *until further notice*, and made sure to convey to Chéri *Madame de La Berche's best regards* . . . He felt mocked, didn't know how to answer, and ended up throwing out this incomprehensible letter; but he didn't go to Neuilly. As April, green and cold, abloom with paulownias, tulips, bunches of hyacinths, and clusters of laburnum, filled Paris with its scents, Chéri sank, alone, into a bleak darkness. Desmond, ill treated, harassed, dissatisfied, but well paid, was assigned the task sometimes of protecting Chéri from overfamiliar young women and indiscreet young men, sometimes of recruiting both parties to make up a gang that ate, drank, and shrieked between Montmartre, the restaurants of the Bois, and the cabarets of the Left Bank.

———————

One night, the Girlfriend, who was smoking alone and bemoaning, that particular evening, some serious infidelity on the part of her friend the Kid, saw a young man with demonic eyebrows that tapered toward the temples entering her home. He demanded "some very cold water" for his beautiful, thirsty mouth, which was parched by a secret ardor. He didn't show the least interest in the Girlfriend's misfortunes when she related them, pressing the lacquered tray and the pipe on Chéri. He accepted only his portion of the matting, the silence, and the semidarkness, and remained there until daylight, as sparing of his movements as one who fears reawakening a wound if he stirs. At daybreak, he asked the Girlfriend: "Why didn't you have on your pearl necklace today, you know, your big necklace?" and left politely.

He fell into the unconscious habit of walking at night, companionless. Quick and broad, his step led him toward a clear but inaccessible goal. After midnight, he would elude Desmond, who would find him toward dawn in his hotel bed, sleeping facedown, his head between his folded arms, in the posture of a morose child.

"Good, he's here," Desmond would say with relief. "An oddball like that, you never know . . ."

One night when Chéri was out walking like this, eyes wide open in the darkness, he went back up the avenue Bugeaud, since he hadn't yielded, the previous day, to the fetishism that led him back there every forty-eight hours. Like fanatics who can't fall asleep without having touched a doorknob three times, he would brush the gate, lay his index finger on the button of the doorbell, call out softly, in a mischievous tone, "Hey-ho!" and leave.

But one night, that particular night, in front of the gate, his heart struck a great blow that he felt in his throat: the electric globe in the courtyard shone like a mauve moon above the front steps, the wide-open door of the service entrance illuminated the pavement, and, on the second floor, the blinds filtering the interior light delineated the form of a golden comb. Chéri leaned against the nearest tree and lowered his head.

"It's not true," he said. "I'll look up again, and everything will be black."

He straightened up when he heard the voice of Ernest, the concierge, who was calling out in the corridor:

"First thing tomorrow morning, I'll carry up the big black trunk with Marcel, madame!"

Chéri quickly turned around and ran as far as the avenue du Bois, where he sat down. The electric globe that he had seen was dancing before him, deep crimson ringed with gold, against the black of the still thinly leafed plantings. He pressed his hand against his heart and breathed deeply. The night carried the scent of half-open lilacs. He threw off his hat, opened his coat, let himself relax against the back of the bench, stretched out his legs, and his open hands fell softly. A crushing but sweet weight had just descended upon him.

"Ah," he said softly, "is this happiness? . . . I didn't know . . ."

He had just enough time to find himself drawn into self-pity and self-contempt, over everything he hadn't savored during his miserable life as a young man of great wealth but little heart. Then he stopped thinking for a moment or for an hour. He was able, afterward, to believe that he would no longer wish for anything in the world, not even to go to Léa's.

When he shivered with cold and heard the blackbirds announcing the dawn, he stood up, staggering but lighthearted, and started back toward the Morris Hotel, without going by the avenue Bugeaud. He was stretching, expanding his lungs, and overflowing with a universal goodwill:

"Now," he sighed, exorcized, "now . . . Oh, now I'm going to be so kind to the girl! . . ."

Up at eight, shaved, shod, feverish, Chéri shook Desmond, who was sleeping, pallid, frightful to see, and bloated in his sleep like a drowning victim:

"Desmond! Hey! Desmond! . . . Enough! You're too ugly when you're asleep!"

The sleeper sat up and fixed eyes the color of turbid water on his friend. He feigned stupefaction so as to prolong a close examination of Chéri, Chéri who was dressed in blue, poignant and superb, pale under a velvety layer of skillfully applied powder . . . There were still times when Desmond suffered, in his studied ugliness, from Chéri's beauty. He yawned intentionally, at length: "What is it this time?" he wondered as he yawned. "This fool's more beautiful than he was yesterday. Those lashes especially, those lashes of his . . ." He gazed at Chéri's lashes, lustrous and thick, and at the shadow they cast on his dark pupils and on the blue whites of his eyes. Desmond noticed, too, that his arched, disdainful lips were parted, that morning, moist, refreshed, a bit breathless, as if after a stolen moment of fleshly pleasure.

Then he relegated his jealousy to the distant plane of his love concerns and questioned Chéri in a tone of weary condescension:

"Might we ask whether you're going out at this hour, or coming in?"

"I'm going out," Chéri said. "Don't worry about me. I'm going to run some errands. I'm going to the florist's. To the jeweler's, to my mother's, to my wife's, to . . ."

"Don't forget the nuncio," Desmond said.

"I know how to behave," Chéri replied. "I'll bring him gold-filled shirt studs and a spray of orchids."

Chéri rarely replied to a joke and always received one coldly. The significance of this lackluster riposte clued Desmond in to his friend's unusual state. He examined Chéri's reflection in the mirror, noted the pallor of his flaring nostrils, the restless wandering of his eyes, and ventured the most discreet of questions:

"Are you coming back for lunch? . . . Hey, Chéri, I'm talking to you. Shall we have lunch together?"

Chéri shook his head. He whistled as he squared his reflection in the oblong mirror, precisely suited to his height like the one in Léa's bedroom, between the two windows. Soon, in that other mirror, against a sunlit pink background, a heavy gold frame would surround its reflection, naked or draped in loose-fitting silk—the sumptuous reflection of a beautiful young man, loved, happy, pampered, who played with the necklaces and rings of his mistress . . . "Is it already there, in Léa's mirror, this young man's reflection? . . ." This thought pierced his overexcitement with such a violence that, dazed, he believed he had heard it aloud.

"What'd you say? he asked Desmond.

"I didn't say anything," his stiff, obedient friend answered. "People are talking in the courtyard."

Chéri left Desmond's bedroom, slammed the door, and returned to his own rooms. The rue de Rivoli, now awakened, filled them with a subdued, ceaseless tumult, and Chéri could see, through the open window, the spring leaves, stiff and transparent as jade blades beneath the sun. He closed the window and sat down on a small, useless chair that occupied a sad spot against the wall, between the bed and the bathroom door.

"Why is this happening . . . ," he began in a low voice. Then he fell silent. He didn't understand why, in the space of six and a half months, he had almost never thought about Léa's lover.

I'm just a big fool! said Léa's letter, reverently retained by Charlotte Peloux.

"A big fool?" Chéri shook his head. "It's strange, I don't see her that way. What sort of man could she love? A guy like Patron? Rather than someone like Desmond, naturally . . . A well-polished little Argentine? Perhaps . . . But all the same . . ."

He smiled naively: "Apart from me, who could really appeal to her?"

A cloud passed in front of the March sun, and the room went dark. Chéri rested his head against the wall. "My Nounoune . . . My Nounoune . . . have you been unfaithful to me? Have you really been unfaithful to me? Have you done that to me?"

He whipped up his hurt with words and images that he assembled laboriously, surprised but without anger. He tried to conjure the morning's delights, at Léa's, certain afternoons of lingering pleasure in perfect silence, at Léa's—the delicious sleep of winter in the warm bed and the sweet-smelling room, at Léa's . . . But in Léa's arms he always saw, in the cherry-colored daylight that blazed behind Léa's curtains in the afternoons, only a single lover: Chéri. He stood up as though resurrected in an impulse of spontaneous faith:

"It's very simple! If I can't manage to picture anyone else besides me with her, it's because there *is* no one else!"

He grabbed the telephone, very nearly called, then gently replaced the receiver.

"No jokes . . ."

He went out, holding himself very straight, throwing back his shoulders. His open car took him to the jeweler's shop, where he gushed over a small fine headband, with sapphires of a burning blue in a barely visible setting of blue steel, "exactly the headpiece for Edmée," which he took away with him. He bought slightly silly, ceremonious flowers. Since it was barely eleven o'clock, he killed another half hour here and there, in a banking establishment where he took out some money, near a kiosk where he leafed through some English comics, in an Oriental tobacco store, at a perfumery. Finally he climbed back into his car, sat down between his spray of flowers and his beribboned packages.

"Home."

The chauffeur turned around in his bucket seat:

"Monsieur? . . . What did Monsieur say? . . ."

"I said home, boulevard d'Inkermann. Do you need a map of Paris?"

The car shot off toward the Champs-Élysées. The chauffeur was overzealous, and his thought-burdened back seemed to be studying, uneasily, the abyss that separated the spineless young man of the past month, the young man of "if you wish" and "a glass, Antonin?" from young Monsieur Peloux, exacting with the staff and mindful of the gasoline.

"Young Monsieur Peloux," leaning back against the morocco leather, his hat on his knees, soaked up the wind and strove not to think. He cravenly closed his eyes between the avenue Malakoff and the Porte Dauphine, so as not to see the avenue Bugeaud pass, and congratulated himself: "How brave I am!"

The chauffeur tooted the horn, at the boulevard d'Inkermann, to ask them to open the gate, which sang on its hinges with a long, low, harmonious note. The concierge rushed around in his cap, the guard dogs' baying greeted the familiar scent of the returnee. Feeling quite at ease, inhaling the green aroma of the mown lawn, Chéri entered the house and climbed with a masterful step toward the young woman whom he had left, three months earlier, the way a European sailor abandons a little native wife on the other side of the world.

Léa cast the photographs she had pulled from the last trunk onto the open desk, far away from her: "My God, how ugly people are! And they dared give me these. And they think I'll set them in effigy on my mantelpiece, in a nickel-plated frame, perhaps, or in a little folding portfolio? In a wastepaper basket, yes, and in four pieces! . . ."

She went to pick up the photographs, but before tearing them up she subjected them to the steeliest scrutiny her blue eyes could manage. On the black background of a postcard, a stout lady in a straight corset concealed her hair and the lower part of her cheeks in a tulle veil lifted up by the breeze. *To my dear Léa, as a souvenir of some exquisite hours at Guéthary: Anita.* At the center of a piece of cardboard as rough as cob, another photograph grouped together a family, large and glum, a sort of penitentiary colony governed by a short-legged grandmother, heavily made up, who raised a small Provençal drum in the air and rested a foot on the outstretched knee of what looked like a stout and cunning young butcher.

"That doesn't deserve to live," Léa decided, breaking the cob-cardboard.

An unmounted print that she unrolled set before her once more an elderly pair of provincial spinsters, eccentric, shrill, and quarrelsome, who would sit every morning on a south-facing bench along a promenade, every evening between a glass of cassis and the square of silk on which they embroidered a black cat, a toad, a spider: *To our lovely fairy! Her little friends from Trayas, Miquette and Riquette.*

Léa destroyed these travel souvenirs and ran a hand across her forehead:

"It's ghastly. And after those, just as before them, there will be others, others that will look just like those. There's nothing to be done about it. It's the way it is. Maybe wherever there's a Léa, the earth sprouts these types like Charlotte Peloux, de La Berche, Aldonza, ghastly old people who were once beautiful young people, people who are, in a word, unbearable, unbearable, unbearable . . ."

She could hear voices, still fresh in her memory, that had hailed her on the front steps of some hotel, that had called out "Yoo-hoo!" in her direction, from far off, across golden beaches, and she lowered her head in a bull-like gesture of hostility.

She had come home, after six months, a little thinner and more sluggish, less serene. A grumpy mannerism sometimes lowered her chin onto her neck, and impromptu dye jobs had caused her hair to blaze too red. But her complexion, the color of amber, whipped by sun and sea, bloomed like a beautiful farmer's, and could have gone without rouge. She still had to carefully drape, if not altogether hide, her wrinkled neck, now ringed with large creases that the tan hadn't managed to penetrate.

As she sat there, she lingered over tidying up small matters and searched around her—as she might have searched for a missing piece of furniture—for her former vitality, her swiftness in inspecting her cozy domain.

"Oh, that trip!" she sighed. "How could I . . . How tiring it was!"

She furrowed her eyebrows and put on her new grumpy pout, noticing that someone had broken the glass on a small picture by Chaplin, the head of a young girl, pink and silver, that Léa found delightful.

"And a tear two hands wide in the appliquéd curtain . . . And that's just what I've seen so far . . . What was I thinking, going away for so long? And on whose behalf? . . . As if I couldn't have gotten over my grief here, quite peacefully."

She stood up to go ring the bell, gathered the chiffons of her dressing gown, addressing herself bluntly:

"Come on, you old errand girl . . ."

Her maid came in, loaded down with lingerie and silk stockings:

"Eleven o'clock, Rose. And I haven't made up my face! I'm late . . ."

"Madame has nothing to rush her. Madame no longer has those Mégret spinsters dragging Madame on excursions and coming in the morning to pick all the roses for the house. Or Monsieur Roland infuriating Madame by throwing bits of gravel into her bedroom . . ."

"Rose, there's enough to keep us busy in the house. I don't know whether three moves equal a fire, but I'm certain that six months away equals a flood. You saw the lace curtain?"

"That's nothing . . . Madame hasn't seen the linen closet: mouse droppings everywhere and the floorboards chewed. And it's really quite strange that I left Émérancie twenty-eight glass cloths and now I find twenty-two."

"Really?"

"It's just as I tell Madame."

They looked at each other with equal indignation, fond as they both were of this comfortable house muffled with rugs and silks, of its full closets and its enamel-painted cellars. Léa slapped her knee hard with her hand:

"That's going to change, my dear! If Ernest and Émérancie don't want their notice, they'll find the six glass cloths. And that big idiot Marcel, did you write to tell him to come back?"

"He's here, madame."

Quick to dress, Léa opened the windows and leaned out to gaze complacently at her avenue with its reawakening trees. No more fawning old maids and no more Monsieur Roland, that slow-witted but athletic young man from Cambo . . .

"Oh, the fool! . . ." she sighed.

But she forgave this casual acquaintance his foolishness, and held against him only his having disappointed her. In her memory, that of a healthy woman with a forgetful body, Monsieur Roland was no more than a strong but slightly ridiculous creature, who had proved to be so inept . . . Léa would have denied, now, that a blinding flood of tears—on a certain rainy evening when the downpour ran fragrant over the pink geraniums—had hidden Monsieur Roland, for a moment, behind the image of Chéri . . .

The brief encounter had left Léa with neither regrets nor embarrassment. At her home, in the rented villa in Cambo, afterward as before, the "fool" and his old scatterbrained mother would have found nicely set-out afternoon teas, rocking chairs on the wooden balcony, the genteel comfort that Léa knew how to dispense and in which she took pride. But the fool, hurt, had gone away, leaving Léa in the care of a stiff but handsome graying officer who aspired to marry "Madame de Lonval."

"Our ages, our fortunes, our tastes for independence and high society—doesn't everything destine us for each other?" the still-slim colonel would say to Léa.

She would laugh, she would take pleasure in the company of this rather dry man who ate well and held his liquor. He had misunderstood, read in the beautiful blue eyes and sustained, confiding smile of his hostess the consent that she was slow to give . . . A specific incident marked the end of their budding friendship, which Léa regretted, frankly blaming herself in her heart of hearts.

"It's my fault! No one treats a Colonel Ypoustègue, from an old Basque family, like a Monsieur Roland. I really sent him packing . . . He would have acted decently and rationally if he'd come back the next day, in his open carriage, to smoke a cigar at my house and tickle my old maids . . ."

She hadn't understood that a mature man accepts a dismissal, but not certain glances that size him up physically, that clearly compare him to another, to the stranger, to the unseen man . . .

Léa, kissed without warning, had not suppressed that dreadful, lingering look of the woman who knows where age inflicts its withering indignities on a man: from his dry and well-manicured hands, crisscrossed with tendons and veins, her eyes climbed to his flaccid chin, to his wrinkle-lined forehead, cruelly returned to his mouth set between angle-bracket wrinkles . . . And all the distinction of the "Baronne de Lonval" burst in an "Oh dear! . . ." so offensive, so explicit and vulgar, that Colonel Ypoustègue crossed her threshold for the final time.

———

"My final romances," Léa mused, propped on her elbows at the window. But the fine Paris weather, the sight of the neat, resonant courtyard and the pruned round forms of the laurels in their green box planters, the warm, fragrant breezes caressing her nape as they escaped from her bedroom, filled her little by little with mischievousness and good spirits. The figures of women went past, going down to the Bois. "Skirts are changing yet again," Léa noted, "and hats are getting higher." She planned visits to the dressmaker's, to Maison Lewis, a sudden desire to be beautiful made her straighten up.

"Beautiful? For whom? Well, for myself. And then, to humiliate old mother Peloux."

Léa was not unaware of Chéri's having run away, but all she knew was that he had run away. While she condemned Madame Peloux's police-like methods, she allowed a young milliner's assistant on whom she lavished attention to pour out her clever gratitude by way of gossip deposited in Léa's ear during fittings, or registered with "many thanks for the exquisite chocolates" across a big sheet of the company's letterhead. A postcard from old Lili had caught up with Léa at Cambo, a postcard in which the crazed grandmother, in a shaky hand, with neither periods nor commas, related an incomprehensible story of love, escape, a young wife confined in Neuilly . . .

"The weather was just like this," Léa recalled, "the morning I read the postcard from old Lili, in my bath, at Cambo . . ."

She could still see the yellow bathroom, the sun dancing on the water and the ceiling. She could hear the echoes of the small, resonant villa casting back a great burst of laughter, rather harsh and not very spontaneous, her own, then the calls that had followed it: "Rose! . . . Rose! . . ."

Her shoulders and breasts out of the water, resembling more than ever—firm, streaming with water, her magnificent arms outstretched—a figure in a fountain, she brandished the damp card in her fingertips:

"Rose, Rose! Chéri . . . Monsieur Peloux's cleared off! He left his wife!"

"It doesn't surprise me, madame," Rose said. "The divorce will be happier than the wedding, where they were all so gloomy . . ."

That day, an awkward mirth accompanied Léa:

"Oh, my pest of a child! Oh, the nasty brat! Well, well! . . ."

And she shook her head, laughing softly, like a mother whose son had stayed out all night for the first time . . .

———

A polished phaeton flew before her gate, gleamed, and disappeared, almost silent on its rubber tires and the delicate feet of its trotters.

"Look, it's Spéléïeff," Léa observed. "Decent fellow. And there's Merguillier on his piebald horse: eleven o'clock. Berthellemy the Desiccated will come along, on his way to loosen up his bones on the Sentier de la Vertu . . . It's strange how people can do the same thing their entire lives. You would think I'd never left Paris, if Chéri were here. My poor Chéri, it's all over for him now. Marriage, women, eating at all hours, drinking too much . . . It's a pity. Who's to say he wouldn't have made a decent man, if only he'd had a pork butcher's nice little pink face and flat feet . . ."

She left the window rubbing her numb elbows, shrugged her shoulders: "Chéri can be saved once, but not twice." She polished her fingernails, puffed "Ha!" on a tarnished ring, examined her hair's botched red and graying roots close-up, jotted down a few lines in a notebook. She was acting very quickly and less coolly than usual, so as to combat a cunning attack of anxiety that she knew well and that she called—denying even the memory of her grief—her mental nausea. She would have wanted, only occasionally and in fits and starts, a victoria with good suspension, hitched to a dowager's horse, then an exceedingly fast car, then a set of Directoire sitting-room furniture. She even mused about altering her hairstyle, which she had worn upswept and short at the back for twenty years. "A little low roll, like Lavallière's? . . . That would allow me to tackle this year's loosely belted dresses. In short, with a diet and my henna redone correctly, I can aspire to ten more—no, let's say five years, of . . ."

An effort restored her common sense, her clearheaded pride.

"Wouldn't a woman like me have the courage to leave it at that? Come on now, we've gotten a proper dressing-down, my dear." She took the measure of the tall Léa standing there, smiling, her hands on her hips.

"A woman like that doesn't settle down in the arms of an old man. A woman like that, who was lucky enough never to dirty her hands or her mouth on a withered creature! . . . Yes, there she is, the 'ghoul' who wants only fresh flesh . . ."

She summoned in her memory the casual acquaintances and lovers of her youth untouched by old men, and thought herself pure, proud, devoted for the past thirty years to radiant striplings or sensitive adolescents.

"And *I* am the one who is owed by this fresh flesh! How many are there who owe me their health, their beauty, normal healthy heartaches and eggnog for their colds, and the habit of making love with attentiveness and variety? . . . And I would now go provide myself, so as not to lack anything in my bed, with an elderly gentleman of . . . of . . ."

She reflected, and decided with a majestic self-deception:

"An elderly gentleman of forty years old?"

She wiped her pretty hands against each other and made a disgusted about-face:

"Ugh! Farewell to everything, it's more fitting. Let's go buy playing cards, some fine wine, some bridge score sheets, knitting needles, all the trinkets that are required to fill a big gap, everything you need to disguise the monster—an old woman . . ."

———

Instead of knitting needles, she bought a great many dresses, and dressing gowns like clouds at dawn. The Chinese pedicurist came once a week, the manicurist twice, and the masseuse every day. People saw Léa at the theater and, before the theater, in restaurants she hadn't frequented in the days of Chéri.

She accepted the invitations of young women and their friends, and of Kühn, her former tailor, now retired from business, to their theater boxes or tables. But the young women showed her a deference she didn't require, and Kühn called her "my dear friend," to which she responded from the first feast:

"Kühn, being a customer obviously doesn't become you."

As if seeking consolation, she caught up with Patron, now the referee and manager of a boxing establishment. But Patron had married a young bar owner, slight, severe, and as jealous as a ratter. All the way to the Place d'Italie, to meet the sensitive athlete, Léa risked wearing her dark sapphire-blue dress heavy with gold, her bird-of-paradise plumes, her impressive jewelry, her hair the color of new-cut mahogany. She breathed in the odor of sweat, vinegar, and turpentine exhaled by the "hopefuls" whom Patron trained, and left, certain she would never again see the vast, low-ceilinged hall where the green gas hissed.

These attempts that she made to return to the active life of the idle cost her a fatigue she didn't understand.

"So what's wrong with me?"

She felt her ankles, slightly swollen in the evening, inspected her strong teeth, hardly loosened in her gums, sounded her inflated lungs, her joyful stomach, with her fist, the way one strikes a barrel. Something indescribable, within her, was tipping, deprived of an absent stay, and pulling her over entirely. The Baronne de La

Berche, come across at a bar where she was washing down two dozen snails with a chauffeur's white wine, finally told Léa about the prodigal son's return home, and the dawn of a new honeymoon on the boulevard d'Inkermann. Léa listened to this moral tale with indifference. But she paled with painful emotion, the next day, when she recognized a blue limousine in front of her gate and Charlotte Peloux crossing the courtyard.

"At last! At last! We meet again! Léa darling! My dear! More beautiful than ever! Thinner than last year! Careful, Léa darling, don't lose too much weight at our age! Just as you are, but no more! And even . . . But what a pleasure it is to see you again!"

Never had that offensive voice seemed so sweet to Léa. She allowed Madame Peloux to speak, grateful for this acid stream, which gave her time. She had seated Madame Peloux in a low, footed armchair, under the soft light of the morning room with its painted-silk walls, as in the past. She herself had automatically taken the straight-backed chair, which forced her to pull back her shoulders and lift her chin, as in the past. Between them, the table covered with a rough piece of antique embroidery held, as in the past, the large engraved decanter half-filled with old eau-de-vie, large resonant glasses, as thin as a mica sheet, ice water, and short-bread cookies . . .

"My dear! We're going to be able to see each other again in peace, in peace," Charlotte wailed. "You know my motto: Leave your friends alone when you're in low spirits, tell them only of your good fortune. All while Chéri was playing hooky, I deliberately stayed out of touch with you, do you hear? Now that all is well, that my children are happy, I shout it out to you, I throw myself into your arms, and we resume our pleasant life . . ."

She broke off, lit a cigarette, as skillful as an actress at this type of suspension:

". . . without Chéri, naturally."

"Naturally," Léa agreed, smiling.

She gazed at her old enemy, listened to her, with a stunned satisfaction. Those large, inhuman eyes, that prattling mouth, that short, plump, fidgety body, all of that, opposite her now, had come only to put her confidence to the test, to humiliate her as in the past, always as in the past. But as in the past, Léa would know how to answer, to disdain, to smile, to hold her head high. Already that sorrowful weight that had oppressed her yesterday and the days before seemed to disappear. An ordinary, familiar light bathed the sitting room and played across the curtains.

"Here we are," Léa thought buoyantly. "Two women a little older than we were last year, the usual malice and the same old talk, the easygoing suspicion, the shared meals; financial newspapers in the morning, scandalous gossip in the afternoon—we must start all of that all over again, since that's life, since that's my life. Some Aldonzas, some de La Berches, and some Lilis and a few elderly gentlemen with no families of their own, the whole lot squeezed together around a gaming table, where the glass of brandy and the card game will sit side by side, perhaps, with a pair of little bootees, begun for a child who will soon live . . . Let's start all over again, since it's inevitable. Let's go cheerfully, since I slip back into it as easily as into the rut of a well-worn path . . ."

And she made herself comfortable, her eyes clear and her mouth relaxed, so as to listen to Charlotte Peloux, who was speaking eagerly about her daughter-in-law.

"You of all people, Léa darling, know so well how my life's ambition was peace and tranquillity? Well, now I have them. Chéri's running away, in short, was a matter of sowing his wild oats. Far be it from me to reproach you for it, Léa darling, but you must admit that between nineteen and twenty-five, he hardly had the time to lead a bachelor's life. Well, he's led that bachelor's life for three months, I'm telling you! So what?"

"It's a good thing, in fact," Léa said, keeping a straight face. "It's a guarantee that he gives his young wife."

"Exactly, exactly the word I was looking for!" Madame Peloux squealed, radiant. "A guarantee. From that day on, he's been a dream. And you know, when a Peloux returns home after having whooped it up, he never goes out again!"

"Is it a family tradition?" Léa asked.

But Charlotte refused to listen.

"By the way, he was made to feel most welcome at home. His little wife, oh, what a wife she is, Léa! . . . You know I've seen my share of little wives, well, I've never seen one who has anything on Edmée."

"Her mother is so remarkable," Léa said.

"Remember, remember, my dear, that Chéri had just left her on my hands for three months—incidentally, she was lucky I was there!"

"That's just what I was thinking," Léa said.

"Well, my dear, not one complaint, not one scene, not one misstep, nothing, nothing! Patience itself, sweetness, the face of a saint, a saint!"

"It's alarming," Léa said.

"And do you think that when our rascal of a child showed up one morning, all smiles, as if he had just gone for a walk in the Bois, do you think she would dare to make one critical remark? Never! None of that! And so *he* was the one who, deep down, was bound to feel a little embarrassed . . ."

"Oh? Why?" Léa said.

"Honestly, come on now . . . He met with a charming reception, and harmony was restored in their bedroom, bam, right then and there. Oh, I assure you, for that next hour, there wasn't a woman anywhere in the world happier than me!"

"Except Edmée, perhaps," Léa suggested.

But Madame Peloux was feeling impassioned and gestured magnificently with her little wings:

"What are you thinking of? *I* was thinking only of the household put back together again."

She changed her tone, screwed up her eyes and mouth:

"By the way, I can't really see that girl in the throes of passion, and crying out in ecstasy. Twenty years old and collarbones hollowed out like saltcellars, bah... at that age you stammer. And besides, between us, I think her mother is frigid."

"Your devotion to family misleads you," Léa said.

Charlotte Peloux ingenuously displayed the depths of her large eyes, in which nothing could be read.

"Not at all, not at all! Heredity, heredity! I believe in it. Take, for example, my son, who is imagination itself... What, don't you know that he's imagination itself?"

"I must have forgotten," Léa excused herself.

"Well, I believe in my son's future. He'll love his home the way I love him, he'll manage his fortune, he'll love his children the way I have loved him..."

"Don't foresee such depressing things!" Léa entreated. "What sort of home do these young people have?"

"Dismal," Madame Peloux whimpered. "Dismal! Purple rugs! Purple! A black-and-gold bathroom. A room without furniture, full of Chinese vases as big as me! And so, here's what happens: they don't leave Neuilly anymore. By the way, in all modesty, the girl adores me."

"She hasn't had any nervous disorders?" Léa asked solicitously.

Charlotte Peloux's eyes sparkled:

"Her? Have no fear... we have a tough opponent."

"Who's 'we'?"

"Excuse me, my dear, habit . . . We're in the presence of what I will call brains, real brains. She has a way of giving orders without raising her voice, of accepting Chéri's whims, of swallowing affronts as if they were sweetened milk . . . I honestly wonder, I wonder whether this doesn't pose a danger, in the future, to my son. I'm afraid, Léa darling, I'm afraid she'll manage to extinguish too completely a nature so original, so . . ."

"What? He's behaving himself?" Léa interrupted. "Take some more brandy, Charlotte, it's from Spéleïeff, it's seventy-four years old, you could give it to babies . . ."

"Behaving himself isn't the word, but he's . . . inter . . . impertur . . ."

"Imperturbable?"

"You said it. And so, when he knew I was coming to see you . . ."

"How did he know?"

Blood leapt impetuously to Léa's cheeks, and she damned her fiery emotionalism and the bright daylight in the morning room. Madame Peloux, her expression sweet, was reveling in Léa's difficulty.

"But of course he knows. You needn't blush because of that, my dear! You're behaving like a child!"

"First of all, how did you know I'd come home?"

"Oh, come on, Léa, don't ask such questions. People have seen you everywhere . . ."

"Yes, but you told Chéri, then, that I'd come home?"

"No, my dear, it was he who told me."

"Ah, it was he who . . . That's strange."

She heard her heart beating in her voice and didn't risk speaking in long sentences.

"He even added: 'Madame Peloux, I should be delighted if you would go ask after Nounoune.' He has retained such an affection for you, that child!"

"That's sweet!"

Madame Peloux, cherry red, seemed to be surrendering herself to the incitements of the old eau-de-vie and was speaking as if in a dream, her head rocking up and down. But her golden-brown eyes remained steady, sharp, intently watching Léa, who, erect, hardened against herself, was awaiting she knew not what blow . . .

"It's very sweet, but it's quite natural. A man doesn't forget a woman like you, Léa darling. And . . . do you want my candid opinion? It would take just one sign from you to . . ."

Léa placed a hand on Charlotte Peloux's arm:

"I don't want your candid opinion," she said gently.

Madame Peloux let the corners of her mouth fall:

"Oh, I understand, I agree with you," she sighed glumly. "When you've arranged your life differently, as you have . . . I haven't asked about you!"

"But it seemed to me that if . . ."

"Happy?"

"Happy."

"True love? Wonderful trip? . . . Is *he* charming? Where's his photo? . . ."

Léa, reassured, sharpened her smile and shook her head:

"No, no, you won't find out anything! Go ahead and try! . . . So you no longer have any detectives, then, Charlotte?"

"I don't rely on any detectives," Charlotte replied. "It's not because this or that person has told me . . . that you had suffered a new disappointment . . . that you were in serious trouble, even money trouble . . . No! No, malicious gossip, you know what I make of it!"

"No one knows it better than I. Lolotte darling, you can leave with no worries. Dispel those of our friends. And wish them half the bagful of money I made on oil shares from December to February."

The alcoholic cloud that was softening Madame Peloux's features vanished; she displayed a face that was sharp, hard, reawakened:

"You invested in oil! I should have known. And you didn't tell me!"

"You didn't ask . . . You think only about your family, it's quite natural . . ."

"I was thinking, too, of compressed coal briquettes, fortunately," the muffled trumpet piped.

"Ah! You didn't tell me, either."

"Disturb a love idyll? Never! Léa darling, I'm going, but I'll come back."

"You'll come back on Thursdays, because for now, Lolotte darling, your Sundays in Neuilly . . . are over for me. Would you want us to have little Thursday get-togethers here? Nothing but close friends, old mother Aldonza, our Reverend Father the Baronne—your game of poker, in a word, and my knitting . . ."

"You knit?"

"Not yet, but I will. What do you say?"

"I'm jumping for joy. See if I don't jump! And you know, I won't say a word to anyone, at home: the boy would be perfectly capable of coming to ask you for a glass of port on Thursdays! One more kiss, my dear . . . God, how good you smell! Have you noticed that when we reach the point where our skin starts to slacken, perfume soaks in better? It's quite nice."

"Go on, go . . ." A trembling Léa followed Madame Peloux with her eyes as she crossed the courtyard. "Go back to your malicious scheming! Nothing will prevent you. You may twist your foot, yes, but you won't fall. Your chauffeur, who is careful, won't skid, and won't run your car into a tree. You'll reach Neuilly, and you'll choose your moment—today, tomorrow, next week—to say the words that you ought never to utter. You'll try to unsettle those who are perhaps at peace. The least you'll be guilty of is making them tremble a little, like me, momentarily . . ."

Her legs trembled like a horse's after a steep ascent, but she wasn't suffering. The care that she had taken with herself, and her retorts, thrilled her. A pleasing vibrancy lingered in her color, in her eyes, and she worried her handkerchief because she still had energy to expend. She couldn't take her mind off Charlotte Peloux.

"We've found each other again," she thought, "the way two dogs find the slipper they're accustomed to tearing apart. How strange it is! This woman is my enemy and it's from her that I draw comfort. How connected we are . . ."

She reflected for a long time, by turns fearful and accepting of her fate. The easing of her nerves granted her a brief sleep. Sitting with her cheek pressed against the chair, she entered her imminent old age in a dream, imagined her days' sameness one to the next, saw herself opposite Charlotte Peloux and for a long time protected, by a lively rivalry that made the hours fly, from the degrading indifference that led mature women to neglect first their corset, then their hair dye, finally their lingerie. She savored in advance the villainous pleasures of the aged, which are only a secret struggle, homicidal desires, keen and ceaselessly rejuvenated hopes for catastrophes that would spare only a single being, a single place in the world—and awoke, surprised, in the light of a rosy twilight indistinguishable from the dawn.

"Oh, Chéri! . . ." she sighed.

But it was no longer the hoarse, hungry cry of the previous year, nor the tears, nor that revolt of the entire body, which suffers and rebels when a spiritual sickness wants to destroy it . . . Léa got up, rubbed her cheek, which bore the imprint of the cushion's embroidery . . .

"My poor Chéri . . . It's strange to think that in our loss—for you of your spent old mistress, for me of my scandalous young lover—we have lost the most honorable thing that we possessed on earth . . ."

Two days passed after Charlotte Peloux's visit. Two gray days that went by slowly for Léa and that she endured patiently, with a novice's soul. "Since this is how I must live," she thought, "let's begin." But she approached it ineptly, and with an excessive sort of diligence well suited to discouraging her novitiate. The second day, she had wanted to go out, walked as far as the Lakes, around eleven in the morning.

"I'll buy a dog," she strategized. "It will keep me company and force me to walk." And Rose had been obliged to search the bottoms of the summer closets for a pair of yellow ankle boots with strong soles, a slightly rough suit redolent of alpine pastures and forests. Léa went out with the determined gait imposed by certain shoes and certain homespun clothes on their wearer.

"Ten years ago, I would have chanced a cane," she thought. Still close by her house, she heard a light, quick step behind her that she thought she recognized. A staggering fear, which she had no time to fend off, nearly made her go numb, and only reluctantly did she let herself be overtaken, then outdistanced, by a hurried young stranger who didn't look at her.

She took a breath, relieved.

"I'm too stupid!"

She bought a dark carnation for her jacket and set off again. But thirty paces ahead of her, standing straight in the diaphanous mist that covered the lawns along the avenue, the silhouette of a man waited.

"This time, I know that cut of jacket and his way of twirling his cane . . . Oh, no, thank you! I don't want him to see me wearing shoes like a mailman's and a thick jacket that makes me look fat. If I have to run into him, I prefer that he see me otherwise. To start with, he was never able to stand brown . . . No . . . no, I'm going home, I'm . . ."

At that moment the man who was waiting hailed an empty taxi, got into it, and passed Léa; he was a fair-haired young man with a small, close-cropped mustache. But Léa didn't smile and no longer sighed with relief, she turned on her heel and went home.

"One of those lazy days, Rose . . . Give me my peach-blossom tea gown, the new one, and the big, sleeveless embroidered cloak. I'm suffocating in all these woolens."

"There's no point dwelling on it," Léa thought. "Twice in a row, it wasn't Chéri; the third time it would have been him. I know these little pitfalls. There's nothing you can do about them, and today I'm not at my best, I'm feeling sluggish."

She returned, for the remainder of day, to her patient attempts at solitude. Cigarettes and newspapers entertained her after lunch, and she welcomed with a short-lived joy a telephone call from the Baronne de La Berche, then another from Spéleïeff, her old lover, the handsome horse trader, who had seen her go by the day before and was offering to sell her a pair of horses.

A long hour of total silence followed, frightening her.

"Come on now . . ."

She was walking, her hands on her hips, followed by the magnificent train of an ample cloak, embroidered with gold thread and roses, that left her arms bare.

"Come on now . . . let's try to assess the situation. I'm not going to allow myself to become demoralized when this kid no longer matters to me. I've lived alone for six months. In the Midi, I managed quite well. First, I moved. And these acquaintances from the Riviera and the Pyrenees did me good, bidding them farewell left me feeling so fresh . . . Starch poultices on a burn: they don't heal anything, but they soothe, provided you keep changing them. My six months of travel are basically the story of the hideous Sarah Cohen, who married a monster: 'Each time I look at him,' she said, 'I think I'm pretty.'

"But before these six months, I knew what it was to live on my own. How did I live, after I left Spéléïeff, for example? Oh yes, we resolutely trailed around bars and bistros, Patron and I, and right away I had Chéri. But before Spéléïeff, little Lequellec had been snatched away from me by his family, who married him off . . . poor thing, his beautiful eyes full of tears . . . After him, I remained alone for four months, I recall. The first month, I cried a lot! Oh, no, it was for Bacciocchi that I cried so much. But when I had finished crying, you couldn't contain me, I was so happy to be alone! Yes, but at the time of Bacciocchi I was twenty-eight, and thirty after Lequellec, and between them, I knew . . . what does it matter. After Spéléïeff, I was disgusted by so much misspent money. Whereas after Chéri, I'm . . . I'm fifty years old, and I was foolish enough to hold on to him for six years."

She wrinkled her forehead, making herself ugly with her sullen pout.

"It serves me right, you don't hold on to a lover for six years at my age. Six years! He ruined what was left of me. From those six years, I could have drawn two or three very agreeable little happinesses, instead of one big regret . . . A six-year liaison is like following a husband to the colonies: when you come back, no one recognizes you and you no longer know how to dress."

To spare her strength, she rang for Rose and they tidied up the little closet where her lace was kept. Night fell, which saw the lamps kindled and called Rose back to the care of the house.

"Tomorrow," Léa thought, "I'll ask for the car and I'll drive out to visit Spéléïeff's Normandy stud farm. I'll take old mother La Berche if she wishes, it'll remind her of her old rigs. And, why, if the younger Spéléïeff makes eyes at me, I'm not saying that . . ."

She went to the trouble of putting on a mysterious, alluring smile, so as to fool the spirits that might be wandering around the dressing table and the formidable bed that shone in the shadows. But she felt completely cold, and full of scorn for others' fleshly pleasures.

Her dinner of delicate fish and pastries was a leisurely affair. She replaced the Bordeaux with a dry champagne and hummed as she left the table. Eleven o'clock caught her unawares as she measured, with a stick, the width of the panels between the windows in her bedroom, where she planned to replace all the tall mirrors with antique canvases painted with flowers and balusters. She yawned, scratched her head, and rang for her nightclothes. While Rose took off her long silk stockings, Léa thought about the day she'd conquered, shed into the past, which satisfied her like a completed chore. Sheltered, for the night, from the peril of idleness, she anticipated the hours of sleep and of insomnia, because the worrier regains, with the night, the right to yawn aloud, to sigh, to curse the milkman's cart, the trash collectors, and the sparrows.

As she got ready for bed, she debated harmless plans that she wouldn't carry out.

"Aline Mesmacker bought a bar-restaurant and it's a gold mine . . . Obviously, it's a job, as well as an investment . . . But I can't picture myself at the cash register, and if you engage a manager, there's no point. Dora and fat Fifi together run a nightclub, old mother La Berche told me. It's quite the fashion. And they wear detachable collars and smoking jackets to attract a particular clientele. Fat Fifi has three children to raise, that's an excuse . . . There's also Kühn, who's getting bored and would certainly take my capital to start up a new fashion house . . ."

Stark naked and tinted brick red by the reflections in her Pompeian-style bathroom, she sprayed herself with sandalwood perfume and unfolded a long silk nightgown with an unconscious pleasure.

"All of that is just talk. I know perfectly well that I don't like working. To bed, madame! You will never have another workplace, and your customers are gone."

She wrapped herself in a white gandoura whose colored lining suffused it with an elusive pink light, and turned back to her dressing table. Her two raised arms combed and held up her dye-stiffened hair and framed her tired face. Her arms had remained so lovely, from their shapely, muscular armpits down to their round wrists, that she admired them for a moment.

"Lovely handles, for such an old vase!"

With a negligent hand she placed a honey-colored comb at her nape and without any great hopes chose a detective novel from a shelf in a dark cabinet. She disliked bookbindings and had never got out of the habit of relegating her books to the bottoms of closets, alongside empty boxes and medicine tins.

As she bent over and smoothed out the fine, cold batiste of her big, turned-down bed, the heavy bell in the courtyard resounded. That deep, full, unaccustomed sound affronted the midnight hour.

"What on earth . . . ," she said aloud.

She listened, her mouth half-open, holding her breath. A second burst seemed louder than the first, and Léa ran, in an instinctual gesture of self-preservation and modesty, to powder her face. She was about to ring for Rose when she heard the front door slam, the sound of steps in the vestibule and on the stairs, two mingled voices, that of her maid and another voice. She had no time to make up her mind, the door opened under a brutal hand: Chéri stood before her, topcoat open over his dinner jacket, his hat on his head, pale and unpleasant looking.

He leaned against the closed door and didn't move. He looked not so much at Léa in particular as at the entire room, his gaze wandering, like a man about to be attacked.

Léa, who had trembled just that morning at a silhouette glimpsed in the fog, didn't yet feel any distress other than the displeasure of a woman surprised at her toilette. She folded her dressing gown around her, fastened her comb, searched with her foot for a fallen slipper.

She blushed, but when the blood left her cheeks, she had already regained a semblance of calm. She raised her head and appeared taller than this young man leaning, all black, against the white door.

"That's a strange way to come in," she said rather loudly. "You could take off your hat and say hello."

"Hello," Chéri said in a haughty voice.

The sound of his voice seemed to surprise him, he looked around more benevolently, a sort of smile descended from his eyes to his mouth, and he repeated softly:

"Hello . . ."

He removed his hat and took two or three steps.

"May I sit down?"

"If you wish," Léa said.

He sat down on a pouf and saw that she remained standing.

"Were you getting dressed? Aren't you going out?"

She signaled that she wasn't, sat down far away from him, picked up a nail polisher, and didn't speak. He lit a cigarette and asked permission to smoke after it was lit.

"If you wish," Léa repeated indifferently.

He fell silent and lowered his eyes. The hand that held the cigarette trembled slightly, he noticed it and rested that hand on the edge of a table. Léa polished her nails with slow movements and from time to time cast a fleeting glance at Chéri's face, particularly at his lowered eyelids and the dark fringe of his lashes.

"It was still Ernest who opened the door for me," Chéri said finally.

"Why wouldn't it be Ernest? Should I have changed my staff because you got married?"

"No . . . You see, I said that . . ."

Silence fell again. Léa broke it.

"Might I know whether you intend to remain on that pouf for

long? I'm not even asking you why you presume to walk into my house at midnight . . ."

"You may ask me," he said sharply.

She shook her head:

"It doesn't interest me."

He got up forcefully, causing the pouf to roll behind him, and advanced on Léa. She was aware of him leaning over her as if he were going to hit her, but she didn't flinch. She thought: "What would I really be afraid of, in this world?"

"Oh, you don't know what I came here for? You don't want to know what I came here for?"

He tore off his coat, flung it onto the chaise longue, and crossed his arms, shouting very near to Léa's face, in a gasping and triumphant tone:

"I've come back!"

She was using a delicate little pair of nail clippers, which she closed calmly before wiping her fingers. Chéri fell back onto his seat, as if he had just spent all his strength.

"Fine," Léa said. "You've come back. That's very nice. Who did you consult about that?"

"Myself," Chéri said.

She got up in her turn to better dominate him. The beating of her quieted heart allowed her to breathe easily, and she wanted to act her part flawlessly.

"Why didn't you ask me my opinion? I'm an old friend who knows your little boorish ways. How is it that in coming here you didn't think you might disturb . . . someone?"

His head lowered, he swept his eyes across the room, inspecting its closed doors, the metal-armored bed, and its bank of luxurious pillows. He saw nothing unaccustomed, nothing new, and shrugged his shoulders. Léa expected better and pushed the matter:

"Do you understand what I mean?"

"Very well," he answered. "Has 'Monsieur' not come home? Is 'Monsieur' staying out all night?"

"That's none of your business, kid," she said quietly.

He bit his lip and nervously shook his cigarette ash into a jewelry dish.

"Not in there, I keep telling you!" Léa cried. "How many times must I . . ."

She broke off midsentence, reproaching herself for having unwittingly reverted to the tone of familiar quarrels. But he seemed not to have heard her, and examined a ring, an emerald that Léa had purchased on her trip.

"What . . . what's this?" he stammered.

"That? That's an emerald."

"I'm not blind! I mean, who gave it to you?"

"Not anyone you know."

"Charming!" Chéri said bitterly.

His tone gave Léa back her full authority, and she allowed herself the pleasure of deceiving him a little longer, since he had ceded to her the advantage.

"Isn't it charming? People compliment me on it everywhere. And the setting, did you notice, the dusting of brilliants that . . ."

"Enough," Chéri bellowed furiously, crashing his fist down on the delicate table.

Roses shed their petals at the impact, a porcelain dish slipped without breaking onto the thick rug. Léa extended toward the telephone a hand that Chéri stopped roughly with his arm:

"What do you want that telephone for?"

"To telephone the police station," Léa said.

He took hold of both her arms, feigned playfulness as he pushed her far away from the phone.

"Come on now, everything's fine, no joking around! I can't say anything without your straight off making a drama out of it . . ."

She sat down and turned her back to him. He remained standing, his hands empty, and his puffy, half-open mouth resembled a sulky child's. A black lock covered his eyebrow. In a mirror, surreptitiously, Léa was watching him; but he sat down and his face disappeared from the mirror. In her turn, Léa sensed, self-consciously, that he was looking at her back, broadened by the loose-fitting gandoura. She returned to her dressing table, smoothed her hair, repositioned her comb, opened a perfume bottle as if absentmindedly. Chéri turned his head toward the scent.

"Nounoune," he called.

She didn't answer.

"Nounoune!"

"Say you're sorry," she commanded without turning around.

He snickered:

"You must be joking!"

"I'm not forcing you. But you're going to leave. And immediately . . ."

"I'm sorry!" he said quickly, aggressively.

"Better than that!"

"I'm sorry," he repeated very softly.

"Marvelous!"

She went back to him, passed a light hand over his bowed head:

"Come on, tell me."

He shuddered and shook off the caress.

"What do you want me to tell you? It's not complicated. I've come back, that's it."

"Tell me, come on, tell me."

He rocked on his seat, clasping his hands between his knees, and lifted his head toward Léa without looking at her. She could see

Chéri's pale nostrils flaring, she could hear his rapid breath attempting to control itself. She had only to say once more: "Come on, tell me . . ." and to push him with a finger as if to make him fall. He called out: "Nounoune darling! Nounoune darling!" and threw himself against her with all his strength, embracing her long legs, which gave way. Sitting now, she let him slip to the floor and surround her with tears, disjointed words, groping hands that clung to her lace, to her necklace, searching beneath her dress for the shape of her shoulder and for the contours of her ear beneath her hair.

"Nounoune darling! I've found you again! My Nounoune! Oh, my Nounoune, your shoulder, and then your same perfume, and your necklace, my Nounoune, oh, it's amazing! . . . And the little burnt taste in your hair, oh, it's . . . it's amazing . . ."

Staggered, he exhaled this stupid word as if it were his last breath. On his knees, he clasped Léa in his arms and offered her his forehead, shadowed with hair, his trembling mouth, wet from weeping, and his eyes, which streamed with joy in luminous tears. She gazed at him so intensely, with such perfect obliviousness to everything that was not him, that she didn't think of kissing him. She put her arms around Chéri's neck and squeezed him gently, to the rhythm of the words she murmured:

"My dear . . . my wicked child . . . Here you are . . . You've come back to me . . . What have you done now? You're so wicked . . . my beauty . . ."

He was moaning softly through closed lips, and hardly spoke: he was listening to Léa and pressed his cheek against her breast. He beseeched, "More," when she suspended her tender litany, and Léa, who was afraid that she, too, would cry, scolded him in the same tone:

"Nasty creature . . . Heartless little devil . . . Big rotten beast!"

He looked up at her with gratitude:

"That's it, bawl me out! Oh, Nounoune . . ."

She pushed him away to see him more clearly:

"Do you love me, then?"

He lowered his eyes with a childlike agitation:

"Yes, Nounoune."

A little burst of strangled laughter, which she was unable to restrain, forewarned Léa that she was very close to surrendering herself to the most terrifying joy of her life. An embrace, the collapse, the open bed, two bodies that fuse like the two living sections of a single severed beast . . . "No, no," she thought, "not yet, oh, not yet! . . ."

"I'm thirsty," Chéri sighed. "Nounoune, I'm thirsty . . ."

She stood up quickly, groped with her hand for the now-lukewarm decanter, and went out, only to return almost instantly. Chéri, curled up on the floor, had rested his head on the pouf.

"They're bringing you lemonade," Léa said. "Don't stay there. Come onto the chaise longue. Does this lamp bother you?"

She quivered with the pleasure of serving and commanding. She sat down at the end of the chaise longue, and Chéri stretched out on it, half leaning against her.

"You're going to tell me a little, now . . ."

Rose's entrance interrupted him. Chéri, without getting up, languidly turned his head toward Rose.

". . . 'lo, Rose."

"Hello, monsieur," Rose said discreetly.

"Rose, for tomorrow morning at nine I'd like . . ."

"Brioche and hot chocolate," Rose finished.

Chéri closed his eyes again with a sigh of contentment:

"Clairvoyant! . . . Rose, where will I get dressed tomorrow morning?"

"In the boudoir," Rose answered obligingly. "Only you probably want the sofa removed and the toiletries put back as before? . . ."

She looked questioningly at Léa, proudly arrayed, who supported, as he drank, the chest of her "wicked infant."

"If you wish," Léa said. "We'll see. Go on up, Rose."

Rose left, and during the moment of silence that followed, they could hear only the confused murmur of the breeze and the call of a bird deceived by the moonlight.

"Chéri, are you asleep?"

He heaved his great hound-dog sigh.

"Oh, no, Nounoune! I'm too comfortable to sleep."

"Tell me, kid . . . You haven't caused hurt, over there?"

"At home? No, Nounoune. Not at all, I swear to you."

"A scene?"

He looked at her from below, without lifting his trusting head.

"Of course not, Nounoune. I left because I left. The girl is very sweet, nothing happened."

"Ah!"

"I wouldn't stake my life on her not having, say, imagined something. This evening she was making what I call her orphan's face, you know, such sad eyes beneath her beautiful hair . . . Do you know what beautiful hair she has?"

"Yes . . ."

She uttered only monosyllables, in a hushed voice, as if she were hearing a sleeper speak in a dream.

"I even think," Chéri continued, "that she must have seen me cross the garden."

"Oh?"

"Yes. She was on the balcony, in her brilliant-white dress, such an icy white. Oh, I don't like that dress! . . . That dress had made me want to clear off ever since dinner . . ."

"Really?"

"Yes, of course, Nounoune. I don't know if she saw me. The moon hadn't risen. She got up while I was waiting."

"Where were you waiting?"

Chéri vaguely extended his hand toward the avenue.

"There. I was waiting, you understand. I wanted to see. I waited for a long time."

"But for what?"

He left her abruptly, sat down farther away. He reverted to his expression of barbaric suspicion:

"Look, I wanted to be sure there was no one here."

"Ah yes . . . You were thinking of . . ."

She couldn't suppress a scornful laugh. A lover at her house? A lover, while Chéri lived? It was ludicrous: "What a fool he is!" she thought vehemently.

"You're laughing?"

He stood in front of her and pushed her head back with one hand against her forehead.

"You're laughing? You're mocking me? You have . . . *Do* you have a lover? Do you have someone?"

He bent over her as he spoke, and pressed her nape against the back of the chaise longue. She felt the breath of an abusive mouth on her eyelids, and made no effort to free herself from the hand that was crushing her forehead and hair.

"Dare to say you have a lover!"

She blinked, blinded by the approach of the refulgent face that was descending over her, and finally said in a muted voice:

"No. I don't have a lover. I love you . . ."

He let her go and began to take off his dinner jacket, his vest; his tie whistled through the air and wrapped itself around the neck of a bust of Léa on the chimney. But he didn't pull away from her and held her firmly, knee against knee, seated on the chaise longue. When she saw him half-naked, she asked him, almost sadly:

"Do you want to, then? . . . Really? . . ."

He didn't answer, consumed with the thought of his imminent pleasure and the desire he had to take her again. She submitted and served her young lover like a good mistress, solemn and solicitous. While she saw with a sort of terror the moment of her own defeat approaching, she endured Chéri like a torment, pushed him away with her powerless hands and held him between her strong knees. At last she grasped him by the arm, cried out feebly, and sank into that abyss from which love rises pale, silent, and full of wistful longing for the annihilation.

They didn't disentangle themselves, and no words disturbed the long silence during which they came back to life. Chéri's chest had slipped onto Léa's side, and his hanging head rested, eyes closed, on the sheet, as if someone had stabbed him on top of his mistress. She, slightly turned the other way, bore almost the full weight of this body, which treated her ungently. She was very quietly gasping for breath, her crushed left arm hurt her, and Chéri could feel his nape going numb, but they waited, each of them, in a respectful stillness from which the decrescent thunderstroke of pleasure had distanced them.

"He's asleep," Léa thought. Her free hand still held Chéri's wrist, which she squeezed gently. A knee, whose uncommon shape she knew, was hurting her knee. Level with her own heart, she felt the even, muffled beating of a heart. Lingering, potent, a mix of rich flowers and exotic woods, Chéri's preferred fragrance drifted. "He's here," Léa thought. And a blind sense of security suffused her. "He's here for good," her thoughts cried out. Her savvy circumspection, the affable common sense that had guided her life, the humiliated doubts of her mature years, and then her renunciations, all receded and disappeared before the presumptuous brutality of love. "He's here! Leaving his home, his silly, pretty little wife, he has come back, he has come back to me! Who could take him away from me? Now, now I'm going to organize our life . . . He doesn't yet know what he wants, but *I* know. We'll almost certainly have to go away. We won't hide, but we'll seek tranquillity . . . And then I'll need time to look at him. I didn't really have to look at him when I didn't know I loved him. I need a place where we'll have enough room for his whims and my wishes . . . *I* will think for both of us—his job is to sleep . . ."

As she carefully extricated her left arm, tingling and painful, and her shoulder, gone numb from immobility, she looked at Chéri's averted face, and she saw that he wasn't asleep. The white of his eye was gleaming, and the little black wing of his lashes fluttered irregularly.

"What, you're not asleep?"

She felt him shudder against her, and he turned over completely in a single motion.

"But you weren't asleep, either, Nounoune?"

He stretched out his hand toward the bedside table and reached the lamp; a layer of pink light covered the double bed, accentuating the depressions in the lace, hollowing out valleys of shadow between the sections of plump padding in a quilt plush with down. Chéri, outstretched, took in the field of his repose and of his voluptuous contests. Léa, propped close to him on her elbow, stroked the long eyebrows that she loved, and tossed back Chéri's hair. Lying that way, his hair spread around his face, he seemed to have been knocked down by a fierce wind.

The enamel clock chimed. Chéri got up abruptly and sat.

"What time is it?"

"I don't know. What does it matter to us?"

"Oh, I was just saying that . . ."

He laughed briefly but didn't go back to bed right away. The first milkman's cart shook loose a peal of glass bells outside, and he moved almost imperceptibly toward the avenue. Between the strawberry-colored curtains, a cold blade of the dawning day crept in. Chéri brought his eyes back to Léa, and studied her with that force and fixity that unsettles us under the gaze of the questioning child and the wary dog. An unreadable thought arose in the depths of his eyes, which, with their shape, their very dark gillyflower hue, their harsh or languorous sparkle, had been of use to him only to conquer, not to disclose. His naked torso, broad at the shoulders, slim at the waist, rose out of the crumpled bedsheets like a swell, and his whole being radiated the sadness of perfect works.

"Oh, you . . . ," Léa sighed rapturously.

He didn't smile, accustomed to receiving tributes without ceremony.

"Tell me, Nounoune . . ."

"What, my beauty?"

He hesitated, fluttered his eyelids, shivering:

"I'm tired . . . And then tomorrow, how will you be able . . ."

With a gentle push, Léa drove the naked torso and the heavy head back down onto the pillows.

"Don't give it a thought. Go to bed. Isn't Nounoune here? Don't think about anything. Sleep. You're cold, I bet . . . Here, take this, it's warm . . ."

She wrapped him in the silk and wool of some small feminine garment that lay bunched on the bed, and put out the light. In the darkness, she offered her shoulder, hollowed out her contented side, listened to the breathing that matched her own. No desire disturbed her, but she didn't want to sleep. "His job is to sleep, my job is to think," she repeated. "I'll organize a very smart and discreet departure for us; my guiding principle will be to cause the least talk and distress . . . For the spring, the Midi will still suit us best. If it were up to me alone, I would prefer to stay here, very quietly. But then there's old mother Peloux, and the younger Madame Peloux . . ." The image of a young wife in her nightclothes, anxiously standing near a window, detained Léa only long enough for her to shrug her shoulders with a cold equitability: "That, I can do nothing about. What makes for the happiness of some . . ."

The silky black head stirred against her breast, and her sleeping lover moaned in a dream. With a firm arm Léa protected him from his nightmare, and cradled him so that for a long time he would remain—without sight, without memories, and without intentions—the very picture of the "wicked infant" that she had never been able to conceive.

He had been awake for quite some time but was careful not to stir. His cheek on his bent arm, he tried to determine the time. A clear sky must have been radiating a premature heat onto the avenue, for no shadow of a cloud passed the fiery pink of the curtains. "Maybe ten o'clock? . . ." Hunger tormented him, he had eaten little the day before. A year ago, he would have jumped up, upset Léa's sleep, uttered ferocious cries demanding his creamy hot chocolate and chilled butter . . . He didn't stir. He was afraid that, if he moved, he would shatter a vestige of joy, a visual pleasure that he was savoring in the pink glow of the curtains, in the steel and copper volutes of the bed gleaming in the tinted atmosphere of the room. His great happiness of the previous night seemed to him to have taken refuge, blurred and very faint, in a reflection, in the rainbow that danced on the side of a crystal vessel filled with water.

Rose's cautious step skimmed the carpet on the stairs. A careful broom cleaned the courtyard. Chéri heard a distant clinking of china in the pantry . . . "How long this morning is," he thought. "I'm going to get up." But he remained absolutely still, because behind him Léa yawned, stretched her legs. A gentle hand came to rest on Chéri's back, but he closed his eyes again, and his whole body began to enact a lie, without his knowing why, as he feigned the limpness of sleep. He felt Léa leaving the bed, and saw her black silhouette pass in front of the curtains, which she opened partway. She turned toward him, observed him, and shook her head, with a smile that was not triumphant but resolute and that accepted all risks. She wasn't in a hurry to leave the bedroom, and Chéri, allowing a thread of light to part his lashes, watched her closely. He saw her opening a railroad timetable and following columns of figures with her finger. Then she seemed to calculate, raising her face toward the ceiling and knitting her brow. Not yet powdered, a thin twist of hair against her nape, her chin double and her neck ravaged, she recklessly offered herself up to his unseen gaze.

She moved away from the window, took her checkbook from a drawer, made out and detached several leaves. Then she placed a pair of white pajamas at the foot of the bed and silently left.

Alone, Chéri, breathing deeply, realized that he had been holding his breath since Léa had risen. He got up, put on the pajamas, and opened a window. "It's stifling," he whispered. He retained the vague, uneasy impression of having committed an ugly act.

"Because I pretended to be asleep? But I've seen Léa just out of bed a hundred times. Only I pretended to be asleep this time . . ."

The brilliant daylight restored to the room its rosy pink, the soft hues of the pale yellow and silver Chaplin shone cheerfully from the wall. Chéri bowed his head and closed his eyes so that his memory might give him back the bedroom of the night before, mysterious and tinted like the flesh of a watermelon, the magical canopy of the lamp, and above all the elation with which, staggering, he had borne intense pleasures . . .

"You're up! Hot chocolate's coming."

He noted with gratitude that in a few minutes Léa's hair had been arranged, her face delicately made up, and her skin suffused with her familiar perfume. The sound of her warm, pleasant voice spread through the room, together with an aroma of toast and cocoa. Chéri sat down near the two steaming cups, took the generously buttered bread from Léa's hands. He was searching for something to say, but Léa suspected nothing, because she had known him to be characteristically silent, and contemplative in front of food. She ate with a good appetite, with the preoccupied haste and gaiety of a woman who breakfasts, her trunks packed, before catching a train.

"Your second slice of toast, Chéri . . ."

"No, thank you, Nounoune."

"Full?"

"Full."

She shook her finger at him, laughing:

"*You're* going to get landed with two rhubarb lozenges, you've got it coming to you!"

He wrinkled his nose, offended:

"Listen, Nounoune, you have an insatiable need to concern yourself with . . ."

"Ta ta ta! That's my business. Stick out your tongue! You don't want to stick out your tongue? Then wipe off your chocolate mustache and let's get straight to the point. Unpleasant subjects must be dealt with quickly."

She took one of Chéri's hands across the table and enclosed it in both of her own.

"You've come back. That was our destiny. Do you trust me? I will take care of you."

She broke off in spite of herself and closed her eyes, as if bowed by her victory; Chéri saw his mistress's fiery blood light up her face.

"Oh," she continued more softly, "when I think of everything I didn't give you, of everything I didn't say to you . . . When I think that I believed you were a mere passing fancy like the others, a bit more precious than the others . . . How stupid I was, not to have understood that you were my love, *the* love, the love we find only once . . ."

She opened her eyes, which appeared bluer, their blue intensified by the shadow of her eyelids, and she breathed unsteadily.

"Oh," Chéri silently beseeched, "don't let her ask me a question, don't let her want an answer now, I'm incapable of uttering a single word . . ."

She gave his hand a shake.

"Come on now, let's be serious. So, I was saying: we leave, we have left. What will you do, *over there?* Have Charlotte sort out the question of money, it's wisest, and generously, please. You will inform them *over there* how? By letter, I imagine. Not easy, but you'll manage if you keep it brief. We'll see to that together. There's also the matter of your luggage—I have nothing left of yours here . . . Those little things are more irritating than a big decision, but don't think too much about them . . . Would you be so kind as to quit constantly tearing off the little hangnails on your toe? It's those bad habits that lead to ingrown toenails!"

He let his foot drop mechanically. His own silence was crushing him, and he was forced to bring an exhausting attention to bear so as to listen to Léa. He scrutinized the animated, joyful, imperious face of his friend, and vaguely wondered: "Why does she look so happy?"

His daze became so manifest that Léa, who was now going on about the advisability of buying old Berthellemy's yacht, stopped short:

"Do you think he would give me an opinion, even? Oh, you really are twelve years old still!"

Chéri, released from his stupor, ran a hand across his forehead and gazed melancholically at Léa:

"With you, Nounoune, I would very likely remain twelve years old for half a century."

She blinked her eyes several times as if he had blown on her eyelids, and let silence fall between them.

"What do you mean?" she asked at last.

"Just what I said, Nounoune. Just the truth. Can you deny it, honest soul that you are?"

She decided to laugh, with a casualness that already masked a great fear.

"But your childishness is half your charm, you silly little fool! Later on it will be the secret of your never-ending youth. And you complain about it! . . . And you have the nerve to come complain about it to me!"

"Yes, Nounoune. Who would you expect me to complain about it to?"

He again took her hand, which she had withdrawn.

"My darling Nounoune, Nounoune my love, I'm not just complaining, I'm blaming you."

She felt her hand being gripped by a firm hand. And his large, dark eyes with their glossy lashes, instead of avoiding hers, fixed on them miserably. She wouldn't yet consent to tremble.

"It's nothing really, nothing at all . . . It takes just two or three curt words to which he will reply with some coarse insult, and then he'll sulk and I'll forgive him . . . That's all this is . . ." But she couldn't find the crucial rebuke she was after, which would have changed the expression in those eyes.

"Come on now, kid . . . You know there are certain jokes that I won't tolerate for long."

At the same time she judged the tone of her voice to be weak and insincere: "How badly I said that . . . It's like bad theater . . ." The ten-thirty sun reached the table that separated them, and Léa's polished nails shone. But the ray also illuminated her large, shapely hands, whose soft, slack skin was incised, on the back, around the wrist, with intricate traceries, with concentric furrows, with tiny parallelograms like those carved by drought, after the rains, in clay soil. Léa rubbed her hands together distractedly, turning her head to draw Chéri's attention toward the street; but he persisted in his miserable, canine contemplation. Abruptly he took hold of the two shameful hands, which were pretending to play with a fold of her sash, kissed them again and again, and then laid his cheek on them, murmuring:

"My Nounoune . . . oh my poor Nounoune . . ."

"Leave me alone!" she cried with inexplicable anger, wrenching away her hands.

She took a moment to master herself, and was terrified by her weakness, for she had nearly burst into tears. As soon as she was able, she spoke and smiled:

"So, you complain about me, now? Why did you blame me a moment ago?"

"I was wrong," he said humbly. "For me, you have been . . ."

He gestured in a way that expressed his powerlessness to find words that were worthy of her.

" '*You have been*'!" she noted emphatically, her tone mordant. "That's the style of funeral oration, my boy!"

"You see . . . ," he reproached.

He shook his head, and she could see very well that she wouldn't anger him. She tensed all her muscles, and bridled her thoughts with the help of the same two or three words, repeated deep down: "He's here, in front of me . . . Come on now, he's still here . . . He's not out of reach . . . But is he still here, in front of me, truly? . . ."

Her thoughts escaped from this rhythmic discipline, and a great inner lamentation replaced the magical words: "Oh, if I could have it back, if I could only have back the moment when I said to him: 'Your second slice of toast, Chéri?' That moment is still so near to us, it isn't lost forever, it isn't yet in the past! Let us start our life over at that moment, the bit that took place since won't count, I'll blot it out, I'll blot it out . . . I'm going to speak to him just as if it were a few minutes earlier, I'm going to speak to him, let's see, about our departure, about the luggage . . ."

She indeed spoke, and said:

"I see . . . I see that I can't treat like a man a creature who, because of his spinelessness, is capable of throwing the homes of two women into disarray. Do you think I don't understand? When it comes to trips, you like them short, eh? Yesterday in Neuilly, today here, but tomorrow . . . Where, then, tomorrow? Here? No, no, my dear, don't bother lying, that guilty man's face wouldn't deceive even a bigger fool than me, if there's such a woman over there . . ."

Her violent gesture, which pointed in the direction of Neuilly, knocked over a shallow cake plate, which Chéri righted. As she spoke, she heightened her pain, transformed it into a stinging grief, aggressive and jealous, the voluble grief of a young woman. The rouge on her cheeks was becoming purplish, a lock of hair, twisted with the curling iron, descended her nape like a thin little snake.

"Even the woman over there, even your wife you won't always find at home when it suits you to go back! My dear, no one really knows how a woman's hand is won, but still less how it's lost! . . . You'd have Charlotte keep an eye on your wife, eh? That's quite an idea! Oh, I'll have a good laugh, the day that . . ."

Chéri stood up, pale and serious:

"Nounoune! . . ."

"Nounoune, what? Nounoune, what? Do you think you're going to frighten me? Oh, you want to stand on your own two feet? Then do it! You're sure to have a hard time, with the likes of Marie-Laure's daughter! She has weak arms, and a flat behind, but that will hardly prevent her from . . ."

"I forbid you, Nounoune! . . ."

He seized hold of her arms, but she stood up, vigorously broke away, and burst into a hoarse laugh:

"But of course! 'I forbid you to say a word against my wife!' Is that it?"

He circled the table and drew very close to her, trembling with indignation:

"No! I forbid you, do you understand, I forbid you to ruin my Nounoune!"

She retreated toward the far end of the room, stammering:

"What do you mean . . . What do you mean . . ."

He followed her, as if he were about to punish her:

"Yes! Is this the way Nounoune ought to speak? What are these manners? Nasty, mean-spirited insults worthy of Ma'am Peloux, now? And they're coming from you, you, Nounoune! . . ."

He threw his head back arrogantly:

"*I* know how Nounoune ought to speak! I know how she ought to think! I've had time to learn. I haven't forgotten the day you said to me, just before I married this girl: 'At least, don't be cruel . . . Try not to cause pain . . . It feels almost as if we're abandoning a doe to a greyhound . . .' What words! *That's* you. And on the day before my marriage, when I escaped to come see you, I recall, you told me . . ."

His voice failed, all his features brightened with the ardor of a memory:

"Darling, don't worry . . ."

He placed his hands on Léa's shoulders:

"And only last night," he continued, "wasn't one of your first concerns to ask me whether I hadn't caused too much hurt *over there*? My Nounoune, I knew you as a kind woman, I loved you as a kind woman, when we first started out. If we must end it, must you go and be like other women? ..."

She vaguely sensed a ruse beneath the tribute, and sat down, hiding her face in her hands:

"How cruel you are, how cruel you are ...," she stammered ... "Why did you come back ... I was so calm, on my own, so used to ..."

She heard herself lying, and broke off.

"*I* wasn't!" Chéri retorted. "I came back because ... because ..."

He spread his arms, let them drop, opened them again:

"Because I couldn't live without you anymore, it's pointless to look for anything else."

They remained silent for a moment.

She was gazing, sunken, at this impatient young man, white as a seagull, whose light feet and open arms appeared ready for flight ...

Chéri's dark eyes wandered above her.

"Oh, you can boast," he said suddenly, "you can boast of having, particularly in the past three months, made me lead a life ... a life ..."

"Me?"

"Who then, if not you? A door would open, it was Nounoune; the telephone, it was Nounoune; a letter in the box in the garden: perhaps Nounoune ... Even in the wine I drank, I looked for you, and I never found anything to equal your Pommery ... And the nights ... God! ..."

He was walking very quickly and without a sound, back and forth, across the carpet.

"I can say that I know what it is to suffer for a woman, indeed! I'm waiting for them, now, those who will come after you ... nothing but dust! Oh, how you have poisoned me! ..."

She was slowly straightening up, following Chéri's to-and-fro with a swaying of her chest. Her cheeks were dry and glistening, their feverish red making the blue of her eyes almost unbearable. He walked, his head bent, and didn't stop talking.

"Imagine, Neuilly without you, when I first came back! What's more, everything without you . . . I would have gone mad. One evening, the girl was sick, I don't remember with what, pains, headaches . . . I felt sorry for her, but I left the bedroom because nothing in the world would have prevented me from saying to her: 'Wait, don't cry, I'm going to go look for Nounoune, she'll cure you . . .' What's more, you would have come, wouldn't you, Nounoune? God, this life . . . At the Morris Hotel, I had engaged Desmond, for good money, and I told him stories, sometimes, at night . . . I said to him, as if he didn't know you: 'My friend, skin like hers doesn't exist . . . And you see that cabochon sapphire of yours, well, my friend, hide it away, because the blue of her eyes, hers alone, doesn't turn gray in the light!' And I told him how you could be vicious when you wanted, and that no one had the last word with you, not even me . . . I said to him: 'That woman, my friend, when she wears the right hat'—your navy-blue one with the wings, Nounoune, from the other summer—'and the way of dressing that she has, you can put any woman beside her, they all go to hell!' And then your amazing way of speaking, of walking, your smile, your kind demeanor, I said to him, to Desmond: 'Oh, a woman like Léa is truly something!' . . ."

He snapped his fingers, with a pride of ownership, and stopped, breathless from talking and walking.

"I never said all that to Desmond," he thought. "And yet I haven't told a lie. Desmond understood all the same." He wanted to continue and looked at Léa. She was still listening to him. Sitting very straight now, in the broad light she showed him her noble, defeated face, shining with dried, stinging tears. An invisible weight tugged at her chin and cheeks, saddened the trembling corners of her mouth.

In this ruin of beauty, Chéri recognized, intact, her lovely, imperious nose, her eyes the color of blue flowers . . .

"So you see, Nounoune, after months of that life, I come here, and . . ."

He stopped, frightened of what he had almost said.

"You come here, and you discover an old woman," Léa said in a faint, calm voice.

"Nounoune! Listen, Nounoune! . . ."

He threw himself onto his knees against her, his face revealing the cowardice of a child who can no longer find the words to conceal a misdeed.

"And you discover an old woman," Léa repeated. "What are you afraid of, then, kid?"

She wrapped her arms around Chéri's shoulders, felt the stiffening, the resistance of this body that was suffering because she had been hurt.

"Come now, Chéri darling . . . What are you afraid of? Of having upset me? Don't cry, my beauty . . . I'm so grateful to you, on the contrary . . ."

He let out a groan of protest and struggled feebly. She leaned her cheek onto his tangled black hair.

"You said all that, you thought all that, about me? So I was that beautiful, then, in your eyes, was I? That good? At an age when so many women have stopped living, to you I was the most beautiful, the best of women, and you loved me? I'm so grateful to you, my darling . . . The kindest, you said? . . . Poor little thing . . ."

He sank and she caught him in her arms.

"If I had been the kindest, I would have made a man of you, instead of thinking only of your body's pleasure, and my own. The kindest, no, no, I wasn't that, my darling, since I held on to you. And it's too late . . ."

He seemed to be asleep in Léa's arms, but his stubbornly shut eye-lids quivered continuously and he clung, with a motionless fist, to her dressing gown, which was slowly tearing.

"It's too late, it's too late . . . All the same . . ."

She leaned over him.

"My darling, listen to me. Wake up, my beauty. Listen to me with open eyes. Don't be afraid to look at me. I'm still that woman you loved, you know, the kindest of women . . ."

He opened his eyes, and his first tearful gaze was already full of a selfish, beseeching hope. Léa turned her head away: "His eyes . . . Oh, let's get this over with! . . ." She rested her cheek against Chéri's forehead.

"That was me, kid, I was that woman who said to you: 'Don't cause hurt needlessly, spare the doe . . .' I didn't remember it. Fortunately you thought of it. You're breaking away from me too late, my wicked infant, I have borne you too long against me, and you have a heavy weight to bear in turn: a young wife, perhaps a child . . . I'm responsible for everything that's lacking in you . . . Yes, yes, my beauty, here you are, thanks to me, at twenty-five, so irresponsible, so spoiled, and so sad at the same time . . . It worries me a great deal. You will suffer, you will cause suffering. You who have loved me . . ."

The hand that was slowly tearing her dressing gown tensed, and Léa felt the wicked infant's claws on her breast.

". . . You who have loved me," she continued after a pause, "will you be able . . . I don't know how to make myself clear . . ."

He pulled away from her to listen; and she nearly cried out to him: "Lay that hand back on my chest and your nails in the wounds they've left, my strength deserts me as soon as your flesh draws away from me!" She leaned on him in turn, as he knelt before her, and went on:

"You who have loved me, you who will miss me . . ."

She smiled at him and looked him in the eyes.

"What vanity, eh! . . . You who will miss me, I would ask you, when you feel close to terrifying the doe who is your possession, who is your responsibility, to restrain yourself, and to imagine, at those moments, everything I didn't teach you . . . I never spoke to you about the future. Forgive me, Chéri: I loved you as if we were both meant to die in the next hour. Because I was born twenty-four years before you, I was condemned, and I dragged you down with me . . ."

He listened to her with an attentiveness that made him look cruel. She ran her hand across his anxious forehead to smooth the furrow from it.

"Can you picture us, Chéri, having lunch together at Armenonville? . . . Can you picture us inviting Madame and Monsieur Lili? . . ."

She laughed sadly and shuddered.

"Oh, I'm as finished as that old woman! . . . Quickly, quickly, kid, go seek your youth, it's only been chipped away at by aging women, it's still there for you, it's still there for that child who waits for you. You've had a taste of it, of youth! It doesn't satisfy, but we return to it . . . Well, it wasn't just last night that you began to make comparisons . . . And who am *I* to give you advice and show you my generosity of spirit? What do I know about the two of you? She loves you: it's her turn to tremble, she'll suffer like a lover and not like a depraved *maman*. You will speak to her as a master and not as a capricious gigolo . . . Go, go quickly . . ."

She spoke in a tone of rushed supplication. He listened to her standing up, planted in front of her, his chest bare, his hair disheveled, so tempting that she interlaced her hands, which were about to seize hold of him. He read her mind, perhaps, but didn't back away. A hope, as senseless as the hope that can strike people mid-descent as they fall from a tower, shimmered between them and disappeared.

"Go," she said softly. "I love you. It's too late. Leave. But leave at once. Get dressed."

She got up and brought him his shoes, laid out his crumpled shirt, his socks. He was aimlessly pacing back and forth and awkwardly moving his fingers as if the tips were numb with cold, and she had to find his suspenders, his tie; but she avoided drawing near him and didn't help him. While he dressed, she looked down into the courtyard often, as if she were awaiting a car.

Clothed, he looked paler, his eyes widened by a halo of fatigue.

"Are you feeling sick?" she asked him. And she added timidly, her eyes downcast: "You could . . . rest . . ." But she corrected herself at once and returned to him as if he were in great peril: "No, no, you'll be better at home . . . Go home quickly, it's not yet noon, a good hot bath will restore you, and then the open air . . . Here, take your gloves . . . Oh, of course, your hat on the floor . . . Slip on your overcoat, the breeze might catch you by surprise. Good-bye, my Chéri, good-bye . . . That's right . . . Will you tell Charlotte . . ." She closed the door on him, and the silence put an end to her vain, desperate words. She heard Chéri stumbling on the stairs, and she ran to the window. He went down the front steps and stopped in the middle of the courtyard.

"He's coming back! He's coming back!" she cried, lifting her arms.

A breathless old woman repeated her gesture in the oblong mirror, and Léa wondered what she could have in common with this madwoman.

Chéri set off again toward the street, opened the gate, and went out. On the sidewalk he buttoned his overcoat to hide the previous day's linens. Léa let the curtain fall back down. But she had just time to see Chéri lifting his head toward the spring sky and the chestnut trees heavy with flowers, and filling his lungs with the fresh air as he walked, like an escapee.

THE END OF CHÉRI

Chéri closed the gate of the little garden behind him and inhaled the night air: "Ah! It's pleasant out . . ." He instantly corrected himself: "No, it's not." The densely planted chestnut trees pressed heavily on the captive heat. Above the nearest gas lamp a dome of scorched greenery stirred. Until dawn, the avenue Henri-Martin, choked with vegetation, would await the faint flow of cool air that rises from the Bois.

His head bare, Chéri gazed at his barren, illuminated house. The sound of roughly handled crystal reached him, followed by Edmée's voice, clear, hardened for the rebuke. He saw his wife approach the bay window in the salon, on the second floor, and lean out. Her beaded white dress lost its snowy hue, picked up the greenish beam of the gas lamp, blazed yellow at the touch of the silk lamé curtain she brushed against.

"Is that you on the sidewalk, Fred?"

"Who else would it be?"

"You haven't taken Filipesco back, then?"

"Of course not, he'd already taken off."

"I would nevertheless have liked . . . Well, it's not important. Are you coming in?"

"Not right away. Too hot. I'm going for a walk."

"But . . . Well, as you wish."

She fell silent for a moment, but she must have laughed, for he saw the frost of her dress shiver.

"All I see of you, from here, is your white shirtfront and your white face, suspended in the darkness . . . You look like a poster for a dance hall. It looks deathly."

"How you like my mother's expressions," he said pensively. "You can let everyone go up, I've got my key."

She waved a hand toward him, and one by one the windows went dark. A particular light, of a muted blue, informed Chéri that Edmée had reached, by way of her boudoir, the bedroom that opened onto the garden at the back of the house.

"Make no mistake," he mused. "The boudoir is now called the study."

Janson-de-Sailly chimed the hour, and Chéri, his face raised, caught the ringing of bells like drops of rain as they flew past.

"Midnight. She's in quite a hurry to go to bed . . . Oh, of course, she has to be at her hospital at nine o'clock tomorrow morning."

He took a few nervous steps, shrugged his shoulders, and calmed down.

"It's as if I had married a classical dancer, in short. At nine o'clock, class: it's sacred. It takes precedence over everything else."

He walked as far as the entrance to the Bois. The sky, pale with suspended dust, softened the pulsing of the stars. A steady step matched his own steady step, and Chéri stopped and waited: he didn't like anyone walking behind him.

"Good evening, Monsieur Peloux," the man of La Vigilante said, touching his cap.

Chéri answered by lifting his finger to the height of his temple with an officer's condescension, which he had learned by socializing, during the war, with his fellow sergeants, and outdistanced the man of La Vigilante, who was pressing his hand heavily on the iron doors of the little walled gardens.

At the entrance to the Bois a pair of lovers on a bench were rumpling fabrics, commingling hushed words; Chéri listened for a while to the gentle sound of a bow cleaving calm water, which rose from the joined bodies and unseen mouths.

"The man's a soldier," he noted. "I just heard the clasp of his cartridge belt."

All his senses, relieved from thought, were awake. The primitive acuity of his hearing had provided Chéri, on certain peaceful nights during the war, with complex pleasures and shrewd terrors. Black with dirt and human filth, his soldier's fingers had been able to discern, with ease, the faces on medals and coins, to recognize the stalk and leaf of plants whose names he didn't know . . . "Hey, Payloux, wanna tell me what I got here?" Chéri could picture the redheaded boy who would slip into his fingers, in the darkness, a dead mole, a little snake, a tree frog, a cut fruit, or some filth, and who would cry out, "Oh, he guesses real good!" He smiled without pity at this memory and this redheaded corpse. He often pictured him, his friend Pierquin, lying on his back, asleep forever with a look of distrust on his face; he spoke of him often. Just that evening, after dinner, Edmée had artfully elicited the brief account, constructed with a studied clumsiness, which Chéri knew by heart and which ended with: "So Pierquin said to me: 'Friend, I had a dream about cats, and then I dreamt again of our river back home, that it was disgustingly dirty . . . You can't get that one past me . . .' It was at that moment that he was snatched, and by a mere piece of shrapnel. I wanted to carry him off . . . Someone found us, him on top of me, a hundred yards from there . . . I'm telling you about him because he was a decent guy . . . It's partly because of him that I received this."

Right after this modest breaking-off, Chéri would lower his eyes to his green-and-red ribbon and shake the ash from his cigarette as if to put on a brave face. He considered it no one's business if a chance explosion had thrown one across the other's shoulders, Chéri living and Pierquin dead. Because the truth, more ambiguous than the lie, had half suffocated beneath the considerable weight of a suddenly motionless Pierquin a living Chéri, outraged and full of hate . . . Chéri bore a grudge against Pierquin. But he had spurned the truth anyway ever since the day, long past, when it had come out of his mouth like a hiccup, to sully and disparage . . .

But that evening, at his home, the American majors Atkins and Marsh-Meyer, and the American lieutenant Wood, seemed not to be listening to him. Their faces like athletic first communicants, their clear, fixed, empty eyes, were only waiting, with an almost painful anxiety, to go to a dance hall. As for Filipesco . . . "Needs to be watched," Chéri reckoned laconically.

A fragrant dampness, exhaled by the mown banks rather than the sluggish water, encircled the Lake. As Chéri was leaning against a tree, a womanly shadow boldly brushed against him. "Evening, kid . . ." He started at the last word, uttered by a soft, smoky voice, the voice of thirst, of arid nights, of dusty roads . . . He made no response, and the indistinct woman took a step toward him on soft soles. But he detected an odor of dirty woolens, soiled undergarments, and sweaty hair, and he set off again with long, springing strides toward home.

The muted blue light was still keeping watch: Edmée had not yet left the boudoir-study. No doubt she was writing, signing pharmacy and bandage vouchers, reading the day's notes and a secretary's brief reports . . . Her frizzly, red-sheened hair, her pretty schoolteacher's face, would be bent over papers. Chéri pulled from his pocket the small flat key at the end of a short gold chain:

"Let's go. She'll make love to me yet again by the book."

———————

He walked into his wife's boudoir without knocking, as was his wont. But Edmée didn't start, and didn't interrupt her telephone conversation, to which Chéri listened:

"No, not tomorrow . . . But you don't need me for that. The general knows you quite well. And at Commerce we have . . . What, I've got Lémery? But not at all. He's charming, but . . . Hello? . . . Hello? . . ."

She laughed, showing her small teeth:

"Oh, come now, you exaggerate! . . . Lémery is friendly with all the women who aren't one-eyed or lame . . . What? Yes, he's come home, actually here he is. No, no, I'll be very discreet . . . Goodbye . . . see you tomorrow . . ."

A housedress, all white, slippery, its white matching the pearls of her necklace, exposed one of Edmée's shoulders. Undone, her fine hair, like a chestnut-brown Negress's, a bit stiffened by the dryness of the air, followed every movement of her head.

"Who was that?" Chéri asked.

She simultaneously questioned him, as she was hanging up the receiver:

"Fred, will you leave me the Rolls tomorrow morning? It'll be better for bringing the general back here to have lunch."

"What general?"

"General Haar."

"He's a Boche?"

Edmée frowned.

"Fred, I'm telling you, those cracks are a bit immature for your age. General Haar is visiting my hospital tomorrow. He'll be able to say in America, on his return, that my hospital certainly compares with the medical institutions over there . . . Colonel Beybert is bringing him. They're having lunch here tomorrow, both of them."

Chéri flung his dinner jacket onto a piece of furniture.

"Couldn't care less, I'm having lunch in town."

"What? . . . What? . . ."

A fleeting aggression appeared on Edmée's face, but she smiled, carefully picked up the jacket, and changed her tone:

"You asked me whom I telephoned? Your mother."

Chéri, toppled into a deep armchair, said nothing. His features wore his most beautiful and most immobile mask. A disapproving tranquillity lay on his face, on his lips, which he took care to close without tension, gently, as in sleep.

"You know," Edmée went on, "she wants Lémery, at Commerce, for her three boatloads of leather . . . Three boatloads of leather that are at the port of Valparaiso . . . Do you know, that's an idea! . . . Only, Lémery won't give the import permit, at least that's what he says . . . Do you know how much the Soumabis are offering your mother as a minimum commission?"

With his hand, Chéri balanced the boats, the leather, and the commission.

"Enough," he said simply.

Edmée didn't push the matter, and tenderly approached her husband.

"You'll have lunch here tomorrow, won't you? Perhaps I'll have Gibbs, the reporter from *Excelsior*, who'll be taking photographs of the hospital, and your mother."

Chéri shook his head patiently.

"No," he said. "General Hagenbeck . . ."

"Haar . . ."

". . . a colonel—and my mother with her uniform. Her tunic—what's it called? jacket?—with the little leather buttons. Her elastic belt . . . Her shoulder straps . . . Her stand-up collar and her chin flowing over it . . . And her cane. No, you understand . . . I can't make myself out to be braver than I am: I prefer to leave."

He laughed softly but seemed cheerless when he laughed. Edmée placed a hand, already trembling with irritation, on his arm, but she became playful:

"You don't mean it, do you?"

"Oh yes I do. I'm going to have lunch at *Brekekekex* . . . or somewhere else."

"With whom?"

"With whomever I want."

He sat down, shook off his pumps without bending over. Edmée leaned against a piece of black-lacquered furniture and searched for the words that would bring Chéri back to his senses. The white satin fluttered against her to the rhythm of her rapid breathing, and she crossed her hands behind her back like a martyr. Chéri gazed at her with a hidden respect.

"She really looks like an attractive woman," he thought. "Her hair any old way, in a shift, in a bathrobe, she looks like an attractive woman."

She lowered her eyes, met Chéri's, smiled.

"You're teasing me," she said plaintively.

"No," Chéri answered. "I won't be having lunch here, that's all there is to it."

"But why?"

He stood up, walked as far as the open doorway to their dark bedroom, fragrant with the scent of the nocturnal garden, then returned to her.

"Because. If you force me to justify myself, I'll raise my voice, I'll swear. You'll cry, you'll let your dressing gown slip off 'in your distress,' and . . . and unfortunately it won't move me in the least."

The same fierceness passed across his young wife's features. But her enduring patience hadn't reached its limit. She laughed and shrugged her round shoulder, naked beneath her hair.

"You can say that as much as you like—that it won't move you at all."

He was pacing up and down, dressed now only in his short drawers of knitted white silk. As he walked, with each step he carefully tested the elasticity of the back of his knees and of his ankles, and he rubbed his hand over two small twin scars, below his right breast, to revive their fading bister. Thin, less fleshy than at twenty years old, but harder and more chiseled, he often strutted around in front of his wife, more as a rival than as a lover. He believed himself to be more beautiful than she, and judged with an air of detachment, like a connoisseur, her weak hips, her rather small breasts, the grace of elongated lines that Edmée dressed so beautifully in slim, straight dresses and silky tunics. "Have you lost weight, then?" he occasionally asked her, for the pleasure of upsetting her a little, and of seeing her stiffen at the provocation, this body that concealed its strength.

His wife's reply annoyed him. He wanted her to be ladylike, and silent, if not unresponsive, in his arms. He stopped, lowered his eyebrows, looked her up and down.

"Nice manners," he said. "Did your physician-in-chief instruct you? Watch yourself, madame!"

She shrugged her naked shoulder.

"How childish you are, my poor Fred! Luckily we're all alone.

Scolding me, for a joke . . . which was a compliment . . . *You* remind-
ing me of propriety . . . *you*! After seven years of marriage!"

"Where do you get the idea it's been seven years?"

He sat down as if for a prolonged discussion, naked, his legs
forming a V, stretched out with an athletic ostentation.

"Madam . . . Nineteen thirteen . . . Nineteen nineteen . . ."

"Excuse me, excuse me! We're not reckoning by the same calen-
dar. Thus *I* calculate . . ."

Edmée flexed a knee, supported herself on one leg, admitting to
her fatigue, and Chéri interrupted her:

"What good does this do us, what we're doing here? Come on,
let's go to bed. You have your dance class tomorrow morning at
nine, don't you?"

"Oh, Fred!"

She crumpled and flung away a rose that was immersed in a black
vase, and Chéri stoked the irascible passion, wet with tears, that
shone in Edmée's eyes.

"That's what I call your flotsam of wounded, when I trip up . . ."

Without looking at him, she muttered, with quivering lips:

"A brute . . . a brute . . . a vile creature . . ."

He wouldn't give in, and laughed.

"What do you want me to say? For you, it's all very well, you're
fulfilling a sacred duty. But for me? . . . If you were obliged to be at
the Opéra every day, in the upper Rotunda, it would make no difference to me. It would leave me equally . . . equally on the outside.
And what I call your flotsam, well, they're wounded, aren't they?
Wounded who were a bit luckier than others, by chance. I have nothing to do with them, either. With them, too, I'm . . . on the outside."

She turned toward him with a start that made her hair fly:

"My darling, don't be upset! You're not on the outside, you're
above everything!"

He stood up, drawn by a carafe of ice water on which azure tears slowly condensed. Edmée fussed:

"With or without lemon, Fred?"

"Without. Thanks."

He drank; she took the empty glass from his hands, and he went toward the bathroom.

"By the way," he said, "the leak, in the swimming pool's cement . . . We'll have to . . ."

"It's taken care of. The man who does the pâte de verre mosaics is the cousin of Chuche, one of my wounded. You can bet he won't need to be called twice."

"Good."

He was about to slip away, he turned around:

"By the way, this business with the Ranch shares that we talked about yesterday morning, should we sell or shouldn't we? What if I had a word with Deutsch senior about it tomorrow morning?"

Edmée erupted in schoolgirl laughter:

"You think I waited for you! This morning your mother had a brilliant idea, when we were taking the Baronne home from the hospital."

"Old mother La Berche?"

"Yes, the Baronne . . . Your mother had a word with her, as you elegantly put it. The Baronne has been a stockholder from the beginning, and is inseparable from the president of the board of directors . . ."

"Except when she's downing a bottle of cheap white wine."

"If you would stop interrupting me at every word! . . . And at two o'clock, everything was sold, my darling! Everything! The little rush on the stock exchange—very short-lived—in the afternoon netted us, easily, two hundred sixteen thousand francs in our pockets, Fred! That will pay for medicines and bandages! I hadn't wanted to tell

you about it until tomorrow, with one of those stunning billfolds . . .
Kiss me? . . ."

He stood, pale and naked, under the folds of a raised portiere, and
looked closely at his wife's face.

"Well . . . ," he said at last. "And my part, in all that?"

Edmée shook her head impishly.

"Your power of attorney is still in place, my love. 'The right to
sell, buy, enter into a lease in my name . . . ,' et cetera, et cetera. My
goodness, I must send a memento to the Baronne!"

"A tobacco pipe," Chéri said reflectively.

"Don't laugh! That good creature is invaluable to us!"

"Who's 'us'?"

"Your mother and me. The Baronne knows how to speak our
men's language, and she tells them stories that are slightly risqué,
but charming . . . They adore her!"

A strange laugh quivered across Chéri's face. He let drop
behind him the dark portiere, whose fall erased him the way sleep
obliterates the vision of a dream. Along a corridor half-illuminated
with blue light, he moved soundlessly, like a figure floating on air,
since he had insisted on thick carpets from top to bottom in his
house. He liked silence and guile, and never knocked on the door
of the small sitting room that his wife had been calling a study
since the war. She evinced no impatience, sensed Chéri's presence,
and didn't give a start.

He showered, didn't linger in the cool water, applied cologne
absentmindedly, and returned to the little sitting room.

He could hear, in the adjoining bedroom, a body rustling the
bedsheets, a paper knife striking a piece of china on the bedside
table. He sat down, put his chin in his hand. Beside him, on a little
table, he read the next day's menu, prepared each day for the butler: " 'Lobster thermidor, cutlets Fulbert-Dumonteil, chaudfroid

of duck, *salade Charlotte*, curaçao soufflé, allumettes with Cheshire cheese . . .' Nothing to object to. 'Six place settings.' To that, I must object."

He corrected the figure, put his chin back in his hand.

"Fred, do you know what time it is?"

He made no response to the soft voice, but he went into the bedroom and sat down in front of the double bed. One shoulder bare and the other veiled with a bit of white linen, Edmée was smiling despite her fatigue, knowing she was lovelier lying down than on her feet. But Chéri, sitting, again put his chin in his hand.

"*The Thinker*," Edmée said, to force him to laugh or move.

"You don't know how right you are," Chéri replied sententiously.

He gathered the tails of his Chinese robe over his legs and crossed his arms fiercely.

"What am I doing here?"

She didn't understand, or didn't want to understand.

"That's what I'm asking myself, Fred. It's two in the morning, and I get up at eight. Another one of those short days, tomorrow . . . It's not nice of you to loaf around the way you do. Come on, there's a bit of wind coming up. We'll sleep in the draft, we'll think we're spending the night in the garden . . ."

He relented, and hesitated only a moment to toss his silk garment away from him, while Edmée switched off the only light. She slipped against him in the darkness, but he turned her around dexterously, took hold of her waist with a firm arm, murmured: "Like that, like on a bobsled," and fell asleep.

———

Through the little window in the linen room, where he kept himself hidden, he saw them leave the next morning. The duck's-egg blue automobile and another long American car were purring softly in the avenue, under the dense, low chestnut trees. A phantom fresh-ness emanated from the watered sidewalk and the green shade; but Chéri knew that a morning in June, Paris's blazing hot month, was wilting the lake of blue forget-me-nots edged with pink dianthus in the garden on the other side of the house.

A sort of apprehension agitated his heart when he glimpsed, com-ing to the gate of the house, two khaki uniforms, some gold stars, a kepi edged in garnet-red velvet.

"In uniform, naturally, the fart!"

This was what Chéri called the chief physician of Edmée's hos-pital, and without knowing him, he hated this strawberry-blond man who spoke technical terms to Edmée in a caressing voice. Chéri muttered vague, hearty insults aimed at the medical profes-sion in particular, and at those who stubbornly wore their uniforms in peacetime. He snickered because the American officer was get-ting paunchy—"For a nation of athletes, what a belly he has!"—but he fell silent the moment that Edmée, animated, dressed in white, with white shoes, appeared and held out her white-gloved hand. She spoke loudly, quickly, gaily. Chéri didn't miss a single word uttered by her laughing red mouth with its tiny teeth. She went as far as the cars, came back, asked a valet for a forgotten notebook, chatted while waiting for it. She addressed the American colonel in English, and lowered her voice, out of instinctive deference, when answering Dr. Arnaud.

Behind the tulle curtain, Chéri watched, standing rigid. His habitual mistrust and untruthfulness would freeze his features when-ever he hid a strong feeling, and he surveilled even his own solitude. His gaze traveled from Edmée to the doctor, from the American col-onel to Edmée, and she lifted her eyes toward the second floor sev-eral times, as if on guard.

"What are they waiting for?" he grumbled to himself. "Ah . . . it's true . . . Oh, for Christ's sake!"

Charlotte Peloux, in a torpedo touring car driven by a cold, flawless young chauffeur, was just arriving. Strapped up tight in gabardine, she held her head straight under a little cap, and you could see the fringe of red hair, cut short, on her nape. She didn't dismount, allowed the others to come greet her, received Edmée's kiss, and no doubt asked after her son, because she lifted her head toward the second floor, revealing as she did so her magnificent eyes, across which played, as in the large eyes of octopuses, an obscure and inhuman dream.

"She has her little cap on," Chéri muttered.

He shuddered strangely, rebuked himself for it, and smiled when the three cars set off. He waited patiently until his "bachelor car" pulled up to the sidewalk, at eleven o'clock, and let it sit there still for quite some time. Twice he stretched his hand toward the telephone and let it drop. His vague desire to summon Filipesco subsided quickly, replaced by the sudden urge to go collect young Maudru and his girlfriend.

"Or Jean de Touzac again . . . But at this hour, he's still sloshed, and he's snoozing. Oh, all that . . . all that doesn't hold a candle to Desmond, to be fair . . . Poor old fellow . . ."

He thought of Desmond as he did of those who had died in the war, but with a pity he denied the dead. Desmond, living but lost to him, inspired in him an almost affectionate melancholy, and the jealous respect owed to a man possessed of a "job." Desmond managed a dance hall and sold antiques to Americans. Pale and weak throughout a war that had seen him carrying everything that wasn't a weapon—paperwork, mess tins, soiled vessels from the hospitals—Desmond bit straight into peacetime with a warlike fury, whose rapid fruits surprised Chéri. Desmond's, situated in a cramped space in a town house on the avenue de l'Alma, gave refuge, within its thick-set stone, beneath its ceilings adorned with swallows and hawthorn, between its stained-glass windows depicting reeds and flamingos, to frenzied, silent couples. People danced at Desmond's, day and night, the way people dance on the day after a war: men, young and old, freed from the anxiety of thinking and fearing, empty and innocent, women devoted to a pleasure greater than the particular pleasures of the flesh: the company of men, the contact of men, their scent, their invigorating warmth, the certainty, sensed from head to toe, of being the prey of a man who is entirely alive, and of submitting in his arms to a rhythm as intimate as that of sleep.

"Desmond went to bed at three in the morning, or three thirty," Chéri calculated. "He's slept enough."

But he once more let drop the hand he stretched toward the telephone. He went downstairs quickly, over the springy, plush wool that covered all the parquet in his house, gazed benignly, as he passed by the dining room, at five white plates, in a ring around a black crystal bowl in which floated pink water lilies, the identical pink of the tablecloth, and didn't stop until he reached the mirror that lined the heavy door of the parlor, on the first floor. He sought out but dreaded this mirror, which was illuminated by the French door facing it, clouded and blue and darkened still more by the garden's foliage. A slight shock would halt Chéri, each time, in front of his image. He didn't understand why this image was no longer strictly the image of a young man of twenty-four. He couldn't detect the precise points where time, with imperceptible strokes, marks on a beautiful face the hour of its perfection, then the hour of a more conspicuous beauty that already announces the majesty of its decline.

There could be no question, in Chéri's mind, of a decline, which he had sought in vain in his features. He would simply stumble up against a thirty-year-old Chéri, not entirely recognize him, and sometimes ask himself, "What's wrong with me?" as if he felt a bit unwell or his clothes were askew. Then he would go on past the parlor door and forget all about it.

————

Desmond's, a dependable establishment, wasn't idle at noon, despite its long nights. A concierge was washing its paved courtyard with a hose; a manservant was pushing away from its front steps the heap of distinguished rubbish—fine dust, tinfoil, corks with spherical metal caps, gilded cigarette butts, and broken straws—that daily attested to the success of Desmond's. Chéri jumped over this residue of the previous night's industry, but the odor of the house blocked the way like a taut rope. Forty couples, tightly packed, had left the odor behind, the memento of their drenched linens, gone cold and permeated with floating smoke. Chéri regained his courage and dashed onto the staircase narrowed by a massive oak handrail and its caryatid balusters. Desmond hadn't wasted any money updating the suffocating luxury of 1880. Two dividing walls knocked down, a refrigerator in the basement, a handsomely paid jazz band—nothing more would be needed for another year yet. "I'll modernize to pull people in when they're dancing less," Desmond would say. He slept on the third floor, in a room overrun with painted bindweed and storks in stained glass; he bathed in enameled zinc alongside a ceramic-tile frieze of riverine plants, and the old water heater snored like an aging bulldog. But the telephone shone like a weapon discharged daily, and Chéri, bounding four at a time up the steps, found his friend, who seemed to be drinking, lips to the chalice, the obscure breath of the receiver. His wandering eyes descended on Chéri, scarcely coming to rest before returning to the cornice of convolvulus. His golden-yellow pajamas made his night watchman's face appear paler, but

Desmond, whose stature had risen with his profits, had gone beyond being concerned about his ugliness.

"Hello," Chéri said. "Here I am. Your staircase stinks. Worse than a foxhole."

"At twelve, you won't get Desmond's business," Desmond was saying to the invisible interlocutor. "I have no trouble getting Pommery at that price. And for my private wine cellar, Pommery should be eleven without the labels . . . hello . . . yes, the labels that came off in the ruckus . . . which is my business. Hello . . ."

"Are you coming to lunch, I've got the car downstairs," Chéri said.

"Absolutely not," Desmond said.

"What?"

"Absolutely not. Hello? Sherry! You're making fun of me. I'm not a liquor store. Champagne or nothing. Don't waste your time or mine. Hello . . . It's possible. Only at the moment I'm in vogue. Hello . . . Two o'clock on the dot. Good day to you, sir."

He stretched before holding out his hand limply. He still resembled Alfonso XIII, but his thirtieth year and the war had settled this wavering blade of grass in its essential soil. To have survived and not fought, eaten every day, taken advantage and dissimulated, were so many victories from which he came away strengthened and self-assured. Confidence, a full pocket, were making him less ugly, and you could count on his giving the illusion, at sixty, of having passed for an attractive man with a big nose and long legs. He would look Chéri right in the eye, scornful yet conciliatory, and Chéri would turn his head away.

"What, you've sunk this low? Come on, my friend, it's noon and you're just getting up!"

"First, I'm ready," Desmond replied, half opening his pajamas to reveal a white silk shirt and a bronze-colored bow tie. "Second, I'm not having lunch in town . . ."

"That's—" Chéri said, "that's . . . I can't find the words! . . ."

". . . But if you wish, I can give you two fried eggs, half my ham, half my salad, stout, and strawberries. A coffee at no extra charge."

Chéri looked at him with a feeble wrath.

"Why?"

"Business," Desmond said with a deliberate nasal twang. "Champagne. You heard what I said. Oh, these wine merchants! If you don't put the screws on them . . . But it's my job."

He laced his fingers together and cracked his knuckles with mercantile pride.

"Is it a yes or a no?"

"It's a yes, you swine!"

Chéri threw his soft felt fedora at Desmond's face, but Desmond picked the hat up and dusted it off with his elbow, to show that it was no longer the time or the place for these childish pranks. They had cold eggs, ham, and tongue, and good black beer topped with beige foam. They spoke little, and Chéri, looking out at the paved courtyard, became respectfully bored.

"What am I doing here? . . . Just not being at home, in front of cutlets Fulbert-Dumonteil." He imagined Edmée in white, the chubby American colonel, and Arnaud, the physician-in-chief before whom Edmée played the obedient little girl. He thought of Charlotte Peloux's shoulder straps, and transferred to his host a pointless sort of affection as Desmond questioned him sharply:

"Do you know how much champagne people drank here last night, between four o'clock yesterday and four o'clock this morning?"

"No," Chéri said.

"And do you know how many bottles came in full and left empty between May first and June fifteenth?"

"No," Chéri said.

"Pick a number."

"I don't know," Chéri grumbled.

"Pick one! Pick a number, guess, come on! Pick a number!"

Chéri scratched the tablecloth as if he were considering. He was suffering from the heat and from his own inertia.

"Five hundred," he said with difficulty.

Desmond tilted back in his chair, and as he did so, his monocle shot a painful shaft of sunlight into Chéri's eye.

"Five hundred! You make me laugh."

He was boasting. The only laugh he could manage was a sort of sob of his shoulders. He drank his coffee, so as to better lay the groundwork for Chéri's amazement, and put his cup down again:

"Three thousand three hundred eighty-two, my friend. And do you know how much that leaves in my pocket . . ."

"No," Chéri interrupted. "And I don't care. Enough. I have my mother for that. And besides . . ."

He got up, and added in a hesitant voice:

"Besides, money . . . doesn't interest me."

"Odd," Desmond said, hurt. "Odd. Amusing."

"If you say so," Chéri said. "No, believe it or not, money . . . doesn't interest me . . . doesn't interest me anymore."

These simple words came out of his mouth with difficulty, and he didn't raise his face. With his foot he pushed a crust of toast across the carpet, and the awkwardness of his confession, his furtive glance, for a moment gave him back the semblance of his marvelous adolescence.

Desmond for the first time accorded him the critical attention of doctor to patient: "Am I dealing with a malingerer? . . ." Like a doctor, he used vague, soothing words:

"A moment to get past. Everyone feels a bit unglued. No one can find his way anymore. Work is a marvelous way to regain your equilibrium, my friend . . . In my case . . ."

"I know," Chéri interrupted. "You're going to tell me I need something to do."

"You yourself admit it," Desmond scoffed patronizingly. "Oh, what damned times! . . ."

He was about to confess to the joy he took in business, but checked himself just in time.

"It's also a matter of education. Obviously, at Léa's side, you didn't learn anything about life. You don't know how to handle things and people."

"So people assume," Chéri said, irritated. "*Léa* wasn't taken in. Proof that I'm not lying, she distrusted me, but she always talked to me before buying or selling."

He stuck out his chest, proud of a time now gone when distrust was synonymous with respect.

"You have only to put your mind to it again—to money," Desmond advised. "It's a game that doesn't go out of fashion."

"Yes," Chéri acquiesced, his eyes vacant. "Yes, of course. I'm only waiting."

"What are you waiting for?"

"I'm waiting . . . I mean I'm waiting for an opportunity . . . a better opportunity . . ."

"Better than what?"

"You're annoying me. A pretext, if you like, for regaining control over everything that the war took away from me for a long time . . . My fortune, which is, in short . . ."

"Rather sizable," Desmond suggested.

Before the war he would have said "enormous," and in a different tone of voice. Chéri blushed with fleeting humiliation.

"Yes . . . my fortune, well, the girl, my wife, takes care of that."

"Oh!" Desmond chided him, shocked.

"And well, I assure you. Two hundred sixteen thousand the

day before yesterday in that little rush of excitement at the stock exchange. So I ask myself, you see, how I can take part . . . What on earth can I do in all this? When I want to get involved in it, they tell me . . ."

"Who's 'they'?"

"Oh, my mother and my wife . . . They tell me: 'Rest. You're a warrior. Would you like a glass of orangeade? Stop by your shirt-maker's, he's making a laughingstock of you. And on your way, pick up my necklace clasp, which is at the jeweler's for repair . . .' And on and on . . ."

He was becoming animated, doing his best to conceal his resentment, but his nostrils were moving along with his lips.

"So, do I have to sell cars, raise Angora rabbits, run a luxury goods business? Do I have to sign on as a nurse or an accountant in that heap there, my wife's hospital . . ."

He walked to the window, came back fiercely to Desmond.

". . . under the orders of Dr. Arnaud, physician-in-chief, and hand around washbowls? Must I buy a dance hall? You see the competition . . ."

He laughed so as to make Desmond laugh, but Desmond, who was no doubt getting bored, kept a straight face.

"Since when have you been in the habit of thinking about all this? You weren't thinking about it this spring, or last winter, or before your marriage."

"I didn't have time," Chéri answered naively. "We took a trip, we began to fit out the house, we bought cars only to see them requisitioned. All of that brought us to the war . . . Before the war . . . before the war I was . . . a rich kid—I was one of the rich, you know."

"You still are."

"I still am," Chéri repeated.

He hesitated again, searching for his words:

"Now, it's not the same. The guys have Saint Vitus's dance. And work, and activity, and duty, and women who serve their country— you're telling me!—and who are crazy about dough . . . They're such businesswomen that they put you off business. They're so hard-working that they make you loathe work . . ."

He looked at Desmond uncertainly:

"Is it wrong, to be rich, and to take life as it comes?"

Desmond was enjoying his role, and compensating himself for his long-standing servility. He placed a protective hand on Chéri's shoulder:

"My friend, be rich and take life as it comes. Tell yourself that you embody an ancient aristocracy. The feudal barons are your models. You're a warrior."

"Shit," Chéri said.

"That's a warrior's word. Just let the working types do the work."

"You, for example."

"Me, for example."

"Obviously *you* don't let women get in your way."

"No," Desmond said curtly.

Because he was hiding from everyone a perverse attraction to his cashier-accountant, a sweet brunette, a bit downy and masculine, hair pulled back, a devotional medallion at her neck, who would confess with a smile: "I would *kill* for a dime. That's how I am."

"No. Certainly not! You can't talk about anything without immediately inserting 'my wife, women . . .' and even 'In the days of Léa . . .' So are there no other topics of conversation, in 1919?"

Chéri seemed to be listening, beyond Desmond's voice, to another sound, already audible, still far away. "Other topics of conversation?" he repeated. "Why would there be? . . ." He daydreamed, subdued by the increasing light and heat as the sun came around. Desmond was speaking, impervious to the stuffy air, his face pale as winter endive. Chéri heard the words "little honeys" and listened.

"Yes, a whole set of amusing acquaintances, which I of course put at your disposal . . . And when I say little honeys, I'm speaking flippantly of a unique selection, you understand, unique . . . My regulars, a fine quarry, refined still more by these four years . . . Oh, my friend, when capital comes back strongly enough, what a restaurant I'll put together! . . . No more than ten tables, which people will snap up . . . I'll cover over the courtyard . . . My lease will underwrite my alterations, you can bet on it! A linoleum-cork floor for dancing, spotlights in the middle . . . That—that's the way of the future! . . ."

The tango trafficker was speaking like a founder of cities, and stretched out his arm toward the window. The word "future" struck Chéri, who turned toward the spot Desmond was aiming at, up high, above the courtyard . . . He saw nothing, and felt weary. The reflected two o'clock sun was sadly punishing the little slate roof of the former stable, where the concierge of Desmond's lived.

"What a hall, eh?" Desmond said fervently, gesturing toward the small cobbled courtyard. "It'll happen soon enough!"

Chéri peered at this man who expected and received, each and every day, his manna. "And what about me?" he thought in frustration . . .

"Look, my swill merchant!" Desmond cried. "You'd better take off, I'm going to warm him up like a Corton."

He gripped Chéri's hand in a hand that had changed. Once narrow and limp, it had become broad, demanding, disguised as a hand of integrity and some firmness. "The war . . . ," Chéri thought mockingly.

"And you're going . . . ?" Desmond asked.

He detained Chéri on the steps long enough to show off to the champagne merchant a purely ornamental client.

"That way," Chéri said, gesturing.

"Mystery," Desmond murmured. "Go on, you great sultana!"

"Oh no," Chéri said. "You're wrong."

He imagined some woman, a sweaty body, nakedness, a mouth . . .
He shuddered with an objectless antipathy, repeated softly, "You're
wrong," and got back into his car.

He took away with him a disquiet that he knew all too well, the
frustration, the abashment of never expressing what he had wanted
to express, of never meeting the person to whom he could entrust
a vague confession, a secret that would have changed everything
and stripped of its ill-fated insignia, for instance, this afternoon of
bleached cobblestones, of asphalt sagging under the midday sun,
high overhead . . .

"Only two o'clock," he sighed. "And it stays light until past nine
o'clock, this month . . ."

The wind generated by his speed hit him in the face with the slap
of a hot dry towel; and he yearned for the artificial night of the blue
curtains, for the little three-note melody of the fountain in the center
of its Italian stone surround, in the garden . . .

"If I move through the vestibule quickly, I can go in without
being seen. *They're* having coffee, downstairs . . ."

He conjured the aroma of a fine lunch, the lingering aroma of
melon, of the dessert wine that Edmée asked to be poured after the
fruit course, and saw in advance Chéri's green-tinged reflection
shutting the mirror-lined door . . .

"Let's go!"

Two automobiles, his wife's and the American car, stood idle
under the canopy of leaves in front of the iron gate, entrusted to a
single, sleeping American chauffeur. Chéri drove his car all the way
to the deserted rue de Franqueville, came all the way back to his
door, which he opened soundlessly, looked his dark reflection up and

down in the green mirror, and nimbly climbed the stairs to the bed-room. It was just as he had wished, blue, fragrant, devoted to rest. All that his parched dash had longed for was to be found there, and much more, because a young woman dressed in white was powder-ing her face, arranging her hair in front of a tall mirror panel. She had her back turned to Chéri and didn't hear him come in; so he had time enough to observe the reflection of her features, animated by the heat and the meal and invested with a singular character of dis-order and triumph, with a look at once thrilled and outraged in its victory. At the same time, Edmée noticed her husband, did not cry out in surprise, and turned around without hesitating. She examined him from head to toe, waiting for him to speak first.

From down below, through the half-open window overlooking the garden, rose the baritone voice of Dr. Arnaud, who sang: "*Ay, Mari, ay, Mari . . .*"

Edmée's whole body was drawn toward this voice, but she forced herself not to turn her head toward the garden.

The slightly intoxicated spirit that appeared in her eyes might have foretold serious words. Out of cowardice or contempt, Chéri demanded her silence by bringing a finger to his lips, then pointed, with the same peremptory finger, toward the staircase. Edmée obeyed, and walked past him resolutely, unable to suppress, at the moment when the distance between them was shortest, a twist of her hips, a quickening of her pace, which aroused in Chéri a vague, fleeting impulse toward punishment. He leaned over the handrail, as serene as a cat at the top of a tree, again thought of punishing, of breaking, of escape, and expected that a flood of jealousy would arouse him. Nothing came but a faint, middling shame, very bear-able. Still, he repeated to himself: "Punishing, smashing every-thing . . . there are better things to do . . . Yes, there are better things to do . . ." But he didn't know what.

Each day, whether he awoke early or late, he began a day of waiting. He had paid no attention at first, believing it to be the persistence of a pathological military habit.

In December 1918, he extended a short convalescent leave, in his civilian bed, for a dislocated kneecap. He would stretch at dawn and smile: "I feel well. I expect I will feel still better. It'll be something, this year's Christmas!"

Christmas having arrived, the truffles having been eaten, and the holly twig doused in eau-de-vie set afire on a silver platter, in the presence of an ethereal, wedded Edmée, to the acclamations of Charlotte, Madame de La Berche, and a nursing staff joined by Romanian officers and athletic, prepubescent American colonels, Chéri waited: "Oh, if only these guys would leave! I'm waiting to go to sleep, my head in the cool air, my feet cozy and warm, in my comfortable bed!" Two hours later, flat as a cadaver, he would wait for sleep, to the calls of the little winter owls, cheerful in the branches, who were hailing the blue light from the half-exposed bedroom. Finally he would sleep, but commandeered from daybreak by an insatiable waiting, he would wait, while outwardly attempting to project a good-natured impatience, for his breakfast: "What the hell are they doing down there with my juice?" He didn't consider that the use of that coarse word and of vocabulary deemed "soldier's talk" always coincided in him with an unnatural state of mind and an evasive sort of geniality. He would breakfast, served by Edmée, but he sensed in his wife's quick movements an impatience, the press of duty, and he would ask for another piece of toast, a warm roll he no longer even wanted, only out of spite, so as to delay Edmée's departure, so as to delay the moment when he would begin to wait again.

A Romanian lieutenant whom Edmée employed, sometimes to

fetch plates of ambrine and hydrophilic cotton, sometimes to plead her case before ministers—"What the government unceremoniously refuses a Frenchman, a foreigner always gets!" she would declare—bent Chéri's ear, extolling the duties of a warrior left more or less unscathed and the heavenly perfection of the Coictier Hospital. Chéri accompanied Edmée, sniffed the antiseptic odor that relentlessly conjures that of hidden putrefactions, recognized a comrade among the "trench foot" victims and sat down on the edge of his bed, doing his best to be cordial the way war novels and patriotic plays teach. Still, he could sense that an able-bodied man, who had pulled through the war, had neither peers nor equals among the disabled. He saw the nurses all in white winging past him, the sunburnt color of heads and hands on the sheets all around him. An unbearable impotence weighed on him, he caught himself bending one of his arms out of guilt, dragging one leg a little. But the next moment, in spite of himself, he would fill his lungs and tread the tiled floor, between recumbent mummies, with a lively step. He revered Edmée with annoyance, because of her authority as a noncommissioned angel and because of her purity. She would cross a room and put her hand on Chéri's shoulder in passing, but he knew that she wanted, through this affectionate and subtly possessive gesture, to make blush with envy and irritation a dark-haired young nurse who gazed at Chéri with a cannibal ingenuousness.

He got bored and felt the weariness of a man who complains, taken to the museum, before row upon row of masterpieces. Too much white fell from the ceilings, splashed up from the tiled floors, obliterated the corners, and he pitied the bedridden men to whom no one would grant the mercy of shade. The noon hour imposes on wild animals rest and refuge, on birds the stillness under the canopies of trees, but civilized man no longer knows the laws of the sun. Chéri took a few steps toward his wife, intending to say to her: "Draw the curtains, put up a punkah, take away the noodle mash from this poor guy who's blinking his eyes and suffering, you will feed him after nightfall . . . Give them darkness, give them a color that isn't white, always this white . . ." Dr. Arnaud's arrival sapped his desire to advise and serve.

The doctor, with his white canvas belly and his reddish-gold hair, had no sooner taken three steps into the room than the noncommissioned angel came down from on high to the office of a humble seraph, rosy with faith and zeal . . . Then Chéri turned toward Filipesco, who was handing out American cigarettes, called out to him disdainfully, "Are you coming?" and whisked him away, not without having bid good day to his wife, Dr. Arnaud, the male and female nurses, with the affable arrogance of an official visitor. He crossed the small, coarse-graveled courtyard, got back into his car, and allowed himself no more than ten words in soliloquy: "It's a fair blow. This blow from the physician-in-chief." He never again crossed the threshold of the hospital, and from then on Edmée invited him only as a matter of courtesy, the way one nevertheless offers snipe, at the dinner table, to vegetarian guests.

———————

He was pondering now, tormented by idleness, so easy before the war, so varied, as resonant as an empty, perfect glass. During the war, too, he had suffered the military regimen of inaction, inaction apart from the cold, the mud, the risk, the watch, even a little combat. Schooled for leisure by his life as a sensual young man, he had watched in safety as vigorous, vulnerable companions all around him wasted away from silence, solitude, and despair. He had witnessed the ravages visited on intelligent beings by the want of printed matter, not unlike the deprivation of a daily toxicant. Whereas he, satisfied by a brief letter, a postcard, a cleverly packed parcel, would once again lapse into silence and contemplation like a cat in a nocturnal garden, some men, his so-called superiors, would exhibit their deterioration like starved creatures. In this way he had learned to use his pride to brace his patience, which was held aloft by two or three ideas, by two or three lingering memories, as colorful as the memories of children, and by the inability to imagine his own death.

Time and time again, during the war, upon emerging from a long, dreamless sleep or a rest disrupted every minute, it happened that he would awake outside the present, stripped of his most recent past, returned to childhood—returned to Léa. Edmée would appear to him a little later, distinct, fully developed, and the resurrection of her image, no less than its instantaneous suppression, put Chéri in a good frame of mind. "That gives me two of them," he would observe. Nothing came for him from Léa, he didn't write to her. But he received postcards signed by old mother Aldonza's deformed fingers, cigars selected by the Baronne de La Berche. For a while he dreamed about a long, soft wool scarf, because of its color, the blue of eyes, and because of the very faint perfume that arose from it through hours of warmth and sleep. He loved that scarf, pressed it against him in the darkness, then it lost its perfume, its fresh blue-eyed tint, and he forgot all about it.

He was unconcerned about Léa for four years. Old lookouts, if the need had arisen, would have noted and passed on to him events that he could scarcely imagine. What was there in common between Léa and sickness, Léa and change?

In 1918, the words "Léa's new apartment," having escaped from the Baronne de La Berche, struck him with incredulity.

"She's moved?"

"Where have you been?" the Baronne replied. "Everyone knows. A spectacular deal, my gosh, the sale of her mansion to some Americans! I saw her new apartment. It's small, but it's cozy. When you sit down in there, you can't get up."

Chéri fixed on those brief words: "small, but cozy." Unable to use his imagination, he laboriously constructed a pink interior, threw in the enormous gold-and-steel vessel, the big bed rigged with lace, and hung on some passing cloud the mother-of-pearl-titted Chaplin.

Since Desmond was seeking a silent partner for his dance hall, Chéri felt a twinge of anxiety and wariness: "That guy's going to tap Léa, drag her into the business . . . I'll phone to warn her." Yet he did nothing. Because it's riskier to telephone an abandoned lover than to stretch out your hand, in the street, to an intimidated enemy who tries to catch your eye.

———

He was still waiting, after the day of the surprise in front of the mirror, after that offense of overexcitement, blushing, disorder. He let time pass, and didn't compound, by putting it into words, the certainty of a still almost chaste complicity between his wife and the man who sang *"Ay, Mari! . . ."* Because he was feeling more light-hearted, and for several days on end he forgot to needlessly check his wristwatch, as he would do at dusk's approach. He got into the habit of sitting in the garden in a straw armchair, as if he had just come into a hotel garden after a trip, and, surprised, he watched the approaching night cause the blue of the aconite to vanish, substituting for it a blue in which the flowers' form melted away but the green of the foliage persisted in distinct masses. The border of garden pinks turned a putrid purple, then darkened quickly, and the yellow July stars shone between the branches of the variegated ash.

He savored at his own home the pleasure of a passerby seated in a public square, and never gave a thought to how long he had rested there, tilted back, his hands hanging. Occasionally he thought about what he called the scene at the mirror, about the atmosphere in the blue bedroom, secretly disturbed by the passage, the gestures, the escape of a man. He said to himself, with a methodical, mechanical inanity: "That's an achievement. It's what you call an a-chiev-e-ment," sounding out the *e* in the middle.

At the beginning of July, he tried out a new open automobile, which he called his spa car. He took Filipesco, and Desmond, for drives along roads bleached white by drought, but he came back to Paris each night, cleaving the warm and cool seams of the air, which surrendered its perfumes as the city approached.

One day, he took along the Baronne de La Berche, a manly companion who, at the octroi tollgates, touched her index finger to her little fedora, pulled well down over her head. He found her easy to get along with, sparing with words, fascinated by wisteria-shaded nightclubs, by rustic shops that smelled of cellars and wine-drenched sand. Motionless, silent, they covered some three hundred kilometers, and opened their mouths only to smoke and to eat their fill. The next day, Chéri invited Camille de La Berche tersely—"Let's beat it, shall we, Baronne?"—and took her along again.

The powerful car sped through the green countryside, returned at night to Paris like a plaything at the end of a string. That evening, Chéri, without taking his eyes off the road, made out to his right the profile of the old woman with the mannish face, as noble as an old coachman from a fine household. He was surprised to find her dignified, because she was forthright, and, alone with her for the first time outside a city, he began to sense confusedly that a woman burdened with a sexual aberrancy bears it not without bravura and a certain grandeur befitting the condemned.

The woman had ceased to wield her malice since the war. The hospital had put her in her proper place, which is to say among males, among males just young enough, just overcome enough by suffering, that she could, among them, live peacefully, forgetting her aborted femininity.

Surreptitiously, Chéri would glance at his companion's large nose, her hairy, graying lip, her small peasant's eyes, which wandered, unconcerned, over the ripe wheat and the mown fields.

For the first time, he felt himself drawn toward the elderly Camille by an impulse that resembled friendship and tender comparison: "She is alone. When she's no longer with her soldiers or my mother, she is alone. She, too . . . In spite of her pipe and her drink, she is alone."

They stopped on the way back to Paris, at a "hostelry" where there was no ice, and where rosebushes parched to a crisp were dying tied to column shafts and ancient baptismal fonts scattered across the lawn. A nearby woods sheltered this dusty place from the breeze, and a small cloud, stoked to a cherry red, floated motionless high in the sky.

The Baronne emptied her short briar pipe against the ear of a marble satyr.

"It'll be hot in Paris tonight."

Chéri nodded in agreement and lifted his head toward the cherry-red cloud. Onto his pale cheeks, his dimple-stamped chin, fell pink reflections, dispensed like the touches of red powder that flock an actor's face.

"Yes," he said.

"Oh, you know, if it tempts you, let's not go back till tomorrow morning. Just give me a minute to buy soap and a toothbrush . . . And we would telephone your wife. Tomorrow morning, we'd take off around four, in the cool night air . . ."

Chéri stood up with unthinking haste.

"No. No. I can't."

"You can't? Come on! . . ."

At his feet he could see her laughter in her small, mannish eyes and big, quivering shoulders.

"I didn't think you were still so reined in," she said. "But since you are . . ."

"What?"

She had gotten to her feet again, heavy and solidly built, and she gave him a hard clap on the shoulder.

"Yes, yes. You go off driving during the day, but you head back to your digs every evening. Oh, you're kept on a tight leash!"

He looked at her coldly. He already liked her less.

"Nothing gets past you, Baronne. I'll bring the car over, and in less than two hours we'll be at your place."

Chéri never forgot their nighttime journey, the cheerless red that lingered for a long time in the west, the fragrance of pastures, the feathery butterflies held captive in the headlights' beam. A black mass darkened by the night, the Baronne kept watch beside him. He drove carefully; the cool breeze of the straightaways, when he slowed down on the curves, became a hot breeze. He trusted in his sharp eye, his responsive limbs, but in spite of himself his thoughts turned to the massive, alien old lady next to him, motionless against his right side, and a kind of fright came over him, a fretting of the nerves, which brought him within a hair's breadth of a cart with no lantern. At that very moment a thick hand came to rest gently on his forearm.

"Pay attention, son."

He hadn't anticipated, certainly, either her gesture or the softness of her tone. But nothing warranted the emotion that followed them, and this knot, this hard fruit in his throat. "I'm an idiot, I'm an idiot," he repeated to himself. He drove on more slowly and diverted himself with the broken beams, golden zigzags, and peacock feathers that danced for a few moments, around the headlights, within the tears that were filling his eyes.

"She told me that I was reined in, that I was on a tight leash. If she saw us, Edmée and me . . . For how many days have we slept like brothers?" He tried to count: three weeks, maybe more? . . . "What's so funny about it is that Edmée doesn't complain, and that she wakes up smiling." To himself, he always used the word "funny" when he wanted to avoid the word "sad." "An old couple, you know, an old couple . . . Madame and her physician-in-chief, Monsieur and . . . his car. All the same, old Camille said I was on a leash. A leash. A leash. If I ever take *her* along again . . ."

He took her along again, because July started to sear Paris. But neither Edmée nor Chéri complained about the scorching heat. Chéri came home each evening, courteous, absentminded, the tops of his hands and the bottom of his face stained walnut-brown. He paced back and forth naked between the bathroom and Edmée's boudoir.

"You must have cooked today, wretched folk of Paname!" Chéri scoffed.

A bit pale and melted, Edmée straightened her pretty, enslaved back, denied her fatigue:

"Well, not really, believe it or not. There was rather more air than yesterday. My office is cool, over there, you know. And then we didn't have time to think about it. My dear little twenty-two who was doing so well . . ."

"Really?"

"Really. Dr. Arnaud has a bad feeling about him."

She never hesitated to toss out the physician-in-chief's name up front, the way someone brings a decisive piece into play on the chessboard. But Chéri didn't bat an eye. So Edmée watched the naked man, his nakedness tinged subtly green by the reflection from the blue curtains. He walked back and forth in front of her, exposed, pale, trailing his cloud of scent behind him, and already out of reach. The very confidence of this naked body, incomparable and haughty, relegated Edmée to a feebly vindictive immobility. This naked body she could now ask for only in a voice from which the tone, the cry of urgency, was lacking: the human voice of mellowed companionship. An arm covered in a fine gold down, a passionate mouth beneath golden hair, now held her back, and she observed Chéri, jealous, restrained, as unconcerned as a lover who covets a virgin inaccessible to all.

They still talked about vacations, about departures, in breezy, conventional rejoinders.

"The war didn't change Deauville enough, and what a crush . . . ," Chéri would sigh.

"You can't find anywhere to eat, and reorganizing the hotel industry is no small task!" Edmée would say.

Around Bastille Day, over lunch, Charlotte Peloux announced the success of some "deal in blankets" and loudly lamented the fact that Léa would get half the profit. Surprised, Chéri lifted his head.

"So you see her?"

Charlotte Peloux bathed her son in a loving look steeped in old port, and called on her daughter-in-law as witness:

"He has this way of talking . . . this way of talking . . . of talking like a gassing victim. Doesn't he? Talking like a gassing victim. It's disquieting sometimes. I've never stopped seeing Léa, my darling. Why would I have stopped seeing her?"

"Why?" Edmée echoed.

He looked at the two women and found in their benevolence a peculiar flavor.

"You've never spoken to me about her, you see . . . ," he began innocently.

"Me!" Charlotte barked. "No, listen . . . Edmée, do you hear him? Well, it speaks highly of the feeling that he has for you. He has so completely forgotten everything that isn't you . . ."

Edmée smiled without answering, bent her head, and pulled up the lace that restrained the décolletage of her dress, pinching it between two fingers. Her gesture guided Chéri's gaze toward her bodice, and he saw that through the yellow lawn, like two identical bruises, the points of her breasts and their mauve aureoles appeared. He shuddered and understood from this shudder that this graceful body, its most immodest details, its unfailing charm, that the whole of this young woman, so near, disloyal, available, no longer aroused in him anything but an absolute repugnance. "Come on now!" But he was beating a lifeless beast. He could hear Charlotte, pouring out nasal streams:

". . . Just the day before yesterday, I said in your presence that, car for car, well, I prefer a taxi, a taxi, do you hear, to Léa's outdated Renault, and it wasn't the day before yesterday, no, it was yesterday that I said, speaking of Léa, that if you must have a male servant when you're a woman by herself, you might as well pick a handsome young man . . . And then Camille, who, in your presence the other evening, regretted having sent Léa a second cask of Quart-de-Chaume instead of keeping it for herself? . . . While I very much compliment you on your faithfulness, my darling, now let me reproach you for your ingratitude. Léa deserves better from you. Edmée will be the first to admit it!"

"The second," Edmée corrected.

"I didn't hear a thing," Chéri said.

He was stuffing himself with July cherries, hard and pink, and was throwing them under the lowered blind at the sparrows in the garden, which was steaming, too zealously watered, like a hot spring. Edmée, motionless, protracted Chéri's last words in her head: "I didn't hear a thing." He certainly hadn't lied, and yet his offhandedness, the feigned childishness of his pinching the cherry pits, aiming at a sparrow, his left eye closed, spoke to Edmée more clearly than words. "What was he thinking about, when he wasn't listening?"

Before the war, she would have looked for a woman. One month earlier, in the aftermath of the scene at the mirror, she would have feared reprisals, some Red Indian cruelty, a bite on the nose. But no . . . nothing . . . he was living, innocent, walking around, at peace in his freedom like a prisoner in the depths of his jail, and as chaste as an animal brought from the opposite side of the earth, who ceases to seek out females of his species in our hemisphere.

"Ill? . . ." He slept enough, ate as he pleased, which is to say fussily, sniffing the meats suspiciously, fond of fruit and fresh eggs. No nervous tic fractured the exquisite symmetry of his features, and he imbibed more water than champagne. "No, he isn't ill. And yet he has . . . something. Something that I would surely guess if I were still in love with him. But . . ." She again straightened the lace at her décolletage, inhaled the warmth, the scent, that arose from her bosom, and saw, as she leaned her head forward, the twin disks of her breasts, mauve and pink, appearing through the fabric. She blushed with sensual pleasure, and pledged this perfume, these mauve shadows, to the redheaded man, dexterous and condescending, whom she would see again in an hour.

———

"They were talking about Léa, every day, in my presence, and I didn't hear anything. So have I forgotten her? I've forgotten her. But forgetting, what does that mean? If I think about Léa, I see her perfectly well, I remember the sound of her voice, the perfume she sprayed herself with and pressed wet between her long hands . . ." He narrowed his nostrils and pushed his lips up toward his nose in a greedy grimace.

"Fred, you just made an appalling face, you look *exactly* like the fox Angot brought back from the trenches . . ."

They spent the least difficult part of their day after waking up and having breakfast. Revived by their morning showers, they listened with gratitude to a heavy rain that advanced the season by three months, a rain that detached the leaves of the false Parisian autumn and knocked down the petunias. They didn't go to the trouble, that morning, of looking for an excuse for their obstinacy in remaining in the city. Hadn't Charlotte Peloux, the day before, rescued them from their predicament by declaring: "We're purebred Parigots, we are! Genuine and unadulterated! We and the concierges—you can say that we've really experienced the first Parisian summer since the war!"

"Fred, are you in love with that suit? You don't take it off anymore. It's not fresh looking, you know?"

Chéri made a gesture with his hand in the direction of Edmée's voice, a gesture that demanded silence and beseeched that no one divert his attention, devoted for the moment to an exceptionally cerebral task.

"I would like to know whether I've forgotten her. But what does that mean, forgetting? A year since I saw her . . ." He suffered a little shock of awareness, a start, and realized that his memory had obliterated the war. Then he counted up the years, and everything inside him fell silent with amazement for a moment.

"Fred, will I never succeed in getting you to leave your razor in the bathroom instead of bringing it in here?"

He turned around listlessly. He was almost naked, still wet, his bared chest dotted here and there with silvery patches of talc.

"What?"

The voice, which seemed to him far away, began to laugh.

"Fred, you look like a badly dusted cake! An unappetizing cake . . . Next year we won't be as stupid as we've been this year. We'll have a house in the country . . ."

"You want a house in the country?"

"Yes. Not this morning, mind you . . ."

As she pinned up her hair, she pointed her chin at the curtain of rain pouring from a windless, thunderless gray storm.

"But maybe next year . . . Right?"

"It's an idea. Yes, it's an idea."

He rid himself of her, politely, to return to his surprise. "I believed that it had been only a year since I'd seen her. I wasn't thinking of the war. It's been one, two, three, four, five years since I saw her. One, two, three, four . . . But have I forgotten her, then? No, since these women were talking about her in my presence and I didn't jump up and cry: 'Wait a minute, it's true, in fact, and what about Léa?' Five years. How old was she in 1914?"

He counted once more, and stumbled up against an implausible total. "That makes her about sixty years old now? . . . You've got to be kidding . . ."

"The key," Edmée continued, "is to make the right choice. Let's see, a pretty area would be . . ."

"Normandy," Chéri finished distractedly.

"Yes, Normandy . . . Do you know Normandy?"

"No . . . Not exactly . . . it's green. There are lindens . . . ornamental ponds . . ."

He closed his eyes, as if dazed.

"Where is that? In what part of Normandy?"

"Ornamental ponds, cream, strawberries, and peacocks . . ."

"You know quite a bit about Normandy! What a place! There's all that, and what besides?"

He looked as if he were seeing what he described, bent over the round mirror in which he daily inspected the polish of his cheeks and chin after his bath. He went on, passive and hesitant:

"Peacocks . . . The moon on the floor and a big, big red mat thrown over a walkway . . ."

He didn't finish, rocked gently, and slipped toward the rug. The side of the bed broke his fall midway, and a lifeless head came to rest against the disordered sheets, its tan tinted an ivory green against their paleness.

Almost as quickly, and without a sound, Edmée threw herself onto the floor, supported the wobbling head in one hand, held an open flask under the blanching nostrils, but two weak arms pushed her away:

"Leave me alone . . . You can see I'm dying."

Yet he wasn't dying, and his hand remained warm between Edmée's fingers. He had spoken murmuringly, with the grandiloquence and affectation of very young suicides who have just, in a single moment, both sought and escaped death.

He had parted his lips over his glistening teeth, and was breathing in and out evenly. But he was in no hurry to come back to life completely. He took refuge, behind his eyelids and lashes, within the green realm that he had conjured at the moment of his faint, a still realm, abundant in strawberry plants and bees, in white water lilies fringed with warm stone . . . When his strength returned, he kept his eyes closed, thinking: "If I open my eyes, Edmée will see all that I see . . ."

Edmée remained leaning over him, one knee bent. She attended to him with an efficient and professional concern. With her free hand, she reached for a newspaper and used it to fan the air around his upturned brow. She whispered trivial and necessary words:

"It's the storm . . . Relax . . . No, don't get up. Wait till I slide the pillow under you . . ."

He sat up, smiled, pressed her hand in thanks. A desire for lemons, for vinegar, dried out his mouth. The ringing of the telephone pulled Edmée away from him.

"Yes . . . Yes . . . What? I'm well aware that it's ten o'clock! Yes. What?"

From the peremptory brevity of her replies, Chéri understood that it was someone calling from the hospital.

"Yes, of course, I'm coming. What? In . . ."

With a glance, she assessed Chéri's recovery.

"In twenty-five minutes. Thanks. See you soon."

She threw open the two glazed casements of the French window, and a few calm drops of rain came into the room, along with a bland river smell.

"Are you better, Fred? What did you feel? Nothing in your heart, right? You must be losing phosphates. It's because of this ridiculous summer of ours. But what can you do . . ."

Furtively she looked to the telephone as if to a witness.

Chéri stood up with no apparent effort.

"Off with you, darling. You'll be late to your job. I'm absolutely fine."

"A light toddy? Some hot tea?"

"Don't worry about me. You've been very kind. Yes, some tea, ask for it on your way out. And some lemon."

Five minutes later she left, after a glance in which she thought she had revealed only solicitude, but which searched in vain for a truth, the explanation for an inexplicable state of affairs. As if the sound of the closing door had severed his bonds, Chéri stretched, felt himself light, cold, and empty. He rushed to the window, saw his wife crossing the small garden, head down, in the rain. "She has a guilty back," he decreed, "she always has a guilty back. From the front, she's a perfect dear. But her back speaks eloquently. My fainting made her lose a good half hour. But let's get back to the point, as my mother would say. Léa, when I got married, was fifty-one, at the very least! So Madame Peloux assures me. She would be fifty-eight, perhaps sixty . . . General Courbat's age? Come on! . . . It's simply absurd."

He tried to combine, with the image of a sixty-year-old Léa, the white horsehair mustache, the graven cheeks, of General Courbat, and his old cab-horse stance.

"It's a scream . . ."

Madame Peloux's arrival found Chéri busy entertaining himself, pale, motionless before the dripping garden, and chewing on an extinguished cigarette. He didn't smile at his mother's entrance.

"You're up early, my dear mother," he said.

"And you got up on the wrong side of the bed, it seems," she retorted.

"Pure illusion. Are there circumstances that extenuate your busyness, at least?"

She lifted her eyes and shoulders toward the ceiling. A small leather hat, impish and sporty, came down like a visor over her forehead.

"My poor little thing," she sighed, "if you knew what I was embarking on at the moment. If you knew what an incredible undertaking . . ."

He scrutinized the deep furrows on his mother's face, surrounding her mouth like pairs of angle brackets, the small soft wave of her double chin, whose ebb and flow covered and then uncovered the collar of her waterproof coat. He weighed the surging bags of her lower eyelids, repeating to himself: "Fifty-eight . . . Sixty . . ."

"Do you know what task I'm devoting myself to? Do you?"

She waited a beat, widened her large, black-pencil-lined eyes.

"I'm reviving the thermal baths at Passy. The Passy Springs. Yes, of course, that says nothing to *you*. The springs are there, under the rue Raynouard, a stone's throw from here. They're dormant, they only need to be reawakened. Extremely potent waters. If we go about it right, it will be the ruin of Uriage, the collapse of Mont-Dore perhaps—but that would be too much to hope for! I've already secured the support of twenty-seven Swiss physicians. The Paris Municipal Council, which Edmée and I have lobbied . . . Incidentally that's why I came, I missed your wife by five minutes . . . What's wrong with you? Aren't you listening to me?"

He was stubbornly trying to light his damp cigarette. He gave up, threw it onto the balcony, where fat drops of rain rebounded like grasshoppers, and eyed his mother seriously.

"I'm listening to you," he said. "I even know in advance what you're going to say. I know all about your business. It's otherwise known as schemes, tricks, bribes, founder's shares, American blankets, dried beans, et cetera. Do you really think I've been deaf and blind this past year? You're wicked, villainous women, that's pretty much it. I don't hold it against you."

He fell silent and sat down, out of habit picking at the two small twin scars above his right breast. He gazed out at the green garden battered by the rain, while on his slack face lassitude and youth struggled, the former hollowing out his cheeks, darkening the sockets of his eyes, the latter still evident in the ravishing arch and fleshy resilience of his lips, in the downy wings of his nostrils, in the black abundance of his hair.

"Well," Charlotte Peloux said finally, "you've given me an earful! Morality shows up in the strangest of places. I've given birth to a censor."

He remained silent and motionless.

"And you judge this poor rotten world from the heights of what? Of your honesty, no doubt?"

Strapped up in leather like a reiter, she was proving to be her old self, ready for battle. But Chéri seemed to be done with all fighting.

"Of my honesty . . . Perhaps. If I had searched for the word, I wouldn't have come up with that one. You're the one who said it. All right, honesty."

She made no reply, deferring the offensive. She fell silent so as to focus her attention on her son's strange appearance. He had his knees apart, his elbows on his knees, and was tightly clasping his hands. He was gazing fixedly at the garden bent under the whipping rain, and after a minute he sighed without turning his head:

"Do you think this is a life?"

She immediately asked him:

"What life?"

He raised one arm and let it fall back down.

"My life. Your life. All this. Everything we see."

Madame Peloux hesitated for a moment, then threw off her leather overcoat, lit a cigarette, and sat down in turn.

"Are you bored?"

Won over by the unaccustomed sweetness of a voice that was ethereal and cautious, he became unaffected and almost confiding.

"Bored? No, I'm not bored. Why do you expect I'm bored? I'm a little . . . what? A little anxious, that's all."

"About what?"

"About everything. About myself, and even about you."

"I must say I'm surprised."

"Me, too. These guys . . . this year . . . this peace . . ."

He spread his fingers, as if they felt sticky or entangled in a too-long hair.

"You say it the way people used to say 'this war . . .' "

She rested a hand on his shoulder, and subtly dropped the pitch of her voice:

"What's wrong with you?"

He couldn't bear the questioning weight of this hand, and stood up, began to move around erratically.

"What's wrong with me is that everyone's a bastard. No," he beseeched, seeing an affected superiority on his mother's face, "no, don't start again. No, present company is not excepted. No, I don't see how we're living in a fantastic time, a dawn here and a resurrection there. No, I'm not angry, I don't love you less, I don't feel under the weather. But I do believe I'm at my limit."

He walked around cracking his knuckles, and inhaled the sickly-sweet mist vaporized by the heavy rain as it hit the balcony. Charlotte Peloux threw down her hat and her red gloves, giving her gesture a conciliatory quality.

"Explain, darling. We're all alone."

She smoothed back her old woman's red hair, cut boyishly, and her dark brown dress hugged her body the way a tarp conforms to a cask. "A woman . . . She was a woman . . . Fifty-eight . . . sixty . . . ," Chéri thought. She looked at him with her beautiful, velvety eyes, full of a motherly flirtation whose feminine power he had long since forgotten. Seeing the sudden appeal in his mother's gaze, he sensed the danger, the difficulty of the explanation toward which she was leading him. But he felt listless and forsaken, urged on by what he lacked. Moreover the hope of offending her drove him on.

"Yes," he answered himself. "You've got blankets, pastas, Legions of Honor. You fool around with the sessions of the Chamber and the Lenoir boy's accident. You're enthralled with Madame Caillaux, and the Passy thermal baths. For Edmée it's her heap of wounded and her physician-in-chief. Desmond wheels and deals in the dance hall, the wine trade, the procurement of honeys. Filipesco wangles cigars from Americans and the hospitals to resell in the nightclubs. Jean de Touzac is in 'inventory,' which says it all . . . What a gang . . . Well . . ."

"You're forgetting Landru," Charlotte suggested.

He casually winked at her in amusement, paying silent tribute to the cruel humor that would rejuvenate the faded combatant.

"Landru doesn't count, that case smacks of the prewar years. It's quite natural to have a Landru. But as for the rest . . . Well . . . Well, in short, everyone's a bastard, and . . . I find it unacceptable. There you have it."

"That was indeed short, but not very clear," Charlotte said after a moment. "You've packaged and presented us well. By the way, I don't say that you're wrong. My flaws are my strengths, and nothing scares me. But that doesn't tell me what you're driving at."

Chéri rocked awkwardly on his chair. He knitted his brows between his eyes, pulling the skin of his forehead forward as if to hold on to a hat lifted by the wind.

"What I'm driving at . . . I don't know. I would want people not to be bastards . . . Or else I would wish simply not to notice it."

He displayed such a self-consciousness, such a need to come to terms with his unease, that Charlotte poked fun at it:

"But why do you notice it?"

"That's the question . . . That's precisely the question."

He smiled a helpless smile at her, and she noticed how the smile aged her son's face. "We should always ply him with tragedies," she thought, "or else infuriate him. Gaiety doesn't become him." In her turn, she let slip, in a puff of smoke, an innocent, equivocal remark:

"Before, you didn't notice all that."

His head shot up:

"Before? Before what?"

"Before the war, of course."

"Ah yes . . . ," he murmured, disappointed. "No, before the war, obviously . . . But before the war, I didn't take the same view of all that."

"Why?"

This simple word left him speechless.

"I'm telling you," Charlotte mocked, "you've turned honest!"

"You wouldn't want to admit, by chance, that I've just remained so?"

"No, no. Let's keep things straight!"

She was speaking, red cheeked, with the conviction of a soothsayer.

"All the same, the kind of life you led before the war—I'm putting myself in the position of people who aren't broad minded and who see things only from the outside, don't get me wrong!—that kind of existence, all the same, it has a name!"

"If you wish," Chéri assented. "So what?"

"Well, it entails a . . . a way of seeing things. You saw existence from the point of view of a gigolo."

"It's quite possible," Chéri said unconcernedly. "And? Do you see anything wrong with that?"

"Of course not," Charlotte protested with a childlike simplicity. "But there's a time for everything, don't you think?"

"Yes . . ."

He let out a deep sigh, his face raised toward a sky obscured by clouds and rain:

"There's a time to be young and a time to be less young. There's a time to be happy . . . Do you think I needed you to make me see that?"

She was suddenly agitated, walked up and down the room, her round buttocks wedged into her dress, thickset and nimble like a fat little dog, and returned to plant herself in front of her son.

"Well, my darling, you're headed toward some mischief, I'm afraid."

"What kind?"

"Oh, there aren't so many options! The monastery. Or a desert island. Or love."

Chéri smiled in surprise.

"Love? You want me to . . . Love with . . ."

He pointed with his chin toward Edmée's boudoir, and Charlotte's face gleamed:

"Who said anything about her?"

He laughed, and reverted to his coarseness out of an instinct for self-preservation:

"In a minute you're going to offer me some American tail!"

With a theatrical start she defended herself:

"Some American tail! Really! And why not a rubber doll like the sailors use, too?"

He approved of this expert chauvinistic scorn of hers. He had known since his childhood that in living with a foreigner, a Frenchwoman didn't demean herself so long as she exploited him or he ruined her. He knew by heart the list of offensive qualifiers with which a native courtesan in Paris sullied the dissolute woman of foreign birth. But he declined the offer, without irony, and Charlotte spread her little arms, stuck out her bottom lip like a clinician admitting his own impotence.

"I'm not suggesting that you work . . . ," she ventured tactfully.

"Work . . . ," he repeated. "Work, that means associating with guys . . . you don't work alone, unless you're painting postcards or taking in stitching at home . . . My poor mother, you don't realize that if men disgust me, I'm no more taken with women. The truth is, I can't see women anymore, either," he finished bravely.

"My God!" Charlotte whimpered.

She clasped her hands as if confronted with a downed horse, but her son sternly silenced her with a single gesture, and she admired the manly authority of this beautiful young man who had just confessed his particular powerlessness.

"Chéri! . . . My little boy! . . ."

He looked toward her with a tender, empty gaze that was faintly begging.

She fixed her gaze on those large eyes whose pure white and long lashes, whose secretive emotion, perhaps exaggerated their brilliance.

She wanted to slip down, through those magnificent breaches, all the way to an obscure heart, which had begun to beat, long ago, close to her own heart. Chéri seemed to give no resistance and to revel in this hypnotic assault. Charlotte had already seen her son ill, annoyed, cunning. She had never seen him unhappy. It produced in her a singular elation, the intoxication that throws a woman at a man's feet at the moment when she dreams of transforming the despairing stranger into a lesser stranger, that is, to make him forget his despair.

"Listen, Chéri . . . ," she murmured quietly. "Listen . . . You should . . . Wait, come on, let me at least speak . . ."

He interrupted her with a furious shake of his head, and she stopped insisting. She broke off the long exchange of looks between them, collected her coat, put on her little leather hat, and started for the door. But as she passed by the table, she stopped and casually picked up the telephone.

"Do you mind, Chéri?"

He signaled his consent, and she began to intone in her nasal twang like a clarinet:

"Hello . . . hello . . . Hello . . . Passy, twenty-nine twice. Twice, mademoiselle. Hello . . . is that you, Léa? But of course it's me. What weather, eh . . . Don't speak to me about it! Yes, just fine. Everyone just fine. What are you doing today? You're staying put? Oh, that's just like you, you great sybarite! Me? Oh, you know, my time isn't my own anymore . . . Oh no, it has nothing to do with that, it's something else entirely! A magnificent project . . . Oh no, not over the telephone! . . . You'll be home all day? Good. That's very convenient. Thank you. Good-bye, Léa darling!"

She replaced the receiver and showed only her convex back. As she moved away, she inhaled, then expelled jets of blue smoke, and she disappeared in a cloud, like a sorceress who has carried out her task.

Unhurriedly he climbed the single staircase that led to Léa's apartment. The rue Raynouard at six in the evening, after the rain, reverberated with the chirps of birds and the shouts of children, like a schoolyard. The thick-mirrored vestibule, the pounced stairs, the blue carpet, the elevator cab as florid with lacquer and gold as a sedan chair—he saw everything with a cold eye that did not even admit to surprise. On the landing he endured that painless moment, detached from everything, that deceives the patient at the dentist's door. He nearly turned around, but the thought that he would perhaps feel obliged to come back displeased him, and he rang with a steady finger. A young maidservant unhurriedly opened the door, a brunette, wearing a fine linen butterfly bow atop her cropped hair, and Chéri, confronted with an unfamiliar face, lost his last chance to express any emotion.

"Is Madame in?"

The young maidservant admired him, uncertain:

"I don't know, monsieur. Is Monsieur expected?"

"Of course," he said with his former severity.

She left him standing there and disappeared. In the shadows, he quickly cast his night-blinded eyes and keen sense of smell around him. No honeyed fragrance wafted, and some humdrum pine resin sizzled in an electric perfume burner. Chéri felt annoyed, like a man who's gotten off on the wrong floor. But a big innocent laugh, in a deep, cascading scale, reverberated, muffled behind a door curtain, and threw the intruder into a turmoil of memories.

"If Monsieur would like to go through to the sitting room . . ."

He followed the white butterfly bow, repeating to himself: "Léa isn't alone . . . She's laughing . . . She's not alone . . . Let's hope it's not my mother . . ." A rosy daylight welcomed him from beyond a door, and he waited, standing, for the world heralded by this dawn to reopen at last.

A woman was writing, her back turned, seated at a bonheur du jour. Chéri made out a broad back, the grainy roll of flesh at the nape beneath vigorous, thick gray hair, cut like his mother's. "So she's not alone. Who is that good woman there?"

"Put the address down in writing for me, Léa, and the name of the masseur. You know how I am with names . . ."

A woman in black, seated, had just spoken, and Chéri felt a premonitory stirring inside him. "So . . . where is Léa?"

The gray-haired lady turned around, and Chéri received the shock of her blue eyes head-on.

"Oh, my goodness, kid, is that you?"

He moved forward in a dream, kissed a hand.

"Monsieur Frédéric Peloux, Princesse Cheniaguine."

Chéri kissed another hand, sat down.

"Is he . . . ?" the lady in black inquired, referring to him as freely as if he had been deaf.

The big innocent laugh reverberated once more, and Chéri sought the source of this laugh, here, there, somewhere else, everywhere else but in the throat of the gray-haired woman . . .

"Oh no, he isn't! Or rather, he isn't anymore! Valérie, come now, what are you talking about?"

She wasn't monstrous, but immense, and laden with an ample expansion in every part of her body. Her arms, like round thighs, hung apart from her hips, heaved up by their fleshy girth beneath her armpits. Her plain skirt, her long, featureless jacket half-open over a blouse with a jabot, announced the natural abdication of and withdrawal from femininity, and a sort of sexless dignity.

Léa stood between Chéri and the window, and her substantial, almost cubic bulk didn't at first appall him. When she moved toward a chair, she revealed her features, and he began to implore her silently as he might have implored an armed madman. Red, of a shade that looked slightly overripe, she was now averse to wearing powder, and laughed with a mouth full of gold. A healthy old woman, in short, with big jowls and a double chin, able to carry her burden of flesh, free from stays and fetters.

"So, kid, where have you come from, dressed like that? You really don't look very well, in my opinion."

She held out a cigarette case to Chéri, beaming at him with her blue eyes, which had become smaller, and he was alarmed to find her so forthright, as jolly as an old man. She called him "kid," and he averted his eyes as if she had said something improper. But he exhorted himself to be patient, with the ill-formed hope that this first impression would give way to a radiant remission.

The two women gazed at him calmly and spared him neither benevolence nor curiosity.

"He looks a bit like Hernandez," Valérie Cheniaguine said.

"Oh, I don't think so!" Léa protested. "Perhaps a decade ago . . . but still! Hernandez had a more pronounced jaw."

"Who's that?" Chéri asked with an effort.

"A Peruvian who was killed in a car, something like six months ago," Léa said. "He and Maximilienne were a couple. She was very upset."

"Nevertheless she got over it," Valérie said.

"Like anybody else," Léa said. "Well, you wouldn't have wanted her to die of it, would you?"

She laughed again, and her cheerful blue eyes disappeared into the folds of her broad cheeks. Chéri turned his head to the lady in black, a stout brunette, common and feline like any number of women from the South of France, and so meticulously dressed as a woman of good taste that she seemed to be in costume. Valérie wore the uniform that had long been favored by foreign princesses and their governesses, a poorly tailored black lady's suit, too tight in the armpits, and a short-sleeved white batiste blouse, very fine, a bit too constricting at the breast. The pearl buttons, the famed necklace, the straight stiffened collar—everything was, like Valérie's legitimate name, princely. In princely fashion, she also displayed stockings of middling quality, sturdy walking shoes, and expensive gloves embroidered in black and white.

She looked at Chéri as if he were a piece of furniture, carefully and inconsiderately. She resumed her critical comparison aloud:

"Yes, I'm telling you, he has something of Hernandez about him. But to hear Maximilienne, Hernandez never existed, now that she's secured her famous Amérigo. And yet! And yet! I speak with full knowledge of the facts. I myself saw Amérigo. I've just come back from Deauville. And I saw them both."

"No! Tell me!"

Léa sat down, filling an entire armchair to overflowing. She had a new habit of tossing back her head and thick gray hair, and with each head toss Chéri could see the lower part of her face briefly dance like that of Louis XVI. She was ostensibly focused on Valérie, but several times Chéri caught her small, shrunken blue eyes faltering as they sought those of the unexpected visitor.

"Yes," Valérie recounted. "She had hidden him, in a villa well outside Deauville, in the middle of nowhere. But that wouldn't do for Amérigo—you understand, monsieur!—who reproached Maximilienne for it. She was piqued, she said: 'Oh, so that's how it is? You want people to see you? Well then, they'll see you!' And she telephoned to reserve a table for the next evening at the Normandy. An hour later the whole world knew, and *I* reserved a table, too, with Becq d'Ambez and Zahita. And we said to ourselves: 'So we're going to see this marvel!' At nine o'clock sharp, there's Maximilienne all in white and pearls, and Amérigo . . . Oh, my dear! What a disappointment! Tall, yes, of course, even rather too tall. You know my opinion of men who are too tall: I'm still waiting for someone to show me one—just one!—who's well built. His eyes, yes, his eyes, I don't dispute his eyes. But from here to there, look, you see, from here to there, something too round about his cheeks, something odd, his ears attached too low . . . In a word, a disappointment! . . . And a stiffness in his back."

"You're exaggerating," Léa said. "His cheeks, what do you mean, his cheeks, they don't matter. From here to there, look, he's really handsome, he's dignified, his eyebrows, the top of his nose, his eyes, he's handsome! I'll grant you his chin, which will get fleshy fast. And his tiny feet, the most ridiculous thing for such a tall boy."

"I can't agree with you there. But I did notice that his thighs are too long, in proportion to the lower part of his leg, from here to there."

They debated calmly, weighing and dissecting the upper and lower quarters of this costly beast.

"Connoisseurs of beef on the hoof," Chéri thought. "They would have done a good job in the Supply Corps."

"For proportions," Léa went on, "there will never be anything to match Chéri . . . You see, Chéri, that you've come at just the right moment. Go on, blush! Valérie, if you can recall Chéri just six, seven years ago . . ."

"But of course I remember him. And Monsieur hasn't really changed much, after all . . . You were quite proud of him!"

"No," Léa said.

"You weren't proud of him?"

"No," Léa said quietly. "I loved him."

She shifted her considerable body and looked at him with cheerful eyes, uncontaminated by any ulterior motive.

"It's true that I loved you. That, and more."

He lowered his eyes, speechless with shame before these two women, the fatter of whom was serenely asserting that she and he had been lovers. But at the same time the sound of Léa's voice, voluptuous, almost masculine, assailed his memory with an almost unbearable torment.

"You see, Valérie, how wretched a man looks when you remind him of a love that no longer exists? Little fool, it doesn't bother me to recall it. I love my past. I love my present. I'm not ashamed of what I had, I'm not sad that I no longer have it. Am I wrong, kid?"

He cried out like a man whose toe has been crushed:

"Oh no, of course not! On the contrary!"

"It's nice that you've remained good friends," Valérie said.

Chéri waited for Léa to explain that he had come to her house for the first time in five years, but she simply laughed, and winked knowingly. An agitation grew within him, he didn't know how to protest, how to cry out at the top of his lungs that he didn't lay claim to the friendship of this enormous woman with hair like an elderly cellist's, and that if he had known, he would never have climbed the stairs, never have crossed the threshold, trodden the carpet, collapsed onto the feather-cushioned bergère, into whose depths he now slipped weakly, and without a word . . .

"Well, I'll be off," Valérie said. "I don't want to wait for rush hour on the Métro, you know."

She stood up, braved the broad daylight that shone benignly on her Roman face, so strongly constructed that its nearly sixty years scarcely affected it, her cheeks enhanced in the old style with white powder in even layers, and her lips with a nearly black, unctuous red.

"Are you going home?" Léa asked.

"Of course. You don't know what she might cook up all alone, my little good-for-nothing!"

"Are you still pleased with your new apartment?"

"A dream! Especially since the bars were installed across the windows. And I had a steel mesh put up on the fanlight in the pantry, one I'd overlooked. With my two electric doorbells, and my alarms . . . Whew! It's about time my mind felt a little at ease."

"And your house?"

"Settled! For sale. And the picture gallery in storage. My little entresol is a sweetheart for eighteen hundred francs. And no more assassins' mugs around me. And what about those two footmen? . . . It still makes me shudder."

"Come, come, you really took too dark a view of that."

"You had to have lived through it to understand, my dear friend. Delighted to have met you, monsieur . . . Stay where you are, Léa."

She enveloped the two of them in her velvety, barbaric gaze and left. Chéri saw her move away and reach the outer door, and did not dare to follow. He remained motionless, almost overcome by the conversation of these two women, who had spoken of him in the past tense, like a dead man. But Léa was already coming back, and burst out laughing:

"Princesse Cheniaguine! Sixty million! And a widow! And she's unhappy! If that's what they call the pleasure of living, really, then no thank you, to tell you the truth! . . ."

Her hand slapped her thigh as if it were a horse's rump.

"What's wrong with her?"

"She's scared to death. Just scared to death. She's a woman who doesn't know how to handle money. Cheniaguine left her everything. But you could say that he did her more harm by giving her money than he would have by taking it away from her. Did you hear her?"

She let herself sink down into the hollow of a soft bergère, and Chéri detested the wet sigh of the cushion beneath her immense behind. She stuck the tip of her finger into the groove of a molding on her armchair, blew on a bit of dust, and grew dark:

"Oh, things are no longer what they used to be, even the servants. Eh?"

He felt pale, and the skin around his mouth tensed, as in the cold of winter. He suppressed a terrible surge of rancor and entreaty, the need to cry out: "Stop! Come back! Throw off this masquerade! You're in there somewhere, because I hear you speaking! Come out! Arise reborn, your hair tinted red in the morning light, your face freshly powdered; put on your long corset again, your blue dress with the delicate jabot, your perfume like a meadow, which I seek in vain in this new house . . . Leave all this, come away, across damp Passy, with its birds and its dogs, to the avenue Bugeaud, where surely Ernest is polishing the copper on your gate . . ." He closed his eyes, his strength extinguished.

"My dear, I'm going to tell you something useful: you ought to have your urine tested. The color of your complexion, and that pinched look around your lips, I recognize the signs: you're not taking care of your kidneys."

Chéri opened his eyes, filled them with the placid disaster settled before him, and said heroically:

"Do you think so? It's quite possible."

"You mean there's no doubt. And then you're not plump

enough . . . They may well say that the best fighting cocks are always scrawny, but you ought to put on ten pounds or so, all things considered."

"Give them to me," he said, smiling.

But his cheeks felt oddly stiff, and rebelled against the smile, as if his skin had grown old.

Léa erupted in happy laughter, the same laughter that had once greeted the "wicked infant's" glaring impertinences. Chéri savored, at the full, deep sound of this laugh, a pleasure that he could have endured only briefly.

"*That*, I could manage without being any the worse for it! I've really packed it on, eh? Look, there . . . And there . . . Can you believe it?"

She lit a cigarette, blew a double jet of smoke out her nostrils, and shrugged her shoulders:

"It's age!"

The word flew from her lips with a casualness that gave Chéri a wild sort of hope: "Yes, she's joking . . . She'll suddenly appear to me . . ." He fixed her with a gaze that for a moment she seemed to understand:

"I've changed, eh, kid? Fortunately it's not important. Whereas *you* look I don't know how . . . Like the quarry struck by the hawk, as they used to say. Eh?"

He didn't like this new staccato "eh?" that punctuated Léa's sentences. But he steeled himself at each interrogation, and each time brought to heel an impulse whose motive and goal he was unable to discern.

"I'm not asking whether you have personal problems. First, it's none of my business, and second, I know your wife like the back of my hand."

He listened to her speaking, but only halfheartedly. In particular he noticed that when she stopped smiling and laughing, she ceased to belong to a definite sex. Despite her enormous breasts and crushing buttocks, she was entering, by virtue of her age, a tranquil virility.

"And I know your wife to be perfectly capable of making a man happy."

He couldn't help betraying an inward laugh, and Léa resumed quickly:

"I said 'a man.' I didn't say 'any man.' Here you are at my house, and without warning. I imagine you're not here for my beautiful eyes, eh?"

She rested on Chéri her "beautiful eyes"—shrunken, criss-crossed with red fibrils, sly, neither wicked nor good, sensible and bright, certainly, but . . . But where was the dewy freshness that used to bathe their white periphery in azure blue, where, their rounded domes like fruit, like breasts, like hemispheres, and as blue as a country through which countless rivers flow? . . .

Playing the buffoon, he said:

"Bah! . . . You're quite the detective! . . ."

And he was surprised to find himself sitting so casually, his legs crossed, like a handsome young man who's cutting up. Because inwardly he was gazing at his frantic twin, on its knees, its arms waving and its chest bared, and howling incoherent cries.

"I'm not the dumbest of women. But you have to admit that you haven't given me a very difficult task today."

She pulled her head back, spilling her double chin over her collar, and the kneeling twin lowered its head as if mortally struck.

"You have altogether the look of someone who suffers from the sickness of the times. Let me speak! . . . You're like all your fellow soldiers, you're looking for paradise, eh, the paradise that's owed to you, after the war? Your victory, your youth, your beautiful women . . . You're owed everything, you were promised everything, well, it's only fair . . . And you find what? A nice ordinary life. So you become nostalgic, spiritless, disappointed, depressed . . . Am I wrong?"

"No," Chéri said.

Because he thought he would have given a finger off his hand to make her shut up.

Léa clapped him on the shoulder, allowed her ring-laden hand to remain there, and since he was bowing his head a little, his cheek felt the heat of this heavy hand.

"Oh," Léa went on, raising her voice, "come on now, you're not the only one! How many have I seen, since the end of the war, guys like you . . ."

"Where?" Chéri interrupted.

The suddenness of the interruption, its aggressive nature, halted Léa's priestly lyricism. She pulled back her hand.

"But there's no shortage of them, my dear. Honestly, how conceited you are! You thought you were the only one to find peacetime lacking? Think again!"

She laughed softly, shook her playful gray hair around the self-satisfied smile of a connoisseur:

"How conceited you are, always wanting to be the only one of your kind!"

She moved away a step, sharpened her gaze, and concluded, perhaps vindictively:

"You were unique only . . . for a time."

Chéri recognized the femininity beneath the vague and carefully chosen insult, and straightened up, quite happy to be suffering less. But already Léa had again become kind.

"But you didn't come to hear that. Did you just decide all of a sudden?"

"Yes," Chéri said.

He would have wanted this yes to be the last word between them.

Diffident, he let his gaze wander around Léa. He picked up, off a plate, a cookie in the form of a curved tile, then put it back, convinced that a siliceous pink-brick ash, if he bit into it, would fill his mouth. Léa noticed his gesture, and the unpleasant way he had of swallowing his saliva.

"Oh, so we've got our back up? And a scraggy cat's chin, and creases under the eyes. Lovely."

He closed his eyes, and cravenly consented to hear her but not see her.

"Listen, kid, I know a bistro on the avenue des Gobelins . . ."

He looked up at her, full of hope that she had gone mad and that he could therefore forgive her simultaneously for her old lady's physical decay and erring ways.

"Yes, I know a bistro . . . Let me speak! But we've got to hurry, before the Clermont-Tonnerres and the Corpechots have declared it fashionable and replaced the good woman with a chef. It's the woman herself who does the cooking, and, my dear . . ."

She brought her fingers together over her puckered lips, and Chéri turned his eyes toward the window, where the shadow of a branch whipped a ray of sunlight in even time, like a blade of grass lashed by the steady ripples of a stream.

"What a strange conversation . . . ," he ventured in a false tone.

"It's no stranger than your presence in my house," Léa countered sharply.

With a wave of his hand he indicated that he wanted peace, only peace, and few words, and even silence . . . He sensed in this old woman newfound strengths, an adaptable appetite, before which he beat a retreat. Already Léa's quick blood rose, purple, to her grainy neck and ears. "She has the neck of an old hen," Chéri observed with the faint, savage pleasure of old.

"That's the truth!" Léa said bluntly, becoming heated. "You show up here looking like Fantômas, and I seek a way to fix things, since I know you, all the same, rather well . . ."

He smiled at her despondently. "And how would she know me? Some who are cleverer than she is, and more so even than I . . ."

"A certain kind of melancholy, my dear, and of disillusion, it's a matter of having the stomach. Yes, yes, you laugh!"

He wasn't laughing, but she could imagine he was laughing.

"Romanticism, depression, world-weariness: stomach. All of that, stomach. And even love! If we wanted to be honest, we would admit that there is well-fed love and poorly fed love. And the rest is literature. If I knew how to write, or speak, my dear, that's what I would say about it . . . Oh, naturally I wouldn't be saying anything new, but I would know what I'm talking about. That would be a departure from some of today's writers."

Something worse than this culinary philosophy struck Chéri: an affectation, a feigned naturalness, an almost studied good humor. He suspected that Léa played at joviality, at epicureanism, just as in the theater a fat actor plays the "broad" characters because he's put on a paunch. As if in defiance, she rubbed her shiny nose, blotched bright red, with the back of her index finger, and fanned her chest with the two panels of her long jacket. In so doing, she was sitting for judgment before Chéri with an excessive complacency, and she even combed her fingers through her stiff gray hair and shook it around.

"Does short hair suit me?"

He deigned to answer only with a silent negative, the way people avert a pointless argument . . .

"So you said on the avenue des Gobelins, there's a bistro . . . ?"

In her turn she cleverly answered, "No," and he saw from the quivering of her nostrils that he had at last annoyed her a little. His animal watchfulness was resurrected within him, soothed him, once more tautened his instincts, up to then horrified and diffuse. He meant to communicate, through the brazen flesh, the graying waves, and the prebendary good humor, with the hidden creature to whom he had returned as if to the scene of his crime. A fossorial intuition kept him around this hidden treasure. "How did this happen to her, becoming old? Suddenly, one morning? Or little by little? And this fat, this weight that makes the armchairs groan? Is it a grief that has changed her this way, and desexed her? What grief? Is it because of me?"

But he put these questions only to himself, and silently.

"She's angry. She's on the way to understanding me. She's going to tell me . . ."

He saw her stand up, walk, gather some papers on the apron of the bonheur du jour. He noticed that she held herself straighter than she had when he came in, and under the gaze that followed her she straightened up still more. He accepted that she was positively enormous, with no discernible curve from her armpits to her hips. Despite the heat, before turning to face Chéri, she tightened a white silk scarf around her neck. He heard her breathe deeply; then she came back to him, with the fluid pace of a heavy beast, and she smiled at him.

"I'm making you feel unwelcome, it seems. It's impolite to greet someone with advice, above all useless advice."

From a fold in the white scarf there suddenly appeared, meandering and gleaming in the daylight, a string of pearls, which Chéri recognized.

Captive beneath the skin of the pearls, an ethereal tissue, the seven colors of Iris danced like a secret flame encircling each precious sphere. Chéri recognized the dimpled pearl, the slightly ovoid pearl, the largest pearl, set apart by its singular pink.

"*They* haven't changed! They and I haven't changed."

"And you still have your pearls," he said.

She was surprised by the foolishness of his words, and seemed to want to interpret them in plainer language.

"Yes, the war didn't take them from me. You're thinking that I could, or should, have sold them? Why would I have sold them?"

"Or 'for whom'?" he joked wearily.

She didn't check a glance toward the bonheur du jour and the gathered papers, and in turn Chéri interpreted this glance, ascribed to it, as end and object, some yellowed carte de visite, the bewildered face of some beardless young serviceman . . . Inwardly he contemplated with disdainful arrogance the image he'd invented: "That doesn't concern me." A moment later, he added: "But what is it that concerns me here?"

The inner turmoil that he had brought with him now radiated outside him, under cover of the sunset, the cries of the swallow huntresses, the glowing shafts of light that pierced the curtains. That incandescent pink, he remembered Léa used to sweep along behind her wherever she went, as the sea takes with it, when it ebbs, the earthly fragrance of hay and grazing flocks.

For a while they didn't speak, rescued by a sweet children's song that they appeared, from their expressions, to be listening to. Léa had remained standing. Massive and erect, she was carrying her irredeemable chin higher, and a sort of uneasiness came across in the frequent batting of her eyes.

"Am I keeping you? Do you have to go out? Do you want to get dressed?"

The question was abrupt and forced Léa to look at Chéri.

"Get dressed? And in what, Lord, do you want me to get dressed? I *am* dressed, once and for all."

She laughed her incomparable laugh, which began at a high pitch and descended in even leaps to the low musical register reserved for sobs and lovers' moans. Chéri unconsciously lifted his hand in entreaty.

"Dressed for life, I tell you! It's what's practical! Blouses, fine fabric, this uniform to top it off, and I'm dressed. As ready for dinner at

Montagné's as at Monsieur Bobette's, ready for the movie theater, for bridge, or for a stroll in the Bois."

"And love, which you've left out?"

"Oh, kid!"

She blushed unequivocally beneath her ever-present arthritic flush, and Chéri, after the cowardly pleasure of having uttered a few insulting words, was struck with shame and regret in the face of this girlish reaction.

"It was a joke," he said awkwardly. "Have I offended you?"

"Hardly. But you know I've never liked a certain kind of dishonesty and tiresome joking."

She took care to speak calmly, but her expression showed her to be hurt, and across her coarsened face stirred what was perhaps an offended modesty.

"My God, if she takes it into her head to cry . . ." He imagined the catastrophe, the tears across those cheeks sunken into a single, deep ravine near her mouth, and her eyelids shot with blood from the salt of her tears . . . He hastened:

"Oh no, come on now! What an idea! I didn't mean . . . come on, Léa . . ."

From the way she moved, he realized that he hadn't yet called her by her name. Proud, as in the past, of her self-control, she interrupted him gently:

"I'm not angry with you, kid. But in exchange for the few moments that you spend here, don't leave me any ugliness."

He was touched neither by her gentleness nor by her words, in which he detected an inappropriate tact.

"Either she's lying, or she's become just what she appears to be. Peace, purity, and what besides? It suits her like a ring in her nose. A heart at peace, grub, movies . . . She's lying, she's lying, she's lying! She wants to make me think that it's convenient, and even pleasant, to become an old woman . . . To other people! To other people she can lie about the good life and the bistro with the honest country cooking, but to me! To me, who was born among fifty-year-old beauties, electric slimming belts, and wrinkle creams! To me, who saw them, all my painted fairies, fighting over every furrow, tearing one another to pieces over a gigolo!"

"Surprising though it may seem, I'm no longer accustomed to your manner of falling silent. Seeing you sitting there, I keep thinking you have something to say to me."

Standing, separated from Chéri by an occasional table and the port service, she didn't shield herself against a harsh scrutiny that she found difficult to bear; but certain scarcely visible signs quivered around her, and Chéri detected between the tails of her long jacket the muscular effort by which she attempted to hold in the weight of her spreading stomach.

"How many times did she put on her long corset, take it off, and bravely put it on again before renouncing it entirely? . . . How many mornings did she change the shade of her rice powder, brush her cheeks with a new red, massage her neck with cold cream and a bit of ice knotted in a handkerchief, before resigning herself to this shiny leather that gleams on her cheeks? . . ."

It was possible that impatience alone caused her to quiver imperceptibly, but because of this quivering he waited, with an obstinate madness, for a miracle of rebirth, a metamorphosis . . .

"Why don't you speak?" Léa pressed.

She lost her calm by degrees despite her resolute immobility. With one hand she fiddled with her string of large pearls, twisted and untwisted their everlasting luster—luminous and seemingly veiled with an inexpressible liquid freshness—around her big, wizened, carefully manicured fingers.

"Perhaps she's just afraid of me," Chéri daydreamed . . . "A man who's silent, like me, is always a bit of a madman. She's thinking of Valérie Cheniaguine's fear. If I stretched out my arm, would she cry murder? My poor Nounoune . . ."

He was afraid to utter this name out loud and spoke to protect himself from a sincerity, albeit short-lived.

"What will you think of me?" he said.

"That depends," Léa answered circumspectly. "Right now I think you look like one of those types who lay a box of cakes in the anteroom, telling themselves, 'I'll still have time to make a gift of it later,' and then pick it up again on their way out."

Reassured by the sound of their voices, she was reasoning like the Léa of the past, clear eyed, shrewd in the way of shrewd country folk. Chéri stood up, walked around the piece of furniture that separated him from Léa, and the broad light from the pink-curtained window hit him full in the face. Léa could readily measure the passage of the days and years in his features, virtually intact but everywhere endangered. A decay this secret might have aroused her pity, stirred her memory, torn from her the word, the gesture, that would throw Chéri into a convulsion of humility; and offering himself up to the light, his eyes nearly shut as if in sleep, he hazarded his last chance for a final affront, a final plea, a final tribute . . .

Nothing came, and he opened his eyes. Once again he had to accept the truthful picture: his spry old friend, at a prudent distance, was showing him a measured benevolence, through small and suspicious blue eyes.

Disabused, distraught, he sought her everywhere in the room where she was not. "Where is she? Where is she? I annoy her, and as she waits for me to leave, she's thinking what a nuisance they are, all these memories, and this ghost . . . But if all the same I called out for her help, and asked again for Léa . . ." Inside him the kneeling twin flinched once more, like a body from which the lifeblood drains . . .

With an effort he had believed himself incapable of, Chéri extricated himself from his tortured image.

"I'll be going now," he said aloud.

With a banal finesse he added:

"And I'm taking back my box of cakes."

A sigh of relief heaved Léa's overflowing blouse.

"As you wish, my dear. But you know, don't you, I'm always at your disposal if you're in any difficulty."

He sensed the rancor beneath the sham magnanimity, and the enormous edifice of flesh, crowned in a silvery herbage, once more produced a feminine sound, her whole being ringing out in an intelligent harmony. But the ghost, restored to its phantom-like sensitivity, insisted, in spite of itself, on fading away.

"Of course," Chéri answered. "Thank you."

From that moment on, he knew, without fail, without thought, how he must take his leave, and the appropriate words came out of his mouth, effortlessly, as in a rite.

"You understand, I came today . . . why today rather than yesterday? . . . I should have done it ages ago . . . But you'll forgive me . . ."

"Naturally," Léa said.

"I'm even more scatterbrained than before the war, you understand, so . . ."

"I understand, I understand."

Because she was interrupting him, he thought that she was eager to see him leave. There still passed between them, during the course of Chéri's retreat, a few words, the sound of a piece of furniture being knocked against, a patch of light, blue by contrast, cast by an open window overlooking the courtyard, a large hand with ring-impressed fingers that rose to Chéri's lips, a laugh of Léa's, which stopped halfway down its customary scale like a fountain suddenly shut off, whose crown, abruptly deprived of its column, cascades to the earth in a shower of evenly spaced pearls . . . The stairway slipped beneath Chéri's feet like the bridge that unites two dreams, and he regained the rue Raynouard, which was unfamiliar to him.

He noticed that the pink sky was mirrored in the still rain-swollen gutter, on the blue backs of the swallows flying low to the ground, and because the hour was becoming cooler, and because the memories he carried away with him were treacherously receding deep within him, so as to attain their strength and final dimensions there, he believed that he had forgotten everything and he felt content.

Only an old woman sitting in front of a mint cordial disturbed, with her phlegmy cough, the peace of this place where the murmur of the Place de l'Opéra fell away, muffled as if by the density of the air, rendered impervious to the sonorous stir. Chéri asked for a soft drink and patted his forehead dry along his hair-line, in a careful manner that came to him from far away, from a time when, as a small boy, he would listen to the music of women's voices exchanging maxims: "If you want cucumber milk with real cucumber in it, make it yourself . . . Don't rub the sweat on your face when you're drenched in it, the sweat will be reabsorbed into the skin and ruin it . . ."

The silence of the bar, its emptiness, created the illusion of cool-ness, and Chéri did not immediately see a couple, leaned in closely over a table, lost in indistinct whispering. After a while he noticed the unknown man and woman because of the sibilants that seeped from their murmuring, and also because of the surfeit of expression that drew attention to their faces, two faces typical of domestic servants, wretched, overworked, and patient.

He sucked down two iced soft drinks, tipped his head back against the plush yellow fabric of the banquette, and with delight felt the mental tautness that had exhausted him for the past two weeks vanish. His burdensome present had not accompanied him over the threshold of this old-fashioned bar, all reddish, festooned with gold garlands and rosettes, adorned with a country fireplace, where the washroom attendant, glimpsed in her tiled domain, inclining her white hair under a green lamp, would mend the linens, counting her stitches.

A passerby came in, did not breach the yellow lounge, drank standing near the bar as if out of discretion, and left without a word. The mint cordial's odor of toothpaste offended only Chéri's nose, and he frowned in the direction of the indistinct old woman. Under a much-handled soft black hat, he made out an old face, enhanced here and there with rouge, wrinkles, kohl, puffiness, all dispensed messily, the way people throw their keys, handkerchief, and loose change pell-mell into a pocket. An abject old face, in short, and ordinary in its baseness, scarcely distinguished by the indifference of savages and prisoners. She coughed, opened her handbag, blew her nose faintly, and placed on the marble table a blackish reticule that resembled her hat, trimmed in the same worn and outmoded black taffeta.

Chéri followed her movements with an exaggerated disgust, because for the past two weeks, everything that was old and female had pained him beyond reason. He thought of leaving on account of the reticule sprawled on the table, wanted to look away but didn't, arrested by a small, shimmering arabesque, an unexpected radiance affixed to the folds of the bag. His curiosity surprised him, but thirty seconds later he was still watching this shimmering point, and he had completely ceased thinking about anything whatsoever. He emerged from his stupor with an involuntary, triumphant start that allowed him to breathe and think freely again:

"I know! It's two interlaced *L*'s!"

He savored a moment of sweet respite, something that resembled the sense of security upon a safe arrival. He actually forgot the close-cropped nape, the vigorous gray hair, and the long, featureless jacket buttoned over a distended stomach, and the innocent contralto laugh, everything that had pursued him so faithfully for the past two weeks and taken away his desire to eat and the freedom of his solitude.

"It's too good to last," he thought. And he courageously regained his place in reality, looked afresh at the offending object, and said to himself without hesitation:

"The two initials in little diamond brilliants that Léa had designed, first for her suede purse, then for her pale tortoiseshell bureau set, and for her stationery!"

He didn't admit for an instant that the monogram on the bag could have stood for another name. He smiled ironically:

"A likely story! No one can tell *me* that this is chance. I come across that bag this evening, by chance, tomorrow my wife will have hired Léa's former valet, again by chance, and after that I'll no longer be able to go into a restaurant, a movie theater, or a tobacco shop without finding Léa at every turn. It's my fault, I can't complain, all I had to do was leave her alone."

He laid some small bills near his glass and stood up before summoning the barman. He turned his back to the old woman as he slipped between the two tables, pulling in his stomach like a tomcat squeezing beneath a gate, expended such reserves of restraint and skill that he barely grazed the glass of mint cordial with the edge of his jacket, said "Excuse me" in a low voice, dashed toward the glass door, toward the verge of breathable air, and, horrified and without the slightest surprise, heard someone call out:

"Chéri!"

Acquiescing to the long-anticipated shock, he turned around, recognized nothing in this slumped old woman that brought to mind a name; but he didn't try to escape for a second time, certain that everything would be explained.

"Don't you recognize me? No? But how would you recognize me? That war aged more women than it killed men, you might say. And yet I can't complain, I didn't risk losing someone, in the war . . . Eh, Chéri . . ."

She laughed, and he recognized her, realizing that what he had taken for decrepitude must have been destitution, and profound unconcern. Straightened up and laughing, she didn't seem older than her likely sixty years, and her hand, seeking Chéri's, wasn't that of a tremulous grandmother.

"The Girlfriend! . . ." Chéri murmured in an almost admiring tone.

"Then you're happy to see me?"

"Oh, yes! . . ."

He wasn't lying, reassured himself by degrees, and thought:

"It's just her . . . The poor Girlfriend . . . I was afraid . . ."

"Would you like something, Girlfriend?"

"Only a whiskey and soda, my dear. But how handsome you are still, all the same!"

He swallowed the bitter compliment, which she tossed at him from the calm edge of old age.

"And what's more, decorated," she added purely out of politeness. "Oh, I knew about it, you know! We all did."

This ambiguous plural didn't wrest a smile from Chéri, and the Girlfriend thought she had offended him.

"When I say 'we,' I'm speaking of those who were your true friends, Camille de La Berche, Léa, Rita, me . . . Mind you, Charlotte wouldn't have told me. I don't exist for her. But then you could say that she doesn't exist for me."

She laid atop the table a pale hand that had forgotten the light of day.

"You understand, Charlotte will no longer be anything more to me than the woman who succeeded in having poor little Rita arrested and held for twenty-four hours . . . Poor Rita, who never knew a word of German. I ask you, was it Rita's fault if she was Swiss?"

"I know, I know, I've heard the story," Chéri interrupted hastily.

The Girlfriend looked at him with her wide, dark, watery eyes, brimming with a habitual complicity and a constantly misplaced compassion.

"Poor kid," she sighed. "I understand you. Forgive me. Oh, you've had your calvary! . . ."

He looked at her questioningly, unaccustomed to the superlatives that provided the lugubrious richness of the Girlfriend's vocabulary, and he was afraid that she might speak to him about the war. But she wasn't thinking about the war. Perhaps she had never thought about it, because the anxiety of war infects only two successive generations. She clarified:

"Yes, I say it's a calvary to have such a mother, for a son like you, a child who has lived a life beyond reproach, before his marriage and after! A child who's quiet and everything, who hasn't passed through umpteen hands and knew how to preserve his inheritance intact!"

She shook her head, and little by little he recalled her, now burdened with the broad, ruined face of a common queen, with an old age lacking in nobility yet free from disease, who had gone through opium and with impunity left it behind, a drug merciful to whoever is unworthy of it.

"You don't smoke anymore?" Chéri asked abruptly.

She lifted her pale and poorly cared-for hand.

"You must be joking! Those foolish things are all well and good when you're not alone. In the days when I was impressing the boys, yes . . . You recall when you used to come at night? Oh, you liked that! . . . 'My dear Girlfriend,' you would say to me, 'another small pipe, well packed!' "

Without protest he received this humble flattery, like the lies of a fawning old servant. He smiled knowingly and searched in the shadows of the faded hat, on a neck encircled in black tulle, for a necklace of big, flimsy pearls . . .

In mechanical little sips he drank the whiskey that had been served to him by mistake. He didn't like hard liquor, but this evening it gave him pleasure and a readiness to smile, removed from under his fingers the roughness of unpolished surfaces and coarse fabrics, and he listened kindly to this old woman for whom the present didn't exist. They were meeting again on the other side of a meaningless era and its importunate young dead, and the Girlfriend built toward Chéri a bridge of names belonging to invincible old men, to old women hardened for battle or ossified under their final guise, to change no more. In minute detail she related a disappointment from 1913, a deceit dating from before the month of August 1914, and something in her voice quavered when she spoke of the Kid, dead—"the week of your wedding, my dear! Can you imagine the coincidence? Fate has us in its grip, you know!"—after four years of pure and peaceful friendship . . .

"We called each other names all day long, my dear, but only in front of other people. Because, you understand, it gave people the idea that we were a couple. Without the screaming matches, who would have believed it? So we went at each other . . . with the devil's own words! And people laughed: 'Oh, how passionately in love they are!' My dear, I'm going to tell you a story that will keep you glued to your seat: you know about Massau's supposed will . . ."

"What Massau?" Chéri murmured languorously.

"Come on, you know all about him! The will that he had—supposedly!—put into Louise MacMillar's hands . . . it was in 1909, and at that time I was part of Gérault's gang, his gang of 'faithful dogs,' there were five of us whom he fed in Nice, every night at La Belle Meunière, come on, we couldn't take our eyes off you on the Promenade, all in white like an English baby, and Léa all in white as well . . . Oh, what a couple! A marvel straight from the hands of the Creator! Gérault used to tease Léa: 'You're too *young*, my girl, and worse, you're too proud, I'll take you on in fifteen, twenty years . . .' And such a man had to depart this earth . . . His funeral was awash in genuine tears, the entire nation cried for him . . . And now I'll finish telling you the story of the will . . ."

A torrent of events, a tide of exhausted regrets and trivial resurrections distilled with a vocero singer's skill, washed over Chéri. He leaned toward the Girlfriend, who leaned symmetrically toward him, lowering her voice for the dramatic passages, suddenly crying out or laughing, and he saw in a mirror how much the two of them resembled the whispering couple whom they had replaced. He stood up, driven by the need to alter their appearance, and the barman mimicked his movement, but from afar, like an unobtrusive dog when its master has concluded her visit.

"Ah yes . . . ," the Girlfriend said. "Well, I'll tell you the rest another time."

"After the next war," Chéri joked. "Tell me, those two letters there . . . Yes, that monogram in little diamond brilliants . . . It's not yours, is it, Girlfriend?"

He pointed to the black bag with his index finger, holding his finger out and drawing back his body as if the bag had been alive.

"Nothing escapes you," the Girlfriend marveled. "Of course. She gave it to me, can you imagine? She told me: 'They're too feminine for me now, these bibelots.' She said: 'What on earth do you want me to do with these mirrors and powders and what have you, with my fat policeman's face?' She made me laugh . . ."

Chéri slid toward the Girlfriend the change from a hundred-franc note to interrupt her:

"For your taxi, Girlfriend."

They emerged onto the sidewalk through the service entrance, and the fading light told Chéri that night was falling.

"Don't you have your car?"

"My car? No. I walked, it does me good."

"Is your wife in the country?"

"No. Her hospital keeps her in Paris."

The Girlfriend nodded her invertebrate hat.

"I know. She's a good woman. She's been recommended for the cross, I heard it from the Baronne."

"What? . . ."

"Listen, stop that one for me, my dear, the closed one . . . And Charlotte really goes to great lengths, she knows people in Clemenceau's fold. It compensates a little for that business with Rita . . . a little, not a lot. She's as black as sin, Charlotte is, my dear!"

He shoved her into a taxi, where she merged with the shadows and ceased to exist. As soon as she stopped talking, he could no longer be certain that they had met, and he looked around him, inhaling the dust of a night that heralded a sweltering day. He believed, the way we believe in a dream, that he would wake up in his home, among the nightly watered gardens, the fragrance of Spanish honeysuckle, and the calls of birds, against the scarcely protruding hip of his young wife . . . But the Girlfriend's voice arose from the depths of the car:

"Two fourteen, avenue de Villiers! Remember my address, Chéri! And you know, I often dine at La Girafe, avenue de Wagram, if you

happen to be looking for me . . . You hear, if you happen to be looking for me . . ."

"She must be joking," Chéri thought, lengthening his step. "Look
for her? No thank you. Next time I'll make a detour if I see her."

Cooled down, rested, he walked effortlessly, and left the banks of
the river only at the Place de l'Alma, from which he returned to the
avenue Henri-Martin by taxi. A dull, coppery fire already tinted the
east and called to mind the setting of a luminous planet rather than
the dawn of a summer day. No cloud crossed the sky, but a mineral
haze, held motionless by its weight, covered Paris and soon took on
the fiery colors, the dark glow, of red-hot metal.

Because the midsummer heat at daybreak deprives the big cities and their outskirts of the watery pinks, floral mauves, and dewy
blues that bathe the open spaces where plants in their masses breathe.

Nothing stirred in the house when Chéri turned the tiny key in
the lock. The odor of the previous night's dinner still lingered in the
tiled vestibule, and cut branches of mock orange, arranged pyrami-
dally in white vases, tall enough to conceal a man, burdened the air
with an oppressive poison. An unfamiliar gray cat made its escape,
stopped on the short walkway, and stood staring at the intruder with
cold indifference.

"C'mere, little puss," Chéri called quietly.

The cat eyed him scornfully without retreating, and Chéri remembered that no animal—dog, horse, or cat—had ever accorded him
any sympathy. Across the space of fifteen years, he heard the husky
voice of Aldonza, who used to prophesy: "Those whom animals dis-
like are damned forever!" But when the cat, wide awake now, began
to bat at a small unripe chestnut with its two front paws, Chéri smiled
and headed up to the bedroom.

It was blue and dark like a night at the theater, and the dawn
didn't encroach beyond the balcony, blooming with trained roses

and pelargoniums restrained with raffia. Edmée was sleeping, her naked arms and legs on top of the light covers, lying on her side with her head inclined, a finger looped through her pearl necklace, and looking, in the half-light, more like a pensive woman than a woman who was asleep. Her frizzled hair was spread across her cheek, and Chéri couldn't hear her breathing.

"She's resting," Chéri thought. "She's dreaming of Dr. Arnaud, or the Legion of Honor, or the Royal Dutch company. She's lovely. How lovely she is! Go on, two or three more hours of sleep, and you'll see him again, your Dr. Arnaud. It hardly matters. You'll be reunited on the avenue d'Italie, in a blessed hole that stinks of carbolic acid. You'll say to him, 'Yes, Doctor, no, Doctor,' like a little girl. The two of you will look quite serious, you'll juggle ninety-nine point three and one hundred two, and in his big coal-tarred hand he'll take your little pheno-salicylic paw. You have the good fortune, my dear girl, to have a romance in your life! I won't be the one to take it away from you, you know . . . I wouldn't mind myself . . ."

Suddenly Edmée awoke, with such a brisk motion that Chéri experienced the choked feeling of a man who's been rudely cut off.

"It's you! It's you! . . . You mean, it's really you?"

"If you were expecting someone else, I apologize," Chéri said, smiling at her.

"Oh! Very clever . . ."

She sat up, threw back her hair.

"What time is it? Are you getting up? Oh no, you haven't been to bed yet . . . you're just coming in . . . Oh, Fred! What have you done this time?"

" 'This time' is a compliment . . . If you knew what I did . . ."

She was no longer in the phase where she would beseech him, her hands over her ears: "No! No! Don't say anything! Don't tell me!" But Chéri, more quickly than she, had moved beyond the innocent, malicious age of free-flowing tears and torments that would drive into his arms, at daybreak, a young wife whom he would carry away with him into a sleep of reconciled adversaries. No more tantrums . . . No more betrayals . . . No more anything but this unavowable chastity . . .

He threw his dusty shoes away from him, presented to his wife a wan face accustomed to concealing everything save his will to conceal, sat down on the bed of fine linen and lace:

"Smell me!" he said. "Well? . . . I've had some whiskey."

She brought their two lovely mouths closer together, laid her hands on her husband's shoulders.

"Some whiskey . . . ," she repeated dreamily . . . "Some whiskey . . . Why?"

A woman of less sophistication might have asked "with whom," and Chéri took note of this shrewdness. He demonstrated that he knew how to play the game by answering:

"With a girlfriend. And do you want the whole truth?"

She smiled, illuminated by the light of dawn, which was growing bolder, touching the edge of the bed, then the mirror, then a picture frame, then the gold of a fish circling within a water-filled crystal sphere:

"Not the whole truth, Fred, no! A dubious truth, a truth for an ungodly hour . . ."

Yet she was reflecting, almost certain that neither love nor base pleasure was luring Chéri away from her. She abandoned her consenting body to Chéri's arms, but on his shoulder he felt a thin, unyielding hand, tensed with circumspection.

"The truth," he continued, "is that I don't know her name. But I gave her . . . let's see . . . eighty-three francs."

"Just like that, right away? The first time you met her? It's princely."

She feigned a yawn, sank languidly into the hollow of the bed, as if she expected no response, and he briefly pitied her, until a bright horizontal ray cast in high relief the almost naked form that lay near him; then his pity disappeared.

"She—*she* is beautiful. It isn't fair."

Leaning back, she half opened her eyes and lips for him. He saw the glint of the expression—narrow, unequivocal, so little what is called feminine—that a woman directs toward a man who gives her pleasure, and it offended his unavowable chastity. Looking down at her, he replied with a different expression, secretive, complicated, the expression of the man who refuses to consent. He didn't want to draw back, and lifted only his head toward the golden daylight, the garden wet from watering, the blackbirds embroidering their vocal arabesques around the sharp, repetitive chirps of songbirds. Edmée could see on his cheek, blue with a nascent growth of beard, the traces of a protracted fatigue and a growing gauntness. She noticed his questionable, noble hands, his nails untouched by soap since the previous day, and the darkish marks, spearhead-shaped, that hollowed his lower eyelids and reemerged in the inside corners of his eyes. She judged that this beautiful, collarless, shoeless boy bore all the marks of physical decline of a man who had been arrested and had spent the night in jail. His good looks had been not ruined but diminished by a mysterious erosion whose spectacle returned to Edmée her authority. She abandoned all voluptuous enticements, sat up, placed a hand on Chéri's forehead:

"Sick?"

Slowly he drew his attention away from the garden, came back to Edmée:

"What? . . . Of course not, I'm perfectly well, just sleepy, so sleepy that I can't manage to go to bed, can you imagine . . ."

He smiled, exposing the pale inside of his lips and his thin, dry gums. But above all, as he smiled, he revealed a sadness that sought no remedy, as modest as a pauper's pain. Edmée very nearly questioned him categorically, then decided against it.

"Come to bed," she ordered, making room for him.

"Come to bed? And what about a bath? I'm as dirty as you can imagine."

He had just enough strength to seize hold of a carafe, take a swig, and throw off his jacket, then collapsed like a wall on the bed and didn't stir again, brought down by sleep.

For a long time, Edmée contemplated the half-clothed stranger, kept close to her by a narcotic stupor. Her scrutiny traveled from his blue-tinged lips to his sunken eyelids, and from his neglected hands to his forehead, sealed over a single secret. She controlled her emotions as if the sleeper might surprise her, and arranged her expression. She got up slowly, and before shutting the curtains against the dazzling window, she threw over the outstretched body a silk bedspread that, concealing a dishevelment that called to mind a burglar knocked senseless, allowed the beautiful, taut face its resplendence, and she carefully stretched the fabric over a dangling hand with a slight reverent disgust, the way she might have hidden a weapon that had perhaps found its mark.

He didn't flinch, spirited away for a few moments to an impregnable shelter; besides, the hospital had taught Edmée professional skills, not gentle but self-assured, that reached their intended target without alerting or grazing the surrounding area. She didn't return to bed, and savored, sitting down, half-naked, the unhoped-for coolness of the hour when the sun would awaken the wind. The long curtains breathed and, in rhythm with the breeze, shed greater or lesser measures of deep azure blue across Chéri's sleep.

Edmée wasn't thinking, as she looked at him, of the wounded, nor of the dead whose peasant hands she had joined over rough cotton sheets.

None among the wounded tormented by nightmares, nor among the dead, looked anything like Chéri, whom sleep, rest, silence, imbued with a singular inhumanity.

Extreme beauty arouses no sympathy, belongs to no country, and time had touched Chéri's only to make it more austere. The intellect, burdened with perfecting human splendor, while eroding it bit by bit, respected in Chéri an admirable edifice consecrated to instinct. What could love, its Machiavellianism, its calculated self-denials, and its brutalities, do against this inviolable bearer of light and his uncultivated majesty?

Endowed with patience, and often subtle, Edmée didn't realize that the feminine appetite to possess tends to emasculate all living conquests and can reduce a man, magnificent but inferior, to the role of a courtesan. Her new-lower-class good sense did not intend to renounce the luxuries—money, peace, domestic despotism, marriage—that it had secured in so short a time and whose savor had been doubled by the war.

She looked at the exhausted, silent, and seemingly forsaken body.

"That's Chéri," she repeated to herself, "yes, that's Chéri . . . How insignificant he is! . . ." She shrugged her shoulders, and added, "That's all he is, their Chéri . . . ," trying to provoke her own scorn for the prostrate man. In her memory she assembled amorous nights, exquisitely languid mornings of pleasure and sunshine, but could summon nothing more, toward this magnificent corpse under the ornate silk and the curtains' cooling wing, than a cold, vindictive homage, because he progressively despised her. She brought her hand to her small, pointed breast, set low on her slender torso, and pressed the supple fruit as if to call upon the most attractive part of her young body to bear witness to this unjust abandonment.

"What Chéri needs is undoubtedly something else . . . What he needs . . ."

But her attempts to scorn him were in vain. A woman herself loses the inclination and power to scorn a man who suffers entirely alone.

Edmée suddenly felt she had had enough of the spectacle that the shade of the curtains, the pallor of the sleeper, and the white bed were tingeing with the romantic colors of night and death. She got up in one fluid motion, alert, strong, but resistant to mounting any impassioned attack on the disordered bed, the traitor, the absent one sheltered in his sleep, in his mute and affronting pain. She was neither annoyed nor despondent, and her blood would pulse more powerfully in her breast, would rise to her pearl-white cheeks, only when she conjured the fiery redheaded man she called "my dear master" and "boss" in a serious but bantering tone. Arnaud's thick, soft hands, his laugh, and the sparks of light that the sun or the operating room lamp kindled in his red mustache, and the white coat that he wore, and even took off in the hospital, like an intimate garment that never crosses pleasure's threshold . . . Edmée stood up as if to dance:

"That, yes, that! . . ."

She shook her head and hair like a mare, and reached the bathroom without looking back.

Devoid of originality and unexceptional in size, the dining room laid claim to luxury through its yellow draperies sprinkled with crimson and green. The white-and-gray stuccowork of the walls cast too much light back onto the guests, already stripped of all shadow by the illumination that fell, unsparingly, from the ceiling.

A crystal galaxy stirred with every movement of Edmée's dress. Madame Peloux, for the family dinner, had kept on her tailored suit with leather buttons, and Camille de La Berche her nurse's veil, beneath which she looked exactly like Dante, only hairier. Because of the heat, the women were silent, but Chéri was silent out of habit. A warm bath, a cold shower, had overcome his fatigue, but the intense light, ricocheting off his cheekbones, betrayed the depressions in his cheeks, and he kept his eyes down so that the shadow of his lashes would cover his lower lids.

"Chéri looks sixteen this evening," the Baronne's deep bass boomed, apropos of nothing.

No one answered, and Chéri acknowledged her with a slight tilt of his chest.

"It's been ages," the Baronne went on, "since I've seen the oval of his face looking so thin."

Edmée frowned imperceptibly.

"I certainly have. Only during the war."

"That's true, that's true," Charlotte Peloux agreed, as shrill as a little fife. "My God, how haggard he looked in 1916, in Vesoul! My dear Edmée," she added without transition, "I saw you-know-who today, and *everything* is going very well . . ."

Edmée blushed in a submissive manner that didn't suit her, and Chéri looked up:

"Who did you see? And what's going well?"

"The pension for Trousselier, my little amputee who lost his right arm. He left the hospital on June twentieth . . . Your mother is handling his case at the Veterans' Office."

She had answered him automatically, and she rested the golden irises of her serene eyes upon him, yet he knew she was lying.

"It's about his red ribbon. After all, poor kid, it *is* his turn . . ."

She was lying to him in front of these two women, who knew that she was lying . . .

"And if I flung the carafe in the midst of all this?" Chéri thought. But he didn't stir. What passion would draw from him the strength that rouses the body, directs the hand?

"Abzac is leaving us in a week," Madame de La Berche resumed.

"It's not certain," Edmée replied somewhat brusquely. "Dr. Arnaud doesn't agree with our letting him go like that on his new leg . . . Imagine him, free to do all sorts of careless things, and the possibility of gangrene . . . Dr. Arnaud knows all too well that careless acts like that, throughout the war . . ."

Chéri looked at her, and she broke off midsentence for no reason. She fanned herself with a leafy-stemmed rose. She waved away the plate that was being passed around, and propped herself on her elbows. Dressed in white, her shoulders bare, she wasn't exempt, even in her immobility, from that secret satisfaction, that self-regard, that marked her as a type. Something offensive shone through her smooth contours. An indiscreet gleam unmasked those women who wish to improve their position in life and have not yet experienced anything but success.

"Edmée," Chéri judged, "is a woman who ought never to have passed the age of twenty. Now she's starting to resemble her mother."

The next moment, the resemblance had vanished. Nothing obvious recalled Marie-Laure in Edmée. Of the venomous beauty, red haired, white skinned, shameless, that Marie-Laure had made use of during her career like a trap, Edmée bore only one mark: shamelessness. Careful to shock no one, she was nevertheless shocking, in the manner of a too-new set of jewels or an inferior steed, to those whose nature or lack of education brought them closer to primitive wisdom. The servants and Chéri feared what they sensed in Edmée to be baser than themselves.

Given permission by Edmée, who lit a cigarette, the Baronne de La Berche laboriously lit the tip of a cigar and smoked with evident pleasure. The white veil with the red cross fell on her manly shoulders, and she was no different from the serious men who, at the end of some revelry, don Phrygian caps, usherettes' kerchiefs, and tissue-paper shakos. Charlotte defied the braided-leather buttons of her jacket, pulled the box of Abdullas toward her, and the butler, respectful of the customs of privacy, rolled within Chéri's reach a small magician's table, full of secret compartments, collapsible false bottoms, and liqueurs in silver vials. Then he withdrew from the room, and the yellow wall lost the long shadow of this white-haired old Italian with a carved-boxwood face.

"He's very distinguished, this Giacomo," the Baronne de La Berche said. "And I know a thing or two about it."

Madame Peloux shrugged her shoulders, a gesture that had long since ceased to stir her breasts. Her bosom strained against her ruffled white silk blouse; her short, dyed hair, still abundant, blazed a dark red above her large, baleful eyes and her handsome French revolutionist's forehead.

"He's as distinguished as all the old, white-haired Italians. You'd think they're all pope's chamberlains, to see them, and they can say the menu in Latin for you, and then you open a door, and you find them busy raping a little seven-year-old girl."

Chéri welcomed this venom like a timely rain shower. His mother's malice broke open the clouds, made the atmosphere bearable once more. Lately he'd been enjoying finding her unchanged from the Charlotte of old, who, from high on her balcony, would call a charming passerby a "two-bit whore," and who, in answer to Chéri's asking, "Do you know her?" would reply: "No! Really, do you think I would know her, that slut!" In a confused way, he had lately developed a taste for Charlotte's superior vitality, in a confused way he preferred her to the two other creatures who were present, but he was not aware that this preference, this partiality, was what might perhaps be called filial love. He laughed, applauded Madame Peloux for being once again, resoundingly, the woman he had known, hated, feared, abused. For a moment, in the eyes of her son, Madame Peloux took on her true character, which is to say that he judged her at her worth, appreciated her as she was, fiery, devouring, calculating, and reckless all at once, like a great financier, capable of taking delight in her cruelty like a humorist. "A scourge, no doubt," he said to himself, "but no more than that. A scourge, but not a stranger . . ." He recognized, their spikes biting into the French revolutionist's forehead, the bluish-black tips that, on his own forehead, accentuated the whiteness of his skin and the blue-black of his hair.

"That's my mother," he thought. "No one ever told me that I resemble her, but I resemble her." The "stranger" in front of him shone with a pearly luster, shrouded and white . . . Chéri heard the Duchesse de Camastra's name, uttered in the Baronne's deep voice, and he saw a fleeting fierceness flare and die on the stranger's face, like a ribbon of fire that suddenly rekindles the form of a burnt vine in the ash. But she didn't open her mouth and didn't join in the chorus of military curses that the Baronne heaped on a rival at the clinic.

"There's some business going on there over antralgesine, it seems . . . Two dead in two days under the needle. I don't think they're blameless!" Madame de La Berche said with a hearty laugh.

"You're imagining things," Edmée corrected her curtly. "It's an old story from Janson-de-Sailly that people are repeating."

"People are judged according to their deeds," Charlotte sighed indulgently. "Chéri, are you sleepy?"

He was dissolving with fatigue, and he admired the endurance of these three women, whom toil, the Parisian summer, activity, and speech didn't put out of action.

"The heat," he said laconically.

Edmée's eyes met his, but she didn't comment and didn't contradict him.

"Pooh-pooh-pooh . . . ," Charlotte sang softly. "The heat . . . Of course. Pooh-pooh-pooh . . ."

Her eyes, resting on Chéri's, overflowed with complicity, with tender blackmail. As usual, she knew everything. The whisperings of the servants, the concierges' accounts . . . Perhaps Léa herself, for the pleasure of lying in a feminine way, of prevailing one last time, had told Charlotte . . . The Baronne de La Berche let a small horsey snicker escape, and the shadow of her large churchman's nose covered the lower part of her face.

"For Christ's sake!" Chéri swore.

His chair fell behind him, and Edmée immediately stood up, ready, watchful. She didn't show the slightest surprise. Charlotte Peloux and the Baronne de La Berche placed themselves on the defensive as well, but in the old-fashioned way, their hands on their skirts as if they might need to hitch them up and flee. Chéri, leaning with both fists on the table, was breathing hard, and turning his head from side to side, like an animal trapped in a snare.

"You, to begin with, you . . . ," he stammered.

He stretched out his arm toward Charlotte, who had seen this many times before and whom the filial threat, in front of witnesses, galvanized.

"What? What? What?" she barked in little yips. "You want to insult me? A little wretch, a little wretch who, if I wanted to talk . . ."

The crystalware quivered at the sound of her shrill voice, but a voice still more piercing cut her off:

"Leave him alone!" Edmée cried.

The silence seemed deafening after three such brief outbursts, and Chéri, having regained his natural poise, made an effort, smiled, covered in a greenish pallor.

"Forgive me, Ma'am Peloux," he said playfully.

She was already blessing him with her eyes and gestures, like a champion at rest at the end of a round.

"Oh, you're quick tempered!"

"He's a warrior," the Baronne said, squeezing Edmée's hand. "I'll say good night. Chéri, my digs await."

She declined a seat in Charlotte's car and intended to return home on foot. Along the avenue Henri-Martin, her tall stature, her white nurse's veil, and her lit cigar would strip the most brazen prowlers of their courage in the dark. Edmée followed the two old women as far as the threshold, a rare courtesy that allowed Chéri to take the measure of his wife's wariness, and her peaceable diplomacy.

He drank a glass of cold water in slow sips, and reflected, standing under a cataract of light, savoring his unbearable loneliness.

"She defended me," he repeated. "She defended me without love. She defended me as she would defend the garden against the blackbirds, her stock of sugar against plundering nurses, her wine against the servants. She probably knows that I went to the rue Raynouard, that I came back, and that I haven't returned there. She hasn't said a word to me about it, and perhaps it doesn't matter to her. She defended me because my mother ought not to have spoken . . . She defended me without love."

He heard Edmée's voice in the garden. From a distance, she tested Chéri's mood.

"Do you want to go up right away, Fred? You don't feel unwell?"

She stretched her head through the half-open door, and he laughed bitterly to himself:

"She's so careful . . ."

She saw his smile and became bolder.

"Come on, Fred. I think I'm almost as weary as you are. The proof is that I lost control of myself a little while ago . . . but I've just apologized to your mother."

She switched off some of the harsh lighting, collected some roses from the tablecloth, and thrust them into water. Her body, her hands, the roses, her inclined head enveloped in a mist of hair whose frizzliness had been diminished somewhat by the heat, everything about her was capable of enchanting a man.

"I said 'a man.' I didn't say 'any man,' " Léa's voice repeated insidiously in Chéri's ears . . .

"I can do anything to her," he thought, following Edmée with his eyes. "She will not complain, she will not divorce me, I have nothing to fear from her, not even love. My happiness is entirely in my own hands."

But at the same time, he shrank with an unutterable repugnance from the idea of living, as a couple, in a sphere that was not governed by love. His bastard childhood, his long adolescence under trusteeship, had taught him that in a world thought to be without restraint, a code almost as narrow as bourgeois prejudice held sway. Chéri had learned there that love was about money, betrayal, sin, and cowardly acquiescence. But he was now on the way to forgetting the old rules and rejecting the unspoken condescensions. So he let slip from his sleeve the gentle hand that rested there. And since he was walking at Edmée's side toward the bedroom, which would witness neither kisses nor reproaches, he felt himself filled with shame, and he blushed at their monstrous understanding.

He found himself outside, and dressed for the street, almost unaware that he had put on a light raincoat and fedora. He was leaving the salon behind him, hazy with suspended smoke, the strong fragrance of women and flowers, the hydrocyanic odor of cherry brandy. He was leaving Edmée, Dr. Arnaud, Filipesco, Atkins, and the Kelekians, two young society women who, having volunteered as truck drivers during the war, no longer cared for anything but cigars, cars, and the camaraderie of garages. He was abandoning Desmond to the company of a real estate agent and an undersecretary of state at the Ministry of Commerce, an amputee-poet, and Charlotte Peloux. A fashionable young couple, no doubt specially apprised, had dined primly but greedily, with knowing expressions and a naive but scandalized avidity that seemed to expect Chéri to dance stark naked, or Charlotte and the undersecretary of state to couple like animals on the salon carpet.

Chéri stole away, conscious of having acted stoically, guilty of no other offense than a sudden loss of connection with the present, an annoying indifference during the course of the meal. Yet this torpor had lasted for only a moment, incalculable as a dream. Now, he was moving away from all these strangers who filled his house, and his footsteps on the sand made the soft sound of nimble paws. The silver-gray color of his coat made him indistinguishable from the fog that had descended on the Bois, and two or three late-night strollers would have envied this hurried young man who had nowhere in particular to go.

The image of his crowded house hounded him. He could still hear the sound of voices, he brought away with him the memory of faces and laughter, and particularly of the shapes of mouths. An elderly man had spoken of war, a woman of politics. He remembered, too, the new understanding between Desmond and Edmée and the interest his wife took in a housing development . . . "Desmond . . . what a husband for my wife . . ." And then, the dancing . . . Charlotte Peloux taking it into her head to tango . . . Chéri quickened his step.

A humid early-fall night enveloped the full moon in a haze. A large milky halo, encircled by a pale rainbow, took the orb's place, disappearing from time to time, obscured behind puffs of scudding clouds. The scent of September arose from the leaves fallen in the midsummer heat.

"It's mild out," Chéri thought.

A bench accommodated his weariness, but he didn't stop for long, joined by an invisible companion whom he denied, on the bench, its seat. A companion with gray hair and a long jacket, whose implacable gaiety rang out . . . Chéri turned his head toward the gardens of La Muette, as if he could hear the jazz band's cymbals from this distance.

The time had not yet come to return to the blue bedroom, where perhaps the two young women of the highest society were still smoking cigars, sitting perched sidesaddle on the blue velvet of the bed, and amusing the real estate agent with supply-truck anecdotes.

"Ah, a good hotel room, a good pink room, very ordinary and very pink . . ." But wouldn't it lose its ordinariness when, after the lamp had been switched off, the utter darkness permitted the entry, lumbering but lighthearted, of the long, featureless jacket and thick gray hair? He smiled at the intruder, because he had passed the stage of fear: "There or elsewhere . . . *she*, too, will remain faithful. But I no longer wish to live with these people."

Day by day, hour by hour, he was becoming more contemptuous, and rigoristic. He already had a harsh opinion of the back-page heroes, and the young war widows who were clamoring for new husbands, like burn victims for cool water. His adamancy extended to the realm of money, though he was unaware of so serious a change. "During dinner, that scheme involving the boatloads of unprocessed hides . . . What a disgusting mess! And they talk about all that aloud . . ." But nothing in the world would have brought him to reveal, by publicly protesting, that he was becoming one of those who no longer have anything in common with their fellow creatures. Wary, he kept silent about it, like all the rest. When he accused her of selling off a few tons of sugar in a questionable manner, hadn't Charlotte Peloux reminded him, in very clear terms, of the time that Chéri, in a tone of cavalier expropriation, had asked: "Léa, give me five gold louis so that I can go get some cigarettes . . ."

"Ah," he sighed, "these women will never understand anything! . . . It's not the same thing . . ."

He was daydreaming like this, his head bare and his hair damp, almost insubstantial in the fog. A womanly shadow passed close by him, running. The rhythm of her footfalls, the scratching sound of her feet biting into the gravel, told of impatience, anxiety, and the shadow of the woman threw itself onto the shadow of a man who came to meet her, collapsed against it, chest to chest, as if shot.

"Those two are hiding," Chéri thought. "Who are they deceiving? Everyone deceives. But I . . ." He didn't finish, but he started to his feet with a repugnance that profoundly signified: "*I* am pure." A vague illumination, falling on stagnant and previously imperceptible regions within him, was beginning to teach him that purity and loneliness are one and the same curse.

The night was advancing, and he felt cold. From his long spells of purposeless wakefulness, he was learning that the night's pungency changes with each successive moment, and that midnight is mild in comparison with the hour that comes just before the dawn.

"Winter will come quickly," he thought, lengthening his step. "It's about time we be done with this interminable summer. Next winter, I want . . . Let's see, next winter . . ." His exploratory effort faltered almost immediately, and he stopped, head lowered, like a horse that sees a hill in the distance.

"Next winter, there will still be my wife, my mother, old mother La Berche, what's-her-name, what-d'you-call-him, and so-and-so. There will be this whole world . . . And there will never again be anything for me."

He stopped to watch the progress, over the Bois, of a throng of low clouds, colored an elusive pink, which a gust of wind brought down, grasped by their wispy manes of mist, twisted, dragged across the lawn, before abducting them to the moon . . . Chéri gazed familiarly at the luminous display of the night, which those who sleep believe to be black.

The appearance, half-veiled, of the large, flat disk of the moon among fleeting vapors, which it seemed to chase and cleave, didn't divert him from an arithmetic digression: he was adding up, in years, in months, days, and hours, a precious time forever lost.

"If, on the day I went to see her again, before the war, I hadn't let her go, that's three, four good years, hundreds, hundreds of days and nights, that would have been saved, put aside for love . . ." So strong a word did not make him flinch.

"Hundreds of days, a lifetime—life. Life as before, life with my worst enemy, as she used to say . . . My worst enemy, who forgave me everything and let me get away with nothing . . ." He wrung his past, squeezed out the remaining juices onto the desert of his present, resurrected, inventing if necessary, his princely adolescence, shaped, guided, by the two large, strong hands of a woman, loving, prepared to punish. A long, protected, Oriental adolescence, in which the pleasures of the flesh flowed like the silences in a song . . . Indulgence, passing fancies, childish cruelties, unconscious loyalty . . . He threw his head back toward the nacreous halo that filled the top of the sky and silently cried: "Everything's ruined! I'm thirty years old!"

He hurried home, cursing himself to the brisk rhythm of his steps: "Fool! The worst part isn't her age, it's mine. For her, it's probably all over, but for me . . ."

He soundlessly unlocked his finally silent house and again confronted, with a sick feeling, the stench of those who had drunk, eaten, and danced there. The mirror in the vestibule, on the back of the door, again brought him face-to-face with a gaunt young man with severe cheekbones, beautiful sad lips tinged blue by a faint growth of black hair, large, tragic, reticent eyes—in a word, a young man who was no longer, inexplicably, twenty-four years old.

"For me," Chéri concluded, "I believe that everything has been said."

"You understand, what I would need is a quiet place . . . Nothing much, a bachelor apartment, a pied-à-terre . . ."

"I'm not a child," the Girlfriend reproached him.

She raised her inconsolable eyes toward the garlanded ceiling.

"A little fantasy, good Lord, a little romance and cuddling for a man's wretched heart . . . How well I understand what you're saying! And you have no preference?"

Chéri frowned.

"Preference? For whom?"

"You misunderstand me, my dear child . . . Preference as to neighborhood?"

"Oh . . . No, I have no preference. A quiet place."

The Girlfriend nodded her large, knowing head.

"I see, I see. Something along my lines, a bit like my apartment. Do you know where I live?"

"Yes . . ."

"No, you have no idea. I was sure you wouldn't write it down. Two fourteen, avenue de Villiers. It's neither beautiful nor big. But you don't look for a bachelor apartment to be noticed."

"No."

"I found mine thanks to a scheme with my landlady. A gem of a woman, by the way, married or all but. A creature with periwinkle-blue eyes, but fate has left its mark on her forehead, and in her cards I've already seen that she used to abuse everything and that . . ."

"Yes. You told me just a moment ago that you knew of a pied-à-terre . . ."

"A pied-à-terre, yes, but it's unworthy of you."

"Do you really think so?"

"Of you . . . of the two of you!"

The Girlfriend sank her suggestive laugh in a whiskey whose smell of wet bridle leather bothered Chéri. He tolerated her joking about imaginary good fortune because on her grainy neck he saw a string of large hollow pearls that he thought he recognized. Every unspoiled trace of the past immobilized him along a path that he was gradually descending, and during these pauses, he would rest.

"Ah," the Girlfriend sighed, "I'd like to gaze at her in passing! What a couple! . . . I don't know her, but I can see the two of you together! . . . Naturally, you'd like to choose the furniture yourself?"

"For whom?"

"I mean for your apartment, of course!"

Puzzled, he looked at the Girlfriend. Furniture . . . What furniture? He had imagined only one thing: having a retreat whose door would open and close for him alone, in a place unknown to Edmée, to Charlotte, to everyone . . .

"Will you furnish it in antiques, or modern furniture? La Belle Serrano covered her first floor in nothing but Spanish shawls, but that's an eccentricity. The fact is, you're old enough to know what you want . . ."

He was hardly listening to her, commandeered by the effort of imagining a future dwelling, secret, cramped, hot, and dark. Meanwhile, he was drinking red currant syrup like a young girl from a bygone era, in the reddish, old-fashioned, unvarying bar, unchanged from the days when Chéri, as a little boy, had sucked his first soft drinks from the end of a straw . . . The barman himself hadn't changed, and if the woman sitting across from Chéri was a faded beauty, at least he had never known her when she was beautiful, or young . . .

"My mother, my wife, the people they see, their whole world changes, and exists to change . . . My mother can become a banker, and Edmée a city councilor. But I . . ."

He hastened to return, in his thoughts, to that future refuge, located at some unknown point in space, but secret, cramped, hot, and . . .

"For me, it's Algerian," the Girlfriend continued. "It's no longer fashionable, but I don't care, especially since it's on loan. I've put up some pictures that you would surely know, and then the portrait of the Kid . . . Come visit, I'd be delighted."

"I'm happy to. Let's go!"

From the front door, he called a taxi.

"But don't you ever have your car? Why don't you have your car? It's really quite extraordinary that people who have a car never have their car!"

She gathered her faded black skirt, pinched the cord of her lorgnette in the clasp of her bag, dropped a glove, and shamelessly suffered the stares of passersby. Beside her, Chéri was subjected to insulting smiles and the commiserative admiration of a young woman who cried out: "Lord, such a waste of a good thing!"

Patient, drowsy, he endured the old woman's chattering in the car. Besides, she told him sweet stories, the one about the little two-pound dog that brought the return trip from the races to a standstill in 1897, the one about old mother La Berche carrying off a young bride, on the day of her marriage, in 1893 . . .

"There it is. Open the car door for me, Chéri, I can't budge it. I'm warning you, the vestibule isn't very bright, and neither is the entrance, as you see . . . But it's a ground-floor apartment, isn't it . . . Stay there a second . . ."

Standing in the darkness, he waited. He listened to the sound of a jumble of keys, the old, wheezy creature's huffing and puffing, her voice like a busy servant's.

"I'm turning on a light . . . What's more, you're going to find yourself among familiar faces. Of course, I have electricity . . . This is my morning room, which is at the same time my drawing room."

He went in, out of kindness blindly praised a low room with vaguely garnet-colored walls blackened by the smoke of innumerable cigars and cigarettes. Instinctively he sought the window, blocked with shutters and curtains . . .

"You can't see in here? You're not an old night owl like your Girl-friend . . . Hang on, I'll turn on the ceiling light."

"Don't go to the trouble . . . I'm just popping in and . . ."

When he turned to the most brightly lit wall, covered in small frames and photographs pierced at their four corners with thumbtacks, he fell silent, and the Girlfriend began to laugh.

"I *told* you that you'd be among familiar faces! I was sure it would delight you. You don't have that one?"

"That one" was a very large photographic portrait, retouched in now-faint watercolors. Blue eyes, a laughing mouth, a blond chignon, a look of serene, well-defended triumph . . . High waisted in a First Empire corselette, legs visible beneath the gauze, legs that never ended, thighs well rounded, slender at the knee, legs . . . And a café singer's hat, a hat that had only a single bit of brim turned up, stretched like a single sail to the wind . . .

"She didn't give you that one, I gather? A goddess, a fairy, up above us! She walks on clouds! And how very like her it is, all the same! That big photo is the most beautiful, to my mind, but I'm just as attached to others—here, for example, this little one, which is much more recent, isn't it a feast for the eyes?"

A snapshot, fastened with a rusted pin, showed a dark woman against a bright garden . . .

"It's the navy-blue dress and the hat with the seagulls," Chéri said to himself.

"I prefer flattering portraits, myself," the Girlfriend went on. "A portrait like that one, come on, in all conscience, doesn't it make you want to clasp your hands together and believe in God?"

A crude, saccharine artistry had polished up the elegant "portrait card," lengthened the neck, slightly narrowed the sitter's mouth. But the nose, just aquiline enough, the lovely nose and its masterful nostrils, the chaste fold, the velvety furrow that carved into the upper lip just under the nose, remained untouched, genuine, respected by the photographer himself . . .

"Can you believe that she wanted to burn everything, on the pretext that no one is interested anymore in knowing how she used to be? My blood rebelled, I let out hellish cries, she gave them all to me, the same day she gave me the reticule with her monogram as a gift . . ."

"Who's that, that guy there, with her?"

"What? What did you say? What is it? . . . Wait till I set down my hat . . ."

"I'm asking who that is, the guy there . . . Hurry it up, come on now . . ."

"Good Lord, but you're rushing me . . . There? That's Bacciocchi, come on! Of course, you'd hardly be able to recognize him, he dates from two go-rounds before you."

"Two what?"

"After Bacciocchi, she had Septfons, and, no, wait, Septfons was before . . . Septfons, Bacciocchi, Spéleïeff, and you. Look at those checked pants . . . It's comical, those men's fashions from the old days."

"And that photo there, when was that?"

He took a step away, because the Girlfriend was leaning over, close to him, her bare head and matted crow's nest of hair smelling like a wig.

"That, that's her outfit at Drags in . . . in eighteen eighty-eight or -nine. Yes, the year of the Exposition. You've got to take your hat off to that one, my dear. They don't make beauties like that anymore."

"Bah . . . I don't find her so breathtaking . . ."

The Girlfriend clasped her hands. Without her hat, she looked older, her hair tinted a green-black above her bare, butter-colored forehead.

"Not breathtaking! That waist that you could hold in your ten fingers! That dove's neck! And just look at the dress! All in sky silk chiffon hemmed with ribbon, my dear, and strings of button roses stitched onto the ribbons, and the matching hat! And the little alms purse matching, too, we used to call that an alms purse . . . Oh, such beauty! We haven't seen debuts like hers since, she was the dawn, the sun of love itself!"

"Debuts where?"

She gave Chéri a gentle poke.

"Come on! . . . How you make me laugh! Oh, life's sorrows must be rosy, around you! . . ."

Turned toward the wall, he could hide his rigid face. He still seemed to be absorbed in a few Léas, one smelling an artificial rose, another bent over a book with a Gothic-style clasp, and revealing a wide nape, a stand-up collar, round and white, like the bole of a birch.

"Well, I'll be off," he said, like Valérie Cheniaguine.

"What, you're going? What about my dining room? What about my bedroom? Take a quick look, my dear child? Make mental notes, for your bachelor apartment?"

"Ah! Yes . . . Listen, not today, because . . ."

He cast a suspicious glance at the rampart of portraits and lowered his voice.

"I have an appointment. But I'll come back . . . tomorrow. Probably tomorrow, before dinner."

"Good. So I can proceed?"

"Proceed?"

"With the apartment?"

"Yes. Right. Let's wait and see. And thank you."

"My word, I wonder what sort of times we're living in . . . The young, the old, each tries to be the most disgusting . . . Two 'go-rounds' before me . . . And debuts, this old spider says, dazzling debuts! . . . All of this out in the open—no, really, what a world . . ."

He noticed that he was maintaining the pace of a foot racer in training, and that he was getting short of breath. Moreover, a thunderstorm, far off and destined not to break over Paris, was holding back the northerly wind behind a purple wall, erect against the sky. On the fortifications along the boulevard Berthier, under trees stripped bare by the summer, a sparse crowd of Parisians in espadrilles and half-naked children in red jerseys seemed to expect that a flood tide would come rushing from Levallois-Perret. Chéri sat down on a bench, unaware that his strength, mysteriously depleted by the dissipations of his sleepless nights and by his failure to limber and feed his body, was now quick to forsake him.

"Two go-rounds! Really! Two go-rounds before me! And how many since? And adding them all together, including me, how many go-rounds?"

He could picture, beside a Léa dressed in blue, wearing the seagull hat, a tall, substantial Spéleïeff, beaming broadly. From his boyhood, he remembered a sad Léa, red with tears, who stroked his hair, calling him "nasty man-to-be" . . .

Léa's lover . . . Léa's new crush . . . Conventional, insignificant words, as ordinary as the weather forecasts, the odds at Auteuil, the servants' thefts. "Are you coming, kid?" Spéleïeff would say to Chéri. "We'll go for a port at Armenonville while we wait for Léa to catch up with us, I can't pull her out of bed this morning . . ."

"She has a gorgeous new little Bacciocchi!" Madame Peloux announced to her son, then fourteen or fifteen years old . . .

But, at once corrupt and pure, accustomed to the ways of love, blinded by the commonplace that love was, Chéri spoke love's language, in those days, in the manner of children who learned all a language's words, sweet or smutty, as pure music, stripped of their origins. No vibrant, voluptuous image rose up in the shadow of this great Spéleïeff, barely risen from Léa's bed. And this "gorgeous little Bacciocchi"—what difference was there between him and a "magnificent Pekingese"?

No photographs, no letters, no stories fallen from the only lips that would have told the truth, nothing had ever encroached on the intimate earthly paradise in which Léa and Chéri had lived together for years. Almost nothing of Chéri's predated Léa; why would he have concerned himself with what, before him, had nurtured or grieved his mistress or made her rich?

A blond little boy with fat knees rested his crossed arms on the bench next to Chéri. They looked at each other with identical expressions of offended reserve, because Chéri treated all children as strangers. The child fixed his pale blue eyes on Chéri's for a long time, and Chéri saw an indescribable sort of smile, full of scorn, rise from the small, anemic mouth to the blue-flax-colored eyes. Then the child turned away, retrieved his soiled toys from the dust, and began to play at the foot of the bench, excluding Chéri from his world, so Chéri stood up and left.

A half hour later he was lying in lukewarm, fragrant water clouded by a milky perfume, and he was taking pleasure in the luxury and sense of well-being, the unctuous soap, the soothing sounds of the house, as if he had earned them through tremendous courage or were savoring them for the final time.

His wife came in, humming, stopped humming when she saw him and did not succeed in hiding her wordless surprise at finding Chéri in his own home, in his terry bathrobe. He asked her without irony:

"Am I bothering you?"

"Not at all, Fred."

She took off her day clothes with a youthful unconstraint, remote from both modesty and immodesty, with a rush toward nakedness and water that entertained Chéri.

"How I had forgotten her," he thought as he looked at the supple, submissively curved back, its sharp edges hidden, of the woman leaning down to untie her shoe.

She didn't speak to him, behaved with the security of a woman who thinks she's alone, and he pictured the child in the dust who, only a little while ago, had played at his feet, determined not to see him.

"Tell me . . ."

Edmée raised a surprised face, a smooth, half-naked body.

"What would you say if we were to have a child?"

"Fred! . . . What are you thinking!"

It was almost a cry of terror, and Edmée held some article of closely woven lawn against her breast now with one hand, while her other hand groped for the first kimono within reach. Chéri couldn't help laughing.

"Do you want my revolver? . . . I won't attack you, you know."

"Why are you laughing?" she asked quietly. "You should never laugh . . ."

"I rarely laugh. But explain to me—we're so peaceful, now, the two of us—explain to me . . . Is it so dreadful, for you, this idea that we could have had, that we could have, a child?"

"Yes," she said cruelly, and her unexpected frankness seemed to wound even herself.

She didn't take her eyes off her husband, lying flopped in a low armchair, and murmured distinctly, to be sure he would hear:

"A child . . . So that it would resemble you . . . Two times you, two times you in a woman's single lifetime? . . . No . . . Oh no! . . ."

He began to make a gesture that she mistook.

"No, please . . . That's all. I won't say another word. Let's leave things as they were. We have only to pay a little attention, and carry on . . . I don't ask anything of you."

"That suits you?"

She answered only with a look that befitted her trapped nakedness, a look full of insulting helplessness and pitiful complaint. Her freshly powdered cheek, her red, youthful lips, the faint brown halo around her brown eyes, the discreet, polished affectation of her whole face, brought out by contrast the disarray of her body, naked save for the crumpled silk undergarment that she clutched to her breasts.

"I can no longer make her happy," Chéri thought, "but I can still make her suffer. She's not completely unfaithful to me. While I, who do not deceive her, I have abandoned her."

With her back to him, Edmée put on her clothes. She had regained her freedom of movement, her deceitful tolerance. A dress of a very pale pink now hid the woman who had so firmly pressed her last veil against her breast, as though against a wound.

She had recovered her elastic resolve, the desire to live, to govern, the prodigious female aptitude for happiness. Once more Chéri despised her, but there came a moment when the evening light, passing through her sheer dress, delineated the form of a young wife who no longer resembled the naked victim, a form striving toward the heavens, powerful and rounded like a serpent ready to strike.

"I can still hurt her, but how quickly she recovers . . . Here, too, I am neither necessary nor expected . . . She has moved beyond me, and gone elsewhere, I was, as the old woman would say, her first go-round . . . It would be up to me to imitate her, if I could. But I can't. And yet, would I want to, if I could? Edmée hasn't stumbled across what a person finds only once and remains forever stunned by . . . Spéleïeff used to say that after a particular fall that had nevertheless cost them no limbs, there were horses that you would put down before a fence rather than make them jump . . . I have met the deadly fence . . ."

He searched for other slightly brutal comparisons to sport that would have likened his downfall and his pain to an accident. But his night, which had begun too early, and his exhausted dreams, were visited by sweet pictures of sky-blue ribbons and the recollections owed to immortal literature that crossed the well-trodden thresholds of the abodes of love, verse and prose devoted to constancy, to lovers whom death could never tear asunder, verse and prose from which jaded courtesans and adolescents drew, equal in their credulity and rapture . . .

"So she said to me, 'I know where the attack is coming from, it's Charlotte who's causing me trouble again . . .' 'That's what you get,' I told her, 'you just have to stop associating with Charlotte the way you do, and not confide everything to her.' She answered: 'I'm more accustomed to Charlotte than to Spéleïeff, and have been so for longer. I assure you that I'd miss Charlotte, Neuilly, bezique, and the boy more than I would Spéleïeff, you can't change the way you are.' 'Nevertheless,' I told her, 'your trust in Charlotte will cost you dearly.' 'Oh, well,' she said to me, 'the good stuff always costs more.' That's just like her, always noble and generous, but not a dupe. And with that, she went to put on her dress for the races, she told me she was going to the races with a gigolo . . ."

"With me!" Chéri cried sourly. "Perhaps I remember it?"

"I don't dispute that. I'm telling you things the way they happened. A white dress, in white silk de Chine, exotic, with a border of clear blue Chinese embroidery, the same dress that you see here in the picture taken at the races. And nothing will get it out of my head that the man's shoulder that you see behind her, that's you."

"Bring it to me," Chéri ordered.

The old woman got up, pulled out the rusted thumbtacks that pinned the photograph to the wall, and brought it to Chéri. Lying back on the Algerian divan, he lifted his disheveled head and only glanced at the snapshot, which he threw across the room . . .

"Have you ever seen me wearing collars that gape at the back, and a morning coat to go to the races? Come now, that's something else altogether! That doesn't amuse me."

She made a "tt! tt!" of halfhearted disapproval, bent her stiff knees to pick up the card, and opened the door that led to the vestibule.

"Where are you going?" Chéri called.

"The water for my coffee is boiling, I can hear it. I'm going to pour it out."

"OK. But come back after!"

She disappeared in a swish of threadbare taffetas and heelless slippers. Alone, Chéri laid his neck against the Tunisian-patterned moquette cushion. A dazzling new Japanese robe, embroidered with pink wisteria on an amethyst-colored background, had supplanted his jacket and vest. A cigarette, smoked too long, was parching his lips, and the fan of his hair, touching his eyebrows, half covered his face.

He presented no ambiguity on account of the feminine garment or the embroidered flowers; but an ignominious sovereignty conferred on all his features their true worth. He seemed to seethe with the need to damage and destroy, and the photograph thrown by his hand had flown like a blade. Harsh, delicate bones shifted in his cheeks with the rhythmic tensing of his jaws. The black-and-white light of his eyes played across the darkness the way the crest of a wave, at night, will beckon and reflect the moon's beam . . .

But when he was alone he pressed his head heavily into the cushion and closed his eyes.

"Lord!" the Girlfriend exclaimed when she returned. "You won't be any more beautiful when you're dead! I have fresh coffee. Would you like some? It has an aroma that will transport you to blissful isles . . ."

"Yes. Two lumps."

He spoke to her curtly, and she obeyed with a sweetness that perhaps concealed a deep delight in servitude.

"You didn't eat much for dinner?"

"I had enough to eat."

He drank his coffee without getting up, propped on one elbow. An Oriental portiere, draped to form a canopy, fell from the ceiling above the divan, sheltering a Chéri of ivory, enamel, and precious silk, lying on an old short-piled wool rug dulled with dust.

On a copper table, the Girlfriend laid out the coffee, an opium lamp topped with its glass cap, two pipes, the paste pot, the silver snuffbox for cocaine, a vial whose firmly driven stopper didn't entirely check the ether's cold and treacherous expansion. To this she added a tarot game, a poker game case, a pair of eyeglasses, and then sat down with the solemnity of a nurse.

"I've already told you," Chéri muttered, "that all this paraphernalia doesn't interest me."

She protested, stretching out her two sickeningly white hands. At home, she adopted, she said, a "Charlotte Corday style," her hair loose, big fichus of white lawn crossed over her dusty mourning, the whole, at once dignified and demeaned, resembling many a heroine of the Salpêtrière.

"That's fine, Chéri. It's just in case. And I'm so happy to see my whole kit here, beneath my eyes, all in order. The arsenal of dreams! The munitions of delirium, the door of illusion!"

She nodded her long head, looked up at the ceiling with the compassionate eyes of a grandmother who bankrupts herself on playthings. But her guest didn't touch any philter. A sort of physical respectability endured in him, and his disdain for drugs echoed his disgust for brothels.

For a number of days he'd lost count of, he had daily come to this black hole, where this enslaved Fate kept watch. He gave the Girlfriend money, with neither good grace nor debate, for her meals, coffee, and liqueurs, and for his personal supply of cigarettes, ice, fruit, and flavored syrups. He had entrusted his helot with purchasing the sumptuous Japanese garment, perfumes, fine soaps. Less greedy than drunk with complicity, she devoted herself to Chéri with a zeal reminiscent of her proselytism of old, the indulgent and culpable eagerness that would undress and bathe the virgin, cook the pearl of opium, pour out alcohol or ether. A frustrated evangelism, because the strange guest brought along no females, drank fruit sodas, stretched out on the old divan, and commanded only:

"Speak."

She spoke, and believed she was speaking as she pleased. But it was he who controlled, sometimes brutally, sometimes subtly, the slow and muddy flow of memories. She spoke like a dressmaker paid by the day, with the persistence, the intoxicating monotony, of women who devote themselves to long, motionless tasks. But she never sewed, and in this respect betrayed the aristocratic negligence of a former prostitute. As she spoke, she would pin a pleat over a hole or a stain, and return to a hand of tarot or patience. She would slip on gloves to grind the coffee bought by the cleaning woman, but handled cards darkened by a glaze of filth without disgust.

She spoke, and Chéri listened to her anesthetic voice, the sound of her felted, shuffling feet. In the chaotic retreat, he reclined in his magnificent robe. His protector didn't dare to question him. His total abstention was enough for her to recognize his monomania. She was in service to a mysterious sickness, but a sickness nonetheless. Just in case, and as if wishing to neglect no detail, she invited a very pretty young woman, childlike and cheerful in her professional demeanor. Chéri paid her no more and no less attention than he would have a little dog, and said to the Girlfriend:

"Are we done with these fashionable gatherings?"

She didn't ask to be scolded a second time, and he never felt the need to demand her secrecy. One day, she came close to the obvious truth and suggested to Chéri the company of two or three friends from the old days, for instance Léa . . . He didn't bat an eye:

"No one. Or I'll find myself somewhere else to go."

Two weeks passed, as funereal and ordered as monastic life, which didn't weigh on either of the two recluses. During the day, the Girlfriend engaged in the frivolous pursuits of an old woman, poker games and whiskeys, clandestine gambling dens, vicious chitchat, provincial luncheons in the stifling darkness of a Limousin or Normandy tavern . . . Chéri would arrive with the first shadows of evening, sometimes soaked with rain. She recognized the slamming of the taxi door, and no longer asked: "But why don't you ever have your car?"

He would leave after midnight, usually before dawn. During his long interludes on the Algerian divan, the Girlfriend sometimes saw him succumb to sleep, remain caught there as if in a trap, his neck twisted onto his shoulder, motionless for a few moments. She wouldn't sleep until after he had left, having forgotten the need for rest. Early one morning when, calmly, bit by bit, he collected the contents of his pockets—the key and its chain, his billfold, the flat little revolver, his handkerchief, and his gold-alloy cigarette case—she ventured to ask:

"Your wife doesn't request explanations when you come in so late?"

Chéri raised his long eyebrows above eyes grown wide with insomnia.

"No. Why? She knows perfectly well that I'm not doing anything wrong."

"A child certainly couldn't be more rational than you are . . . Are you coming this evening?"

"I don't know. I'll see. Act as though I'm coming for sure."

He fixed his eyes once more on all the blond napes, all the blue eyes, that decorated one wall of his sanctuary, and left, to return faithfully some twelve hours later.

———————

When, in a roundabout way that he deemed clever, he had led the Girlfriend to speak about Léa, he would clear the account of the smutty dross that slowed it down. "Skip, skip . . ." He would scarcely utter the word whose sibilant *s* alone interrupted and lashed the monologue. He wanted to hear only reminiscences free from venom, purely descriptive glorifications . . . From the chronicler he demanded a documentary respect for the truth, and would reprimand her bad-temperedly. In his memory he would take note of dates, colors, names of fabrics, towns, dressmakers.

"What's poplin?" he would ask, out of the blue.

"Poplin? It's a fabric of silk and wool, with a dry hand, you know, that doesn't cling . . ."

"Yes. And mohair? You said 'of white mohair.' "

"Mohair is like alpaca, with better drape, you see? Léa couldn't stand lawn in the summer, she claimed that it was good for underclothes and handkerchiefs . . . She had queenly underclothes, you remember, and at the time that picture was taken . . . yes, the beauty with the long legs . . . we didn't wear plain underclothes the way they do today. It was ruching and more ruching, a froth, a bit of snow, and bloomers, my dear, that would make you dizzy, the sides in white Chantilly, the middle in black Chantilly, you can imagine the effect! . . . Can you imagine it?"

"Sickening," Chéri thought. "Sickening. The middle in black Chantilly. A woman doesn't wear black Chantilly in the middle for herself alone. She wore that in front of whom? For whom?"

He could picture Léa's gesture when he would come into the bathroom or boudoir, the furtive gesture of folding her gandoura across her body. He could picture the chaste confidence of her rosy body, naked in her bath, reassured by the milky water clouded with an essential oil . . .

"But for others, bloomers in Chantilly . . ."

With a kick of his foot, he pushed one of the straw-stuffed moquette cushions to the floor.

"Are you too warm, Chéri?"

"No. Give me that photograph for a minute, the big one, in the frame . . . Turn the whatchamacallit on your table lamp. More . . . there!"

Shedding his habitual wariness, with his sharp eye he studied details that were new and almost refreshing to him.

"A high belt, with cameos . . . Never saw that on her. And old-fashioned buskins. She had tights? No, of course not, her toes are bare. Sickening . . ."

"Whose house did she wear this outfit to?" he asked.

"I don't rightly know anymore . . . An evening at the club, I think . . . Or at Molier's . . ."

He handed back the frame, at arm's length, outwardly disdainful and annoyed. He went off shortly after, under a still-impenetrable sky, into a night that smelled of woodsmoke and washhouses as it drew to a close.

He was changing noticeably and hardly realized it. By eating and sleeping little, walking and smoking a great deal, he was losing weight, exchanging his apparent vigor for an airiness, a false rejuvenation, that the light of day refuted. At home, he lived as he pleased, welcoming or fleeing from invited guests, from passing visitors who knew nothing of him but his name, his gradually petrifying beauty, seemingly corrected by an accusing chisel, and the unthinkable ease with which he ignored them.

Thus he bore, up to the last days of October, his serene and bureaucratic despair. He was overcome with hilarity, one afternoon, because he caught out his wife in an involuntary impulse to flee. He brightened up suddenly with an anesthetized gaiety: "She thinks I'm insane, what luck!"

His gaiety didn't last, because it occurred to him that, between the wicked man and the madman, the wicked man has the advantage. Frightened by the madman, wouldn't Edmée have remained there, biting her lip and choking back her tears, so as to win over the wicked man?

"They no longer even think me wicked," he thought bitterly. "It's because I no longer am. Oh, what pain the woman I left has caused me . . . Yet others left her, she left others . . . How do Bacciocchi, for example, Septfons, Spéleïeff, and all the others now live? . . . But what do all the others have in common with me? She called me 'petit bourgeois' because I kept count of the bottles in her cellar. Petit bourgeois, faithful man, noble lover, these are my names, these are my true names, and she, all glistening with tears when I left, is still the same Léa, who prefers her old age to me, who counts on her fingers, by the fireside: 'I had what's-his-name, what-d'you-call-him, Chéri, so-and-so . . .' I thought she belonged to me, and I didn't realize that I was just one of her lovers. Who is there, now, that I can be unashamed of? . . ."

Practiced in the gymnastics of impassivity, he devoted himself to suffering these capricious devastations in the manner of a possessed man worthy of his demon. Proud, dry-eyed, his steady hand holding a lighted match, he would observe his mother obliquely, sensing her to be kindly disposed. Having lit his cigarette, he would nearly have strutted before an invisible public, he would have taunted his tormentors "So?" Obscurely, the strength born of dissimulation and resistance was painfully taking shape in his deepest being, and he was savoring the extremes of his detachment, with the vague intuition that a paroxysm of emotion can be used and profited from just like an interlude of calm, and that in these moments a person can find in himself the counsel that serenity denies him. As a child, Chéri had often taken advantage of a genuine anger to cultivate a self-serving displeasure. Today, he was already coming close to the point where, having reached an unequivocal distress, he would rely on it to resolve everything . . .

———

A September afternoon, swept by brisk winds and leaves sailing level to the ground, an afternoon of blue fissures in the sky and scattered raindrops, beckoned Chéri toward his black shelter, toward his servant clad in black with a bit of white across her chest like an alley cat. He was feeling lighthearted, eager for confidences that were as sweet as arbutus and, like it, armed with thorns. He was already singing to himself words and phrases imbued with an ill-defined power: "Her monogram embroidered on her underclothes in hair, my dear, in blond hair from her own head . . . fairies' work! The masseuse removed the hairs from her calves with tweezers, one by one . . ."

He came away from the window and turned around. Charlotte,

seated, was gazing up at her son, and he saw take shape, in the unappeasable water of her large eyes, a convex, mobile, crystalline, prodigious glimmer, which broke away from her golden-brown iris and which the blaze of her flushed cheek no doubt vaporized . . . Chéri felt flattered and cheered: "How sweet she is! She's crying for me! . . ."

An hour later, he found his old accomplice at her post. But she was wearing a sort of priest's hat, wrapped with black oilskin, and she held out to Chéri a blue paper, which he pushed aside.

"What? . . . I don't have time. Tell me what's on it."

The Girlfriend gave him a perplexed look.

"It's my mother."

"Your mother? Are you joking?"

She tried to be offended.

"I'm not joking at all. Show respect for the spirits! She has died."

She added by way of excuse:

"She was eighty-three."

"My condolences. Are you going out?"

"No, I'm leaving."

"For where?"

"For Tarascon, and from there I catch a small local branch line that will take me . . ."

"For how long?"

"Four, five days . . . at least . . . There's the notary to see, about the will, because my younger sister . . ."

Arms to the heavens, he burst out:

"A sister, now! Why not four children?"

He could hear his own voice crying out in a high, unintended pitch, and he controlled himself.

"Well, all right. What do you want me to do about all this? Go, go . . ."

"I was going to leave you a note, I'm taking the seven thirty."

"Taking the seven thirty."

"The hour of the funeral isn't written in the telegram, my sister tells me only about placing the body in the coffin, the climate is very hot down there, we'll be forced to move quickly, the formalities are all that would keep me. With formalities, it's out of your control . . ."

"Of course, of course."

He walked from the door to the wall of photographs, from the wall to the door. Along the way he knocked against a sagging overnight bag. The coffeepot and cups sat steaming on the table.

"I made you some coffee, just in case . . ."

"Thank you."

They drank standing up, as in a train station, and the strain of departures choked Chéri, whose teeth secretly chattered.

"Good-bye then, my dear," the Girlfriend said. "Rest assured that I'll hurry."

"Good-bye. Have a good trip."

Their hands touched, but she didn't dare kiss him.

"You won't stay here a little while?"

He looked around him restlessly.

"No. No."

"Take the key?"

"Why would I?"

"You're at home here. You have your habits. I've told Maria to come at five o'clock to light a fire and make coffee every day . . . Take my key anyway?"

He limply took a key that he found enormous. Outside, he was tempted to throw it away or take it back to the concierge.

Emboldened, the old woman gave him instructions that she would have given a twelve-year-old child.

"The lights are on the left as you enter. The kettle is always on the gas stove in the kitchen, you have only to put a match under it . . .

I've given orders to Maria to leave your Japanese robe folded on the corner of the divan, and the cigarettes in their place."

Chéri nodded "yes, yes" in reply, with the carefree, courageous look that teenagers wear on the first morning of the fall term. And when he was alone he didn't laugh at his servant with the dyed hair, who ranked at their proper value the last privileges of the dead and the pleasures of the abandoned.

He awoke, the following morning, from an unfathomable dream in which passersby were in a rush and all running in the same direction. He knew them all, even though he saw them only from behind. As they passed, he identified his mother, a breathless and strangely naked Léa. Desmond, the Girlfriend, the Maudru boy . . . Edmée was the only one to turn around and smile the sardonic little smile of a marten. "But it's the marten that Ragut caught in the Vosges!" Chéri cried out in his dream, and this discovery gave him an inordinate delight. Then he again identified and counted those who were running in the same direction, and thought: "There's one missing . . . There's one missing . . ." By now beyond the dream, on this side of waking again, it dawned on him that the missing one was none other than himself: "I'm going to return there . . ." But an entangled insect's exertions, which tensed all his limbs, extended a blue line between his eyelids, and he emerged into a reality in which he was squandering his strength and his time. He stretched out his legs, bathed them in a cool swath of the sheets: "Edmée got up long ago."

Beneath the window, a new garden, of yellow anthemis and heliotropes, surprised him, he remembered only the summer garden, blue and pink. He rang, and his ring roused an unfamiliar housemaid, whom he interrogated:

"Where is Henriette?"

"I took her place, monsieur."

"Since when?"

"But . . . a month ago . . ."

He said, "Ah!" as if to say, "That explains it."

"Where is Madame?"

"Madame is coming, monsieur, she's ready to go out."

Edmée indeed came in, briskly, but stopped short on the threshold, to Chéri's inward amusement. He allowed himself the pleasure of further alarming his wife by exclaiming, "But it's Ragut's marten!" and her beautiful eyes wavered for an instant under his own.

"Fred, I . . ."

"Yes, you're going out. I didn't hear you get up."

She blushed very faintly.

"There's nothing unusual about that, I sleep so badly these nights that I've had sheets put on the divan in the boudoir . . . You aren't doing anything special today, are you?"

"Yes, I am," he said somberly.

"Is it a serious matter?"

"Quite serious."

He waited a beat, and finished in a breezy tone:

"I'm going to have my hair cut."

"But you'll be home for lunch?"

"No, I'll eat a chop in Paris, I've booked an appointment at Gustave's at a quarter past two. The employee who usually comes is sick."

The lie blossomed effortlessly on his lips, courteous, childish. Because he was lying, he recovered his boyhood mouth, rounded for a kiss and stuck out coquettishly. Edmée looked at him with a masculine sort of complacence.

"You look well this morning, Fred . . . I'll be on my way."

"You're taking the seven thirty?"

She stared at him, stunned, and left so quickly that he was still laughing about it when she shut the front door.

"Oh, that does me good!" he sighed. "How easily you laugh when you no longer expect anything from anyone . . ." Thus he formulated, as he was dressing, the essence of his asceticism, and the little made-up song that he hummed, closed-mouthed, kept him company like a simpleminded nun.

He went down into Paris, which he had forgotten. The crowd staggered his paradoxical stability, which demanded a crystalline void and grief's routine. His reflection in a window, on the rue Royale, hit him head-on, at full length, when a spell of midday sun parted the rain clouds, and Chéri did not argue with this harsh new image, set against a backdrop of seamstresses and newspaper sellers, with jade necklaces and silver fox furs on either side. He thought that a certain fluttering inside him, which he compared to a lead bead bouncing around inside a celluloid ball, arose from inanition, and he took refuge in a restaurant.

His back to the wall of windows, shielded from the light, he lunched on delicate oysters, fish, fruit. Young women nearby, who took no notice of his presence, gave him a pleasure analogous to that produced by a bouquet of cold violets laid across closed eyelids. But the aroma of coffee suddenly reminded Chéri of the urgent need to get up, to go to the appointment to which this aroma of fresh coffee summoned him. Before obeying, he went to his barber's, held out his hands to the manicurist, and slipped, while expert palms substituted their will for his own, into a moment of precious rest.

The enormous key clogged his pocket. "I won't go, I won't go . . ." To the cadence of this refrain, repeated over and over, cleansed of all meaning, he reached the avenue de Villiers without difficulty. His clumsiness in groping around the lock, the scratching of the key, quickened his heart for a moment, but a vibrant warmth, in the vestibule, settled his nerves.

He advanced cautiously, master of this empire of a few square feet, which he possessed but did not know. The well-trained cleaning woman had arranged the useless daily arsenal on the table, and the embers were dying under a velvet of hot cinders around an earthenware coffeepot. Methodically, Chéri pulled from his pockets and arranged his cigarette case, the big key, the little key, the flat revolver, his billfold, his handkerchief, and his watch. But having donned the Japanese robe, he did not stretch out on the divan. He opened doors, examined cupboards, with the silent curiosity of a cat. A rudimentary yet feminine bathroom caused his singular prudishness to recoil. The bedroom, furnished chiefly with a bed, and covered as well with that sorrowful red that creeps in around deteriorating lives, smelled of old bachelors and cologne, and he returned to the sitting room. He lit the two wall lamps, the chandelier decorated with ribbon bows. He listened to the faint sounds, tested on himself, alone for the first time in the mean abode, the power of those, deceased or disappeared, who had inhabited it. He thought he heard and recognized a familiar footstep, its slippered or old-animal-paw sound, then shook his head.

"It's not her. She won't be here for a week. And when she has come back, what more will I have in this world? . . . I'll have . . ."

In his head he listened to the Girlfriend's voice, the weary voice of the down-and-out . . . "And so let me finish the story of the shouting match at the races, between Léa and old Mortier. Old Mortier thought that with some publicity in *Gil Blas*, he would get everything he wanted out of Léa. My goodness, boys and girls, was he split on a rock! . . . She showed up at Longchamp, a dream in blue, as composed as a picture in her victoria hitched to two piebald horses . . ."

He lifted his head toward the wall where, before him, so many blue eyes were smiling, so many soft necks were proudly displaying themselves above impassive breasts:

"I'll have that. I'll have only that. It's true that it's perhaps a great deal. I'm very lucky to have found her again, on this wall. But after having found her again, I can no longer do anything but lose her. I'm still hanging, like her, from those few rusted nails, from those pins stuck in askew. How long will that last? Not long. And then, I know myself, I dread needing more than this. I might all of a sudden cry out: 'I want her! I need her! At once!' What will I do then? . . ."

He pushed the divan toward the wall of pictures and lay down there. When he lay like this, the Léas that had their eyes lowered appeared to be concerned about him. "But I know perfectly well that they just look that way. Just what did you intend to leave me with after you, my Nounoune, when you sent me away? Your magnanimity cost you very little, you knew what a Chéri was worth, you didn't risk much. But we've paid the price, you for being born so long before me, I for having loved you above other women: there you are, finished, your consolation a disgrace, and I . . . I, whereas people say, 'There was the war,' I can say, 'There was Léa, the war . . .' I had believed that I thought no more about one than about the other, yet both of them have pushed me outside these times. From now on, I will everywhere take up only half a place . . ."

He pulled the table toward him to check his watch.

"Five thirty. The old woman won't be here for a week . . . And this is the first day. And if she were to die along the way? . . ."

He tossed around a little on his divan, smoked, poured himself a cup of lukewarm coffee.

"A week. All the same, I shouldn't expect too much of myself. In a week . . . what story will she tell me? I know by heart the one about Drags, the one about the shouting match at Longchamp, the one about the rift—and when I've heard them all, over and over again, what will come after? . . . Nothing more. In a week, this old woman whom I already await as if she were supposed to give me an injection, this old woman will be here . . . and she'll bring me nothing."

He turned a beggar's gaze toward his favorite portrait. Already the lifelike picture inspired in him no more than a dwindling rancor, and rapture, and agitation. He turned from side to side on the moquette bed, and unwittingly mimicked the muscular contractions of a man who wants to jump from a great height but doesn't dare.

He worked himself up to moaning aloud and repeating, "Nounoune . . . My Nounoune . . ." to make himself believe that he was feverish with emotion. But he fell silent, ashamed, because he knew all too well that he had no need for fevered emotion to pick up the flat little revolver on the table. Without getting up, he searched for an advantageous position, in the end lay down on his folded right arm, which was holding the revolver, pressed his ear against the barrel in the cushions. His arm promptly began to go numb and he knew that if he didn't hurry, his tingling fingers would refuse to obey. So he hurried, let out some choked moans of complaint at the undertaking, because his right forearm, crushed beneath his body, was bothering him, and he knew nothing more of life beyond the strain of his index finger against a small projection of threaded steel.

NOTES

Some of the information in the following notes was drawn from the "Notes et variantes" sections accompanying *Chéri* and *La fin de Chéri* in volumes 2 and 3 of the Bibliothèque de la Pléiade edition of Colette's *Œuvres* (Paris: Gallimard, 1986 and 1991).

TRANSLATOR'S NOTE

XX "MUDDIED THE WATERS": Julia Kristeva, "Colette, une sensation," *Revue des Deux Mondes* (May 2002): 80. My translation.

XX "UNCOMPROMISING ZEAL": Angela Carter, "Colette," *London Review of Books* 2, no. 19 (October 2, 1980): 15.

XX "OBSCENE GERMAN POSTCARDS": Margaret Crosland, *Colette: The Difficulty of Loving* (Indianapolis and New York: Bobbs-Merrill, 1973), 47.

XX "TRUNK LOADS OF PORNOGRAPHIC BOOKS": Yvonne Mitchell, *Colette: A Taste for Life* (New York: Harcourt Brace Jovanovich, 1975), 65.

XXI "TO THE TENSION IN FRENCH CULTURE": Diana Holmes, *French Women's Writing, 1848–1994* (London and Atlantic Highlands, NJ: Athlone, 1996), 133.

XXII "LOVED CERTAIN WORDS": Maurice Goudeket, *Close to Colette* (New York: Farrar, Straus and Cudahy, 1957), 20.

XXII "HOMELY TECHNICALITY": Goudeket, *Close to Colette*, 92.

XXII "CAPABLE . . . OF WORKING": Goudeket, *Close to Colette*, 18.

XXII "A STUBBORN ERADICATION": Colette, *Œuvres*, vol. 3, Bibliothèque de la Pléiade (Paris: Gallimard, 1991), 1823. My translation.

XXII "YOU BECOME A GREAT WRITER": Colette, *Paysage et portraits*, in *Œuvres complètes*, Édition du Centenaire, vol. 8 (Paris: Flammarion, 1973), 439. My translation.

XXIII "A LOVELY PIECE": Colette, *Sido*, in Colette, *Œuvres*, vol. 3, 517. My translation.

XXIV "YOU KNOW, I READ": Roger Stéphane, *Portrait souvenir de Georges Simenon: Entretien* (Paris: Quai Voltaire, 1989), 71. My translation.

XXIV "WHAT I PARTICULARLY LIKE": Gide to Colette, December 11, 1920, quoted in Colette, *Œuvres*, vol. 2, Bibliothèque de la Pléiade (Paris: Gallimard, 1986), 1548. My translation.

XXV "LOOSE, RAPID, MALLEABLE DIALOGUE": Colette in *Journal de Monaco*, 1924, quoted in Mitchell, *Colette*, 146.

XXVI "PREFERENCE FOR AN IDIOM": I. T. Olken, "Imagery in *Chéri* and *La Fin de Chéri*," *Studies in Philology* 60, no. 1 (January 1963): 115.

XXVI "A LITTLE NOVEL": Colette, *Lettres à ses pairs*, ed. Claude Pichois and Roberte Forbin (Paris: Flammarion, 1973), 69. My translation.

XXVI "TO BE DRAWN TOWARDS": Mitchell, *Colette*, 145.

XXVIII "PROBABLY THE GREATEST": Judith Thurman, *Secrets of the Flesh: A Life of Colette* (New York: Knopf, 1999), 353.

XXVIII "IN *CHÉRI*": Colette to Frédéric Lefèvre, "Une heure avec Colette," *Les Nouvelles littéraires*, March 27, 1926, quoted in Colette, *Œuvres*, vol. 3, 1354. My translation.

XXX "IT IS I WHO AM PROUD": Marcel Proust to Colette, letter of November 1920, quoted in Julia Kristeva, *Colette*, trans. Jane Marie Todd (New York: Columbia University Press, 2004), 373.

XXX "THE GREATEST LIVING WRITER": Paul Claudel, quoted in "Colette Is Dead in Paris at 81: Novelist Wrote 'Gigi' and 'Chéri,' " *New York Times*, August 4, 1954.

XXX "THE GREATEST LIVING MASTER": Thurman, *Secrets of the Flesh*, 409.

XXXI "THE PRIESTESS": Kristeva, *Colette*, 17.

XXXI "HYMN TO JOUISSANCE": Kristeva, *Colette*, 7.

XXXI "APPALLINGLY DIFFICULT TO TRANSLATE": Mitchell, *Colette*, 189.

CHÉRI

6 WEDDING BASKET: "An extremely important tradition in 19th century France, the *corbeille de mariage* was a gift basket given by the groom to the bride

upon the signing of the wedding contract." Katy Werlin, "The Corbeille de Mariage," *The Fashion Historian* (blog), http://www.thefashionhistorian .com/2012/01/corbeille-de-mariage.html. Here, Chéri is appropriating the wedding basket for himself.

6 BONHEUR DU JOUR: Literally "happiness of the day," a bonheur du jour is a lady's small writing table with a cabinet top. Bonheurs du jour were extremely popular in eighteenth-century France.

7 DRAGS DAY: Drags Day at the Auteuil Hippodrome was a meet that took place on the Friday preceding the Grand Prix. It was the tradition to arrive at the meet in a mail coach, or *drag*, whose name derived from the English verb "to drag."

7 GIL BLAS: *Gil Blas* was a Parisian literary periodical founded in 1879. Colette wrote for *Gil Blas* in 1903 under the name of "Claudine."

8 PAÏVA: Esther Pauline (Thérèse) Lachmann, best remembered as La Païva (1819–1884), was born in Moscow to Polish and German Jews. Taking her name from the Marquis de Païva, to whom she was briefly married, she rose to notoriety and wealth as perhaps the most famous Parisian courtesan of the nineteenth century. Her lavish Second Empire mansion on the avenue des Champs-Élysées was famous for hosting the literary and political figures of the day and for its over-the-top decor.

10 NEUILLY: Officially Neuilly-sur-Seine, Neuilly is an affluent residential suburb northwest of Paris, bordering the Bois de Boulogne.

14 RUBELLES: Rubelles was a faience manufacturer founded in 1836 in Rubelles, a commune in the département of Seine-et-Marne, southeast of Paris. The company ceased operations in 1858.

14 THE AVENUE BUGEAUD: Located in the Passy neighborhood of Paris's sixteenth arrondissement, the avenue Bugeaud begins at the avenue Foch (formerly the avenue du Bois de Boulogne), near the Porte Dauphine, at the edge of the Bois de Boulogne, and ends at the Place Victor-Hugo. Passy was and is home to some of Paris's wealthiest residents.

15 THE BOIS: A former royal hunting ground, the Bois de Boulogne is a large public park situated in the west of Paris, comprising gardens, lakes, restaurants and cafés, and the Auteuil and Longchamp Hippodromes. It is bordered on the east by Passy and the sixteenth arrondissement, and on the north by Neuilly.

15 THE OCTROI: Historically, goods entering Paris were charged a duty, or *octroi*, which was paid at various entry points to the city. The building where the duty was collected was by extension called the octroi.

15 THE BOULEVARD D'INKERMANN: Located in Neuilly-sur-Seine, the boulevard

d'Inkermann begins at the present-day Place Winston-Churchill and ends at the Place du Duc-d'Orléans.

16 FIFTH POSITION: Fifth position is the most difficult of the five basic ballet positions, and the one with which most classroom exercises begin and end. It requires the legs to be turned out and crossed, and the feet to be placed one in front of the other, so that the heel of each foot is against the toes of the other.

19 KHALIL-BEY: Khalil-Bey (1831–1879), an Ottoman diplomat and art collector, had been ambassador of the Sublime Porte (the government of the Ottoman Empire) in Saint Petersburg. He commissioned Gustave Courbet's graphic painting of a reclining woman's genitalia, *L'origine du monde* (The Origin of the World).

22 ABOUT: Edmond About (1828–1885) was a French journalist and author. His *Le roman d'un brave homme* (The Story of an Honest Man) is a moralistic portrait of a virtuous smallholder who through his honesty and hard work secures the wealth and happiness of his family.

22 GUSTAVE DROZ: Gustave Droz (1832–1895) was a French popular writer, author of light sketches of everyday life and novels extolling the virtues of the family.

22 "LITTLE MASTERPIECE": In French, *petite chef-d'œuvre*. The American lady speaks French imperfectly: she has used a feminine adjective to modify a masculine noun.

26 HONFLEUR? THE CÔTE DE GRÂCE?: Honfleur is a picturesque coastal town situated on the southern bank of the Seine estuary, in Normandy. The Côte de Grâce is a plateau overlooking Honfleur and its port.

29 RENOUHARD: A short-lived luxury car brand.

36 MR. BRACKET: An allusion to the brackets traditionally used by accountants in manual calculations.

46 SCHWABE'S: No jeweler's shop by the name of Schwabe's is known to have existed in Paris in 1912.

48 HER ASSETS PROTECTED: In French, *le régime dotal*, which limits the husband's rights over the property the wife brought into the marriage through her dowry.

54 PIQUET: A two-player card game with strongly middle-class overtones.

55 THE CEINTURE: The Petite Ceinture was a rail line that encompassed Paris, located inside the boulevards des Maréchaux, the series of boulevards that encircle the city just inside the city limits.

56 BRETON: A Breton, or Breton hat, is a felt or straw hat with a round crown and curved brim, typically worn tilted to the back of the head.

66 DUBARRY OR POMPADOUR: Madame du Barry (1743–1793) became the mistress of the French king Louis XV following the death of Madame de Pompadour. Condemned during the Revolution, she was guillotined in 1793. Madame de Pompadour (1721–1764) was the mistress of Louis XV from 1745 until her death.

68 HOSPITAL GREEN: According to Judith Thurman, Colette reported that the walls of her and Willy's apartment on the sixth floor of 93, rue de Courcelles, were painted a "hospital green." Judith Thurman, quoting from *Lettres à ses pairs*, in *Secrets of the Flesh: A Life of Colette* (New York: Knopf, 1999), 104.

71 THE AVENUE HENRI-MARTIN: Located in Paris's sixteenth arrondissement, between the Place du Trocadéro and the Porte de la Muette, close to the Bois de Boulogne, the avenue Henri-Martin still boasts town mansions with front gardens, like Chéri and Edmée's.

76 LA BOURBOULE: Located in central France, in the Auvergne region, La Bourboule was a popular spa town during the Belle Époque.

80 YOU MUSN'T TOUCH THE AX: An allusion to *"Ne touchez pas à la hache"* (Don't touch the ax), a quotation from Balzac's novel *La duchesse de Langeais*, said to be the words of Charles I of England to his executioner before his decapitation. The phrase implies that something is sacrosanct. That Edmée knew the allusion reminds us that she has her secondary-school diploma (*baccalauréat*), which was rare for a woman at this time.

83 THE PORTE DAUPHINE: One of the city gates of Paris, at the edge of the Bois de Boulogne.

86 ADVERTISING FAN: An inexpensively made hand fan that displays an advertisement. Advertising fans were produced in France from the mid-nineteenth century to the Second World War.

86 POMMERY: A champagne brand of high repute, founded in 1858 in Reims.

88 *PETITS BLEUS*: *Petits bleus*, or *télégrammes pneumatiques*, were cheap, handwritten telegrams sent pneumatically for rapid communications within Paris.

89 THE MORRIS HOTEL: Colette's model for the Morris Hotel was Le Meurice, a luxury hotel that opened on the rue de Rivoli in 1835.

89 THE WEBER: The Café Weber, no longer extant, was located at 21, rue Royale. It was a favorite of Marcel Proust.

97 THE AVENUE DU BOIS: Fashionable then as now, the broad avenue du Bois de Boulogne, today the avenue Foch, in the sixteenth arrondissement, runs from the Arc de Triomphe to the Porte Dauphine, at the edge of the Bois de Boulogne.

103 GUÉTHARY: A Basque fishing village located on the Atlantic coast between Biarritz and the border of Spain.

104 TRAYAS: Le Trayas is a small village along the Côte d'Azur, the Mediterranean coast of southeastern France.

105 CHAPLIN: Charles Joshua Chaplin (1825–1891) was an extremely successful Academic painter best known for his sensual portraits of young women.

106 CAMBO: Cambo-les-Bains is a spa town in the Pays Basque.

108 MAISON LEWIS: Maison Lewis, proprietor Louise Lewis, was located at 16, rue Royale, Paris, with its entrance at 422, rue Saint-Honoré. It was "one of Paris's most prestigious milliners." Lisa Chaney, *Coco Chanel: An Intimate Life* (New York: Penguin, 2011), 72.

109 THE SENTIER DE LA VERTU: One of the main promenades in the Bois de Boulogne, located near the avenue Bugeaud.

110 LAVALLIÈRE'S: Eugénie Fenoglio, stage name Ève Lavallière (1866–1929), actress who became the star of the Théâtre des Variétés in Paris as well as the mistress of its director, Fernand Samuel. After separating from Samuel, she had a religious conversion to Catholicism, joined the Third Order of Saint Francis, and traveled as a lay medical missionary to Tunisia, where she nursed Arab children. Colette lived in Lavallière's former home on the boulevard Suchet in Auteuil between 1916 and 1925 and therefore during the composition of *Chéri*.

111 KÜHN: There was a furrier by the name of Kühn at 134, rue de Rivoli, in 1912, but no tailor or dressmaker of that name.

111 NEW-CUT MAHOGANY: In French, *acajou neuf. Bois neuf* is defined in the *Trésor de la langue française informatisé* as "*bois transporté par véhicule et non abîmé par le flottage*" (wood transported by vehicle and not damaged in a log drive).

120 THE LAKES: That is, the Lac Inférieur and the Lac Supérieur, the two lakes in the Bois de Boulogne.

121 SARAH COHEN: If this is an allusion to an actual person, she has not been identified.

122 BACCIOCCHI: Colette's inspiration for this name was either Félix Pascal Bacciocchi (1772–1841), husband of Élisa Bonaparte, sister of Napoléon I, or Félix-Marnès, Comte de Bacciocchi (1803–1866), the nephew of Félix Pascal Bacciocchi, and first chamberlain of Napoleon III.

123 A PARTICULAR CLIENTELE: That is, a lesbian clientele.

139 RHUBARB LOZENGES: Rhubarb is a stimulant laxative, and rhubarb lozenges were used to treat constipation.

149 ARMENONVILLE: A posh restaurant at the entrance to the Bois de Boulogne. In *Where Paris Dines* (1929), Julian Street called it one of the "most attractive restaurants actually within the Bois," adding, "Prices are not low." Quoted in John Leland, *A Guide to Hemingway's Paris* (Chapel Hill: Algonquin, 1989), 13. "At the Armenonville restaurant, Swann and Odette listened to the 'little

phrase' of music that would become a recurring motif in *In Search of Lost Time*." Jessica Powell, *Literary Paris: A Guide* (New York: New York Review Books, 2006), 102. "Hundreds of times, without my leaving this room, the little phrase has carried me off to dine with it at Armenonville." Marcel Proust, *Within a Budding Grove*, vol. 1, trans. C. K. Scott Moncrieff (London: Chatto and Windus, 1929), 150.

THE END OF CHÉRI

154 JANSON-DE-SAILLY CHIMED THE HOUR: A reference to the Lycée Janson-de-Sailly, a celebrated lycée located at 106, rue de la Pompe, in Passy, whose facade is surmounted by a clock.

155 LA VIGILANTE: A company called La Vigilante appeared in the *Annuaire du Commerce Didot-Bottin* for 1919; it advertised home watch services and was located at 100, boulevard Arago, in the fourteenth arrondissement.

156 GREEN-AND-RED RIBBON: An allusion to the Croix de Guerre, a French military decoration established in 1915.

156 THE LAKE: The Lac Inférieur (or Grand Lac), the largest lake in the Bois de Boulogne, facing the Porte de la Muette.

157 LÉMERY: Henry Lémery (1874–1972) was among the politicians whom Colette met through her marriage to Henry de Jouvenel. He served in both the French Chamber of Deputies and the Senate and was undersecretary of state for maritime transport and the merchant marine from November 16, 1917, to November 28, 1918, in the cabinet of Clemenceau.

158 *EXCELSIOR*: An illustrated French daily newspaper that ran between 1910 and 1940, to which Colette contributed numerous articles in 1917 and 1918.

159 *BREKEKEKEX*: No restaurant by this name is known to have existed. The name is borrowed from the call of the frog chorus in Aristophanes's *The Frogs*.

161 THE UPPER ROTUNDA: This rotunda is still used as a rehearsal studio for the corps of the Paris Opera Ballet.

162 RANCH: A fictitious company whose name Colette may have derived from the names Royal Dutch or Rand Mines.

162 DEUTSCH SENIOR: Probably an allusion to a member of the Deutsch de la Meurthe family, a family of wealthy industrialists and philanthropists.

163 CUTLETS FULBERT-DUMONTEIL: Named for Jean-Camille Fulbert-Dumonteil (1831–1912), celebrated French food writer.

166 TORPEDO TOURING CAR: In French, *une torpédo*. Produced between 1908 and the mid-1930s, the torpedo was a four- or five-seated touring car with a long, sleek design and a detachable soft top.

167 THE AVENUE DE L'ALMA: Located in Paris's eighth arrondissement, the avenue de l'Alma runs from the Place de l'Alma, near the Seine, to the avenue des Champs-Élysées. It was renamed the avenue George V in 1918.

169 ALFONSO XIII: King of Spain from 1902 to 1931. Photographs show a tall, thin figure with a disconcertingly narrow head.

174 SAINT VITUS'S DANCE: Chorea, a neurological disorder marked by involuntary spasmodic movements of the limbs and facial muscles. Here, Chéri is undoubtedly using the term to describe the characteristic tremor seen in victims of shell shock.

175 CORTON: A grand cru appellation in the Côte de Beaune district of Burgundy.

176 YOU GREAT SULTANA: In French, *grande sultane*. One of Colette's nicknames for her second husband, Henry de Jouvenel, was the feminine *"ma sultane."*

176 RUE DE FRANQUEVILLE: The rue de Franqueville intersects the avenue Henri-Martin at its westernmost end, near the Porte de la Muette.

179 AMBRINE: A paraffin wax preparation for the treatment of burns, frostbite, and trench foot, popularized during the First World War.

179 COICTIER HOSPITAL: Colette derived this name from that of Jacques Coictier, physician to Louis XI of France.

182 ACONITE: A perennial grown for its attractive dark blue flowers, aconite (or monkshood) is poisonous in all its parts, being highly toxic to the cardiovascular and nervous systems.

183 BURDENED WITH A SEXUAL ABERRANCY: The description of the Baronne de La Berche clearly evokes Missy, the Marquise de Belbeuf, a strikingly masculine lesbian transvestite and Colette's lover from 1906 to 1911.

186 PANAME: A colloquial name for Paris. It is variously said to have had its origin in the Panama hats popular in Paris in the early twentieth century or the Panama Scandal of 1892–93, which exposed corruption in France's Chamber of Deputies.

187 GASSING VICTIM: Allusion to the neurological symptoms exhibited by victims of poison gas attacks during the First World War. The use of chlorine gas by the Germans at the Second Battle of Ypres, April 22 to May 25, 1915, marked the first effective use of poison gas in warfare.

188 QUART-DE-CHAUME: A sought-after sweet white wine from the western Loire Valley.

190 PARIGOTS: A colloquial term for Parisians.

194 THE PASSY SPRINGS: Passy was made famous in the seventeenth and eighteenth centuries by the thermal waters discovered there around 1650. Jean-Jacques Rousseau and Benjamin Franklin were both visitors to *les Eaux de Passy*. The springs began to dry up during the Second Empire, owing to urbanization, and the spa shut permanently in 1868.

195 URIAGE: Known since Roman times for its thermal waters, the spa town of Uriage (or Uriage-les-Bains), located in the département of Isère, in the Rhône-Alpes region of southeastern France, was very fashionable in the late nineteenth century. Colette went there in 1896, with Willy, and again in July 1946.

195 MONT-DORE: Known for its healing springs, Mont-Dore is a commune in the département of Puy-de-Dôme, in the Auvergne region of central France.

195 SCARS ABOVE HIS RIGHT BREAST: Colette has lost track of the location of Chéri's twin scars: on p. 160, the scars are located below his right breast (*sous*), but here they are above it (*au-dessus de*).

195 REITER: A German cavalry soldier, especially of the sixteenth and seventeenth centuries.

197 THE CHAMBER: The Chamber of Deputies, the legislative assembly of the French parliament during the Third Republic.

197 THE LENOIR BOY'S ACCIDENT: In 1917, Pierre Lenoir, the son of a wealthy publicity agent, was indicted on charges of trading with the enemy after it was discovered that he had used money from German sources to purchase the French newspaper *Le Journal* in July 1915. He was sentenced to death in 1919. The "accident" may have been the temporary paralysis he suffered on September 19, 1919, a few weeks before his execution.

197 MADAME CAILLAUX: Henriette Caillaux (1874–1943), wife of the French cabinet minister Joseph Caillaux, assassinated the editor of *Le Figaro*, Gaston Calmette, at the newspaper's offices on March 16, 1914, after Calmette launched a campaign damaging to her husband's reputation in the paper. Her arrest and subsequent trial riveted the nation. She was acquitted of murder on July 28 of that year, on the grounds that it was a crime of passion.

197 LANDRU: Henri Désiré Landru (1869–1922), one of France's most notorious serial killers, lured his female victims by means of personal advertisements placed in Paris newspapers. Arrested on April 12, 1919, he was tried for the murder of ten women and the teenage son of his first victim, convicted on all counts, and executed by guillotine in February 1922. Colette covered his trial for *Le Matin* in 1921.

207 IN THE MIDDLE OF NOWHERE: Colette has Valérie say *au diable vert*, a popular alteration of the more correct *au diable Vauvert*. *Au diable vert* may have arisen from the blending of the expressions *au diable* and *au vert*, to mean both very far away and out in the country.

207 THE NORMANDY: Opened in 1912, this palace hotel still operates in Deauville.

211 QUARRY STRUCK BY THE HAWK: According to *Le Littré*, the French expression *battu de l'oiseau* is used to describe someone who has lost his courage as a

result of misfortune or failure. The term is said to come from falconry, specifically an avian predator's manner of beating its prey with its wing.

214 THE CLERMONT-TONNERRES: Colette was probably thinking of Élisabeth de Gramont, Duchesse de Clermont-Tonnerre (1875–1954), a writer whom Colette would have known through their common friend (and lover) Natalie Clifford Barney and others. Élisabeth's house was on the same street as Léa's, the rue Raynouard.

214 THE CORPECHOTS: Lucien Corpechot (1871–1944) was a French journalist, editor, and author of a number of books, among them the three-volume *Souvenirs d'un journaliste*. Colette may have known him through their friend Anna de Noailles.

215 FANTÔMAS: An elusive criminal genius and master of disguise, Fantômas is the protagonist of thirty-two hugely popular novels by Pierre Souvestre and Marcel Allain, published by Arthème Fayard between February 1911 and September 1913, as well as of five films by Louis Feuillade, released in 1913 and 1914.

216 THE SEVEN COLORS OF IRIS: Iris was the Greek goddess of the rainbow and messenger of the Olympian gods. The seven colors, therefore, are the colors of the rainbow: red, orange, yellow, green, blue, indigo, and violet.

217 CARTE DE VISITE: A small photographic portrait mounted on a piece of board, meant for use as a calling card. Colette calls it a *portrait-carte*, a rare usage according to the *Trésor de la langue française informatisé*, which gives a quotation from *Claudine à Paris* as its sole illustrative example.

218 MONTAGNÉ'S: According to the editors of volume 3 of the Pléiade edition of Colette's *Œuvres*, there was a restaurant called Montagné at 169, rue Saint-Honoré, near the corner of the rue de l'Échelle. Prosper Montagné (1865–1948), the famed restaurateur, cookbook author, and first editor of the *Larousse gastronomique* (Paris, 1938), opened his own restaurant, Montagné Traiteur, in Paris in 1920, purportedly at the corner of the rue Saint-Honoré and the rue de l'Échelle; it would seem, therefore, that the reference is to Prosper Montagné's restaurant.

218 MONSIEUR BOBETTE'S: Bobette is noted as the manager of an establishment that would have been suited to cocaine trafficking in the political satire *Satan conduit le bal* (Satan directs the dance) (Paris, 1925), by the lawyer, journalist, and publisher Georges Anquetil. Mixing fact and fiction, the book associates the names of eminent French figures of the day with acts of extreme debauchery, to imply that France's own government leaders were destroying the country.

229 VOCERO: A Corsican funeral dirge calling for vengeance after a murder or violent death.

230 THE CROSS: That is, the Cross of the Legion of Honor.

230 CLEMENCEAU'S FOLD: Georges Clemenceau, known as the Tiger (1841–
1929), French premier (1906–9, 1917–20) and minister of war (1917–20)
whose strong leadership helped secure the Allied victory in the First World
War. His many visits to the trenches inspired the devotion of the poilus, or
French infantry soldiers.

230 TWO FOURTEEN, AVENUE DE VILLIERS: The address numbers on the avenue
de Villiers, located in the seventeenth arrondissement, stop at 147.

230 LA GIRAFE: No restaurant by this name is known to have existed at this time.

232 COAL-TARRED: An antiseptic made from coal tar was used topically to prevent
infection in flesh wounds during the First World War.

232 PHENO-SALICYLIC: Pheno-salicylic acid was a form of salicylic acid, used to
treat rheumatism, neuralgia, and septic diseases and, in large doses, to prevent or reduce fever.

240 VESOUL: Capital of the Haute-Saône département in eastern France. The French
auxiliary hospital no. 8 was located in Vesoul during the First World War.

240 VETERANS' OFFICE: The Office national des anciens combattants et victimes
de guerre (National Office of Disabled and Discharged War Veterans), created in 1917.

241 ABDULLAS: Though their name suggests an Egyptian origin, Abdulla cigarettes were first produced in London in 1902 and were available in Egyptian, Turkish, and Virginian blends. Stanford University, Research into
the Impact of Tobacco Advertising, "Abdullas," http://tobacco.stanford
.edu.

242 THEIR SPIKES BITING: Probably a reference to the spiky bangs falling across
the foreheads of men in Revolutionary France. It was during this era that men
began to "wear their own hair"—that is, to forgo wigs.

243 ANTRALGESINE: No drug by the name of *antralgésine* is known to have
existed. Colette appears to have invented the name from other drug names
such as *analgésine* and *névralgésine*.

243 JANSON-DE-SAILLY: In October 1914, Colette volunteered as a night nurse at
the temporary military hospital set up at the Lycée Janson-de-Sailly, where
she tended soldiers critically wounded in the war.

247 HYDROCYANIC ODOR: That is, a bitter-almond odor. Hydrocyanic acid, also
called prussic acid, is a highly poisonous solution of hydrogen cyanide in
water. A systemic chemical asphyxiant and chemical warfare agent that can
rapidly cause death, hydrogen cyanide also has numerous commercial appli-
cations, including fumigation, electroplating, mining, and the production of
plastics, dyes, and pesticides.

248   THE GARDENS OF LA MUETTE: Probably the Jardin du Ranelagh, near the Porte de la Muette.

258   THE EXPOSITION: The Exposition Universelle of 1889, a world's fair held in Paris.

259   THIS OLD SPIDER: According to the *Trésor de la langue française informatisé*, in French argot, *araignée* (spider) means *"une femme maigre et mal bâtie"* (a thin, badly built woman).

259   THE BOULEVARD BERTHIER: A street in the seventeenth arrondissement and part of the boulevards des Maréchaux, the series of boulevards that encircle the city of Paris just inside the city limits.

259   LEVALLOIS-PERRET: A northwestern suburb of Paris on the right bank of the Seine, Levallois-Perret borders on Neuilly.

260   THE ODDS AT AUTEUIL: That is, the Auteuil Hippodrome, a horse-racing venue that opened in 1873 at the southern end of the Bois de Boulogne.

263   HER LAST VEIL: An allusion to the biblical character of Salomé. In Oscar Wilde's eponymous 1891 play, Salomé is an inscrutable femme fatale, and Edmée's refusal to let go of "her last veil" indicates that she is unwilling to let down her guard before Chéri.

267   CHARLOTTE CORDAY: Marie-Anne-Charlotte Corday d'Armont (1768–1793), a member of the impoverished aristocracy and a Girondist, was the assassin of the radical Jacobin Jean-Paul Marat. She was executed by guillotine four days after the murder.

267   THE SALPÊTRIÈRE: Before the Revolution, La Salpêtrière comprised a poorhouse for the homeless, a girls' reformatory, prisons for prostitutes and female criminals, and an insane asylum. The prison component was eliminated in 1795.

271   MOLIER'S: Perhaps a reference to the Cirque Molier, an amateur circus founded by Ernest Molier and operated out of his mansion on the rue Benouville in Paris between 1880 and 1933. The Cirque Molier's fashionable galas attracted Parisian socialites and men and women of the literary and theater worlds.

279   MORTIER: Michel Mortier (1845–1925), who established and directed between 1900 and 1906 the Théâtre des Capucines and founded the Théâtre Michel in 1906.

279   LONGCHAMP: The Hippodrome de Longchamp, located along the Seine in the Bois de Boulogne, opened in April 1857. Both Édouard Manet and Edgar Degas painted horse-racing scenes there.